P9-DZO-991

The gun was locked in my fist, cocked.

"Let's see empty hands."

Neither man moved nor showed sign of doing so. The woman's fear was overpowering. I lightened my voice. "Your idea? Leaving with them?"

The slight movement of her head meant no.

"You fellows best do like I said."

The gun was steady. My eyes held a deadly message most could read. But the larger man couldn't or wouldn't; he was setting himself. The damned fool was going to try to take me, gun and all. My mouth pulled into a tighter, nastier slash. "I hit good up to thirty yards." Three feet lay between us.

I leaned forward, letting my finger take up the last bit of slack in the trigger.

• • •

FATAL GAMES

FATAL GAMES

Bob McElwain

PAGEANT BOOKS

Publisher's Note: This is a work of fiction. The characters, incidents and dialogues are products of the author's imagination and are not to be construed as real. Any resemblance to actual events or persons, living or dead, is entirely coincidental.

♪

PAGEANT BOOKS
225 Park Avenue South
New York, New York 10003

Copyright © 1989 by Robert McElwain

All rights reserved. The right to reproduce this book or portions thereof in any form must be obtained in writing from the Permissions Department of the publisher.

PAGEANT and colophon are trademarks of the publisher

Cover artwork by Howard Koslow

Printed in the U.S.A.

First Pageant Books printing: April, 1989

10 9 8 7 6 5 4 3 2 1

To the readers:
I hope you enjoy this tale as
much as I enjoyed writing it.

FATAL GAMES

Monday

‖‖ ‖‖ ‖‖ ‖‖ ‖‖

The door of the bank closed behind me. I examined the faces of those walking toward me.
There was no need; the cash was in the bank, not my pocket. But habits, even those no longer useful, are tough to set aside.

I turned north, checking each face approaching and those in cars nearest the curb. Part of me laughed at myself. What was there to fear? The flustered mom herding three little ones into the yard goods store? Or the two young lads trying to act as if they didn't belong in school? Screeching tires and blaring horns declared normalcy. I watched the faces anyway and held a pace that gained ground on those behind me.

An old man, chin up, watery eyes scanning bright blueness overhead, sensed my approach

and moved toward the curb, just as I did. We
both had to stop. He grinned sheepishly. "Sorry.
I should pay more mind to things."

"No problem. It's worth a look." I joined in his
search of the sky, glad for someone with whom
to share it. To the north, a gliding hawk lifted
swiftly on unseen air currents high above, then
wheeled toward the mountains.

"Lived here in L.A. most of my life," said the
old-timer. "I seen it lots a times. But damned if
it ain't pretty today."

"For sure." Those behind me were catching
up. As if it had a mind of its own, my hand
brushed lightly across the butt of the Colt,
tucked into my waistband under the shirt. "Take
care," I said, glancing behind me.

"I surely will," the old man replied, still looking up at the sky.

I stepped around him and moved on. Ahead
was Artie's. Images of thick juicy hamburgers
added length to my stride.

Inside, I was relieved to see the lunch hour
was over. Aromas from onions on the grill and
rolls in the oven blended, an enticing invitation.
Only three booths by the long row of windows
were occupied. Two men lingered over coffee at
the L-shaped counter. At the far end I took the
middle of the three seats facing the entrance.
They give a good view of the door, the counter,
and the booths along the windows.

In the mirrored wall in front of me, reflections
of pies and cakes mingled with the view of the
six booths behind me against the back wall.

Only one was occupied. A man crowded against the woman next to the wall. I could see only the back of the second man. I looked away, then back into the mirror. Something jarred, clashing rudely with the day. I let the feeling linger, peeking at the edges of it. The tall waitress in the pale blue uniform repeated, smiling, "What will you have, sir?"

"Sorry." Her smile was delightful, inviting attention to laughing eyes. "Make it a super burger with trimmings and a large milk."

"Coming right up," she said, scribbling on her pad as she turned away. I watched her move and liked it. Few women look better walking away than toward you. I was surprised when I found my eyes focused on the mirror instead of the waitress.

The man with his back to me was large and broad. Thick curly black hair added width to the massive head. The high collar of his pin-striped shirt hugged his neck well above the light brown suit coat, filled with shoulders and upper arms.

The man facing me was taller. A black turtleneck sweater extended above the charcoal gray sport coat, providing better proportion between his long neck and shoulders. Pale blond hair streaked with white was combed straight back, making the baldness on the front of his head seem an extension of his forehead. He watched the woman intently, thin lips set in a slight tight smile.

Her white blouse buttoned down the front;

one of the buttons was undone. Strands of dark brown hair touched her shoulders. With her head tilted down, most of her face was hidden. What could be seen appeared unnaturally pale. The ugly aura of conflict emanating from the three was nearly tangible.

"Enjoy." The waitress set the burger and milk in front of me, then whirled, grabbed a coffee pot, and started down the counter in search of customers wanting refills. I picked up the burger with my left hand and took a bite. It was a chore best suited to two hands but my right felt comfortable in my lap near the Colt.

I looked again in the mirror and saw more of her face. The light even tan failed to hide paleness. The tendons in her hands were rigid, holding the empty glass. She lifted her head to say something. Hair hid her ears and much of her cheeks, disguising breadth of face. The slender nose contrasted with width of mouth. Tension accented deep crescent-moon clefts at the corners of her lips.

The man beside her lifted his arm possessively to the back of the seat, behind the slumping shoulders. He watched with the same tight smile as she pleaded with the man across the table.

She shook her head in an urgent no. The man leaned forward, spreading his elbows to support huge arms, straining the seams of his coat. She cradled her head in her hands, looking down at the table, listening. Long slender fingers massaged her head at the temples.

So she's in trouble? So what? Whole bunches of people are. I stabbed angrily with the fork at the chunks that had fallen from the burger. I should damn well have used both hands. My right wasn't doing anyone any good in my lap.

Surely everyone feels this way, uneasy at the quarrels of others. Most want to step in to quiet angry screams directed at a defenseless child or hold back the heavy fist raised for another blow. I pulled my glance away. Even in public, people have a right to privacy. I swallowed the rest of the milk, counted out some bills, and stood.

In the mirror, her pale blue eyes locked with mine. Fear was there and something else. Was she pleading for help? I knew what I ought to do. Get out. Staying alive brings its own troubles; only a fool looks for more. This wasn't my affair. I concentrated on subduing the inexplicable feeling that I had to stay. I wasn't surprised when I found myself sitting again, my hand back in my lap. I motioned to the waitress for coffee and looked back into the mirror at the woman. The waitress set coffee in front of me, picked up the bills, and turned away.

Every man's dream. Lady in distress. Hero to the rescue. And they live happily in the castle forever. Crap. Besides, who in hell's got a castle these days? Still, I watched in the mirror.

Then I saw it. The right hand of the man facing me had been below the table. While shifting his arm, the barrel of the pistol lifted above the tabletop. The woman cringed at what must have been the gun pressing into her side. She recoiled forward, away from the arm that moved off the back of the seat to embrace her shoulders. What little could be seen of her expression shouted terror.

My hand trembled, spilling coffee. Fine sweat erupted from pores in my palms. There wasn't enough air to breathe. Feelings fled, leaving me bitterly cold in that odd way thermometers can't measure. Unwanted memories rushed in. They had to be stomped ruthlessly aside. I focused what attention could be diverted from mental chores to my hand. In time the trembling stopped. I settled the cup on the counter precisely. I wiped my hand on my pant leg and eased it up under my shirt. The butt of the Colt Python was cool; it melded into my palm as if part of my fist.

I kept my head down, hoping bushy eyebrows hid my attention within reflections of pies and cakes. It wouldn't do to let them see my face or the emptiness stealing color from my eyes. I reviewed the path they must take to the door. I was sure of only one thing. A mistake would bring thundering explosions, gushing blood, and the anguished cries of pain and dying.

The large man slid out of the booth and looked toward the entrance. His broad features matched the width and power of his shoulders. Dark eyes were set deep under thick black eyebrows. The full mustache drooped below the corners of his mouth. I picked up the coffee cup and looked down at the counter. I could feel it, his hard, calculating inspection. Hopefully my worn shirt and denims excused me from serious consideration.

The hand steady, I took a sip and glanced in the mirror. The taller man, one hand on the gun in his coat pocket, drew the woman out of the booth. It wasn't easy; terror had nearly immobilized her. I caught a glimpse of slender hips and long legs in snug-fitting jeans, tapering down to running shoes. I concentrated on my hand, took another sip of coffee, then lowered the cup to the counter.

I could hear them now, moving toward the entrance. The woman's heavy breathing eclipsed other sounds, tearing at me, soul deep. Six feet. Four. Two. I reached again for the coffee as they came up beside me. When they passed the mirror, I set the cup down, slipped off the stool, and closed behind them. In a half-crouch, arms low and well forward, I did all I could to stifle sound from the crepe soles of my loafers.

The waitress saw my face and froze. She couldn't see the Colt, held low, near the counter. The big man caught her look. His massive head whipped around, his glance darting to my gun. He stopped and turned as I closed. His left hand was tucked to the knuckles in his coat pocket, giving him a courtly look that rang false, as if practiced in front of a mirror. The taller man holding the woman also stopped, turning awkwardly, his grip firm around her shoulders.

I saw what I desperately needed. The muzzle of the gun in the pocket moved away from the woman toward me. "Don't." I cocked the Colt to accent the demand. The tall man's gun stopped moving, pointed neither at the woman nor at me. Could this be ended without blood flowing? "Even if you're cops, let's see empty hands."

Neither man moved nor showed sign of doing so. They weren't any kind of cops. The woman's fear was overpowering. Much of it seemed to be of me. I lightened my voice. "Your idea? Leaving with them?"

The slight movement of her head meant no.

"You fellows best do like I said."

The man with the gun waited on the larger, whose face was rigid with lethal anger.

"I pour these slugs myself, then add a little mercury," I said, struggling for patience. My mouth was dry and I could feel the muscles of my face pulling at my lips, flattening them against my teeth. "With an extra bit of powder, they get it done."

My eyes didn't waver. The gun was steady. I tried to ignore the woman's terror. Rage marred the face of the large man; uncertainty clouded the eyes of the other.

My face wasn't nice to look at. The eyes held a deadly message most could read. But the larger man couldn't or wouldn't; he was setting himself. The damned fool was going to try to take me, gun and all. My mouth pulled into a tighter, nastier slash. "I hit good up to thirty yards." Three feet lay between us. I leaned forward, tired of waiting.

The taller man eased his hand out of his pocket, leaving the gun behind. He released the woman and let his hands fall to his sides. The larger man remained still, his eyes locked with mine. He was six feet with at least two hundred solid pounds. I had a couple of inches on him and about the same weight, but this wasn't the time to test him physically. The muzzle of the Colt drifted upward and to the right, until pointed at the center of the bright red tie. "Figure it's your time?" I leaned closer, letting my finger take up the last bit of slack in the trigger.

As though chewing a baby's messy diaper, he grimaced, took a deep breath, then sought to erase all emotion from his face. He failed only with his eyes. To kill was what he wanted. The beefy hand lifted slowly from the coat pocket and dropped to his side.

I glanced around the restaurant. None of the diners had noticed. No one gaped through the windows. "Let's sit back down." I let the Colt drop to my side, gripping it by the cylinder and barrel, hiding it from casual view. I backed toward the counter, motioning with my head.

The two men moved. The woman did not. I stepped to her side, pressed a fifty into her hand, and said, "Time to go."

I shook the hand gently to be sure I had her attention; it was clammy, cold. The pale blue eyes, wide with terror, turned to mine but focused on the wall behind me. "There's a place down the street," I said. "The Palms Motel. If you want help or some talk, check in. Use the name Mary Jackson."

She gave no indication she'd heard. The two

men were halfway to the table. I placed my hand on her slim waist and turned her gently toward the door, as if directing a reluctant child. "Go on. Now."

I nudged her waist. When she took a tentative step, I moved up behind the two men. As the taller one started to take the seat at the far side of the table, I said, "That's mine."

He shrugged and slid in beside the big man, his hands flat to the tabletop. The woman turned toward the door, walking stiffly. Then she was gone, leaving behind a haunting impression of slimness. I sat down, the gun butt back in my palm, hidden under the table. "You," I said, watching the large man. "Some I.D."

The giant paw reached under his coat and withdrew the thin leather billfold. He tossed it disdainfully toward me and returned the hand to the table. The manicurist had tried, but these were the hands of a dock worker or stone mason. They clashed with the expensive tailored coat.

I flipped the billfold open and looked at the driver's license. "Salvadore Rosta," I murmured, studying the rigid face. I ignored the eyes and dropped the billfold on the table.

"Now you," I said, turning toward the taller man. He took out a small I.D. wallet and laid it open on the table. Dell Vickers was the name on the gun permit. I had names for the faces and the woman was gone. It was time to go.

"You're dead, hero," Rosta said. The gravelly voice added weight to the sinister statement.

"You ain't nothing but fucking fish food, ass-hole." His smile was more ominous than his anger had been. "I'd take you right now but I want you nervous, waiting for it. I'll tell 'em to put 'em low in the gut, slow-like."

"Send people you don't need real bad," I responded, wondering about the man's arrogance. He's close to fifty. I'd watched him kidnap a woman; it wasn't the first time he'd unleashed violence. Surely others have opposed him, in dark corners of the night where a body could be safely abandoned. How in hell has he lived so long? I tucked the gun away, hooked my thumb beside it, and stood. "You best stay a while."

For the first three steps, I watched them in the mirror. Halfway to the entrance I paused, reaching for a toothpick on the counter. Neither man had moved. I strode quickly out the door and ran, ignoring curious gawking stares.

At the corner I dashed right, then left into the alley leading to the parking lot behind the bank. At the end of the alley I stopped behind a trash bin, watching. I gave it four minutes, breathing deeply. No one entered the alley. I trotted across the lot to the car.

It's a '66 Dodge, a classic, with its 426 Hemi. It's nicked and scarred from city driving. Once a metallic brown, dust and rust now confuse the issue. The chrome on the roll bar is pitted, peel-ing in places. It looked particularly good to me just now. I climbed in, crossed my arms over the wheel, cradled my head, and waited. It began with a slight tremble in my hands that spread

up the arms and across the shoulders. When
only the dull pounding ache in the kidneys remained, I slipped the key into the ignition. The
powerful engine smoothed into a steady, even
rumble. Half my attention was focused on the
rearview mirror as I drove off.

In the Palms Motel no one notices anyone,
even should friends or fellow workers find
themselves riding in the same elevator. And
there's good reason. The usual duration of stay
is measured in hours, not days. Massive wispy
artificial palms turn the lobby into someone's
sterile vision of a tropical paradise. Sandy col-
ored deep pile carpets erase the sound of any
step. The light is too dim to read by, hiding
blemishes, blotches, and wrinkles. There was no
sign of the woman from Artie's.

Walking toward the desk, I heard subdued
sounds from the bar and dining room beckon-
ing. I felt uneasy. I couldn't say who or how
many were in the lobby. When I don't know
such things, I'm edgy. The only person to be
seen was the man behind the counter. Farcical
attempts at elegance ended here; a motel desk
is, after all, a motel desk.

My shirts are a size too large. The slope to the
shoulders makes them gather at the back and
sides like drapery. It's not stylish. The brown
plaid is faded from many washings, as are the
tan denims. The loafers are scuffed and scarred.
The clerk behind the counter made his judgment: I was of no significance to the Palms

Motel. He turned his back to rummage through
a stack of papers at the desk. I waited, wondering where one finds these pompous pinheads.
Are they all that's available? Or are they spe-
cially trained for the role?

When he could no longer reasonably ignore
me, he turned back to the counter and asked,
"May I help you, sir?"

"Mary Jackson?"

His Adam's apple was pronounced, enhanced
by thin lips closed tightly, pulling skin up across
the jaw. "I don't believe we have a Ms. Jackson
registered," he said, forgetting the sir.

"Tall. Long brown hair. About thirty."

"I haven't seen the lady," the clerk replied
haughtily. But he saw the folded twenty peeking
out from under my palm.

"I'd like to see the registration cards for the
last hour."

He hesitated, looking at the bill. When I
pushed it closer and took my hand away, his
glance swept the lobby. He laid a stack of cards
on the counter, slipped the bill into his pocket,
and turned back to the desk.

I ignored names. Only three of the cards had
been filled out by women and two were over an
hour old. The remaining card showed a check-in
time of ten minutes ago. The script was bold
and crisp, not that of a terrified woman. "Is that
the lot?" I asked.

"It happens," the clerk said, without turning.
"The ladies don't always keep their promises."

"I need a phone."

"In the bar," he replied, turning back to the counter.

As I neared the arched entrance, sounds from inside grew more distinct; those of ice cubes against glass and soft laughter mingled. There were only a few cozy booths occupied. Without walking past each one and peering at the occupants, I couldn't be certain the woman wasn't here. But she didn't show herself. Relief flowed over me; I hadn't realized how much I'd been hoping she would solve her own problem. But the feeling didn't last. It was erased by a nasty twinge of the guilties. She might not need my help but she sure in hell needed someone or something.

I turned to the phone and dialed. "Foothill Division. Sgt. Acton."

"Sgt. Haggen?" I asked, wondering if I'd ever feel comfortable talking with cops.

"Sorry, sir. He's out. Can I help?"

"Ask him to call. The name's Scott Macklen."

"Does he have your number?"

"Yeah." I hung up, wondering what Tony Haggen would tell me about Rosta and Vickers. Since the woman wasn't here, there wasn't much point. Still, Rosta had said he'd kill me. There'd be no harm in knowing more about him. I took a step toward the entrance, then stopped.

I didn't owe her a thing. If I left now, I'd be free of it. If she'd wanted to talk, she'd be here. I don't win many of these arguments with myself.

I walked to the bar. Waiting might leave me feeling better about myself. Besides, a shot might chase away the tail end of the shakes.

The stool near the wall provided a good view of the room and entrance. The large man approaching behind the bar looked even larger in his white ruffled shirt and long burgundy vest.

"Bourbon and cubes," I said.

When the drink arrived, the twenty I'd laid on the counter was replaced by three fives. The tab was high at the Palms Motel. And either the ice melted quickly or they watered the whiskey. I sipped absently and studied what I could see of people hidden away in cleverly designed seclusion.

A woman entered, paused, and looked around the room. The pale yellow dress accented her hips and revealed deep cleavage between lovely breasts. Dark black hair glistened in the dim light, framing a face worthy of being sculptured in marble. She caught me watching and held my glance, the hint of a playful smile tugging at the corners of her lips.

I smiled in return, enjoying the attention. When I shook my head with the barest movement, she shrugged and walked on. I swallowed the rest of the drink, put the glass down, and turned on the stool to leave, only to face slim hips and long legs embraced by tight jeans. That her face could be lovely, there was no doubt. Now it was deeply marred with tension and fear. The button was still undone on

her blouse and a shoelace was about to come
loose. The hands, holding the purse tightly,
were trembling. The pale blue eyes were unnaturally bright.

As the silence built, I became increasingly uncomfortable, certain I should be someplace else.
" 'Lo," I said, knowing there had to be something
better to say. "Would you like a drink?" Silently
I cursed the absence of fine words.

She looked toward the entrance, as a wilderness creature poised for flight. Hesitantly she
turned back and perched herself on the far edge
of a stool, away from me. The bartender approached and picked up two fives. "Something
for the lady?" he asked politely.

"Whatever he's having, please." When the bartender turned away, she continued, looking
down at the bar. "Don't tell me; let me guess.
You're Don Quixote reincarnated." She spoke
softly but with good projection. She knew how
to use her diaphragm, as a trained singer does.
It provided depth to what otherwise might be a
ridiculously thin soprano.

Her head snapped up and around. Her gaze
locked with mine. "You've disposed of the
dragons, the fair maid's at hand, and you now
expect to be rewarded in customary fashion."

I hadn't noticed how hard and lumpy the bar-
stool was. I shifted position; it didn't help. My
cheeks flushed. I hoped it didn't show in the dim
light. "Not exactly," I said finally.

"Then why this phony sexual playhouse?" she
demanded.

"It was handy." I was grateful for the inter-
ruption of the bartender depositing two glasses
in front of us. She reached eagerly for her's and
swallowed a hefty portion. She choked, then
grimaced, but took another swallow.

"It'd be handier if we were talking in a room
with a bed, wouldn't it? You're a fair-sized specimen. All that black wavy hair and those bushy
eyebrows. The tan adds to the impression of
healthy vigor. And a voice to please the gods:
deep, rich, and full. Only a few words and they
roll back on their heels. It's really too bad about
the bed, don't you think?"

"Expect I shouldn't have butted in." I've never
expressed my feelings more honestly. Partly my
discomfort stemmed from the realization she
was right, in a way. I couldn't remember a
woman who'd interested me so quickly, so in-
tensely.

"I'm no raving beauty but I suppose some
men aren't particular. I wonder if you'd have
helped if I'd been seventy, instead of thirty."

"I'd like to think so."

"Is your confidence slipping? There's a good
deal of confusion in those slate-gray eyes. What
a shame. You thought I'd be panting and trembling by now." She emptied her glass. "You
should have grabbed for that black-haired
beauty. I suspect she knows how to please a
man."

The tall, broad-shouldered figure in a blue
plaid sport jacket stepped inside the room and
leaned against the wall, watching us. He was of

a size. At least six-four. Two-fifty or more. He looked fit and competent. He had bouncer written all over him. The bartender was watching us, too.

"Look," I said. "If you want, I'm gone."

She made no reply, reaching for my untouched drink.

"Do you like scotch?" I asked, as she swallowed with a grimace.

"I'm a cocktail waitress; we drink anything," she snapped.

"What's your name?"

"Lori Adams."

"Sure. A cocktail waitress who can't tell the difference between scotch and bourbon. You borrowed the purse; that's why the initials on it are L.L., instead of L.A. And you won't call a cop because you're a princess, traveling incognito."

"Now listen here." She whipped around to face me, leaning forward at the waist. "I did not come here for a roll in the hay or to hear clever remarks. Is that clear?"

"Why did you come?"

"Because I'm frightened, you fool. Now that I'm here, I don't know who frightens me more, you or those...those...animals." She finished with a shudder, whirled back to the bar, grabbed the glass, and swallowed deeply. She didn't grimace this time. "Why do you carry a gun?" she asked, seeking a more reasonable tone and failing.

From my wallet I pulled the gun permit and laid it on the bar near her elbow, remembering

Dell Vickers had one, too. This didn't seem the time to tell her so. I laid a business card beside the permit.

She scrutinized both. "According to this card, Mr. Macklen, you work for Nelder, Inc., whatever that is. And the permit gives you the legal right to carry the gun. But bits of paper don't answer my question. Why do you have it unless you plan to shoot someone?"

"I carry money, sometimes important documents." I took a deep breath, thinking of the other reasons. I picked up the card and permit and tucked them away. The big fellow behind us shifted restlessly. "Look," I said, patience fading. "Is there much point to more of this?"

Her eyes were focused on the drink held with both hands. Long slender fingers were wrapped tightly around the glass. She sat rigidly, shoulders back, her head tilted down. The white blouse, pulled taut, revealed small thrusting breasts. Her hair hid her face except for her nose. I let my glance drift downward. There was no doubt. The long slender legs were her most intriguing feature.

I remained puzzled by my keen interest. I usually hesitate, even given good opportunity. And by the time I've thought it through, the invitation's been withdrawn. True, there was the childlike innocence about her that contradicted her age. But that didn't explain it. All I could be sure of was how badly I wanted to take her in my arms, to hold her gently, to watch terror and fear subside, to bring forth a smile, if for no other reason than to see if her face was as lovely as I thought a smile would make it.

She's alone with her thoughts. She probably doesn't even know where she is. Would I ever learn not to butt in? Rosta is a vicious dangerous type with nasty plans for her. But she doesn't want my help. I slipped off the stool. Her head snapped around, the eyes brimming with confusion. "I'll be going," I said. "Need a lift?"

She jumped up off the stool. Her upper body jutted toward me until her nose nearly touched my chin. The eyes focused on each of mine in turn. The man by the entrance strode toward us. "Would you have shot those men?" Her voice raised in pitch and volume on each word. "Would you have killed them without even knowing what they'd done or planned?"

"I can't say." It was a lie; she'd have to be a fool not to know it. I knew what had been written on my face, with the Colt leveled and cocked. Even Rosta had read it finally and understood there were no options but mine.

"I could see it in your eyes. You wanted to shoot them. You'd have enjoyed it!" A couple in the booth in front of me turned to gawk at us through the lattice partition. The man who'd been at the entrance was close. "My God," she cried. "You're no ..."

Broad shoulders draped with blue plaid interrupted her, partially interposed between us. "Trouble, Miss?" The eyes were cautious, watchful. They ignored Lori.

A male tends to be intimidated by another who's two inches taller with fifty more tough pounds. All I felt was his presence, his availability. He was an eminently suitable target. Tightness in my neck flowed downward through my shoulders and into my arms. The fingers of both hands locked straight.

When I wiped my palms on my denims, he tensed, shifting his weight. It would be good to pound someone. Anyone. Hard. I took a deep breath and rubbed the broad white scar in the palm of my hand. Sometimes it helps, remembering how I got the scar. "I'm leaving," I said.

I stepped around the man, half hoping he'd try to stop me. Anger added length to the stride. I was within a few steps of the street when I heard heavy breathing behind me. I whirled, ready. She crashed into me with her hands against my chest, then backed away, awkwardly, shyly. She looked down at her purse, nervously opening and closing it with both hands. When she looked up, her eyes held a silent plea I couldn't read. She looked back down, shoulders drooping. "I'd appreciate a ride." She looked up again, like a kicked dog, one that had been kicked before.

Anger evaporated as if it had never existed. The peculiar tightness in my gut would have to be examined later. "Why not?" I replied, more gruffly than intended.

I turned and walked out the door. She scurried to my right, positioning herself between me and the wall of the building. She apparently had nothing more to say, which suited me fine.

At the car, I debated whether or not to open the door for her. I was still undecided when I slid inside and fired the engine. She was slow to get in, carefully inspecting the tarnished beast. She eased herself cautiously onto the torn seat. She seemed to have equal concern for all she'd noticed about the car.

"It runs good," I said bluntly.

"I'm sure it does," she replied, so softly I could hardly hear.

Once out of the parking lot, I drove north on Van Nuys. Traffic was light. I could have saved time with a few judicious lane changes. But as was my habit, I stayed in the right lane, waiting for vehicles to park or move, when halted. I watched in the rearview mirrors. We left most of the traffic behind when I cut up Vesper toward Woodman. "Do you have any idea where you want to go?" I asked.

"Do you know where San Jose crosses Woodman?"

I nodded.

"Turn left there." She leaned her head back over the top of the seat and closed her eyes. I glanced at her, more puzzled than ever. Who in hell is she? What's she into? More importantly, what am I into? Jesus H. Christ. I'm nothing but a goddamned do-gooder.

At San Jose, I turned left onto the residential street. She straightened in the seat. As we slipped by each house, her tension grew. Again I had the feeling she was unaware of me. Whatever lay ahead, she dreaded it. How much more could she take? She grabbed the dash with both hands. "Turn," she demanded. "Turn now."

I did, but I'd seen it too. Two police black and whites were parked in front of the third house in the next block. An ambulance was backed up near the porch. I caught the address of the corner house. It was then she broke.

Tears flooded into her lap, leaking from around palms driven hard into her cheeks. The only sounds to be heard above the rumble of the engine came from her deep sobs and gasps for air.

What in hell should I do? I couldn't dump her at the bus station or in front of a hotel. What about the police? We were close to Foothill Division. Tony Haggen might be in by now. But what if they asked why she hadn't reported a kidnapping? The smart move was to get rid of her somehow, no doubt about it. Excellent reasons abounded but I didn't bother looking for them. I turned back toward Woodman and home.

Once out of Panorama City, Woodman slants north and east. It becomes Fox Street and passes through the eastern part of the old mission community of San Fernando. With each turn of the wheels, I felt better; I was closer to the hills and home.

The San Gabriel Mountains are the northern boundary of the San Fernando Valley and the sprawling city of Los Angeles. Early Indians had called them the Smoking Hills. Lightning storms start brush fires and the smoke lingers. It can be seen for miles. These days, vandalism is the major cause of fire but the mountains remain. A few oaks and pines gallantly survive.

Lori's bitter sobs eclipsed the wonder of the hills and the day. Maybe she'd feel better once we got to the house. I turned right on Foothill and then left onto Lopez Canyon Road. As we climbed deeper into the foothills, we left housing tracts behind and were soon passing individual homes on land measured in acres, not feet. They vary in age and worth, tending toward older and modest.

At the upper end of the canyon, where the road turns right, then back into the valley, I pulled left, across the noisy cattle guard. The racket startled Lori. She sat back and looked around. Tears still leaked from bloodshot eyes and her face had an unhealthy reddish tint, but the sobs had ceased. I smiled to myself. She had a right to be confused. When she'd last noticed anything, we'd been in the heart of the city. Here there wasn't a building in sight, except my house. There were the hills, the horses, and a little graze. The rest was brush, rock, lizards, and sandy desert soil.

"Where in the world are we?" she asked.

"My place," I answered, slowing the car, uncertain of the intention of two romping colts charging the car.

"Those are magnificent animals," she said, lost in watching the horses. "Do they belong to you?"

"No," I said. "They belong to my neighbor, Ned Early. He breeds, raises, and trains them."

"They're beautiful."

When we crossed the second cattle guard, leaving the horses behind, she turned to watch through the rear window. The drive steepened, winding up the last two hundred yards to the house. I dropped into second and continued up the hill. When the pasture was lost to view, she turned back to look absently out the windshield. The animation triggered by the colts was gone. Her lips and the clefts that bounded them drooped heavily. She seemed defeated in that markedly painful way that most people fortunately never experience. Men who've survived battle their buddies did not often have that look. And I've seen it in the faces of those who've lost more than they could afford, or everything.

The house is perched on a knoll. Its white aluminum roof makes it seem more a large shed or warehouse. A fifty-foot width of gravel circles the house. The only plantings are two dozen fruitless mulberry trees. Still bare of leaves in the late winter sun, they were ready to explode, to create a canopy of great green leaves, bringing the miracle of cooling shade to the desert summer.

The black Doberman rushed at us from behind the house. At least Bobbie was glad I was home. Lori perked up, watching the dog. As I drove around the house, Bobbie dashed from one side of the car to the other, delighted to see me but determined to know more about our guest. I parked beside the oversized garage I use as a workshop, alongside the charcoal gray Chevy Blazer.

"I figured you could stay the night. At least no one can get at you here."

She shrugged, opened the car door, and got out. I did the same, then squatted on my heels and tried to rub the hair off Bobbie's head and back with both hands. When I stood, the dog dashed around the car to check on our guest. I followed them up to the crest of the knoll. Lori made a slow full circle, examining the hills, the horses, and the valley below. She looked at me strangely, idly scratching the dog between the ears. "You must like being alone," she said.

"Mostly."

She looked down at the dog. "What's her name?" she asked.

"It's Roberta on her papers; she answers to Bobbie."

"What a silly name for such a beautiful dog."

"Expect you're right."

"Then why did you choose it?"

"I didn't. A buddy dumped her off on his way to Africa. The name came along with her."

I couldn't tell if the answer satisfied her but she said nothing more. I seized the opportunity to break away and start toward the house, the dog beside me. Although Bobbie has her own private doggy door, she waited impatiently, one grand continuous wiggle, for the honor of entering through the people door. When I had unlocked the heavy steel hinge and opened the door, she trotted happily inside. Lori had walked around to the front of the house for a better look at the colts below.

The sun had dipped behind the hills, shadowing the house. I turned on a small lamp, opened two windows, then went into the kitchen. I dumped instant coffee into the cup, added water from the electric coffee pot, then sat down at the kitchen table, letting the legs stretch, slumping comfortably on my spine. From where I sat, I could only see Lori's head and shoulders through the window. Bobbie lay down in the open doorway, watching her, but with ears attuned for a clue to what I might do next.

When Lori finally turned toward the house, her shoulders slumped. Unspoken words, but faintly heard, assured me it'd be a long night. The dog stood to let her pass.

Inside she paused, studying what is essentially one large room. Spanish tile covers the floor; an occasional throw rug adds wild color. Windows dominate all four sides, except for the bathroom behind the kitchen counter. Bookcases and cabinets are built in under the windows. Books for which there's no vertical space are tucked over the top of those standing. Beyond the bathroom, in the corner, is a king-sized bed. There's a short partition, window high, providing a sense of privacy. When I'd built it, I'd assumed I'd use it. It hadn't worked out that way. I use the day bed in the front corner of the house.

Furniture is scattered randomly; nothing

really matches anything else. Each piece is massive and old, with an abundance of hardwood showing. The three tables in the room are also wood. The only formica allowed inside was on top of the kitchen counter. A large Franklin stove dominates the center of the room and there are ten cords of oak in the shed out back to feed it.

I don't have many visitors. And I've never paid any attention to their opinion of the place. I wanted Lori to like it. I watched as she wandered absently about, stopping occasionally to brush the finish on a chair or table, or to read a book title. Her face was expressionless, even when she stared at the massive bed. She passed from sight into the bathroom and closed the door firmly behind her.

I drank the last of the coffee as the bathroom door opened. When she stepped into the kitchen, I could see she'd made an attempt to comb her hair. She'd probably washed her face as well. She looked terrible. "Do you have anything to drink?" she asked, without emotion.

"Bourbon?" I asked, standing.

She nodded.

I poured a double shot into a small glass, dropped in an ice cube, and handed it to her. "I think I'll fix a steak and some greens. Want one?"

She shook her head and walked back into the main room. If Rosta was to be believed, I too was in trouble. But I was hungry. I pushed the button on the radio. Muddy Waters drifted crisp sounds of guitar throughout the room. I whistled through my teeth in accompaniment.

I didn't see or hear her while I cooked and ate. I was tucking away clean dishes when she wandered back into the kitchen. She looked at the radio. The cut was Shelly Mann, featuring light staccato drum. "Do you really like ... that?"

I nodded.

"I guess Mozart has been forgotten."

I punched the radio off, wondering what else she'd seen and objected to. She probably didn't like me whistling through my teeth, either.

"You wanted to hit that man in the motel bar, didn't you?" Her voice had a cutting edge. "You wanted to beat and batter him into unconsciousness."

"I thought about it."

"Is that how you deal with those who oppose you? With violence?"

How do you answer something like that? A frightened woman is not usually beautiful; Lori was no exception. Yet there was a special quality about her, beyond the aura of innocence. It occurred to me she seemed completely unaware of her sexuality. "Anything else you'd like to lay on me?" I asked. As with most of my attempts at cute and clever, this one fell to the floor, unnoticed.

"I'd like another drink."

I refilled her glass and handed it to her. Her hand brushed mine. She recoiled, as if touching another was evil. It brought a glimpse of where she was coming from. Life, as she'd known it, had been destroyed. Nothing would ever be right again. I wanted to reach out and hold her close. "A bit of advice?"

She looked up with a sharpness I'd seen before. "Do you have any worth hearing?"

I felt my cheeks redden but continued. "I'd bet heavy drinking's new to you. That bourbon can have you cuddling with the toilet before long. It sneaks up on you."

"I appreciate your concern, Mr. Macklen," she said, turning and walking back into the main room. What the hell? She wasn't slurring yet. I grabbed a beer from the fridge, stepped out onto the porch, and settled into the old oak rocker to sip and think and to watch the sun's rays disappear from the hills. Bobbie sat beside me until I tired of scratching her head, then lay down.

When Lori came outside, she stopped to watch the colts play. Things were looking up; she'd noticed the undone button on her blouse and had fastened it. She sat down in the captain's chair on the other side of the doorway. She crossed her legs and propped her elbows on the armrests, holding the drink with two hands. I watched, trying not to be obvious about it. With tension partly dissipated, she seemed without direction, without purpose. Yet I sensed a core of inner strength, that essential human trait some call guts. All she needed was time.

"You're what they call a bush vet, aren't you?" she asked abruptly.

I shifted lower in the rocker. She didn't seem to notice.

"All this gravel and not a single bush," she continued. A hint of previous vitality showed in the quickness of her speech. "Then there are the locks on the windows and the elaborate steel hinge locks on the doors. You have enough Seconal in the bathroom to kill a dozen people."

"I have trouble sleeping sometimes," I replied, shifting once again in the rocker.

She continued as if she hadn't heard. "And all of this." Her gesture encompassed the mountains and the valley below. "You've set up a defensive perimeter, or whatever it's called. With those rifles over the door you could stop an army, couldn't you?"

There was no appropriate reply. Some things can't be explained easily. I let the silence grow, hoping her interest would drift elsewhere.

"I marched against that terrible war in Vietnam."

"You probably did the right thing. It wasn't a good war."

"A good war?" she snapped. "What's a good war as opposed to a bad one?"

I stood and stepped to the edge of the porch. Anger perched on my shoulder without bidding. Why didn't she just shut up?

"How many did you kill?" she demanded. Fear had returned.

"You want too much."

"How many?"

I whirled to face her. "I didn't keep count. Who in hell would?"

I stalked into the house and into the kitchen.

How in hell do you answer such questions? Not a soul who'd been there would ask. Who'd want to remember out loud? The night thoughts are more than enough. I needed something with more punch than beer.

I poured bourbon and drank half of it in one swallow, then disgustedly tossed the rest into the sink. Bourbon wouldn't help; I'd tried that and more.

I walked into the main room and began pacing beside the windows. I concentrated on taking deep breaths. In time the pulse rate slowed. I looked down at the tiled floor. The miles I've walked along this path have not marred the ceramic surface. How could there be no trace of so many passings? She was something, all right. With two words she'd loosed unneeded anger.

It was full dark when I poured more coffee, turned off the lamp, and sat down in the chair at the foot of the day bed to watch the flickering lights of the city. She came inside and poured another drink. I'd have to pour her into bed, if she kept this up. Or maybe I'd leave her right where she passed out. She walked over and stood beside me. Bobbie, sensing the mood, chose to lie down at the opposite end of the room.

"Where would you like me to sleep?" she asked politely.

"Pick a spot. The bed's comfortable. Or you can take the keys and lock yourself in the car." I looked up at her, baffled. "Exactly what kind of a monster do you think I am?"

She shrugged and took a long swallow.

"Are you going to tell me about the trouble you're in? And why you won't call a cop?"

"No."

"And tomorrow?"

"That will have to wait."

Were there tears in the corners of her eyes? I tried to hold her glance. She looked away and took another swallow.

"Do you want to try the bed?" I asked.

She nodded.

"Are those clothes washable?"

She nodded again. I walked into the bedroom area, rummaged in the closet, found the brown terrycloth robe, and tossed it on the bed. "The sheets may be a bit musty but they're clean. Try one of my shirts for PJs if you like. Dump your clothes outside the bathroom door and I'll wash them."

She cocked her head to the side; her eyes filled with an expression I couldn't define. A single tear had left a shiny trace down her cheek. "Thank you," she said.

I returned to the chair as the bathroom door closed behind me. Moments later it opened, then closed again. When I heard the shower go on, I walked over and scooped up the clothes. I dumped them into the washer, added soap, and turned it on. I damned well hoped everything would shrink. There was no doubt about it; she had a way.

Back in the chair, I punched a button on the recorder by the phone. One call was from the

bank; they were sending out a form that required my signature. The other was from Vance
Coggswell, about a house that could be had at
the right price. Tony Haggen hadn't called.

The water in the shower went off. I could picture her stepping out of the stall and toweling
herself. I thought of long slender legs. I wondered if her breasts sagged or if the bra was only
a formality.

I didn't want more coffee but it was something to do. I kicked off my shoes, pulled off my
socks, and padded barefoot to the kitchen, the
tile cool to my feet. If I'd been alone, all but the
shorts would have long since been stripped.
Likely Lori would have objected.

I made a project of building another cup. I
even took time to tidy up things that didn't need
tidying. But Lori was still in the bathroom when
I returned to the chair. When the door finally
opened, I resisted the impulse to turn and look
at her. " 'Night," I said.

"Good night, Mr. Macklen." Was there more
tension in her voice? More fear? Of me? I listened while she made herself comfortable in the
bed. Then all sounds ceased. I was left with my
coffee, the dog dozing beside me and the riotous
roar of crickets through the window over the
day bed.

The ringing phone startled me. The recorded
message was interrupted with, "There's no way
I'm goin' to talk to a machine, buddy. You've got
ten seconds to pick up or forget it."

I reached for the phone, grinning. Sgt. Tony

Haggen was one of the few constants in my life, a great rock in windy storms of shifting sand. "What's wrong with my recorder?"

"Tapes make me nervous, even those I know about. Now let me point out, it's been one of those days. Was there somethin' you needed? Or am I just the evenin' clown act?"

"Tell me about Sal Rosta and his gun hand, Dell Vickers."

"Are you fixin' to zip yourself into a body bag?"

I waited. Tony would get to it.

He sighed. "Rosta's a killer for hire. There's half a dozen arrests. Two trials. No convictions. We can tie him to a lot of action but nothin' good enough for a judge. Witnesses disappear. Permanent-like. Vickers is muscle with a rod, license and all. He likes to beat on people. He's legally clean. The truth is, he's sewer dirty.

"Rosta owns a clap joint, The Office, on Santa Monica, near the beach. Broads, drugs, and more broads. He likes blackmail when he gets the chance. Lately I hear he's lookin' for somethin'. It sounds big so it's probably drugs.

"Now, rememberin' it's been one of those days, tell me what you're doin', messin' with those two assholes."

I told him what had happened at Artie's. When I'd finished, he asked, "Where's the girl?"

"I don't know." I whip Tony in poker, seven out of ten times.

"Right," he muttered. "I hope I don't destroy your last link to sanity when I call you a liar."

"I can handle it."

"A little advice?"

"That too."

"Rosta will bury you in tiny little pieces nobody'll ever find, if you give him the chance."

"Got it, Tony."

"Is she good lookin'?"

"Was she good looking," I corrected. "Probably not real high on your scale, but I thought so."

"Uh huh."

The line went dead. Rosta thinks Lori has what he wants. Or knows where it is. Or is holding out. But the combination of Lori and drugs made no sense at all. It had to be something else. Only one thing was certain: She'd end up badly hurt or dead or both if she got near Rosta again. The day's beauty had been destroyed by the terror of a woman, Tony's caution, and a deep, not unfamiliar sense of futility.

Tuesday

IIII IIII IIII IIII IIII

I tried to snuggle closer to the wall below the window, to ignore the sun thrusting up over the mountains. Usually it's simple. But it sure as hell wasn't working now. She'd been quiet, digging for her clothes in the dryer and dressing. But it was unaccustomed sound.

To wake is a nasty unpleasantness. To be awakened before ten is the pits. I rolled out of bed, slipped on my pants, and padded across to the closet for clean clothes. Bobbie was nowhere in sight; she knows better than to come near so early in the morning. She was probably with Lori on the porch.

Coffee was the key; it was a multicup morning. I cleaned up and dumped dirty clothes in the washing machine, my version of a clothes hamper. I poured coffee and added cold water. I don't know why I bother; I never get it right. The first sip burned my tongue.

Lori was sitting in the captain's chair with elbows propped, her chin cupped in her hands, watching the colts. Even with the morning grumps, she looked fine. With what little courage I can muster so early in the day, I stepped onto the porch. " 'Lo," I mumbled, slumping into the rocker.

"Good morning," she responded politely.

Bobbie had raised her head to watch me in the doorway and her eyes had followed me to the rocker. She decided it was too soon for a morning greeting and put her head back down on her paws.

Without turning, Lori said, "I gather you like to sleep late. I'm sorry if I disturbed you."

"No problem." I sipped coffee, looking at her back. It was a nice-looking back.

"You were right about one thing, Mr. Macklen."

"Yeah?"

"I had too much to drink last night."

"There's aspirin in the bathroom."

"I tried that."

"Food helps."

Her head snapped around. "Are you serious?"

"It might."

Her eyes filled with disgust before she turned back to watch the colts, shoulders rigid.

It's not a lot of fun talking to a back. I rose and made my way to the kitchen. It was just as well; she wouldn't like my cooking. I poured more coffee, tossed a chunk of leftover steak into the cast-iron frying pan, and sliced green peppers on top of it. When the steak was newly browned, I scrambled four eggs beside it with a fork and set the pan on the table. It's a rule. If you eat out of what you cook in, there's less to wash.

As I swallowed the last mouthful, she came inside and stared disapprovingly at the skillet on the table. So far as I could tell, she hadn't liked a thing I'd done or said. It wasn't a good beginning to a significant relationship. She sat down and gazed out the window at the bare trees and hills.

I washed the pan and utensils, tucked them away, poured more coffee, and sat down opposite her. I searched halfheartedly for something friendly to say and came up blank. There was tiredness in her face and the eyes were bloodshot, but she looked to have put the worst behind. Her hair was lovely, highlighted by the morning sun streaming through the window. "Have you decided what to do?"

She turned from the window and stared at my cup. "When you grow up," she said with sugary sweetness, "you'll be a coffee bean."

"Yeah. I like coffee. You didn't answer the question."

She shrugged, her eyes avoiding mine. "Are those the only clothes you have? Tan denims and brown plaid flannel shirts?"

"It simplifies things." She wasn't being fair. She'd seen what was in the closet. There are two good sport jackets, three decent pairs of slacks, and a fine pair of black dress loafers. "What did Rosta want?"

"It was all a mistake," she replied finally. "I'm not the one he wants."

"And how did he find you? By mistake, I mean."

"I don't know."

I tried to find a hint of fact in what she'd said and failed. "I need some things in town. Want to come?"

She shook her head.

"You've got to move sometime."

She met my glance; fear was back.

"You'll need clothes. It'd be a start."

For reply, she cupped her head in her hands and stared down at the table. I locked up and stood by the front door, waiting. She wouldn't look at me but she did stand and walk toward the door. Bobbie watched unhappily, knowing she was being abandoned.

The Northridge Shopping Center is one of those grand malls with acres of parking, vast covered interior walkways between shops, and usually not enough customers to justify operating costs. I parked near an entrance and handed Lori six fifties, thinking how foolish I'd feel if she turned out to be a missing heiress. Without comment, I climbed out of the car. As I walked away, she was still looking down at the bills. She could use them to move on, or for clothes. I hoped she'd opt for clothes. If she'd stop snapping, she'd be nice to have around.

If I could only get inside her defenses. No matter how bad things might be, there would be options, if not solutions. The empty feeling in my gut told me she must move decisively and make no mistakes. The sight of bodies, in various states of destruction and decay, is not new to me. But once it flashed on the mental screen, I couldn't erase the image of her tall slender figure crumpled, motionless, cold.

When I returned to the car with a copy of the *Los Angeles Times*, she was gone. I tried to decide how long I'd wait but gave up. If she came back, I'd be here. I scanned the headlines, feeling a familiar sense of discontent. To start your day with terror, read a newspaper.

Things were slow today. Two trials on charges of child molesting, each weakened the news

value of the other. Only half a dozen killings
were reported. But a third of a village in Hon-
duras had been massacred in the name of someone's definition of peace. A sacred dagger,
reputed to have belonged to Mohammad himself, had been stolen. It was worth forty million
dollars, according to an unnamed source. The
Saudi prince who'd been its caretaker swore it
was an American plot and that no Saudi
would ever again sell oil to us. And it seemed
certain Iran and Iraq could, without Russian
assistance, give rebirth to the Middle Ages by
blowing up the rest of the Middle East. Every
time I look at a paper, the same conclusion is
thrust upon me. The human experience is one
of nature's modest little experiments that isn't
going to make it.

It was there, in the Valley section, down toward the bottom of the page. Ms. Beth Dobsen
of 11412 San Jose Street had been murdered.
The address was about where I'd seen the police
cruisers and ambulance yesterday. I folded the
paper open on the seat and set off in search of a
phone.

I found three booths together in a corner of
the parking lot. The first one devoured my
quarter but refused to emit a dial tone or return
the quarter. The cord and handset were missing
from the second one. I approached the third
phone, distinctly wary. At the first hint of a dial
tone, I punched out the number rapidly.

"Foothill Division. Sergeant Haggen."

"Macklen here."

"So how's it go?"

"Good enough."

"Bill's got a game on tonight. Want in?"

I tugged at my ear with thumb and forefinger. If I didn't go, Tony would be suspicious. It's poker winnings that make the real estate work so well. Tony's invitations generally lead to profits. "Expect I'll have to pass."

"Is that so?"

I could almost hear the mental gears whirling. "This way there'll be more for you."

"Yeah. Sure," he grunted. "So what do you need?"

"What happened to Beth Dobsen?"

"Why the interest?"

"Curious, is all. I caught the address in the paper this morning. I was driving by when your people were there."

"When's the last time you read a paper?"

"It's been a while."

"How come I've got this feelin' you're not tellin' all of it?"

"Maybe you could just answer the question?"

Tony hesitated. "Take my word. You don't want to hear it all. She was beaten, tortured, and raped. Repeatedly. We'll never know which killed her."

"A bad one, then?"

Tony was silent for several moments. When he spoke, it was with uncharacteristic softness. "You. Me. We've seen ugly. Nam and all. But nothin' like this. Nothin' even close." After another long silence, he continued. "We've had two others the last ten years. Same MO. What we've got is one sick perverted sonofabitch walkin' loose. A lot of boys are lookin' to bury him."

"Any ideas?"

"Not a fuckin' one. You?"

"Why would I?"

"This is Tony. Remember? Now what have you got?" There was an edge to his voice that made me glad I was on the phone, not standing beside his desk.

"Not a thing, Tony."

"How's this connect to Rosta and that weasel Vickers?"

"Tony, I haven't a thing."

"But you'll get back when you do, won't you?"

The connection was broken with an authoritative slam. Sergeant Tony Haggen was mad. Someone, somewhere, had better duck.

I had to walk a long block to find a market. As I picked up what was needed, the picture of Lori, demanding I turn when she saw the squad cars, chilled me. The memory of her back and shoulders, heaving from sobs, was vivid. If she didn't return, I'd have to get back to Tony. She undoubtedly had information. She might even be able to connect Rosta to the killing.

When I got back to the car, she was staring out the windshield at nothing at all. I don't think she saw me walk past the front of the car. I was belted with a grand twinge of the guilties. I'd left the paper open on the seat where she'd be sure to see the article about Beth Dobsen. She didn't look at me when I tucked the two bags of groceries on the floor in back. The seat was covered with her purchases. She struggled to hold back tears and fear all the way back to the house.

When finished putting away the groceries, I walked back outside. She stood, arms crossed, watching the colts. I stepped up beside her and waited. It was her move.

"Do you suppose Mr. Early would let me ride a horse?"

"Now?"

"Yes."

For me, there's always better things to do than ride a horse. And she damn well had things to do. I would tell her so, tell her to move quickly, without error. But the words that slipped off my tongue were, "Let's go see."

She walked beside me down the draw. Questions collided with one another but I left them unasked. Bobbie roamed happily.

When we rounded the last bend, the old weathered ranch house came into view, nestled among a grove of eucalyptus. It's a long rambling structure with wood siding. Many layers of paint have been applied; the latest coat, a desert tan, still serves well. The roof is Spanish tile; the mass gives the impression it's driving the old house into the ground. The porch is deep, spanning the front, with the roof extended over it.

Ned Early stepped into the door of the barn below the house, watching us approach. Even at this distance, I could see the patches on the worn shirt and jeans. The clothes fit the tall, thin, wiry frame as if tailored. The ancient Stetson shadowed his eyes. Now that we were here, Lori was apprehensive, like a small child approaching a department store Santa, somehow knowing the hair and beard are false.

" 'Lo," I said. Bobbie had returned from foraging and stood beside me, panting contentedly.

"Howdy," Ned replied in a whispery voice, stretching the word into three syllables. The eyes were invisible under the brim of the hat.

"This is Lori, Ned."

"Pleased," the old man acknowledged, watching her closely, smiling.

"I'm very glad to meet you, Mr. Early," Lori responded hesitantly.

Ned lifted his head and reached for a cigarette. His smile interfered with the deep weathered lines etched in his leathery skin, forcing a greater squint to the eyes. What little hair showed below the hat was nearly white.

"She'd like to ride some," I explained.

"Thet so?" Ned tucked the cigarette into the corner of his mouth, struck a wooden match, and lit it. Smoke drifted up, spreading under the brim of the hat. "Ya ride much?" he asked, long spaces of time between words.

"I rode every chance I had when I was younger," Lori answered in a rush. "But I haven't been near a horse in years."

"Seems like ya're still near ta young," Ned commented. He took a drag on the cigarette.

He'd leave it tucked in the corner of his mouth until it burned down to his lips. "Let's see if'n I got anythin' worth time."

He turned toward the barn, his ungainly crablike gait an awkward way to cover ground. But on a horse, the man was grace personified. I stepped inside. Lori followed uncertainly. Bobbie lay down outside the door, content to watch the horses from a distance.

Ned picked up a bridle and stepped into a stall. When he led out the chestnut mare, he said, "This 'n 'll mebbe do."

"She's beautiful. Simply beautiful," Lori responded in a hushed reverent tone.

Ned nodded approval of her judgment and reached for the saddle blanket, then for the saddle. When he handed her the reins, she looked at me, confused. "You're not coming?"

Before I could reply, Ned said, "Him? On a horse?" He removed the cigarette butt from the corner of his mouth, dropped it, and ground it out with the toe of the worn dusty boot. "He's a scared a horses."

"Anything big, powerful, and stupid can be trouble," I said. She twisted the reins in her hands, dividing her attention between us and the mare.

"Don't pay him no mind, gal. Jest ease up thet draw an' drift left at thet ol' oak. It'll open up." Ned stepped up beside her. "Go on. Ya'll do fine."

"Are you sure?" she asked uncertainly.

"Ain't been wrong in more 'an twenty years."

She mounted with a graceful sweeping motion. Even I could see Ned had judged well; the stirrups were the right length. "Thank you, Mr. Early," she said, eyes bright. She gave me a soft look I couldn't fathom, then seized the mare with her knees and kicked lightly. The mare moved out smartly at a trot, head high, testing the long-legged rider on her back.

Ned lit another cigarette and leaned against the door of the barn. "She handles thet mare real good, don't she?"

"Hell. I don't know anything about horses."

"What about women?" Ned asked innocently.

"I'm not much better with them."

"Ya ain't too ol' to learn some." We watched until horse and rider disappeared around the curve in the draw. "She's got trouble, ain't she?"

I nodded, wondering how many people had gravely underestimated this lean, wiry old man.

"Mark the words," he said with special slowness. "She's a good 'n. Do right by her, ya hear?"

"So far, it hasn't been easy."

Ned chuckled. "It never is. Truly, it ain't. Ever."

I nodded agreement and walked back up the draw, Bobbie beside me.

Lori had ridden down the draw an hour ago with shoulders back and a smile brightening her face as I'd known it could. Bobbie had rushed out to join her, despite the presence of the mare. By now she'd finished brushing down all the horses in the barn and anything else Ned would let her do.

I was hungry whether she was or not. I laid down the book I was reading and turned off the stereo. In the kitchen I unwrapped the two chops I'd bought this morning, trimmed and readied them for the broiler. If she didn't get back soon, I'd eat them both. I rinsed two large potatoes and put them in the oven, then cut asparagus into a pot.

I poured coffee and sat, stretching my legs out under the table. I looked down at the cup, trying to picture what a coffee bean looked like close up. From the look of her, coming down the draw, she was in good spirits. I hoped it'd last. If she could find something nice to say, it would be a pleasant change.

Lori, striding briskly up the draw, saw me through the window, smiled, and waved. I waved back. Bobbie frolicked at her side, grateful for an occasional scratch between the ears. They made a nice picture. If a horse was all it took, I'd buy one from Ned. If I could keep her smiling, I might define the storms that shadowed her, even whip up hard winds against them.

She swept inside and into the kitchen, her face radiant. She placed her hands flat on the table and looked back up the draw where she'd been riding. "It was wonderful. Absolutely wonderful," she said, her voice filled with excitement. "Ned even let me brush her down."

"It sounds great," I said. "Hungry?"

"Starved," she replied decisively.

"There's chops in the broiler. You've time for a shower."

"I'll only be a minute." She whirled from the room. Bags were ripped open on the bed where I'd left them. Then the bathroom door closed. The water went on an instant later. I slouched further down in the chair, contented. This is who she is. The beaten, broken woman was gone. The task was clear: Keep her smiling.

When the shower went off, I gave it five minutes, then fired the flame under the asparagus. I'd timed it right. She stepped into the kitchen minutes later wearing white duck slacks that hugged her waist, hips, and thighs, flaring from the knees down. The bright yellow blouse had half-sleeves and ruffles down the front. She gestured with her dirty clothes. "May I put these in with your things?"

"Sure," I replied, bending to turn the chops a last time.

"It smells marvelous. Do you like to cook?" she asked, brushing by me on the way to the dryer.

"I hate it."

"Then why do you do it?"

"Do you spend much time in coffee shops?"

"I see the point." She rinsed and dried her hands, then began serving the asparagus. When I put the potatoes on the counter, she sliced them open. "Butter?" she asked.

"The fridge," I said, easing the chops out of the broiler and onto the plates. She found the butter, bread, the bottle of A1 sauce, and carried them to the table.

"Dig in," I said, setting the plates down. She poured a dash of sauce and started. She nodded, her left cheek bulging, to acknowledge approval of what her mouth contained. It was never completely empty until her plate was cleaner than the dog could have licked it. I'd given her the larger chop and she'd chosen the largest potato, yet she finished before I'd made a fair start. She jumped up from the table and made coffee, adding milk and sugar.

"When did you build this place?" she asked brightly.

"It comes with the job at Nelder," I said, working at cutting meat close to the bone.

"That's the first lie you've told me, Scott."

My cheeks reddened. At least I'd been promoted to Scott and she was still smiling. "What makes you think that?"

"The place fits you too well. Besides, no one builds like this to rent."

Uncomfortable with her curiosity, I bent my head down to the plate. It didn't help; it was too small to hide in.

"You built this house. And I suspect you bought the land from Ned."

I took a bite and chewed.

"Am I right?" she demanded.

I swallowed and said, "I am Nelder, Inc. It's a Nevada corporation. It keeps my name out of things."

"And what does Nelder do?"

"I buy houses, then fix them up to rent or sell."

"How much land do you have here?"

"About a hundred acres."

She looked out the window behind her, then down toward the road. "Ned said the national forest begins near the foot of the mountains. You must own his pasture."

I swallowed the last of the chop, uncomfortable with the conversation.

"Does he lease from you?"

"No. I caught him in a money bind. His wife died badly. There were bills. All he had was his horses. All I wanted was room. When he started the new fence, I stopped him. We put in the cattle guards instead." I stood to escape her thoughtful gaze and carried the plates to the sink.

She jumped up and grabbed the washcloth. "You dry," she commanded.

When we'd finished, I reached for her hands. "I'm glad you enjoyed yourself. Real glad." She looked down at the floor. "It seems wrong to spoil it but we've things to deal with."

She looked up finally, the difference in her face startling. The sparkle and lightness were gone but it wasn't fear that had returned. What dominated was grim anger. She pulled her arms back gently, freeing them of my hands, and said, "I've decided what must be done. It can wait for tomorrow."

"Expect I need more than that."

"It's my problem. I'll handle it."

"Rosta claimed he'd kill me. It might help to know what's going on."

She turned and reached for a glass and the bottle of bourbon. She didn't bother with ice. I poured coffee and sat back down. She sat opposite me, her features softening in the growing darkness. "What would you like to know?" she asked cautiously.

"What does Rosta want from you?"

"I don't know," she responded, looking down at the table.

"Lori, you're so turned off you can't trust anyone. You'll have to deal with that. And soon."

"I know."

I reached for the money and keys I'd pocketed earlier and laid them in the center of the table. "You've got to get out of here. There's a cop; he's a good buddy but still a cop. He's figured you're here. He'll be by. There's a couple thou there. Take it and the car and go, if that seems best."

"And what am I expected to do to earn this money?"

"Lori, I've damn well heard enough of your bullshit." I didn't raise my voice but there was a brittle snap to each word. "I'm not one to push but you've a choice. Tell me what in hell's going on or take the money and leave."

"Yes," she said. "You've heard more than enough bullshit." She stared at the drink she'd hardly touched. "I saw Rosta murder a man."

"That's a fair start."

"That's all I'm going to say."

I rubbed the scar on my palm. I couldn't afford anger now. "Look, your name's not Lori Adams and you're no cocktail waitress. Beth Dobsen planned to meet you at Artie's, maybe bring some money or help of some kind. But Rosta beat on her until she told him what was planned. That's how he found you at Artie's."

"She was...a very dear friend," Lori said, burying her face in her hands.

"She was more than a friend. I saw you come apart at the sight of those squad cars."

God. What a heel. Teardrops gathered on the table beneath her head. "And there's a lie in what you left out. Rosta wants something and he thinks you know where it is. Otherwise you'd be dead. He has a way with witnesses."

She made no reply. The pool of tears grew larger.

"Look, if you're involved some way..."

"What is that supposed to mean?" she snapped, whipping her head up.

"How in hell do I know? I was going to say I know a great attorney. And the cop I mentioned, he'd help. Goddamn it. I don't know what to say or do or think. And I won't until you tell me what's going on. I know this, though. If you don't pull the act together fast, you'll likely end up very, very dead."

"To trust is difficult for me," she said. "It wasn't always that way. Things happen. People change."

"If you don't want help or the money, what do you want?"

"To stay the night. I'll leave in the morning."

It was a polite statement but there was a firmness behind it I hadn't heard before. She'd made up her mind to something. I only wished I knew what it was. With a catch in my voice, I asked, "You'll just walk out? Like we'd never met?"

"I must." She stood abruptly and left the kitchen. She stepped back into the entry and said, "Do you know what I'll remember?"

I shook my head without looking at her; I didn't trust my voice.

"In Artie's, when you looked at me in the mirror, I knew you'd try to help. I didn't think you had a chance. But you made it possible for me to stand and walk with those monsters." She turned and was gone. Later, there were soft rustlings in the bed, then nothing.

Much later, I reached again for the bourbon and discovered the bottle was empty. It didn't matter. What I wanted doesn't come in a bottle. I told myself she knew what she was doing. She could handle it. And I was better off out of it. I told myself the same things, over and over and over. I took two Seconals, stripped, climbed under the rumpled bedding, and set myself to the task of sleep.

If it rains in hell, it rains like this. They were closing. I lost ground with each faltering step. Black raisin-sized drops sheeted into my face, blocking vision; they stole muddy ground from beneath my feet. The cap and fatigues were glued to the exhausted, flagging body.

The open ground suddenly tilted upward, becoming a cliff. Neither hands nor feet could hold purchase in the slippery cascading mud. And they were closer. I unslung the rifle, my nose filled with the stench of my own sweaty fear. I fought to suck soggy air into aching lungs.

A burst of fire ripped through the bleak blackness, driving me down to mushy open ground. I rolled, then fired. Three Cong regulars went down. They had to be Cong! I couldn't see more than vague body outlines behind gun flashes, but only the Cong could be here. Fierce cries accented the throb of pounding rifles. Misty figures surged forward. Bodies stacked on bodies, and they closed.

I was hit, my leg lost to slamming, throbbing pain. Over the barrel of the bucking gun, I stared with unendurable horror. They aren't Cong! They're my own people!

I recognized some, even through the near-blinding rain. Jake McQuire fell, then Nate Washington. And still they came, most nameless, but with faces too well remembered. I took another hit. All of me was burning, molten waste. The gun jammed. I gathered last remnants of strength, surged up for the final effort, and woke.

Her hand was cool on my wrist. The trembling began to ebb. The crickets argued excitedly outside the window and night air cooled my bare, sweated skin. I opened my eyes. Her long hair was black in the moonlight, her face milky white.

"'Lo," I said, the voice hoarse to my ears. I was embarrassed at laying the consequences of unwanted memories on another.

"You were thrashing so, I was afraid to wake you." She wasn't wearing my shirt; a sleeveless knee-length satiny whiteness lay about her in deep folds, pulled together at the neck. "Does this happen often?" she asked, concerned, not morbidly curious as others had been.

"Not as often, since I moved here."

"Who are Nate and Jake? When you called out their names, I half expected them to break through the door."

"Fellows I knew in Nam. Jake was a laughing, devilish Irishman who took the point on my order, once too often. Nate was a great giant of a black man, mostly heart. I bent down to check some sign and he died instead of me."

"I am sorry."

"There's not much point now."

"I meant if I hadn't brought up the war, this might not have happened."

"There's no way to know. I've never found any kind of trigger." Cautiously I reached over and clasped her bare forearm. "I don't want you to leave."

"Why in the world not? I've been nothing but an absolute pain in the ass."

"That's just a now kind of thing."

"And in what psychological science did you get your degree?"

I tightened my grip on her arm and pulled her closer. "Sarcasm doesn't suit you."

"I know." She leaned down and kissed me lightly, then pulled free of my hand.

I rubbed my lips with my fingers, trying to discover why they felt cool and warm at the same time. "I liked that."

I reached out and pulled her toward me once more. She tucked both hands behind my neck. Her kiss was long, filled with eagerness. She lay her head on my shoulder, her breath warm on my skin. Her left breast snuggled with my chest. I could feel myself growing. With considerable reluctance, I said, "I don't think I can handle much of this without wanting a bunch more."

"I hope not," she murmured shyly, reaching to kiss my neck.

My hand moved down her thigh and under the fluffy whiteness of the gown. Her skin was satiny smooth to my restless fingers.

"Please don't stop," she murmured, lifting her head and pulling herself against me. Her lips came gently to mine with the same eagerness but more demand.

There was cautious exploration on both sides. Much of the usual fumblings were strangely absent. It was as if we'd studied each other with loving care over endless time. But the needs, the demands, were too great. Our tension had been pressed passed our limits. It was over too soon. She lay with her head cradled on my arm, exploring my chest with long slender fingers. Contentment was the feel of her thigh beneath my hand.

Later, before the moonlight disappeared, it

was much better for both of us. She was a wondrous guide, leading us down the best paths. When it was no longer possible to delay it, we let the storms descend. She fell asleep with her head on my shoulder, my arm embracing her. The moonlight faded, blurring the crisp, clear outline of her breast and nipple. Gently I freed my arm. There was no way she would leave tomorrow, at least not alone.

Wednesday

‖‖ ‖‖ ‖‖ ‖‖ ‖‖

When I awoke, the room was bathed in sunlight. Where was Lori? I lunged up, turning. She was watching from the kitchen table, her smile brighter than the day.

"Good morning," she said, laying down the pencil. She wore the same white slacks and yellow blouse she'd worn last night.

I reached deep inside, searching for sign of the the usual morning grumps. I couldn't find much except a vague uncertainty about feeling so good. "Come here and say that."

She laughed, tossing her head back. There was a rich, free sound to it. Her hair floated and settled slowly. "We can accomplish more if I stay right here."

I wanted to hear her laugh again. "It depends on the objective." She'd used the word "we." It sounded good.

"You tempt me, sir."

She hadn't laughed but I could hear lingering echoes. "Not enough?"

She shook her head. "You're much too greedy." Her eyes were bright. "But then, so am I."

"What's that mean?"

She laughed again. "It means you should put clothes on and not tempt me further."

"You're hard, woman." I rolled out of bed, brushed the hair back out of my eyes, and padded naked toward the closet. Bobbie, lying beside Lori, watched, puzzled. She, too, knew something was different about this morning.

When I'd cleaned up, I walked into the kitchen. Bacon was frying on the stove. What I wanted was coffee. But the sketch stopped me. Lori watched as I rotated it for a better look. It was a penciled drawing of the old oak. With sharp bold slashes, she'd caught the essence of the ancient tree. The huge root dug determinedly downward into the rocky draw in balance with massive branches thrusting upward for light. "I really like this."

"Do you?" she asked, with a shyness I'd heard for the first time last night. "I haven't done much drawing lately."

I turned to face her. "You're quite a package."

"I'm glad you think so." She leaned forward and kissed me lightly on the cheek.

"That's no good." I stepped into her, pulled her close, and kissed her long and thoroughly. "The bed's still there."

"The bacon is burning," she replied.

Reluctantly I released her, poured coffee, and sat down to look at the sketch again. It showed more about her than all I'd learned thus far. It extended perspective. She was one who sought reality, dealt with it boldly, and worked at not caring what others thought of her view.

It was a quiet meal, partly because she ate continuously. Quick looks, soft smiles, and twinges of embarrassment accompanied sounds of forks. I'm well acquainted with my uncertainties in sexual matters. I was strangely pleased at her's. I liked the way her forehead wrinkled, whenever she glanced up.

"Don't look at me that way," she said, putting her fork down.

"How's that?"

"I'm not the goddess of love; don't put me on an altar."

"I don't know all that much about altars and such, but you're really something. Words like exceptional and fantastic come to mind."

"You don't know much about me, Scott."

"I can see goodness when it jumps up and bites me. And there's an innocence about you, a basic honesty."

"What an odd thing to say." She glanced down at the table, then reached for my plate and glass, stood, and turned to the sink. She picked up her dishes but didn't look at me. Working at the sink, she said, "I'd like to borrow your car."

I looked down, not wanting to see her reaction. "Are you planning to bring it back?"

She turned to face me. "Yes. There's no place I'd rather be."

The words hit solidly, enveloping me. They were wonderful words, opening grand vistas to be explored. "Let me take you."

"No. I'd rather handle it myself."

"There could be trouble."

"I don't see how."

"But if there is, I can deal with it better than most."

"You can. But at what price? After last night, I know the peace you've found is fragile."

"It's not so different for others. Some make good moves, establish solid careers, end up with a nice home and family, and a flock of friends. They've got it all. But it's an illusion. One worth living, but still illusion.

"Life's more a crapshoot than a planned process. If you roll sevens at the wrong time, the illusion is destroyed, replaced by some grim version of reality that changes your life forever."

I stood and moved to stand beside her, tucking my arm around her waist. It felt good, like it belonged there. "Expect that's what happened to you; sevens came up at the wrong time."

She nodded, laying her head back against my shoulder.

"You best let me come with you."

"I think you're being chauvinistic, but company would be reassuring."

"The offer stems from self-interest, not chauvinism."

She tried for a smile that failed only because of nervousness.

"Where are we headed?"

"A bank in Panorama City. There's a safety deposit box I must get into."

"Need a briefcase?"

"I've no idea."

"Take mine."

She nodded acceptance and turned to the counter to finish the dishes. I hunted up the black case and paused to console Bobbie, unhappily watching us get ready to leave. I scooped up the Colt from the windowsill. At the door, I handed Lori the case and let her step outside before grabbing two speed loaders from the shelf. I locked the door, wondering if two extra loads would be enough. It was silly speculation; there's no such thing as too much ammo.

She made no comment when I drove off the graveled road and through the edge of the small pond that was water for the horses. I held the wheel full right, slamming through the edge of the pond on each circle, until my side of the car was sloshed with mud. I left the motor running, got out, and examined the results. I tossed more mud against the back of the car until the license plate was unreadable. I rinsed my hands and climbed back inside.

I hesitated, looking out at the pond, muddied

now. Ned had always wanted to enlarge it, to
create a home for trout to be hunted savagely
with a good fly rod. He'd even bought the dynamite to blast a larger hole. Right now, I wished
the three of us were building it. I didn't like the
feel of what lay ahead. From the look on her
face, Lori didn't either.

Inside the First National Bank in Panorama
City, there were two empty desks. The name-
plate on the nearest one read JANET FELDING,
LOAN COUNSELOR. Mr. Salters, seated at the next
desk, had a small, pinched mouth that looked as
if it were accustomed to saying no. I asked him
when she'd be back. He was happy to tell me
Ms. Felding had left for lunch five minutes ago. I
thanked him and said I'd wait. I took a chair
against the wall from which I could see the
counter, the vault area, and the entrance to the
bank.

Lori entered and walked to the counter.
Watching her peripherally, I concentrated on
molding my face into an expression of boredom
and let my gaze drift absently around the bank.
No one seemed out of place or interested in anything other than their own business. The memory of Rosta's angry eyes kept me alert.

The tall lean man in the gray three-piece suit
who'd entered behind Lori stood at the counter,
talking earnestly with the teller. An elderly lady,
angry, stalked toward Mr. Salters' desk. A young
couple finished their business and left. Lori followed a woman into the vault area. Hours of

practice at the green felt of the poker table helped cover inner tension with the mask of disinterest.

Two more men entered, each with a handful of cash and checks. The tall man in the gray suit was directed to another window. If something was wrong, I couldn't spot it.

When Lori reappeared from the vault area, her features were marred by grim slashes. It was decision time. Should I precede her out the door? Step up beside her? Or follow? The tall man in gray made decision unnecessary. He turned away from the teller in the middle of her explanation and walked toward the door, pacing himself to reach the entrance behind Lori.

The angle was wrong. I couldn't move for fear of being noticed. The seconds dragged on. My glance swept the bank. There was no other sign of interest in her.

When the man looked around for what I earnestly hoped was the last time, I followed. Lori reached for the bar on the door and pushed her way through. The man caught the door swinging back, pulled it toward him, and followed her into the hall. I couldn't move faster without arousing suspicion. I hooked my thumb next to the Colt; a bullet travels faster than I can. It wasn't a good option but it existed.

I was several feet behind them when I cleared the door. We were in the wide hallway connecting the street with the parking area. I checked to the left. Nobody was in sight. I lengthened my stride, gaining on Lori's slower pace. When I saw the long slender arm reach under the back of the coat and produce a short-barreled .38, I palmed the Colt and lunged.

With his free hand, the man grabbed Lori's arm. I tried to ignore her look of pure terror. I slammed the gun into the side of his head. He crumpled, his head clunking solidly against the concrete walk. The .38 skittered across the walkway. Lori froze.

"Move," I commanded, tucking my gun away. "Now!" Would I have to carry her? She turned as if in a trance. Her first step was tentative.

"You've got to," I urged. She squared her shoulders and lifted her head. Each step was more determined than the last.

Discovery could come any moment. The urge to run was nearly overwhelming. But I had to know this new face. I reached down, flipped the man's coat up, slipped the black wallet from his hip pocket, and tucked it into mine.

Our luck held. There was still no one in sight. I tucked my thumb into my waistband and followed Lori. Once clear of the building, I studied anything that moved. No one seemed to notice her. But no one had seemed interested inside the bank, either.

She got into the car, fumbling for the key. The engine roared to life as I reached the front fender, glad I'd thought to back into the narrow parking slot. I took precious time to consider everything in sight. If anyone was watching, I missed it. Lori moved to the passenger side. I slid behind the wheel and pulled out. She was

rigid in her seat, her head tilted down as if
studying the pavement beneath the car. She
didn't seem up to conversation. It was just as
well. I was busy.

Several cars had been behind us when we'd
pulled out of the lot. In the rearview mirror, I
watched cars parked on the street. One, then another, began to move. I turned right, then right
again, and waited for the light at Van Nuys. The
cars behind us included some I'd seen when
we'd left the parking lot, but this is a natural
route back to the principal north-south street.

On the green I turned, watching three cars behind us make the same light. I stayed in the
right lane, slowing as required. Most of my attention was on the mirrors but I also watched
Lori. She was looking out the side window;
tenseness had not faded.

Behind us, the tan Ford was holding our
speed. Could it be coincidence? Another unusu-
ally cautious driver who happened to be right
behind us? The car was too far back for me to
see anything of the driver; the sun visor was
down, adding shadow to the interior of the car.
Traffic moved left to pass both of us. I pulled the
Colt and shoved it down between my thighs. I
had to know about the Ford.

At the next corner, the light flashed red while
we were still ten feet from the intersection.
Without changing speed, I drove on through.
The Ford closed behind us, running the light to
the accompaniment of blaring horns. I caught a
brief glimpse of the driver and jammed the ac-

celerator to the floor. "Dell Vickers is right behind us, Lori."

"What should I do?" she asked in a rush.

"Be ready."

"For what?"

"I don't know yet."

At the last instant I slipped through a gap in
oncoming traffic, whipping onto Vesper, north
toward Woodman, the same route we'd followed
leaving the Palms Motel. Vickers lost ground,
waiting for room to turn. Given an open road, I
could easily outrun the small Ford. But in the
heavily congested area ahead, it would be far
too risky. If we didn't get killed, chances were
good I'd kill someone else. And a shootout
wasn't appealing. I thought back to the scene at
Artie's and the white hate in Rosta's eyes. It was
certain violent decisive action was planned. I
pictured the maze of streets ahead, rejecting
route after route. One filtered in and remained.
A possibility, nothing more.

Tires screamed as I slid to a stop at Woodman.
Cross traffic was heavy with no break in sight.
While I waited for an opening, tension mounted
as I watched the Ford coming up fast.

When Vickers hit the brakes, he drifted left to
the wrong side of the road. I saw the gun. "Get
down!" I looked both ways, dismayed at the unbroken flow of traffic. There wasn't any room
but there wasn't any time, either. I floored the
accelerator.

The front of the slowing Ford was even with
our rear fender when our tires screamed. Lori

had her head under the dash and was pulling
her back after it. The sound of shattering glass
coincided with two harsh cracks from the gun. A
round tore through my shirt and left upper arm.
Another passed over my shoulder. Both ripped
through the windshield. The Dodge leapt in
front of the cross traffic bearing down on us
from the left.

I wanted to turn west but first I had to clear
the truck and car, nearly into the left side of the
Dodge. Horns blared and tires squealed as
brakes were applied. Our tires smoked from
power applied, the car shuddering violently.
Clear of the truck, I wheeled left to straddle the
double line, creating a new traffic lane in the
middle of the wide street. The car kissed our
rear fender and I heard the tortured sound of
metal tearing. Shoved off course, I fought the
wheel with both hands, refusing to let up on the
gas. It was easy to ignore the pain in the arm.
"You might as well try the seat again, Lori." She
began wiggling out from beneath the dash.

There was still no room for us on the right.
Several oncoming cars squeezed past, horns
wailing. When no further cars were headed our
way I drifted left, letting the engine wind. In the
mirror I watched Vickers use the same gap in
traffic to cross half the street and accelerate
down the wrong side as I was doing. I had better
than a hundred yards and was gaining as the
engine wound out toward max revs. But Vickers
was too close for us to escape with the turn I'd
hoped to make. Blood from the torn arm pooled

in the elbow of my shirt. Lori watched anxiously through the rear window.

On the gradual curve north, I was able to slip back to the right and avoid the next cluster of oncoming traffic. And we had room. The speedometer showed one-ten; I let it climb. The Ford was forced to wedge its way to the right into slower traffic. We had nearly a three-hundred-yard lead, coming up to Devonshire.

The curve of the road made it impossible for Vickers to see us. I braked hard. We were down to fifty and slowing when I slipped left through oncoming traffic, half sliding, onto Devonshire. I continued to brake and made a skidding U-turn. I almost lost it but the heavy-duty shocks paid their way. A moment later we were nosed out toward Woodman, peering through the brush at the corner. The anxiety in Lori's face became alarm when she saw blood dripping through the elbow of my shirt. She dug into her purse, producing a pair of nail scissors.

There were two options I could see. If Vickers missed our turning, we'd be free to lose ourselves back in Panorama City. If he turned after us, down Devonshire, we might well do the same. He might not see us or be much too late doing so. Lori reached across my stomach and cut with the scissors. She ripped a strip loose from the bottom of the shirt.

I'd miscalculated. I'd pulled too far forward. The options evaporated when Vickers saw the Dodge and began slowing. There was a break in traffic. The intersection would be our private playpen.

"Brace yourself, Lori." I didn't wait for her to move. I stomped the accelerator to the floor and the car surged forward, tires billowing smoke. I'd ram the sonofabitch, then use the Colt if necessary. But Vickers saw what I intended. The compact Ford was meat to the heavy Dodge. He whipped a right, onto Devonshire, running from a contest the Ford would lose.

He had turned late; he was forced to keep pulling the wheel tighter as he closed on the power pole at the corner, occupying space he might need. We were gaining; a chance was all I needed. His car tilted dangerously, right wheels nearly off the pavement. When I rammed the right rear, the Ford rolled up over the sidewalk. I eased off the gas, watching in the mirror. The sides of the car crumpled nicely; the top collapsed halfway to the seat tops. It rolled three times, out into the vacant field. Although Vickers was strapped in, he was jounced about in fine fashion. If appendages weren't broken, some would at least be unusable for a considerable time. Lori's face was pasty white as she watched through the rear window.

I turned north at the first opportunity. I held the speed below the limit; we didn't need a cop's attention. I tucked the gun back into my waistband. The wound was only a gash, more blood than pain. I opened the window to hide the bullet-shattered glass. There was nothing to be done about the windshield.

Lori took the piece of shirt she'd torn, tore it again, and knotted the strips together. She found a handkerchief in her purse and folded it into a pad. When I felt reaction begin, I turned off onto a quiet residential street and parked. I slumped in the seat, my head back, and let the trembling have its way. I lifted my arm, strangely heavy, across my chest. Lori tied the makeshift compress tightly.

"Your face is awfully pale," she murmured. "Should I drive you to a doctor?"

"I need a minute, is all. I've been shot before. But it's not something you get used to." Within moments, the trembling had faded noticeably.

"Do you think Vickers is dead?" she asked.

"I doubt it. The bastard only rolled; he didn't hit anything."

"And the man at the bank?"

"He'll do time in the hospital." I reached with my good arm for the man's wallet and began going through it.

Lori cradled her face in her hands. "I might know what you're thinking," I said. "Two men were nearly killed and you feel it's your fault some way."

She turned to look at me, face pale, eyes pensive. "That may be part of it, but I was thinking of how close you came to dying."

"It's only a scratch."

"Don't give me that; you could have been killed."

"It didn't happen." I counted the money. Ninety-seven dollars. Credit cards and driver's license agreed. The man in the gray suit called himself Sergio Landis. I handed Lori the license. "Did you ever see him before?"

She studied the picture. "It hardly looks like the same man."

"I.D. pictures are like that." According to the business card, Landis worked for Krutz Import & Export. His title was purchasing agent.

"No," Lori said, handing back the license. "I've never seen him or heard his name."

I tucked the business card into my shirt pocket and returned everything else to the wallet, and the wallet to my pocket. I climbed out to survey the damage. A jagged foot of steel had been ripped off the left rear fender and the back bumper was gone. The front bumper had a number of new nicks. Considering we could have been killed, there was nothing here to cry about.

I got back in and drove off. "I want to stop at Doc's. Then, Lori, we have to talk."

She was silent. Several blocks slipped by. "Yes," she said finally. "We must." Her features were drawn and stern.

"What was in the safe box?" I asked, testing to see how things might be between us.

"Money. A lot of it. Your briefcase is full of one-hundred- and five-hundred-dollar bills."

"You weren't expecting money?"

"No. I wanted what Rosta is looking for."

I had stayed on minor streets and was now at the edge of central San Fernando. "It's only a few minutes to Doc's."

"Won't he have to report a gunshot wound?"

"That's the law. But Doc Tilden breaks a lot of laws."

"I don't understand."

"You will when you meet him. His people are mostly Barrio Mexicans, a lot of them illegals. Many can't pay. He's always hustling bucks to support himself and the little clinic he runs for anyone too torn up to make it on their own."

"And you contribute?"

"He picks me clean every time I see him."

I parked behind a worn and beaten two-story building on Cellis, two blocks off the end of the mall. What the graffiti covering the wall lacked in artistic merit was compensated for by quantity. The downstairs was a small bar, Del's, near-empty this time of day. Doc's office was the second floor. I left the keys in the ignition and turned, lifting my arm to the back of the seat.

"Are you thinking of running?" I asked.

She nodded, then looked up sharply. "How did you know?"

I shrugged. "You didn't find what Rosta wants. Running could be the smart move. The money would help. I'll leave the keys, if it's what you want. Or I'll go with you."

"No."

"That's probably best. I did some running. It's a lousy way to live. There's too much fear."

"Yes, I know the feeling too well."

"So stay."

"Let's not forget Mr. Rosta and friends."

"We can handle it."

"Why on earth do you want to become involved? You risked your life in Artie's when you
stopped those animals. And a few minutes ago
you were nearly killed. The risks won't dimin-
ish."

"I'd still like you to stay. We can figure something."

"I simply don't understand."

"It seems like I can't dig up good words when
I need them. It's a bit soon to talk of love and
all. But those kinds of words keep popping into
my head. Let's just say running doesn't fit with
what I know of you, and your staying would suit
me fine."

Her hand brushed my thigh as she yanked the
car keys and handed them to me. "I think you
use words very well. And I think it's time to
meet Doc." She opened the door and got out,
carrying the case.

Once again she'd made the decision I wanted.
I only hoped it was also best for her. One thing
was certain. Any punk that hurt her had better
be a whole lot better than me.

During the drive back to the house we kept
our own thoughts, although they probably
weren't much different. Bobbie was glad to see
us. She romped excitedly about the car as we
drove around back. We took time to respond to
her welcome and assure ourselves we were safe.

Inside, Lori looked up at the rifles over the
door. She laid the briefcase down on the oak
coffee table and walked to the window near the

day bed. Watching the colts in the pasture, she asked, "Are those rifles loaded?"

"Yeah."

"And you know how to use them?"

"Better than most."

She turned to face me. Her smile lacked warmth. "I detest guns and all they represent, but right now I wish you had more."

"When Ned and I built the cattle guards, I made sure they were noisy. You can hear anyone driving in. And if someone tried walking, Bobbie would give us ten minutes at least. Even she can't cross the gravel without my hearing her."

"I thought it strange you'd build so far from others. Now I think I understand. The distance adds to freedom, a sense of control, of security."

"That about says it," I said. "I'm going to take a shower and grab a shirt in a little better shape than this one."

She nodded and looked back out the window.

In the bathroom, I pulled off the bandage and examined the arm in the mirror. The stitches were tight and even. The scar would be unnoticed among the others etched in my hide. I rotated the arm slowly. A little stiffness, a pulling at the stitches, but no pain of consequence. I dropped down and did twenty pushups on my fingertips, driving hard. The arm would do.

When I came back out, Lori had counted the money. "Two hundred thousand dollars," she said in an awed tone.

"I've played in some big games but I've never seen that much cash in one place." I sat down on the couch beside her, looking at the neat stacks of bills. "Do you know anything about it? Like where it came from?"

"Nothing," she said wonderingly. "I thought we were close to being broke."

"Are you sure this isn't what Rosta's looking for?"

"Yes." She paused, thinking back. "He used the term shipment, as if something had been lost or not delivered."

"Could it be drugs?"

"He didn't use the word."

"A moment ago, you said *we* were going broke. Who's we?"

She stiffened against the back of the couch, staring at the money. I reached out, gathered her hands together, and clasped them in mine.

She smiled faintly, freed one hand, and stroked the back of mine. She looked away, then turned back decisively. "My real name is Lorraine Livingston. My husband's name was Matt."

"You said *was*. Is he the man you saw Rosta kill?"

"Yes. We met in Houston three years ago, married, and moved to Los Angeles. He bought a lovely home in Chatsworth. Between Matt, entertaining, the house, and the yard, I was busy and content."

"When did it go wrong?"

"You know too much."

"Not usually." I gave her hand a gentle

squeeze of encouragement, wishing I could erase the sadness in her eyes.

"Either I didn't satisfy him or he wanted variety. I do know there were other women. When I found I had gonorrhea, it ended any hope of continuing the relationship."

"Then you'd decided to leave before he was killed?"

"Yes. I even hired a private investigator."

"Evidence for a divorce?"

"Yes. I'm ashamed of that. It was over. I should simply have left."

"What did he find?"

"I was to call him. There doesn't seem much point now."

"What business was Matt in?"

"He worked for Exton Industries. He had a talent for arranging profitable contracts for off-shore production of electrical components. He spent a great deal of time in Asia and Mexico."

"Tell me how he died."

She withdrew her hands and cupped her face in them. "Sunday afternoon, Matt came home with another man. They went straight into the den. I'd planned to be out, so I don't think they knew I was home. I could hear conversation but not what was said. When I heard two shots I ran to the den. A third man, who turned out to be Rosta, stood with his back to me, just inside the door. Matt, with a gun in his hand, was looking down at the man on the floor. There was a great deal of blood." She shuddered.

"Matt yelled, 'Wait. That's not it!' I think he

was referring to the package Rosta was holding. Rosta didn't wait. He shot Matt three times in the stomach. At first I couldn't move, watching Matt crumble in agony, dying.

"When Rosta saw me, I ran. He shot once, before I got out the side door to the kitchen. I climbed the fence into the Latterman's yard. I knew they were out of town, so I hid in the bushes until dark. I don't know where I found the courage, but I went back into the house, changed clothes, and collected what money I could find.

"There wasn't much. It made me think of Matt, lying in the den. He always carried several hundred dollars. I'm not sure I could have taken a dead man's wallet but I never found out. Both bodies were gone." She reached for my hand and gripped it.

"I thought it must be a monstrous trick. I'd seen Matt die. I felt reality slipping away, until I forced myself to look at the bloodstains. No one could survive, having lost so much blood. Someone had taken the bodies away. I was more terrified than ever. Matt's car was parked in the drive, the keys in the ignition. I made sure no one followed and spent the night in a motel."

"This was the day before we met at Artie's?"

"Yes."

"The man with Matt, you didn't know him?"

"No."

"You didn't see Rosta come in?"

"No, and I've no idea how he did it."

"Could Rosta have killed the man on the floor?"

"That's odd. When you put it that way, I can't say. At the time, I thought Matt had shot him. What made you think of that?"

"Was Rosta's gun a revolver like mine or an automatic?"

"A revolver."

"If Rosta fired the two shots you heard and the three that killed Matt, the one he fired at you would have been six, max for most revolvers. If he had to reload, it could explain why you had time to get over the fence."

"What is it?" she asked.

I realized I'd been tugging on my ear, looking down at the floor. "I don't think Rosta's trying to kill you."

"You said he was in the habit of eliminating witnesses."

"Yeah. But he could have blown you away as you went into Artie's. And Vickers was trying to stop us, not kill you. If I'd died, it wouldn't have mattered. It's you they want. Rosta didn't believe Matt when he said, 'That's not it.' So he killed him and tried to get you, too. Now he knows different. With Matt dead, you're his next best lead. He plans to kill you but only after he's found out what you know."

She shuddered and looked down at the money. I waited for her to look up. When she did, I said, "Why didn't you call the police?" I gave her hand a squeeze. "You could have gotten over another fence and found someone with a phone."

"I guess I wasn't thinking clearly." She looked back down at the money.

"And later, when I shook you loose from Rosta? Why bother with me? Why not go straight to a cop?"

"Rosta told me police couldn't help, that he had connections." Her lips trembled. "He said if police became involved, I'd die, horribly. I believed him."

I reviewed what she'd said. Possibly I was biased, so taken with her that the hunches I live by weren't receiving fair hearing, but I believed most of what she said. "And you felt the safe box was your last hope?"

"Yes. I thought if I gave Rosta what he wanted, I'd be free of him."

I reached out for a stack of bills, fanned it with my thumb, and tossed it back to the table. "I'm surprised Matt left this where you could stumble onto it. I'd have used a bank you didn't know about and kept the only key."

"When we first arrived, we opened a joint account and rented the safety deposit box. About a month later, I misplaced my key. I didn't give it much thought because Matt handled the money. But when I saw his key with the car keys, I knew I had to check the box."

"Could he have taken your key?"

"I don't generally lose things."

"And you never guessed he had this kind of cash?"

"Never."

"Did he ever mention any names?"

"Sometimes. What are you looking for?"

"I'm not sure." I shoved hair out of my eyes. "Did any of those names seem particularly important?"

"No. His boss, surely, Finley Quale."

"What do you know about him?"

"Nothing, really. Matt didn't often share his work. I never met the man."

"I can't figure where he got this money. Legitimate businesses pay with checks."

She picked up a sheaf of papers I hadn't noticed and handed them to me. The company name was Stillson Imports. "They're shipping invoices," she said.

I studied each one carefully. There were eight in all. The cargos appeared to have been electrical components. The earliest date was nearly two years ago. "Have you any idea what these mean?"

"Perhaps. Matt kept a scrapbook of letters and orders as mementos of highlights of his career. It was like a diary. He may have kept these for his scrapbook."

I looked through them again. "If these brought him two hundred thou, they'd be worth remembering." I laid them on the table and walked over to the phone. I opened the Valley directory, looking for Stillson Imports. "What city is given there?"

She leaned over for a closer look. "Sherman Oaks."

I moved to the bookcase in the corner. "Then it should be in that directory but it's not." I pulled out the city map and checked the address. "Hell. I remember that block. It's vacant; the address is a phony." I tried the number.

"Ellen's Stationery."

"Dialed wrong," I said, then hung up. "Looks like you really didn't know him."

"I thought I did. Then came his girlfriends. Now this. I guess I didn't know him at all."

"Could he have been a courier or smuggler? He could have buried drugs or whatever in the middle of these shipments."

"It would never have occurred to me, but he had a secretive side. He enjoyed any maneuver that surprised people, particularly when competing with others."

"If he decided to keep a shipment for himself, it could explain why he died. Men like Rosta don't play games."

"With two hundred thousand dollars, would a man risk his life for more?"

"There's one thing you learn from poker. Everyone wants more. Especially when it looks easy. When a player thinks I'm easy, it costs him money. If Matt thought Rosta was easy, it may have cost him his life."

I stood and began pacing. I pulled the business card from my shirt pocket and dropped it to the table. "Sergio Landis was carrying that." Lori picked it up. "Anything there?" I asked. "In Krutz Imports & Exports, I mean?"

"No," she said. "But with all his travels, Matt

may have known or had dealings with them. He never mentioned it."

"Rosta's for hire. Since Vickers and Landis were both at the bank, it looks as if Rosta is working for Landis or someone tied to Krutz Imports & Exports." I reviewed what we had. There wasn't much. "Any thoughts?" I asked.

"About what to do?"

I nodded.

"Nothing constructive, I'm afraid. Do you?"

"Have you got the number of that detective?"

"Yes. Should I call him?"

"No. Let me do it. We'll drop in and see if he found anything useful."

She reached into her purse and produced a business card. I took it to the phone and dialed. A man answered on the second ring. "Slawson here. It's your quarter."

"The name's Johnathan Smith. I was told that for cash you might handle something special."

"Smith, you said?"

"Yeah. I also said cash."

"Sure thing, Mr. Smith."

He was eager. Too eager. "Tomorrow morning at your office?"

"Ten-thirty?"

"That'll do."

"That cash, it's up front?"

"Yeah." I hung up and turned back to Lori. "Where'd you find that slug?"

"In the phone book. The large agencies wanted too much information. I'm afraid I don't know much about private investigators."

I looked again at the business card. Carl
Slawson might be helpful. Anything was possible. I tucked the card into my shirt pocket and
said, "Our best chance is to find what Rosta's
looking for and try to trade. If we don't find it or
someone beats us to it, we'll have no leverage.
Either way, we have to face the fact that Rosta
wants you dead. If your testimony could put
him behind bars, could you deal with that?"

"It would be extremely difficult."

"But you could do it?"

"If it was the only way."

I packed the money back into the briefcase,
along with the invoices. "Come watch, in case
I'm not around when you need this."

She followed me into the bathroom. I loosened a screw inside the medicine cabinet at the
top and lifted the cabinet from the wall to get at
the safe behind it. "Write the combination down
in some trick way."

She watched and made notes as I twirled the
knob. When the heavy door swung open, I asked,
"Got it?"

She nodded.

I slipped the case inside and closed the door.
"Try it."

Without reference to her notes, she opened it
on the first attempt. "Good," I said. I closed the
safe, fit the cabinet back into the wall, tightened
the screw, and restored order to the few items
on the shelves. She followed me into the
kitchen. "Coffee?" I asked.

She nodded and sat down at the table. I

poured two cups and joined her. "We ought to run through it again," I said. "We might have overlooked something."

"Yes," she said, with obvious reluctance. "I think we should."

I couldn't find much enthusiasm either. She had carefully avoided giving any information about herself prior to marrying Matt Livingston. I wanted to ask several things that could be important. Where did she grow up? Her clipped way of speaking assured me it hadn't been Texas. Had she gone to college? It seemed likely. But mostly I wanted more about Beth Dobsen. She'd been much more than a friend. And I needed to know why she was afraid of cops.

We continued into the growing dusk and through a dinner neither of us paid much attention to. The net result was zero. I thought of Sergeant Tony Haggen. We needed his help. But I couldn't risk it without knowing what other trouble Lori was in.

It was growing dark when we walked up the draw to the old oak. Bobbie ranged happily ahead of us. We sat on the giant root, watching the lights of the city grow brighter as night fell about us.

"A couple of things got left out in all that talk," I commented, tucking my arm around her shoulders.

"I know," she replied, leaning into my side.

"I hope it has nothing to do with this mess."

"It doesn't."

"When do I get the rest?"

"Later."

"Why not now?"

"I don't want to lose you."

It was much later when we went back inside. Naked, she interrupted my shower and claimed she was helping wash my back, which was absurd. All she accomplished was to make it necessary to cuddle on the sheets of the big bed sooner than planned. When she fell asleep in my arms, I was tempted to wake her. I began listing the ways that might please her. But the sandman returned from childhood before I finished the list.

Thursday

‖‖ ‖‖ ‖‖ ‖‖ ‖‖

I woke at Lori's touch on my shoulder. The sun highlighted her hair and shadowed her face. "I hate to wake you," she said.

"It can be dangerous." I reached and pulled her down beside me.

"It's nearly nine." She kissed me lightly on the neck and snuggled closer.

I didn't want to get up. What was the point? Seeing Carl Slawson would be a waste of time; it might even mean trouble. I didn't need that. I needed the long-legged woman cuddled beside me, nothing more. I pulled her to me and kissed her.

"It's after nine now," she said firmly.

Reluctantly I released her and struggled up and across the room. I grabbed clean clothes and stumbled into the bathroom.

When I entered the kitchen, Lori was frying sausages and eggs. She was half smiling at private thoughts. What they might be was beyond me. I cleaned my plate before I realized I'd begun.

"I've got to make a couple calls," I mumbled, standing. I poured coffee and carried it to the phone. Bobbie lay watching, her head on her front paws, judging my mood and her distance accordingly. I dialed Tony.

"Foothill Division. Sergeant Haggen."

"It's me," I said, distinctly unenthusiastic.

"What have you got?"

"I need help is all. Can't you be friendlier?"

"A grump shouldn't make early calls."

"Krutz Imports & Exports. What do you know?"

"Only what I hear at the tables."

"What's that mean?"

"That Hank Krutz is good at poker. He could break laws without comin' apart but nobody ever said he did. A tough old bird. I sort of like him. What else do you need?"

"What's he worth?"

"A bunch."

"Where can I find him?"

"He doesn't show himself much."

"I need to see him."

"I'll think on it. I might even get back to you. Now, in this new spirit of friendly cooperation, what else can you tell me about the girl? Or Rosta?"

"Nothing. There's a bit of news, though."

"Yeah?"

"Do you have a body tagged as Matt Livingston?"

"What the hell do you want with a body?"

"Just answer. Try yes or no."

"No," he said. "I never heard of him, alive or dead."

"Do you have any John Does?"

"There's always a couple. So?"

"So check. One could be Livingston. 17431 Beldane in Chatsworth."

"Where'd you get this?"

"Here and there."

"Right." He sighed. "Any more seed for the starvin' birdies?"

"Another could have worked for Rosta."

"What makes you think two citizens are dead?"

"Check that address. There's blood on the carpet that didn't come from shaving."

"Buddy, you can't leave it hangin' here. Give. What the hell are you into?"

"Let me check a couple things. I'll get back."

"You're stallin'."

"So? I'll get back."

"Make damn sure it's soon."

The line went dead. Maybe this time I'd pushed too far. Hopefully it was only as Tony had said; it was simply too early in the day. I sighed and dialed again.

"Vance Coggswell, Investment Counselors," said the young voice.

"Macklen here. I need to talk to Vance."

"I'm sorry, sir. Mr. Coggswell is in conference. May I take a message?"

"Tell him I'm on the line."

"But, sir, I . . ."

"Look. You're new but take my word. He won't fire you. Buzz him."

She placed the line on hold. Seconds later, Vance Coggswell said crisply, "Scott. It's good to hear from you. How can I be of service?"

"Exton Industries and Krutz Imports and Exports. I need financial details and whatever else you find. I'll pay a premium for fast."

"I will get right to it," he said. "Now, about that house, can I give you the particulars?"

"Let me get back. I'm jammed right now." A real estate deal at nine-thirty in the morning? Vance was working the wrong side of the day.

"Right. And I'll get this other information as soon as possible. Have a good day, Scott."

I hung up, knowing I didn't expect one. I grabbed the Colt from the windowsill and went back into the kitchen. I pecked at Lori's cheek as I passed, set my cup on the counter, and turned back to her. "Ready?"

"Not really."

"Me neither."

I tucked my arm around her waist and walked her toward the door. She smelled good and I liked the pale blue blouse she was wearing. Her new jeans fit every quarter-inch of her, from waist to ankles. I ushered her outside before picking up three speed loaders. The Colt seemed too small. Today was an Uzi day, a day for machine guns and all the clips that could be carried.

I drove the Dodge. Lori followed in the Blazer. I pulled into Perez's Body Shop and parked. Ricardo, a large, smiling man, increased his smile an impossible inch when he saw me. *"Amigo! Como stas?"*

"I'm getting by," I replied. "I need some glass, a rear fender and bumper."

"Caray! Bullet holes, no?"

"Yeah. But don't notice them."

"Si." He shrugged. "But the car, Scott. It is such a wreck. Pay only for the paint; it will be beautiful. What you can't see, the engine, it's *magnifico.* The car should look as good."

"I need glass, a fender and bumper, is all."

"But *amigo.* For only a few bucks more? It's not right."

"But you'll do it."

"Si. I will do it." Ricardo walked back into the shop, shaking his head.

I climbed behind the wheel of the Blazer. Lori faced directly front, the smile deepening the clefts bordering her lips.

* * *

We were ten minutes late when I parked in the underground garage. One glance at the four-story building told me it didn't matter. It wasn't old, but it showed more than a fair share of abuse. Tenants would not be fussy types. The elevator didn't work; we walked up to the third floor. SLAWSON INVESTIGATIONS was painted on the wooden door. Much of SLAWSON had peeled off. It was a door to be opened carefully, hoping it wouldn't drop off its hinges. I did so and let Lori enter.

"I'm Smith," I said to the red-faced man behind the desk. "You know her." Slawson's tight automatic smile stayed in place but the pale eyes narrowed to slits.

"How do you fit in?" he asked cautiously.

From in front of the small scarred desk I could see only the upper part of his thin frame. The pinstripe pattern in the coat of what may once have been a good suit clashed with the lined face and the few strands of oily pale red hair combed carefully back over the balding pate. The wine-and-silver-striped tie should have been replaced two years back. "I'm a friend. Leave it there."

I made sure Lori sat in the chair least likely to collapse and sat down gingerly in the other one. Slawson watched me, never looking at Lori.

"Lady," he said. "You didn't say nothing about this guy." His voice was scratchy, as if he'd been out too late last night and struggled through too many years of similar nights.

"Mr. Slawson," Lori said firmly. "I paid for information. Both Mr. Smith and I would like to hear what you found."

"Well, you see, it ain't that easy."

"Start somewhere," I said bluntly. "And see where it ends up."

"Well, she was right," he said slyly. "There's one broad I know about. But I got a whole lot more into this than the thou she gave me."

"How much more?" We were dealing with a leech. It might work in our favor, if my money held out.

"Well, you see, it's this way. I had no place to start. Christ, it took more than . . ."

"I need a price, not a story."

Slawson studied me, trying to decide how much I was good for. I hoped he was taking a good look at my eyes and giving adequate consideration to my size.

"Five bills? A name and address?"

I pulled a wad of bills from my pocket, counted out five hundreds, and laid them on the desk. When Slawson reached for the money, I covered it with my hand. "The name?"

"Sure thing. Got it right here. Let me tell you, she's a looker. Any guy'd like to see these goods close up. Know what I mean? Guess your old man's really into it. A whole closet's full of his stuff." He pulled a slip of paper from his coat pocket and laid it out on the desk.

I picked it up. "Rachelle Nestrum. Does it mean anything, Lori?"

She shook her head, distinctly uncomfortable.

"Did you find anything besides clothes when you searched her place?"

"Hey. I don't do break-ins. No way. There's a thing called the law."

"Stuff the bull and tell us what you found."

He tapped the desk with his fingers as his glance flicked between the two of us. "Well, you see, it's heavy stuff. Know what I mean?"

"How heavy?"

"Six hundred?" Slawson asked cautiously.

"You talk. Then we'll decide."

His gaze shifted restlessly between the money in my hand and my eyes. Years of making similar delicate decisions didn't seem to be helping.

"Well, sure," Slawson said nervously. "Why not?" He reached into the bottom drawer of the desk, lips tight in a cat-about-to-taste-the-canary grin. "I think maybe your old man was cheating some other ways, lady."

The package he set on the floor a few feet from the desk was the size of a two-pound box of chocolate, covered with a polyurethane fabric. A snap catch secured the top to each side. On the desk, Slawson placed what looked like an electric garage door opener. He shoved the gadget toward me. "Go ahead. Push the button."

When I did, the four catches popped free. The ominous sound of escaping gas filled the room. I shifted in the chair, uncomfortable, watching the top of the box slowly fill and expand into a balloon, nearly four feet across. Dropped off a ship at sea, it would lift several hundred pounds to the surface. Lori stared at it with curiosity and distaste.

"Neat," I said, watching the smug look on Slawson's face. "Were there others?"

"One."

"I'd like to take it along."

"Well, I was thinking to keep it. You know? Like a souvenir?"

"Keep the one on the floor. How much for the other one?"

"How about an even thou for the info and the toy?"

I counted out the money. Slawson reached into the drawer and pulled out another package and transmitter. He laid them on the desk and picked up the money.

"Do you have anything else?" I asked.

Slawson stared at the wad of bills in my hand and leaned out over the desk. "I get good pictures, if you want. I'm real good with videotape."

I believed him. From the expression on Lori's face, she did too. "Maybe later." I stood up. Lori rose quickly beside me. I counted out another five hundred and laid it on the desk.

"What's that for?" Slawson asked suspiciously.

"No one's to know anything about this."

"Hell. I wouldn't say nothing. We got a code."

"Let's say we want to support this code of yours."

"I don't even know you."

"You know Mrs. Livingston. And Ms. Nestrum. We want to talk with her. Alone. We don't want to bump into any strangers on the way in or out. And if we want you, we'll call."

"Hey. You got it."

I turned Lori toward the door with a touch at her waist, picked up the package and transmitter, and followed. At the door, I glanced back. Slawson had gleefully counted the bills once more and was tucking them into his coat pocket. He started to stand, then noticed me watching. He sat back down, trying for a warm, friendly smile. I closed the door fast to cut off the view.

Lori walked swiftly away, down the hall. I had the same need for distance between myself and the redheaded man.

"What did you call him yesterday?" she asked.

"A slug."

"There must be a better word."

As we started down the stairs, I heard what I'd expected. A door opened and closed. It could have been any door on the floor but it could also have been Slawson's. As we walked down the stairs, my ears were attuned to those above. I didn't hear anything but almost anyone can be silent on concrete steps. When we reached the ground floor, I handed the package and transmitter to Lori. "I need to check something. Will you wait in the car?"

She nodded uncertainly and turned down the last flight of steps to the garage. I could be wasting time, but I could afford it. I stepped to the lobby side of the stairs and waited. Someone was coming. Fast and quiet. I pulled the Colt.

When the head of thinning red hair peeked

around the corner down the steps to the garage,
I was ready. When Slawson looked toward me,
my left arm was already moving. He drew back,
terror flooding into the eyes, but I'd expected
that. With a lot of shoulder, hip, and thigh behind it, I drove my fist to a point a foot beyond
his head. There was a grinding crunch of small
bones of the nose, breaking, and the snapping
pop of cartilage being rearranged. Blood exploded in all directions, as if from his entire
face. His head slammed against the wall. The
eyes glazed. He slid slowly down the wall into a
heap on the floor.

Each slack arm lay across a step. With a lift of
my heel and a downward thrust, the threat of
this little man would be eliminated. Broken
arms take time to heal. I caught myself considering those points where a simple blow would
be fatal. I shook my head sharply and took a
deep breath. The pistol would give us time.
Slawson wouldn't even know who he was for a
day or two. I brought the Colt crashing down
over his left ear. Remaining tension fled; the
body lay as if dead.

Disgustedly I dug for the bills so recently
counted onto the small scarred desk. Maybe losing the two thou would hurt worse than two
broken arms. I hoped so. I tucked the Colt away
and used the one clean place on his shirt to wipe
the blood from my fist, then hurried on down
the stairs.

As I approached the car, Lori watched with a

mixture of suspicion and concern. I climbed inside without meeting her glance. It didn't help.

"What was the delay?" she asked.

"Some fellows live in a sewer. Others will kill for a dime. Slawson has a foot in both worlds. He was following us." I started the engine.

"And you stopped him?"

"Hard." I pulled out and drove up the ramp to the street.

"How could he hurt us?" she asked, staring at the smear of blood on my middle finger.

I eased into traffic and turned toward the San Diego freeway. "Lots of ways. When the news hits about Matt, he might be able to make points with the cops by leading them to you, points he probably needs. If he finds out Rosta wants you, he could make a buck. But first, he'd try blackmailing us."

She stared out the windshield, shoulders rigid.

"Lori," I said, slowing for a car pulling from the curb, "those I've seen in this are cold. Real cold. To them, people are mere objects to be bought, sold, or discarded according to convenience. Talking won't get it done."

"You're right," she said. "I was only hoping I'd never meet such people again."

I thought of several questions but said nothing.

When I suggested it might be better if I visited Rachelle Nestrum alone, Lori agreed before I finished the sentence. It wasn't unexpected;

wives and girlfriends seldom become close. But I didn't want to leave her waiting in the Blazer. As we passed a large shopping center, she suggested the supermarket on the corner. I drove around the block and let her out.

She tried for a smile when I suggested she might find something for the house but the lines in the face and the shadows in the eyes spoiled the effect. I watched until she disappeared inside, wishing for her sake that Slawson hadn't found Rachelle. As I drove off, I realized I had no desire to see her either.

The apartment house was on Beverly Glen, in Westwood, an affluent community from border to border. The worn and battered Blazer was out of place parked between a Mercedes and a late-model Corvette.

In recent years, smiling, amiable doormen, ready to help for a buck or two, have given way to private uniformed security guards, armed and wary and capable. One glance at this man's broad, craggy features told me money wouldn't get me inside. I built a friendly smile, fished out the embossed business card that gives my title as special assistant to the president, and handed it to the frowning guard. He was sure that, in scuffed loafers and worn casual clothes, I didn't belong here. "Rachelle Nestrum, please."

"Is she expecting you?" the guard asked skeptically, his right hand resting on the butt of the holstered .38. The gray-blue uniform was nicely tailored, sharp, and professional looking. It had

also been designed for easy movement of powerful arms and legs. The silver name tag read
SIDEL HINDERLING.

"I don't think she knows me, Hinderling. A
friend of hers, Matt Livingston, gave me her
name and address. I have some information."

Hinderling didn't like it but the name was
right. He turned to the house phone, watching
me.

"She wants to know how come you know Livingston," Hinderling demanded.

"Business. He's arranging to get some electrical components built for us."

When the burly man hung up, he grudgingly
opened the door. If he'd had his way, I'd be
leaving, not entering. "Third floor. Number
thirty-one." He turned his back as I stepped
inside and went up the stairs, ignoring the elevator.

In front of her apartment, I knocked. When
she opened the door, I handed her the card. "The
name's Macklen."

I'd heard what Slawson said but it hadn't prepared me. She was stunningly beautiful, ready
to step into an ad photo layout for *Esquire* or
Playboy. She looked at the card, rubbing her
thumb over the embossed logo. Long red nails
were done to perfection. Dark brown hair was
cut short and immaculately groomed. Makeup
had been applied meticulously, adding to the
sense of aloofness.

"Won't you come in," she said, her voice
pitched low. If its husky sexiness had been prac-

ticed, it was well learned. She hit the first of each word with a soft rush of breath. I stepped inside onto gold carpet, wanting to pause to take my shoes off.

"Please. Have a seat." She gestured toward the ermine-white couch. I felt like a dumb, awestruck kid amid opulence, sexually challenged by this strikingly beautiful woman. I glanced around the room and sat down gingerly. The cost of the furnishings would cover the down payment on a modest house.

She sat in the matching chair, right-angled to the couch, and fixed dark brown eyes on me, neither accepting nor rejecting. The tight-fitting turquoise blouse accented proud, thrusting breasts unconstrained by a bra. Pale beige slacks fit snugly at the waist, billowing about her legs as might be the fashion in chic Middle Eastern garb. A belt of turquoise stones, set in delicately crafted silver, decorated her waist.

"You said you had information?" she asked formally.

"Some. But I need some, too," I began, with no idea how to continue.

She nodded slightly, her eyes empty of emotion.

Surely she could see my discomfort. Was she laughing at it? I half-thought she was. She crossed her legs, the rubbing sound startling in the quiet room. I tried to focus, to find words suitable to the woman and surroundings. "I only used Livingston's name to get past the guard," I blurted out. "We don't have business. I never met the man."

"It would seem," she said with a wry smile, "you have achieved your objective. You're here."

I shifted uncomfortably on the couch. Where in hell were the goddamned words? "Have you found anything unusual Matt left here?"

"Why should that concern you?"

"Something he had cost three lives and threatens at least one other."

"I don't believe you."

"You've got to," I said, leaning toward her. "When did you hear from him last?"

She tried not to let it show but worry announced itself in the tensing of her shoulders. "Friday of last week," she said finally.

"Did he call or stop by?"

"He stopped by. How that could be your business escapes me."

"And he didn't leave anything?"

"No. Please tell me what this is about or you'll have to leave."

"And he hasn't contacted you since?"

"No. He has not."

Her impatience showed; she didn't like the way things were going. Neither did I. "Did you expect him to?" I continued in a rush.

A worried frown briefly creased her forehead. "I think you'd better leave."

"I've a hunch Matt was using you, Ms. Nestrum. I can't prove it, but everything I know says he made a big score. I'd bet he told you he was leaving his wife, and he would have. But he'd have left you behind, too."

"That is preposterous. We are to be married as soon as he can be rid of his shrewish wife. Do I look to be the sort of woman who could be used, as you put it?"

"Don't tell me it hasn't been tried. Matt just made it where others struck out. And it's clear you haven't met Lori Livingston. If you had, you'd never call her a shrew."

With nostrils flared she tossed me a haughty look and stood. "I don't believe you know anything of interest to me."

I stood to face her. I hadn't handled it well; I knew that. This was a task for he of the silver tongue, not this clumsy oversized beast, awed by spectacular beauty. She might know nothing but I couldn't leave it like this. There had to be a way. "Did you know you were burglarized recently?"

"You are absurd. No one has broken into this apartment."

I studied her face. She was mistaken but she wasn't lying. Slawson was better at burglary than at following people. Her heavy breathing thrust her breasts against the front of her blouse in disconcerting fashion.

"Now will you leave? Or must I call security?"

"Ms. Nestrum, I'd bet there's a nice woman under all those fancy clothes and makeup. I need to talk to her. But I can't get through the facade." I watched her angry face and eyes, searching for a way to proceed.

"Okay. I'm leaving." I paused, needing to stifle an anger of my own. "But if one more dies, I'll be back to point out how you could have helped."

I stepped around her toward the door. I stopped with my hand on the knob and I turned back to face her. "If you weren't burglarized, how do I know you have a closet full of Matt's clothes?"

"You broke in here?"

"No. It was a fellow named Slawson."

"I don't understand. Nothing is missing. What was he looking for?"

"Anything helpful in a divorce case. What he found was evidence Matt was a smuggler."

"You are utterly unbelievable. Matt has an excellent position with Exton Industries. Why would he jeopardize his success by smuggling?"

"Money." I took two steps forward. I described the balloon device and what it looked like when triggered. I didn't need to explain its function; she saw it.

She turned her back to me and said softly, "I remember the packages. They reminded me of chocolate. I thought he'd brought them to surprise me." She walked to the end table beside the couch and wrote briefly on a slip of paper. When she handed it to me, she said, "I think you're wrong about Matt. But if it's any use, that's the address of his apartment. Recently, he spends more time there than at home. I'd appreciate it if you'd leave now."

"Thank you, Ms. Nestrum. Thank you very

much." I stuffed the note into my shirt pocket. "There is one more thing."

"I suppose you feel you must."

"You could be in danger. Leave the city for a while; visit friends or relatives. Two men and a woman are dead and someone made a try for Lori Livingston. They may come for you."

"Do you seriously expect me to believe that?"

"I was hoping you would. Matt had something others want. Someone's checking everyone he knew. I'm no pro but I found you. So will they."

"You're ridiculous. You can see this apartment is well protected."

I wanted to grab her by the shoulders and shake hard, to tear her loose from her private world. Words were the only available weapons. "How did Slawson get in?"

She did not reply. Confusion and uncertainty filled her lovely face.

"What about me? How good is this security you're counting on?" I took another step, reducing the space between us to inches. "What's to stop me from doing whatever comes to mind? Could you? Can the guard hear silent screams?"

There was fear now, replacing uncertainty. "We could visit the morgue to see what was done to the woman before she died. It might give you some idea of what you're up against."

"I cannot believe this. Any of it," she said finally, straightening her shoulders. "Please leave."

"Did you notice I used the past tense when I

mentioned Livingston? 'He was.' 'He had.' That kind of thing?"

Her face paled.

"He's dead, murdered. You should get clear."

I waited, hoping for response, something to grab hold of, an opening I could use. She stared at me in granite silence. I turned to the door and left.

Downstairs, Hinderling watched me approach, distinctly wary. Maybe I wasn't doing a good job of hiding frustration. His beefy hand rested on the butt of the holstered .38.

"You any good with that?" I asked coldly, pointing at the gun.

"You fixing to try me?" There was quick eagerness in the dark brown eyes. His shoulders bowed forward.

"Someone will."

"Who?" he demanded suspiciously, the eyes watchful, disbelieving.

"Sal Rosta and friends."

"Why would a big-time hood come messing here?"

"Rachelle Nestrum."

"What are you talking about?"

"Rape and murder. One woman's down and Rosta tried for another. Two men are dead. One was Matt Livingston. Rachelle's name could be on a list."

"Go on." There was a cop watchfulness in the eyes, and skepticism, but he was listening.

"Rosta wants something Livingston had. He'll find out about Rachelle and drop by."

"Did you tell her this?"

"Yeah. She wasn't buying."

"She can be that way," he said, showing concern for the first time. "Say I believe you. Why not call a cop?"

"If you want to know about me, check with Sergeant Tony Haggen at Foothill Division. But there's no case; he can't help."

"Why lay it on me?"

"I don't see anyone else. If you stay alive, she might, too."

"Reasonable," he said thoughtfully. "What's Rosta looking for?"

"I don't know, but it's big." I reached into my pocket, pulled out five hundred of what I'd taken back from Slawson, and offered it to Hinderling. "I'd get a good backup, the next day or two."

"This is the damnedest thing ever. Who are you? Some loony do-gooder type? Out to save the world?"

"Say I don't like seeing people wasted, and leave it there. You want this or not?"

Slowly the beefy hand reached for the money. "I guess I have to take you seriously."

"Do that. It might keep you both alive." I left.

When I came up behind Lori in the supermarket, I said, "You look kind of familiar." She whirled, lunged for my neck, and kissed me. In contrasting her warmth and aliveness to the sterile beauty of Ms. Nestrum, Rachelle didn't fare well. I lifted her chin gently and said, "Time to go."

Reluctantly she released me and began pushing a cart heaped with groceries toward the checkout counters. "It's a small kitchen," I pointed out. "Have you figured where you're going to put all that?"

"Yes, and in time, half of it will go into your stomach."

She wanted to ask about Rachelle but she kept up a fast, snappy, idle chatter until clear of the checkstand and back at the Chevy. It was not until we were nearly to the San Diego freeway that she asked, facing forward, "Was she pretty?"

"Very young and very beautiful. A bit of a snob, but there's probably a nice person under all the trimmings."

She was silent for several blocks. I turned onto the freeway, north, toward the Valley.

"All right," she said finally. "She's young and beautiful. What did you find out?"

I repeated the conversation. It didn't sound any better describing it than it had in Rachelle's apartment.

"You're absolutely right," she said firmly. "She is in danger. Is there anything we can do?"

I told her what I'd said to Hinderling. "If I read him right, he's good. He'll get someone in with him. He half thinks I'm a nut but he won't bet against me. I don't see anything else we can do." I handed her the slip of paper. "It's supposed to be Matt's apartment. We ought to check it out."

"Now?"

"There's no point putting it off."

"Are you going to break in?"

"If I can."

On Saticoy, the apartment building we wanted was almost hidden between two newer, larger units. I could see through the entrance into the courtyard. Parking was in the rear, at the end of the long narrow drive. Walls of flaking ivory paint begged to be scraped and repainted and the plantings needed to be replaced or cut back drastically. Each ground-floor apartment had a separate narrow patio extending across its width. The second-floor apartments each had a small balcony. There were twelve on each floor. Since it was a weekday, most tenants would be at work.

I drove around the block. "Any ideas?"

"None," Lori replied, "except I wish we were someplace else."

"Me, too." I took another right, back onto Saticoy. "If I can get in, do you still want to come along?"

"Yes. I might see something you would miss."

I turned down the narrow drive. At the back, I took the left behind the building. Only one car was parked in the carport garages. I pulled into slot 204, the number of Matt's apartment.

"Let me look around. If someone drives in,

duck down. Rosta probably doesn't know about this place, but there's no need to take chances."

When she nodded, I got out and walked toward the back entrance. I took out a business card and pretended to study it as I entered the courtyard and turned up the stairs. I couldn't see that anyone noticed me.

In front of 204, in the back corner of the building, I knocked, feeling foolish. Dead men seldom answer doors. I knocked again. Rachelle could have written the wrong number. I tried the knob. It was an older, inexpensive lock. A pro could be inside in seconds. Short of breaking the door down, the lock would keep me out. I thought again of the balconies. I had to be sure of the apartment number.

Passing the small swimming pool, I felt dangerously exposed. That strangers often check apartment directories did not ease the tension in my gut and shoulders. From beyond the door marked MANAGER, a television soap commercial blared. The name on the mailbox for apartment 204 was M. Livingston.

Back in the Blazer, I asked, "I don't suppose you know how to pick a lock?"

"Be serious," Lori replied with a wan smile.

"I was afraid of that."

I turned and looked again at the building. The balcony was bordered with a four-foot ornamental iron fence. The patio below had a gate, hinged to the four-by-four attached to the wall of the building. "I'm going to try to get to that balcony. With luck I can unlock the glass slider with my knife. If I make it, you come on up the front."

I got out and walked to the corner. No one would see me from the street. Only someone in the neighboring apartment buildings had an opportunity. Drapes had been pulled against the morning sun. It was unlikely they'd be opened until tenants got home. It was a risk I'd have to take.

I considered the route. If I could plant my feet on top of the four-by-four, against the wall, then crouch, the lower part of the balcony railing would be within reach. The gate was locked. I reached over it with both hands, bracing myself on the two-by-four top rail, to which the grape stakes were nailed. It was no trick to get my right foot on top of the four-by-four post. It was harder to balance and muscle the left foot and leg up over the gate and under the right. The stakes took part of my weight.

I inched my hands down the gate toward the wall. The gate slipped in the worn latch with annoying unpredictability. As my hands got closer to my feet, my back arched like an inchworm. It was tough to maintain balance. If I lost it, the only option was to tumble into the small patio, hoping to avoid the two metal chairs and barbecue. The thought of falling increased my concentration.

When my hands were within two feet of the wall, I was teetering dangerously. I looked up but I couldn't tilt my head back far enough to see the railing. I bent my knees, seeking balance, wanting to move my left foot a few inches away from the wall. The gate suddenly shifted again. I was falling. I lunged for the remembered railing. Extended hands found only air. Then my right made painful contact, grabbing at a decorative scroll. My left slammed into the bottom rail as my feet slipped off the gate. I dangled. A stitch popped loose in my arm; the others smarted nicely.

The rest was relatively simple. I pulled myself up until my chin was even with the bottom rail. I reached up for another scrolled pattern and continued pulling. The iron tore into my palms. When I was able to lift my foot to the floor of the balcony, I used it to lunge for the top rail. Seconds later my back was to the sliding door. There was no sign I'd been noticed.

I dug out the Buck knife, opened it, and tried the slider. I'd been right. It was as old and worn as the building. I was able to force a gap, slip the blade through, and lift the plastic hook latch. I tucked the knife away, opened the slider, and stepped inside.

Free of the drape, I looked about the room. To my left was a small kitchen. I was standing in the living room, which extended to the door in front of me and to my left beyond the kitchen. Although the blue couch and chair were nearly new, they were inexpensive pieces. The blue shag carpet was faded into purple tones in places. Two small end tables supported matching lamps with yellowed shades. The coffee table was nicked and scarred.

Moving further inside, I could see the part of the living room that balanced the kitchen. The only furnishings were a large console television set and an office desk. Both looked out of place. They, too, were inexpensive pieces, but new and unmarked. I walked to the door and opened it an inch. I wasn't expecting anyone but Lori. Still, my hand rested on the butt of the Colt.

She stepped inside, her expression a mix of uncertainty, caution, and curiosity. I locked the door behind her.

"It seems unlived-in," she commented nervously.

"Yeah. It's got less personality than a motel room."

I followed her through the archway into one bedroom. I reached down and slapped the bedspread. Fine dust drifted upward. I lifted the spread; there was no linen or blanket under it. The closet was empty and dust layered the small end table beside the bed.

"No one has used this room in a while," I commented.

Lori nodded agreement and walked into the other bedroom. It was a duplicate of the first room but someone had been using this one. The bedding had been casually pulled up over the pillows. Looking at the clothes in the closet, Lori said, "These are Matt's things."

I opened the top drawer of the dresser; shorts, T-shirts, and socks were neatly stacked. The other drawers were empty. In the bathroom, a set of towels was laid out. The medicine cabinet contained only the minimum required for a single man with few needs. There was no sign Rachelle or any other female had been here. Lori went back into the living room.

Thoughtfully I walked into the bedroom and pulled down the bedding. They were there, the stains of sustained lovemaking. I tried to picture Rachelle naked, in this bed with Matt, and couldn't get it done. The apartment was worn and shabby. Rachelle would demand finer accommodations.

In the living room, Lori was seated at the desk with the contents of a file folder spread in front of her. "The top drawer is locked," she said, continuing to read. "Can you open it?"

The lock was standard. The flat metal bar projected upward into the pressboard top of the desk. The hole cut into the top was larger than necessary. There was play when I shoved, then pulled on the drawer. I used the knife to enlarge the hole. I shoved the drawer in, then yanked hard. Something gave. I yanked again. The drawer flew open, the lock dropping inside; the small screws holding it had pulled loose.

I picked up the two scrapbooks it contained, walked to the couch, and laid them on the coffee table. Lori followed and sat beside me. She reached out and opened one. "This is what I told you about, Matt's souvenirs," she said. "I saw it only a month ago." She thumbed idly through pages of correspondence, orders, invoices, and awards. She turned to the last filled page and said, "There's nothing new."

She closed the scrapbook and laid it to one side. She sat unmoving, looking at the second one. "I haven't seen this before," she said in a small thin voice. She flipped open the cover, then leaned back on the couch.

The smiling sultry faces of four women looked up at us. They were not nude shots but the adornments were minimal. Little of their lovely attributes were left to the imagination. As amateur photography goes, the shots were excellent. Even in the indoor poses the lighting was good, bringing out rich skin tones and fine detail. The photos were mounted on a sheet of black felt paper, covered with clear plastic. Locks of hair were tucked under two of the shots.

Lori's face was pale. Slowly she reached out and turned the page. There were three photos on the left and four on the right. She turned another page, then another. She looked at her own picture several pages later.

She'd been captured in tension, pulling herself from the swimming pool. Her hair was plastered to her head and water streamed off her slender body. She wore a brief bikini that accented her breasts and narrow hips. A lock of hair was mounted by the photo. In the picture, she was smiling. She wasn't smiling now. "This was taken in Houston, before we were married."

Disgust etched her face as she examined the

photos beyond her own. Some of the women were older but most were younger than Lori. All were posed with care. All were beautiful through the lens of the camera. There were a couple dozen photos mounted after hers. "Which is Rachelle?" she asked, as if not wanting to know.

I flipped back a page and pointed. She leaned forward. There were three photos mounted beyond Rachelle's. I hoped it helped. Lori hadn't been the only one fooled. The other photos could explain the apartment. Rachelle would not be content here but there were those who would be. The last photo had been taken by the small pool downstairs. I leaned forward and closed the album. "That's enough."

"Yes. It is," she said tonelessly. "It would seem I'm not very good at picking men."

"You picked me."

She tried to match my attempt at lightness but could only come up with half a smile. "As I recall, you did the picking."

"Me? You've got it all wrong. Women do the picking. Men only think they do." I pulled her to me. She tucked her arms around my back and pulled herself tightly against me, burying her face in my neck. I waited until taut muscles began to slacken, then kissed her lightly on the cheek. "Now tell me what you found in the file."

She pulled away slowly, stood, and walked back toward the desk. I liked the way she forced her shoulders back, the way she squared her head. "This looks important," she said in a more natural tone. "It's a letter from Hank Krutz."

The figure of five hundred thousand dollars stunned me. I read the letter again. There was nothing else of note. Krutz was raising his previous offer, not mentioned, for the "merchandise discussed."

"Five hundred thou is one hell of a chunk of money," I commented. "More than enough to get determined attention from a lot of serious-minded people." I read the letter again, concentrating on each word. It didn't help. I laid it back on the desk.

Lori handed me another, saying, "Everything else seems routine, the sort of thing I've seen on his desk many times. This one suggests Matt saw his boss, Finley Quale, shortly before his last trip."

"Where did he go?"

"Japan, but he mentioned he might also visit Hong Kong."

"Did he?"

"I didn't see him until last Sunday." She was racked by a tremble that faded slowly.

I read the letter thoughtfully. Quale congratulated Matt for the arrangement of a recent contract. The important line was a request Matt stop by before leaving. It might help to know what they'd discussed.

When I laid the letter down, Lori said, "Nothing else seems important. Should you look these over?" She pointed to the correspondence and papers laid out on the desk. "You might find something I missed."

I tugged on my ear. "I'm edgy," I said finally. "Maybe it's only this burglary bit, but I've got the feeling we've been here too long. Gather up everything you can find. We'll take it with us. Then let's see how well we can search this place."

"We have no idea what we're looking for."

"I know. How big was the package Rosta was carrying?"

"About the same size as the box Slawson gave you. It could even have been the same sort of device."

"Maybe that gives us a max size, then. But it may be stashed somewhere, say in a different safe box. So we could be looking for a key."

I left Lori at the desk, gathering up papers, and walked into the kitchen. Searching an apartment is not my forte but I've seen Tony Haggen and his team at work. I began mimicking what I remembered. A few minutes later, Lori joined me. Together, we emptied the refrigerator and every shelf in the kitchen. We dumped the contents of each open container on the counter and poked through it carefully. I took the ice trays out and held them under hot tap water, wondering if it was true that diamonds can be hidden in ice. The answer was not revealed; the ice melted into water. There wasn't a whole lot of drama in the process.

I left the bathroom to Lori and tore apart both

bedrooms. I used the knife to examine suspicious firmness in mattresses and clothes. All drawers were removed and examined, as was the cabinet space behind them. When I tipped the cabinet over, I was puzzled.

Matt's passport was taped to the bottom. Why? What could be secret about it? I leafed through the last few pages. Lori'd been right. Matt had gone to Japan, then on to Hong Kong. He'd also been in Kuwait for two days. Asia and Mexico, Lori had said. Entry and exit to Kuwait must have significance, but what? The only things they had there in abundance were sand and oil. Sand is hardly worth smuggling and oil can't be brought out in a suitcase.

I was headed for the bathroom to show the passport to Lori when I heard it. Sound from the lock on the front door. I stepped to her side, touched my forefinger to my lips for quiet, motioned for her to stay out of sight, and closed the door behind me without latching it. I moved soundlessly to the front door and flattened back against the wall, lifting my left hand above the door frame. The Colt came free as the door swung open.

My only impression of the man was size: huge. I slammed my hand down on the back of his neck, grabbed, and yanked. He tumbled into the room. My right arm drove under my extended left, the Colt pointed at the chest of the second man, reaching under his coat. "Go for it," I snarled.

They were wasted words. He was motionless. I reached for the tie and led him into the room, trying not to think of what might be happening behind me. As if rehearsing a dance step, I rotated back to the wall, pulling the man with me, desperately wanting to know what the first man was doing.

I needn't have worried. He was on hands and knees, blood dripping from his scalp. His head had slammed into the corner of the television cabinet.

"Close the door," I said to the man I faced, my voice flat, harsh.

He didn't move. Using the tie, I pulled him toward me until the muzzle of the Colt was nestled between two ribs. I nodded toward the door and jabbed sharply with the pistol. With studied motion, he reached out and closed the door. The muzzle of the Colt remained buried in his ribs.

"Smart," I said. My smile was one I reserve for punks with guns. "Grab the back of your neck and turn around."

With deliberate slowness, he did as directed. Lori had come out of the bathroom and was standing in the archway, watching fearfully. The man with his back to me was about my height but heavier.

The big fellow had struggled to his feet, still out of touch, and more puzzled at his partner's position than concerned. He tried to focus on the Colt. When he shook his head, long brown hair fluttered in feminine fashion. Apparently he decided it was a gun, then looked up at my face.

"Lori," I said flatly. "Ever see either of these fellows?"

She shook her head.

"Take the stuff from the desk and get the car started. Duck when you're between me and the big fellow."

She did as directed, crouching below the barrel of the gun as she passed in front of me. She was badly frightened but she was handling it. There was no need for her to know why I wanted her out of the apartment.

When the door closed, I reached out with the gun barrel and tapped the shoulder of the man in front of me. I watched the big man. "You aren't cops. Who sent you?"

"Fuck off."

"I don't generally ask twice. Who sent you?"

"Fuck you, asshole."

I palmed the Colt and drove it up and across my body, slamming it into the side of his head. The gun butt crushed the ear and blood flooded downward, changing direction as the body crumpled silently into a motionless heap. With my eyes locked on those of the big man, I took three quick steps forward, the bloodied hand and gun pointed at the middle of a stomach some twenty pounds too heavy.

"Ya killed him," he mumbled, staring at the twisted, lifeless-looking body.

"Hope so," I said bluntly. "Who sent you?"

"Like he said, fuck ..."

He couldn't finish. The upward swing of the Colt shattered his nose. I drove my fist to a spot well beyond his solar plexus. He was suddenly without air to breathe. He grabbed his stomach, folding forward. I met the downward motion of the head with my knee, driving. He arched upward and back, sprawling across the television cabinet. His head cracked wallboard. I stepped up and slammed my knee into his crotch. When his mouth opened to cry out, I jammed the muzzle of the Colt into the gaping cavity, shattering teeth.

"Who sent you?" I asked in the same flat voice. The steel of the pistol ground against jagged bloody whiteness. "Who?" I demanded, accenting the word by driving the pistol deeper.

It was difficult to understand but the gasping word spit out around the bloody pistol was what I'd expected. Rosta.

I grabbed hair, yanked, then dropped the butt of the gun to the base of his skull. His body crashed face first onto the carpet.

In the bathroom, I wiped blood off the pistol with a towel, tucked it away, and washed my hands. I locked the apartment door, then forced a casual pace down the stairs and out the back entrance. When Lori saw me, she backed the Chevy out, then slid to the passenger side. I climbed behind the wheel and concentrated on steadying the trembling of my hands. I turned right on Saticoy at the first break in traffic. Several turns later, I knew no one was following.

"Was it bad?" she asked tensely.

"Yeah."

"You didn't kill them, did you?"

"No."

She was silent for several blocks. "What are we going to do now?" Fear raised the pitch of her voice.

"It's time for a chat with Rosta. Those were his boys; I'm bored with the type."

"What good will that do?"

"I'm not sure. Maybe nothing."

The shudder was brief but intense. "Scott," she said, placing a hand on my thigh. "This is getting out of hand."

"We've still some moves left."

"More violence?"

"It wouldn't come as a big shock."

I wanted to reach down and hold her hand. But only by keeping both of mine tightly on the wheel could I control the trembling. I tried to enjoy the feel of her hand and concentrate on driving. Images of Rosta's hate-filled face interfered with both efforts.

I'd let Lori off in front of Rothland General Hospital and stood beside the Blazer, watching until she was inside. I was to meet her in the waiting room outside emergency. If something went wrong, she had Tony's number. She also had the combination to my safe.

She had wanted to say more, to change my sense of things, but she'd said nothing. I was grateful. Explanations of gut feelings are tough to put together. About all I could have said was

there are too many Rostas out there, warlords
bent only to their own wants and lusts. I plain
don't like them. I'd told Rosta those sent against
me might not return. I had to be certain he
knew he risked even more, coming for Lori. But
the man seemed convinced no other could stand
in his way. If so, the visit would be futile.

Still, I might get a better feel for him. It's
always best to know those already at the green
felt before sitting into the game. And I might
discover what he wanted, find it, and end his
threat to Lori.

I caught a whiff of the Pacific, crossing the
summit of Sepulveda Pass, then began descending into the Los Angeles basin. Once on the
Santa Monica freeway, the air became damper
as I got closer to the ocean. I could almost taste
the saltiness. It tasted fine. Southern California
beaches had been part of my growing up. I roam
them now only at night; people crowd the days.

I turned off at Lincoln and, three turns later,
drove past the front of The Office. It's a clever
name for a bar, if not original, particularly one
noted for its willing women. Large neon signs,
ugly in daylight, promised all manner of wondrous things to those who would but enter.

Once past the front, I turned to circle the
block. There was an alley that was promising. I
passed it by, then went all the way around and
past the front again. It was a three-story building without windows on the ground floor. Large
ones accented upper floor rooms, all heavily
draped.

What I needed was a way to get inside with a chance of staying alive. The front door seemed a bad bet. I turned into the alley behind the building. The second- and third-floor windows were duplicates of those in front. They were inaccessible. The four-story building next door might help. I could climb down from the top of it to the roof of The Office. There had to be a better way.

When I came to the end of the alley, I turned left and parked on the street in front of the row of apartments. I walked back to the rear of the building. The familiar feeling taking hold was not new to me. Things were about to happen. This time, I would be the cause. My skin tingled and the eyes roamed constantly.

There were two emergency exits at the rear. Without explosives, they were useless. I walked briskly past the corner of the building and found cover in a doorway in the next building. In shadow, I examined the parking area and service entrance at the side of the building.

A custom-built black Cadillac limo was parked near the door. A burly young Mexican stepped outside carrying a trash can, black hair combed tightly back against his head. The cook's apron was soiled from a day of chores. Muscles rippled as he lifted the can and emptied it into the trash bin. Would he make another trip?

I stepped out of the doorway and walked back past the Caddy, turned, and walked between the car and building toward the entrance. I stopped at the front of the car, ready to run or shoot or both. Exposed, vulnerable, I felt tension mount. If it didn't happen soon, I'd have to try something else.

The young man stepped outside again. Up close, he was younger than I'd thought, no more than eighteen. He looked up and stopped as I approached, large brown eyes wary.

"Do you like the job?" I asked.

"I've had better," he said, the trash can forgotten. "Ya taking a survey or just butting in?"

"Do you know if Rosta's inside?"

"So he's in there. So what?"

I fished out a hundred and showed it. "I need to see him."

"I ain't stopping ya."

"He's got people who'd try."

"Ya're right there, man."

"Can you help without getting hurt?"

"Shit. He already done that. He hit me up alongside the head so hard the ringing lasted two days." He looked back at the door, then set the trash can down and turned back to face me. "I just signed on to eyeball the broads." He grinned. "I heard they even stroked, man, right on stage." He shrugged. "It didn't work. They keep me in the kitchen." The look in his eyes reinforced the calculating grin. "Ya gonna hurt the man?"

"It might come to that."

He nodded, as if he understood the whole of it. Maybe he did. "I don't like the fucker. The job ain't no better. Give me three of them," he said, pointing to the bill, "and I'll make it real easy."

I dug out two more bills. The young man stripped off the dirty apron. He handed it to me, took the bills, and passed me the white cap.

"Walk through the door like ya own the joint. Know what I mean?"

I nodded.

"It's like six steps to the hall. Take a right. There'll be a big dude there. Rosta's in the first booth on the left. If he ain't, take the stairs. His office is on the second floor, to the left at the top of the stairs. Got it?"

"Yeah. And thanks."

The young man grinned. "Hurt him good, if ya get the chance." He trotted to the alley, turned right, and was gone.

I wasted little time putting on the apron. When I'd tied the drawstring, I tucked the Colt under the front flap. It bulged awkwardly but it was easy to reach. The cap was too small but I wasn't planning to wear it long. I snugged it down and walked toward the door. The heartbeat picked up. Adrenaline flowed.

I opened the door and walked straight ahead. To the left, two men in white worked at the stainless steel counter. My luck held; both had their backs to me. I grabbed a serving tray, laid the Colt on it, and covered it with a napkin. "Hey, Francisco," one of the men in white called out, turning. But I was in the hall before he saw more than the apron.

I looked left. Nothing, only the emergency exit. The man leaning against the wall was big. His heavy arms were crossed, straining the fabric of his coat. My fist was wrapped tightly around the butt of the Colt under the napkin. I glanced up the stairs as I passed; no one was in sight. I pressed the serving tray against the man's back, then jabbed the gun barrel into his neck. "Sit," I said.

He didn't move. I dug harder with the pistol, grinding the steel against bone. Slowly he unfolded his arms and stepped forward. Rosta looked up. At sight of me, his face flushed furiously. The drooping mustache trembled.

"It's good to see you, Rosta." I prodded with the gun. When the man started to sit, I slid into the opposite side of the booth. The gun under the table pointed midway between the two men. "Like old times," I said. I pulled the cap off and brushed my hair.

Two men moved toward us from the far end of the bar. Both had their hands up under their coats. "Expect those two fellows best sit somewhere. Right soon."

Rosta swung his huge head, nodded slightly, then turned back to face me. The two men sat down on barstools, twenty feet away. They placed their backs to the bar, watching, their hands on their knees in clear view.

"What the fuck you doing here, asshole?"

I wanted to say something slick and glib about vocabulary. That of Rosta and his punks was limited. Words like fuck and asshole were overly abundant. Instead I said, "I want a couple of answers..."

"You get duck shit from me."

"Like what are you looking for?"

"Fuck off. You're just a bug in my soup, still wiggling. You were lucky with Vickers. Next time'll be different."

"Vickers had the luck. I should have killed him."

"You? Take Vickers? That's fucking bullshit."

"There's two punks lying on the floor of an apartment on Saticoy that might say different."

"What the fuck's that mean?"

"One's busted up some."

"Who the fuck are you, hero?"

"Someone better than anyone you've got."

"How come you're in this?"

"The woman. I want her left alone."

"You busted in here for a broad?"

"That's so."

"You're wasting time you ain't got much of."

"Why not tell me what you want and let me get it for you? She saw you waste Livingston. I can move her out of town. Permanently."

"I don't want either of you moving at all. Ever."

"That doesn't leave me much choice, does it?"

"What the fuck you talking now?"

"It looks like the only way out is to put you down." The gun felt good in my hand. "I've been thinking on that."

"You'd be burned before you got off your ass."

"There'll be other times, other places. It'd be best to work out something."

"You got nothing to deal with."

"You're not thinking, Rosta. You're overconfident. I'll have to move against you if we can't deal."

"Shit. Who's overconfident? One half-salty dude against all my boys?"

"You've got three less now."

"Fuck off, asshole. Move on or you'll die right here."

"I doubt it. You'd have to answer too many questions, if you were still alive." So far, I hadn't scored a point. "You know what I think?"

"Who gives a fuck?"

"This is too big for a dumb punk like you. You're working for someone. Hank Krutz?"

"I work for anybody with the bread for heavy action."

It wasn't working. I guess I'd known it wouldn't. He hadn't taken me seriously and he wasn't going to. I stood, slipped out of the cook's outfit, and hid the gun under it. The two men at the bar rose to their feet. Rosta and the man beside him tensed.

"Climb out of there."

The big man looked at Rosta, waited for a nod, then slowly rose to his feet.

"Now you, punk," I said to Rosta. "We're going out the back."

"The fuck I am."

I could feel my lips tighten against my teeth. All else faded from view except the broad chest in front of me. How else could Rosta be dealt with? My finger took up the slack in the trigger. Rosta dead would solve a lot of Lori's problems. Without looking down I knew my fist had turned white, gripping the Colt. I leaned forward.

He moved and nearly died. For an instant, I saw it. Fear. Then it slipped from view. He slid out from behind the table and stood.

"Too bad," I said, my voice hoarse. "I kind of wish you'd stayed there a bit longer."

When he was close enough, I hooked my left arm under his right and drove the pistol into his ribs. Even shot, I could get a round off.

I led him down the hall, across the kitchen, and out the side door. Thinking of the flash of fear that had showed briefly, I said, "Ever noticed those apartments over there?" I nodded toward the three fourteen-story towers in the next block.

Rosta looked at me, confused. "I used to get paid for shots like this." I didn't tell him where I'd done that kind of shooting. Let him think what he wanted. Hopefully Mafia and hit men would come to mind.

"Like what?"

"I could take you easy from one of those windows. If I was you, I'd figure another way in and out of here."

Rosta made no reply. I released him and ran. I drove hard, half expecting shots. At the street, I slowed long enough to glance first right, then left, then behind me, back down the alley. No one was in sight. I stuffed the gun into my waistband and charged the Blazer. Once inside, I had it moving in seconds. When

I was certain no one followed, I turned onto
the Santa Monica freeway and let the engine
wind.

In the second-floor waiting room at the hospital, Lori was standing at the floor-to-ceiling
window. I couldn't tell if she was studying the
scene below or images in her mind. The sun was
low, its rays providing a halo effect around her
head. Her arms were folded under her breasts,
adding to the delightful natural uplift. Shadowed light silhouetted long slender legs. To hell
with Matt's scrapbook. If I were to begin an
album, I'd like this shot as the first of an ongo-
ing study of the same lovely subject.

I lost track of time, watching her. When she
turned from the window, she looked directly at
me, her face expressionless. Her eyes examined
my parts, looking for rips and tears and holes
and blood. She walked toward me, stopping two
feet away, her arms still folded. "Invading
Rosta's court was a damned fool thing to do."

"You're right."

"An hour ago, I decided you weren't coming
back. I don't want to deal with that again.
Ever."

"Sorry. It took longer than I expected."

"And you gained nothing, am I right?"

I nodded.

We tucked our arms around each other's waist
and walked slowly down the hall.

In the Blazer, she slid over beside me. We cuddled, as younger lovers are wont to do, all the

way back to the house. When we pulled across the cattle guard, I stopped.

"What is it?" Lori asked, stiffening.

"Up there," I nodded. "The red Porsche." Fifty coats of lacquer and the sun not yet behind the hills created an exploding blaze of color in front of the house. The man sat in the captain's chair, leaning back against the wall.

"Who is it?" Lori asked, frightened.

"Sergeant Tony Haggen. Homicide. He wants to talk."

"Oh my God. What can we do?"

"Tell him everything we know or even guess."

"You sound as if we have a choice?"

"We do."

"I don't understand."

"We can leave. He won't follow."

"What are you saying?"

"That he's a friend. He'll leave this to me if you want."

"That doesn't sound like policemen I've known."

"Even with strangers, he makes up his own mind, sometimes his own rules."

"And you think we should talk to him?"

I nodded.

I couldn't tell what she was thinking; her eyes were fixed on the man in the chair. Her knuckles whitened as her fingers dug into my thigh. "Let's meet this unusual man," she said, her words tinged with grim determination.

I put the Blazer in gear and drove up the hill. Lori's eyes remained fixed on Tony. I could feel her tension and fear. I wanted to tell her not to worry. I couldn't. The things she hadn't told me might be much more than worrisome.

As we came up to the house, Bobbie, who'd been lying on the porch beside Tony, charged the Blazer and happily pranced about us as I drove around back. Walking to the house, Lori ignored the dog. I tried to make up for her inattention with extra rubs and scratches.

When we stepped onto the porch, Tony stood, smiling, studying Lori. He wore a tan sport coat and dark brown slacks that looked as if he'd slept in them, three nights running. His tie was loosely knotted, halfway between his chin and belt. Anyone who knew the man could tell the time of day by the distance the knot in the tie had dropped below his chin. The coarse blond hair was brushed back without regard to style. But the frumpy casualness did not disguise his self-assurance. Only the eyes hinted at harsh capabilities. I couldn't help but contrast this lanky figure with Rosta's big goons. Rosta was wrong about size. He'd find out how wrong if he ever tackled this man.

" 'Lo, Tony," I said.

"So how's it go?" he asked. His voice, though pitched high for a man of his height, was rich and full, carrying hints of past chuckles and those yet to come.

"Getting by," I said.

Tony's dark blue eyes never left Lori's face. His deep tan was darker in the shadow of the porch. The scar on his cheek was white against the tan. "And you'd be Lori Livingston," he said.

"Yes," she said firmly. "I am."

"Scott probably told you we don't have to talk." His disarming smile was having its effect on her. She was beginning to relax. "But it might be good to get together on a couple of things."

"I think we should," Lori replied.

"Great. Now if we can get this big lug to open up the fort, we can get in out of the cold."

"Cold?" I said. "It's near eighty today. You don't know what cold is." Tony's lightness was meant to reassure me. It wasn't his fault he failed.

I opened the door and ushered Lori inside. Tony followed and was nearly knocked to the floor when Bobbie slipped through beside him, hammering his right leg out from under him.

Lori turned into the kitchen and sat down at the table. Tony chose the seat opposite her.

"Something to drink?" I asked, looking at Lori.

She nodded.

"A little of that stuff you call coffee?" Tony asked.

I poured coffee and bourbon, grabbed a beer, and sat down.

"How do you figure we ought to run this here inquisition?" Tony asked, his eyes mocking me.

I'd been wondering the same thing. "Best if I start." Lori would know what I'd said before giving what she wanted of her story.

"Go for it. It'll do you good to get it off your chest, sort of like goin' to confession."

I ignored the comment. Lori listened intently. Tony moved restlessly in his chair from time to time. His glance wandered about the room, brushed Lori's face occasionally, but focused most often through the window behind her. He didn't appear to be listening, but I knew better. He plays poker the same way, never looking at a card more than once and never forgetting what it had been. He'd remember every word I said for as long as he wanted to. And he'd fill in the gaps with speculations of uncanny accuracy. I ended with my visit to Rosta.

"Like to have seen that," Tony said, chuckling. "Mostly our boys don't go inside unless there's three or more. You yanked his tail some."

"That's all. I wanted to know what he's looking for and to see if he's working for Hank Krutz, but I struck out."

"Rosta's a roach," Tony commented. "A killing roach but still a roach. He could be eatin' anybody's crumbs."

I tossed Matt's passport out onto the table. "I was going to show that to Lori when we were interrupted. He went to Japan, then on to Hong Kong. But why Kuwait?"

"He's never been to the Middle East before, so far as I know," Lori said, puzzled.

"You're the detective, Tony," I said. "Show us how it's done."

He began at the beginning of the passport and examined each page. When he looked up, he said, "All I see is Asia and Mexico, except this last entry. I don't think I'm goin' to dazzle you with this one. I'm stumped."

"So am I," I said. I picked up Lori's empty glass and moved to the counter. I set a fresh drink in front of her. "Open your coat, Tony."

"What for?" he demanded, pulling his lapels out as far as they'd go.

"I want to leave you two alone but I have to be sure you don't have a rubber hose." I saw no need to comment on the 9mm Beretta with its fifteen round clip, tucked under the left arm.

"Me? A rubber hose?"

"Lori's tougher than she looks, buddy. She's whipped better than you."

"Hey. Whose side are you on?"

"Hers."

Lori's smile showed more confidence. At least with me gone, she'd be free to talk without worrying about what I thought. I headed for the door.

"Honest," Tony said to my back. "I'll be good." I wasn't all that worried about Lori handling Tony. What bothered were the things she hadn't told me.

In the workshop, I tried to ignore the old Ford tractor I'd been working on for Ned. The engine should be rebuilt. I'd invested three times the energy required for the job finding ways to duck it.

I puttered about, trying not to think of Tony and Lori inside. What tools I found, I put away. I could sweep the floor but it would only get dirty again. In a way, I hoped Tony would discover what so frightened Lori about her past. But I didn't want to hear it from anyone but her.

It was half an hour later when Tony yelled out the window. "Come on in. There's no blood to speak of."

I hurried from the shop, up the knoll, and into the house. Lori looked tired and a little frightened, but she met my look with a smile that said not to worry. Tony had already poured more coffee and freshened her drink. I grabbed a beer and sat down, glancing back and forth between them. "So what can you add, Tony?"

"I took some boys into her place this mornin'. We got what we could. But without a body, it's tough to convict. And I checked the John Does. Nothin' comes close. Her testimony might do it. I can't say. Her personal phone directory is missin'. I'd bet Rosta got to the Dobsen woman usin' it but I'd never prove it. From your calls, I guessed some of it. Of course I didn't know about the fun you had today."

"I would have called."

"Yeah. But when?" He grinned. "Anyway, I'll lean on Rachelle Nestrum. I think you're right. She could be a target and should be movin'. For sure, I'll check on Matt's apartment. And I'll need the stuff you took."

"It's still in the car. I'll get it on the way out." I took a sip of beer. "Do you know anything about Finley Quale?"

"I never heard of him until Lori mentioned the name."

"Tell me more about Krutz."

"I don't know much about his business. Imports and exports, the way he deals, is a game out of my league. Like I said, he plays poker. I've dealt him a few hands. He does good. If the stakes are high enough, he'll play. He never squawks at losin'. The book says he's ready to help a friend or walk right through somebody that's out of line. His word's good. If he says he'll do somethin', it gets done, whether it's a promised delivery or a leg that needs breakin'."

"How can I get to him?"

"I'm workin' at it. Slim's settin' up a game for tomorrow night. He's pushin' Krutz to be there. If he's comin', I'll get you in."

I nodded. "I wish to hell we knew what Rosta's looking for."

"Funny about that. When you called, I thought it was drugs. After hearin' you and Lori, it must be somethin' else." He stood, looking down at Lori. "Until we figure it out, keep close to her, buddy."

I stood also. "Will do."

Tony looked at me and grinned. "It shouldn't be too tough."

My cheeks began to redden. The unreadable look Lori gave me didn't help. "Come on," I said. "I'll get that stuff."

Tony said, "Lori, hang loose. Okay?"

She nodded solemnly.

"And do what this bum says?"

"I will."

"Good. We'll get you clear of this, one way or another."

Tony followed me out the door. Bobbie remained protectively beside Lori, a worried doggy look on her face. I got the folders and scrapbooks from the Blazer and handed them to Tony. As he opened the door of the Porsche, he said, "I guess you know she's not tellin' it all."

I nodded.

"It could all sort of blow up in your face. She might have killed her husband."

"Bullshit."

"I think so too. But my hunch is based on a little more than sack time." He climbed behind the wheel and fired the engine. "I'll give you this. She's more than likely worth the effort. A little on the skinny side but sort of interesting. Stay in touch and keep that Colt handy." He slammed the car into a sliding turn and plunged down the narrow drive, dust billowing up behind him. Moments later, tires squealed as he accelerated down the canyon road. Lori had come up beside me.

"You're right," she said. "He is an unusual man."

"Yeah. But he's going to kill himself, the way he drives that car."

"Did he tell you he took my fingerprints?"

I wheeled toward her. "No. He didn't."

"He showed me fresh photos and asked me to identify Rosta. Later, he only touched the edges as he put them away in an envelope." She reached out and tucked her arm around my waist, turning me back toward the house. "If he discovered others were looking for me, he'd report it, wouldn't he?"

"He'd give you warning and time to split."

"That's unreal. I'd think he'd find himself in all kinds of trouble doing that sort of thing."

"Tony doesn't mind trouble. And his boss, Captain Greer, likes his arrest-to-conviction ratio too much to let anyone get in the way. Tony works alone, probably because he doesn't want to explain the rules he breaks. He gets the sharks, almost as if he doesn't notice the little fish. In exchange, those little fish owe him. They form an intelligence network that's unbelievable."

"I wonder if he'll decide I'm a little fish."

"Believe me. He'll call before doing anything."

"Strange. How very strange."

We carted in the groceries. The meal was a silent affair. It was full dark when the dishes were finished and put away. She sat down beside me on the small couch that faces the windows overlooking the valley.

"Your friend gives the appearance of being an easygoing man, slow to anger. Yet I sense in him some of what I see in you. I think he's dangerous."

"If there's trouble, it's good to have him beside you."

"That's enough of him," she said, cuddling closer. "Tell me more about yourself."

I don't often talk of myself. The subject bores hell out of me. But it might help Lori get to what I had to hear. "There's not much to tell. I grew up in these hills, a few miles west of here. Mom died when I was little but Dad made up for it. I tried some college but gave it up and enlisted. I did my time and got nailed with three extra years as a prisoner of war. When I got home, they promoted me to major, told me how the world had changed, and cut me loose.

"You called me a bush vet. It fits in some ways. Like the gun. Sometimes I go for weeks without thnking about it. Then I can't pull into a gas station without it."

"You said you knew what it meant to run. Is that part of it?"

"Probably. I wasn't home but a few months when I was arrested for murder. I skipped bail and bummed it for a couple years, paying my way with poker. That's when I started carrying the gun. Every face was a threat.

"When I came home, Tony helped nail the killer. Living's been better since. I keep busy fixing up houses. And every now and then, I get into a good poker game. My time's my own. That alone leaves me better off than most."

"You didn't mention any women."

"I thought you'd get to that." I smiled, trying to console myself with the thought that when I finished, it would be her turn. "I was married before the war; it fell apart. There've been a couple of fine girls since but it never seemed to work out into a long run."

"That's a rather brief synopsis."

"It's all you get." I reached over and kissed her lightly on the cheek.

The silence grew, lying comfortably between us. She laid down with her head in my lap, then rubbed my hand lightly with hers. When she rolled over she cuddled, then leaned back on her elbow. "Clothes are a nuisance," she said shyly. She reached out and undid the top button of my shirt. "I want to feel you next to me." She undid the next button, watching my eyes.

We played a private pleasant game, quietly, earnestly seeking more of each other. Gentleness and serenity enfolded us. It took time, because of interruptions, to be rid of clothes. Later, I scooped her up in my arms, held her close, and carried her to the big bed. When I laid her down, her arms around my neck pulled me to her.

Much later, she lay cuddled against me, her head on my shoulder. Her fingers drew light patterns on my chest, then were still. I could feel a sudden tautness have its way with her, fading ever so slowly. I dared not move to look at her.

"Perhaps you're stronger than others I've tried to tell. With the war, then running from a prison cell, you might understand."

I was afraid to say anything. I squeezed her thigh gently, hoping to encourage her.

"Beth Dobsen was my younger sister," she said finally. "I grew up in that house with her. Mom and Dad were killed in a plane crash when I was eighteen. Beth was all I had left.

"I wanted to go to college and there was a little money from insurance. I chose the State University at Northridge because it was close; Beth needed someone near. By the time I'd graduated and earned my masters degree in chemistry, she was well into her own college career.

"I could have found a job in industry but I wanted to teach and study. My applications were turned down because I didn't have the Ph.D. Then a friend of Mom's found a position in Houston.

"I loved it. It was simple to earn the respect of my peers and students. I enjoyed my studies. My apartment was modest but it was mine. I'd met several interesting men. I had all anyone could ask for. I didn't know it was only cotton candy." The last words were loaded with bitter anger. She rolled away from me and sat on the edge of the bed, her naked back bowed toward me.

"One night, a man got into my apartment. I've no idea how, unless I forgot to lock the door." Her words were cold, lifeless.

"I let him maneuver me into the bedroom and onto the bed. Behind his back, I fumbled for the .32 in the bedstand, then shot him.

"I called the police." Bitterness overrode anger. "I should have known better. No one believed my story. There was no sign of forced entry. I couldn't prove I hadn't invited the man into the apartment, then into the bed.

"The court-appointed attorney was a disgusting little man who smiled knowingly at my story and didn't believe any of it. He pointed out

I could have torn my own clothes, broken up the furniture, even caused the bruises on my body.

"The man had been accused by other women but for reasons I'll never understand, this information could not be used in court. It was recommended we plea bargain, so these facts could be part of the judicial decision. I agreed to serve six months in jail and a year's probation. It was the only truly foolish thing I have ever done. The judge I faced was a Texas judge with Texas ideas about women. He sentenced me to fifteen years in the state penitentiary.

"I spent three long terrible years there, then was released on probation. I couldn't teach, because of the conviction. I'd been working as a secretary for two years when I met Matt. When he asked me to marry him and move to California, I gave it no more than seconds before saying yes."

"So if you're found," I said, "you'll be taken back to serve the balance of your sentence."

"Yes."

"You weren't kidding. It'd cost you a bunch to testify against Rosta."

She rose suddenly and walked into the bathroom. The door closed quietly and the shower went on. I knew what she was trying to do. She wanted to wash it away, to be clean. She knew there wasn't enough soap or water in the whole of the world to do the job.

I watched the moon climb free of the hills to the east, then went into the bathroom and joined her. It was much different than our last shower together. For the longest time, I merely held her tightly, letting the warm spray do what it could to wash the filth and chill away. Later I dried her, using the towel to caress.

Once again in the great bed, I sought to arouse her. It was not that she rejected me. It was as if she'd lost the ability to respond. I didn't push. It felt fine to lay beside her for long periods of time with only a hand on an arm, a thigh, or holding her hand. When I sensed her growing demand, I began to withhold, to slow the process. In tiny increments, she became more aggressive, more demanding. Restraint was the watchword as I judged the feel of her, the tension, pain, and love. I tried to anticipate her every gesture, to subvert demand to softness. Only when she yielded totally to gentleness did I embrace her. She fell asleep, cuddled on my shoulder, the sheet beneath my arm, soggy wet with soundless tears.

Friday

IIII IIII IIII IIII IIII

It was after ten when I poured the first cup of the day and added water. The front door had opened and closed hours earlier; Lori and Bobbie were probably up by the oak. I'd added too much water; the coffee was cold. The bright cheery sunlight flooding through the windows clashed with my thoughts. Keeping Lori alive was one thing. But ten years in prison?

I rose heavily and poured another cup, concentrating on things to be done. It didn't take long; there wasn't much to think about. There was but one immediate imperative. Lori must agree to meet with Stephen Weinberg. The man could charm a jury into believing up was down, then reverse their opinion. Within the interwoven structures of law, government, power, and society, he derived good solutions.

Lori was sitting on the root of the oak. As I came closer, I could see her smile of welcome was strained. My own was more worried than warm. I pulled her close and kissed her.

"You're a good listener," she said, leaning back against my arms. "Your follow-up technique can hardly be improved on."

"I'm glad you like it," I said gruffly. "Things are supposed to look better in daylight. Do they?"

"No. I feel abused and betrayed. And ashamed, as if it were all my fault in some grotesque fashion. And I'm frightened so badly I can't think straight. I believe that sums it up."

"It sounds normal to me."

She looked away, out over the valley. Her grip on my arms tightened. "Be honest. You feel differently about me now, don't you?"

"More worried, is all."

She buried her face in my chest and hugged herself to me, searching for reassurance. When she showed no sign of letting go, I said, "Come back inside." I urged her down the draw with my arm around her shoulders. "You find something to eat while I set up a meeting."

Stephen Weinberg doesn't believe in earthquakes. His office is on the eighteenth floor of the Rockwell Towers Building in Century City on Wilshire, six stories above building heights allowed in Los Angeles, when people still believed California ground moves occasionally and suddenly and violently. As we were ushered into the office by the smiling receptionist, I wondered if I was the only one uncomfortable this far above ground. I grit my teeth mentally and smiled. " 'Lo, Steve."

The slender, elegantly dressed man stood to greet us. Black wavy hair burst forward and up from low on his forehead, lending youth to his smooth, nearly beardless face. Those who'd decided youth was equivalent to ignorance had paid dearly. Others noticed the thickness of the bifocals in the dark bronze frames and reconsidered initial judgments. Only a few recognized his radiant self-confidence came from winning. He was good in the courtroom, better in negotiations.

Weinberg stepped around the desk and gripped my hand firmly. "You look terrific. I envy you the fresh air you live in and the time you take to enjoy it."

"Bull," I replied, smiling. "You love this stinking rat race. Even if you weren't paid ridiculous fees, you'd still play the game."

"Of course," he said, his smile broadening. "But don't tell my clients. The fees are useful." He turned to face Lori, taking both her hands gently in his. Tension drained from her shoulders and face as Weinberg held her hands, smiling into her eyes. "I'm delighted to meet you, Lori."

"Thank you," she replied nervously.

"Don't get too attached," I commented. "I've plans that don't include you, Steve." I watched delightedly as the last of her tension faded, replaced with shyness.

He escorted her to one of the three overstuffed chairs that faced the massive desk. "Frankly, Lori, I believe you're wasting your time with this man. He's an incorrigible recluse. And look at the way he dresses. Disgusting."

Smiling now, Lori said, "I see you're also fond of him."

He spread his hands, palms up in mock surrender, and walked around the desk. "Unfortunately, he does somehow capture the good wishes of a number of unsuspecting souls."

I ignored it all with a grin and sat down in the chair next to Lori, extending my legs, slumping comfortably. Weinberg sat behind the desk. He's a slender man of less than a hundred forty pounds and the only such man I know who doesn't seem aware of his slight stature.

He leaned forward in his chair and turned his attention completely to Lori. This ability to focus, even in the midst of courtroom dramatics, was one of his greatest assets. "Lori, it's difficult to speak of matters best kept private. Yet this is precisely what you must do." He paused, watching her until convinced she had heard, understood, and believed. "Are you aware of the confidentiality that exists between an attorney and client?"

"Yes."

"Then you know nothing you say here will be repeated."

"I do."

"Fine. Then start at the beginning. Give me every detail. Even the slightest fact, meaningless of itself, could prove to be fundamental."

She was hesitant at first but Weinberg had his way. He listens with such intensity, such total concentration, it's impossible to ignore his concern, his commitment. Lori was no exception. Encouraged with an occasional nod or question, I watched her lose all sense of self-consciousness, all fear.

It was an uglier tale, broken down and analyzed in its smallest parts. When Lori had answered his final question, Weinberg leaned back in his chair. When he spoke, his voice resonated warmly off the walls. "I won't insult your intelligence by suggesting there may be a simple solution. Parole violation is seldom treated lightly. Your fears of being returned to prison are valid."

He leaned forward in the chair, placed his elbows on the desk, and focused his total being.

"I cannot let you misunderstand. In the end, I may fail."

"Unfortunately, I understand you perfectly," Lori said.

"Good. I'll contact associates in Houston. They'll examine the case for any possible strategy. Perhaps we can appeal or find grounds for a retrial. These are unlikely possibilities but they should be explored.

"There are two other avenues that seem more promising. Both amount to preventing extradition. If the governor can be persuaded, that would end it. It's difficult to arrange but not impossible.

"The second notion, the one that appeals to me, is for you to testify against Rosta in exchange for the right to remain in California." He turned to me. "Does Tony have a case?"

"I'm not sure. He needs a body most of all."

"Technically, a body isn't necessary," Weinberg said thoughtfully. "I'll get with him and work with whatever he can pull together."

He picked up two of his business cards and laid them in front of Lori. "One last thing."

"Yes?"

"Don't talk about this to anyone without my being there."

"No exceptions?"

"Yes. Two," he replied, smiling. "This man is trustworthy." He nodded toward me. "As is Sergeant Haggen. Tony will tell you if it becomes necessary to call me. But if anyone else approaches you, refer them to me. And should you be taken into custody, not a word until I get there."

"I understand."

Back at the house, I sat down at the phone. I wanted to get to Finley Quale. What he and Matt had discussed before that last trip could contain a scrap of needed information. But how do you get hold of the president of a multi-million-dollar corporation? I found the listing for Exton Electronics in the directory and dialed.

Several secretaries later, I was connected to Quale's private secretary. I said that Nelder, Inc., had a business arrangement with Matt Livingston and that I couldn't seem to locate him. Mr. Quale was not in but she gave me a number where he could be reached. So much for drawing fine battle plans.

I dialed again. A deep male voice answered, "Who's calling?"

"Scott Macklen. I'd like to speak to Mr. Quale."

"Why?"

"Matt Livingston is doing some work for me but I can't seem to find him. I've been trying to trace his recent movements. He met with Mr. Quale before his trip to Japan. I'm hoping Mr. Quale can help."

"Help? How?"

"To be honest, I don't know."

"Hold on."

I was put on hold. A minute later, the deep voice returned. "He says you should be here at two. Mulholland Drive. 1457." The line went dead.

I hung up thoughtfully. Strange. On the one hand, Hank Krutz keeps to himself. But here is a man with an estate on Mulholland Drive who had time for questions merely because I felt them important.

Still thinking about it, I played back my calls. Lori came into the living room and sat down near me. One call had ended with a disconnect, someone wanted to sell me the finest insurance program the world would ever see, and Vance Coggswell had called. I dialed Vance. His secretary answered.

"Macklen. Let me talk to Vance."

"Right away, sir." She learned fast.

Moments later, Vance said heartily, "How are you, Scott?"

"Good. What did you find?"

"I can't be of much help with Krutz Imports & Exports. Mr. Krutz emigrated to this country shortly after World War II and began his business. He's been very successful but since the company is wholly owned, there's no public record to speak of. To further complicate matters, most of his business is transacted abroad where records can be buried completely.

"He's well known and has a reputation for delivering as promised. Much of his profit derives from his role as agent. Someone calls. He finds what they need and delivers, without ever handling the merchandise."

"Did you get anything about his private life?"

"He married here in Los Angeles and has two sons. One's a lawyer, the other a stockbroker. Beyond that, little is known. He's a very private man, inaccessible to all but his trusted associates."

"What would you guess he's worth?"

"It's impossible to say. Millions, certainly. I'm sorry I can't be more specific. If you feel it necessary, there's a firm in Beverly Hills that has resources not available to me."

"No. Until I know more, let's drop it." I paused. "Any opinions about him as a person?"

"Not really. He could be a major arms dealer. Would that be a mark against his character? I can't say. Apparently many of his contracts are mere verbal agreements. I'd have to begin with this trust he's earned. It suggests a certain honesty, rare these days. Beyond that, I couldn't extrapolate."

"How about Exton Industries and Finley Quale?"

"I'm on firm ground here. Exton has been one of the dream stocks over the last twenty years. As with so many high-tech companies, earnings have been up, up, up. Dividends have been small but that's not unusual. Earnings are typically reinvested. Finley Quale is the president and principal stockholder, holding some forty percent."

"What's that worth?"

"At yesterday's closing price, some sixty million. Naturally sale in the open market would bring considerably less."

"Still, that's rich country."

"And the future is bright, at least on paper."

"Only on paper?"

"Let me put it this way. I wouldn't advise purchase at this time."

"Can you be more specific?"

"Yes. But I can't support it."

"Your guesses are good enough for me."

"Fine. To begin with, Mr. Quale has always been something of a wastrel. He was born with the proverbial silver spoon, inheriting four companies upon his father's death. He had always been a womanizer. With his new wealth, he became a leader in the jet set. Few could match his extravagances. Subsequently, all but Exton have been sold. Each company was in a period of stress at the time of sale, due primarily to limited liquidity. To put that simply, Mr. Quale was taking profits that should have been retained by the company."

"What do you figure he got for those three companies?"

"Over twenty million. And apparently he's spent most of it in as many years, an unusual, nearly impossible feat."

"If he's doing the same thing with Exton, he won't have any assets left."

"Exton was and is much the stronger company. But many well-established high-tech firms have fallen on bad times. I have no real evidence but I feel Exton is not nearly as solid as it appears. If you wish, I can gather specific details."

"No. I think you've given me all I need. I'll get back if I want more."

"Fine. Would you like the details on the property I spoke of? It's a modest house in the most deplorable condition but the price and terms could make it an attractive acquisition."

"Sure." I grabbed the note pad and pen. "Ready." When Vance had finished, I said, "It sounds possible."

"Very good, Scott. I'll look forward to hearing from you."

The house wasn't important; it'd keep. I turned to Lori. Telling her what Vance had said helped clarify the facts. It didn't bring any new insights. Krutz is a millionaire, a loner, who does a lot of business on verbal contracts. Quale is a high roller. Whether or not Exton was sliding from its lofty position had not been established. I couldn't see how it could matter.

I caught the phone on the third ring. " 'Lo."

"Tony here. The game's at the Holiday Inn on Sepulveda. Room 436. Do you want in?"

"Yeah. I've got to get to Krutz."

"Don't forget the stakes. With a little luck, you could pick up a bundle."

"Will you be there?"

"I've an invite but I don't want to cramp your style."

"No problem. Pick me up?"

"About seven?"

"Sounds good."

A silence built that puzzled me. If Tony had more to say, he usually plunged right in.

"About Livingston's girlfriend?" he began.

"Rachelle?" I felt Lori tense on the couch beside me.

"Yeah. I dropped by early this mornin'. That guard, Hinderling, must have used your dough. There was another guy on her floor who looked good to me. Anyway, I gave her the same advice you did. But I'm not sure she heard me any better than you. On my way out, I talked to both guards. If there was any doubt, I think I got rid of it. They were both lookin' pretty serious when I left."

"So?"

"So a couple of our guys took the squeal. The word is Hinderling and his backup are shot up pretty good. The girl's gone."

"Do you mean Rosta's got her?" Lori's hand gripped my thigh.

"I can't say. She could have left on her own. We're lookin' but we'd have to get lucky. There's a good team coverin' Rosta. He won't fart, we don't know about it."

"That doesn't mean his people can't do what they're told." I tried to picture Rachelle laid out on a stone cold slab.

Tony sighed, obviously frustrated. "What we do is keep swingin' and hope for a hit or somebody to muff it. Right now I've got three phones ringin'. I might know more for you tonight." He hung up.

"What is it?" Lori demanded.

"Rachelle is missing. Tony went by this morning. Now she's gone and he doesn't know if she took his advice or Rosta's got her. The security guards are in bad shape."

She was pale, speechless, her entire body trembling.

"Are you any good with a gun?" I asked grimly.

"Not really," she said in a whisper.

I knew of one occasion on which she'd used one effectively. "You ought to carry one."

"I don't know how to handle that."

"First, get mad. The madder, the better. I've got to see Quale this afternoon and I'll be out with Krutz tonight. I want to leave you with Ned. He's good with a carbine but if enough come, it'll be up to you. I've a Colt .38 you should be able to handle. Shooting a couple hoods Rosta sends is a lot easier than dealing with what they have planned."

"I don't believe I could ever kill again."

"It can come down to you or them."

"Even so, the choice would be difficult."

"It always is. But one way you live, the other you die. There's really no choice at all."

I found the pistol in the back of the corner cabinet. I cleaned and oiled it, grabbed a box of shells, and said, "Let's see how you do."

Reluctantly she followed me out the back. In the shop, I grabbed some paper targets. On the stump across the draw, I used the rusty nail there to hold one. I handed Lori the pistol and shells. "Try it."

She looked down at the gun as if it were alive, a deadly snake writhing against her grip. Finally she released the cylinder and loaded the pistol. Trembling fingers dropped two rounds. The eighteen-inch target was twenty feet away. She missed it entirely with her first three rounds but the last three notched paper.

I offered suggestions on stance, showed her how to hold the weapon with two hands and how best to sight on the target. She'd shot before; it was fear and revulsion that interfered now. In the end, she punched out six scoring rounds with two in the bull.

I explained that accuracy with a good stance was one thing, while snap shooting, without time to set, was another. I asked her to point with her forefinger, as I identified a target. She did. I loaded the pistol and asked her to try it with the gun, to point as if with her finger. Targets I selected ranged from ten to thirty feet. She did well, as if moving brought the necessary extra concentration. If the targets had been people, five would have been hit.

I looked up at the sound of the horse in the rocky draw. It was Ned, the Winchester carbine cradled in his elbow. The eyes were hidden under the brim of the worn hat. He rolled gently in the saddle as the giant stallion picked his way between rocks. As he came up, he slipped the carbine into the saddle holster. He reined in the great horse, curled a leg around the saddle horn, and reached for a cigarette. When he had it going, he dragged deeply and asked, "Ya expectin' trouble?" He was smiling but the look in his eyes, fixed on Lori, carried no warmth.

"It might come to that," I replied. "I've got to leave for a while. And I'll be out late tonight. I'd like Lori to stay with you."

Ned took another deep drag. "Thet's no problem."

"It could be," I said.

"Thet so?"

"People have been dying. And some heavy types are looking for her."

"Ned," Lori said firmly. "It could be very dangerous. You could even be killed."

The old man smiled, the eyes narrowing. "It's been tried," he said.

"Are you sure about this?" I asked.

He nodded, smoke curling up under the hat.

"Then we'll be down in about half an hour."

"Thet'll do." The old man slipped his foot back into the stirrup, turned the black with his knees, and started down the draw.

Lori followed me back into the house. I cleaned and oiled the gun, loaded it, and handed it back to her, along with a fresh box of shells.

"I still don't like this," she said.

"I don't blame you. But put them in your purse and keep it close. Ned can probably deal with anything that comes his way but if even one gets by, you're going to need it."

When I'd showered and shaved, I put on my best sport coat and slacks. Meeting two millionaires—Quale, and later Krutz—seemed sufficient cause for extra effort. I tucked the Colt in my waistband at the back, letting the coat drape

over it. I took an extra moment to console Bobbie, wishing I could explain things to her.

With Lori beside me, I drove slowly down the
draw with the Blazer in four-wheel drive, ducking larger rocks. Ned was sitting on the porch,
the carbine propped beside him. Lori kissed me
on the cheek.

"Best tell Ned some of it," I said. "I wouldn't
want him to underestimate things."

"I will."

"Remember," I said, as she got out. "They
don't know you're here. It's probably all the
edge we need."

I drove off, watching her in the mirror until
the dirt drive curved, erasing the scene.

I found Quale's estate a few minutes before
two. Heavy plantings extended across the front
of the five-hundred-foot property. All was meticulously maintained. Behind the plantings was
an eight-foot iron fence. I turned into the drive
and stopped at the guard station. Nothing but
grass was planted within twenty feet of the
fence on either side. Large signs listed the near-
fatal dose of current flowing through the iron
bars.

One of the two armed guards remained in the
station, watching. The other walked around the
front of the Blazer, face expressionless. He appeared capable and properly wary. He asked politely for identification. I produced my driver's
license. He carefully compared the picture to

my face before handing it back. "Thank you,
sir."

As he walked back to the station, the second
guard disappeared from view. I saw the array of
television monitors and other assorted elec-
tronic gear beyond where he'd been standing. I
leaned forward in the seat and looked up. Behind the guard station, a television camera rotated back and forth across the entry. The guard
pressed a button. The heavy gate began to roll
open. When space was sufficient, I drove on up
the drive.

The grounds were maintained with even
greater care than the front. Except for several
massive shade trees with their first branches ten
feet above the ground, none of the landscaping
was taller than a man's knee. The open areas
were planted with grass, cut closely, as on a putting green.

The house was nearly centered on the lot,
three hundred feet back from the fence. It reminded me of a Southern plantation manor,
more recently built. Eight large columns rose
from the front edge of the deep porch to support
the extended roof. The first-floor windows were
covered with flowery wrought iron that failed to
disguise steel bars.

The large porch was surfaced with slabs of
white marble, streaked with a twisting, swirling
grain the color of red wine. Camellias bordered
the porch, extending across the front of the
house on either side. Paint, in large chunks, had

broken loose from the wall over the massive double front doors. A new coat was overdue.

Before I could ring the bell, the door opened. The man was tall with white hair swept back from his forehead, brushed down and back at the sides. The narrow shoulders were deceiving, giving the impression of fragility. Some basketball players have the look. He was over six-six and clearly a powerful man, particularly in hips and thighs. The butt of the large-caliber automatic bulged through the thin blue fabric of the suit coat. The eyes were expressionless. It could be only the gun that lent the aura of menace, but I couldn't be sure. I handed him my card and he stepped aside to let me in.

The floor of the entry was tiled with small pale blue ceramic hexagons. A large tapestry covered one hall. Paintings hung in a pleasing pattern on the opposite wall.

"Right to the first room," the tall man behind me said, the deep voice emotionless, as colorless as the eyes had been.

The room was done in near-white, from the fine-napped carpet, up the walls, to the drop ceiling. There was a narrow channel around the ceiling that hid the fluorescent fixtures. The three couches and several chairs were upholstered in shades of brown. A giant six-foot television screen dominated the far end of the room. I could see only the top of the man's head, much of the dark hair turned gray. He was watching the tape of a football game.

I coughed politely. Finley Quale snapped the

set off, stood, and turned to face me with a Hollywood smile of exquisitely capped teeth. "I'm terribly sorry. That was rude, Mr. Macklen. I'm afraid you've caught me enjoying one of my vices. Please. Join me," he said, gesturing to the chair beside the couch.

I approached with more than casual interest. I'd never met anyone who'd burned a million a year for twenty years. Quale was nearly six feet and probably twenty pounds overweight but it was difficult to tell. The colorful Hawaiian shirt was cut full and draped well below his waist. The white linen pants and bare feet revealed little. He wore a flashy diamond ring on the middle finger of his right hand that couldn't have been larger without being designed to bend with the finger.

I sat down, examining the video gear. Three recorders were linked to each other and to the television set. Two custom-made cabinets held several hundred cassettes behind ornately trimmed glass doors. "Quite a setup," I commented.

"A weakness, I'm afraid," Quale responded, smiling. "I'm a fanatic about football. I spend a ridiculous amount of time editing tapes, extracting the most exciting segments, and adding my own commentary as if I had actually announced the game. It's a bit foolish, I suspect."

"I wouldn't say that. At least they haven't found a way to fake it."

"Marvelous. You understand." He brought his hands together as if to clap but made no sound.

"But you didn't come to discuss my aberrations. How can I help?"

"I'm not sure. I'm trying to find Matt Livingston. Either he doesn't want to be found or he's not in town. If I don't find him, I could be looking for a job."

"Your boss is something of a tyrant, I take it?" His smile invited me to speak freely.

"That about says it. I'm the one who set this deal up with Livingston. He was supposed to bring back some prototype boards for a radar tracking system. Top security and all. If those boards end up in the wrong place, the company could be in serious trouble."

"Can you be more specific about the boards?"

I fidgeted in the chair, crossing my legs. "To tell the truth, I can't tell one circuit board from another. I'm paid to find people who can and solve their problems."

"I see," Quale said thoughtfully. "And may I ask what you've discovered thus far?"

"Not much. I know he went to Japan and on to Hong Kong. He also spent two days in Kuwait before returning to the States."

"Kuwait?" Quale asked, puzzled. "We have no business with the Saudis. Why would he have gone there?"

"I haven't a clue. I was hoping you might."

"It's a complete mystery to me," he replied, shaking his head. "Did you find anything else?"

"Not much. I can't find anyone who'll admit they've seen him since he returned. And I can't find his wife. I did find a girlfriend but she was no help. I was hoping you might have a suggestion to get me pointed in the right direction."

"A girlfriend? Fascinating. I thought Matt was happily married, but I guess boys will be boys." He winked solemnly and leaned forward. "I'm an incurable snoop. Tell me about her."

"Her name's Rachelle Nestrum. She's spectacularly beautiful." I didn't like this turn to the conversation but I couldn't see how to duck it, if I wanted to hear more. "Judging from her apartment, she's got bread or else she's damned expensive."

Quale leaned back, saying, "Interesting. How very interesting." The eyes were bright. I sensed he wanted to hear more but held back for reasons known only to himself.

Out of the corner of my eye, I saw a tall woman enter the room. I meant only to glance at her politely but found myself half turning to watch closely. Her broad face was cold and coarse. The whole of her asked one single question: "Can you handle it?" And added the comment she was certain most could not. She'd used little makeup, but what there was darkened and widened the brows and added a deep bright pinkness to the lips. The bleached blond shoulder-length hair was straight. The longer strands, falling to her chest, directed attention downward.

She wore what looked like two large vertical scarves knotted behind her neck, joining below the navel, and drawn up snugly between the legs. She was braless. Broad foundations of

ample breasts were boldly revealed on either
side of the silky material. The nipples were erect
and large. When I noticed Quale watching me, I
turned back to face him, keenly aware of my
discomfort, hoping it didn't show.

"Don't be surprised at your reaction. She
always has that effect on men," he said with a
chuckle. "Let me introduce Char Killen." He
nodded toward me. "This is Scott Macklen, my
dear."

She nodded slowly and sat down next to
Quale. Her eyes focused deliberately on my
crotch. If there'd been any question of Quale's
sexual preferences, all was answered here. Only
hard sex and lots of it would satisfy this woman.

"Now," said Quale, still chuckling, "let's get
back to your problem." He began stroking the
inside of her tanned naked thigh. "Unfortunately I have precisely the same difficulty. In
fact, I was hoping you could be of help. Matt
was to have delivered an important contract to
us. But we haven't heard from him. Is there anything you could add?"

"There was one thing. But I don't see how it
could help."

"And that is?"

"Some tough street types are looking for him,
too. I bumped into a couple of them and damn
near ended up in the hospital or worse."

"That's amazing. Why do you suppose they're
looking for Matt?"

"I've no idea. Since you didn't say different, I

figure you had no objections to Matt working for us while working for you?"

"Heavens no. I've always encouraged it. It brings us new contacts and hence new business. Matt is always careful to see there's no conflict of interest. However, I had no idea he was representing you. And that's surprising. Matt keeps me informed."

"Maybe that explains the street types."

"I don't believe I understand."

"He might have been representing another party you don't know about, someone capable of heavy action."

"I suppose it's possible." He looked beyond the wall of the room, thinking. His hand absently stroked the inside of the tanned thigh. I tried not to watch directly but it was difficult to ignore the overt sexuality. The whole of it was disconcerting. Weird, to put a simple word to it. I'd never seen the like of it, but then my friends continue to point out how naive I am about contemporary sexual behavior. Conscious of the woman's continuing stare, of her callous speculations, I shifted position in a fruitless effort to distract her. I hoped Quale's hand wouldn't explore further.

He rose suddenly. I did the same. I could feel the woman's eyes continue their calculating examination. I felt exposed, not embarrassed. I simply wanted to be free of the blatant sexuality.

"I will keep your card convenient, Mr. Macklen. If I hear anything, I'll contact you."

"I'd appreciate it," I said. "And I'll do the same. But frankly, you were the last idea I had. All I can do now is wait for Matt to show and hope I don't get fired."

"I'm sure it won't come to that," Quale said, smiling. He escorted me into the entry, extracted a cigar from the humidor on the table, and began unwrapping it. The tall, powerful man who'd let me in was by the door. "I know he didn't say much; he never does. But I'd like you to meet Otto Gillis, my friend and bodyguard."

Gillis nodded almost imperceptibly, then opened the front door before I could respond. Quale stopped in the middle of the porch, bending to light the cigar. When it burned to his satisfaction, he looked about the grounds and said, "A lovely day, don't you think, Mr. Macklen?"

"You can't beat this time of year," I replied, extending my hand.

Quale took it lightly, shook it once as if for appearances, then pulled back. "You know," he said, "Matt's a secretive man. I often don't know where he is for several days. To be frank, I suspected a girlfriend. However, I've never worried. He's never let me down. He generates more profit than any other three of my people. Now with these others looking for him, and this mysterious visit to Kuwait, I'm extremely concerned. And quite puzzled. I want to thank you, Mr. Macklen, for dropping by. The matter is far more serious than I had thought it was."

"Thank you, too," I said, speaking to his back disappearing beyond the door.

At the Blazer, I noticed the TV cameras at each corner of the roof, scanning the front and sides of the house. Somewhere inside, at least one man was sitting, bored, eyes fixed on the monitors. Watching me might be his only break in the day. I resisted the impulse to wave at the cameras and climbed behind the wheel. Before I got to the front gate, it rolled open.

Once on the street, I began to relax. It wasn't the lies I'd told that had tightened me up. I'd done that often enough to carry it off effectively within limits. Was it Char Killen? She would create tension in only a certain kind of man. I shuddered, certain I wasn't that kind. What was it that rubbed the nerve endings in irritating fashion? What made me feel as if I had been in some other world, one in which I could never belong?

Quale looked older than his years. His love of booze, probably drugs, and certainly hard sex, had deeply etched the face prematurely. That couldn't be it. Carefully I reviewed the conversation. I'd learned nothing helpful. He hadn't drawn a map with a red dot appropriately located. But then I hadn't given him anything either, except confirmation of Matt's extramarital sex life. Matt's visit to Kuwait had surprised him but there'd been nothing more I'd caught hint of. There was no single reason I could point at to justify my tension. I let it go, glad to be free of the estate.

I turned north on the San Diego freeway toward the Valley. True, Quale's home needed a coat of paint but so did mine, and probably one in nine houses in the city. Still, I found myself asking what was owed against his estate. I couldn't even guess at its value. I turned off the freeway at Burbank and pulled up near a phone.

Moments later, I asked Vance Coggswell, "Can you find what's owed against Quale's place?"

"I should have mentioned it earlier. There are two notes against the property. The balance due is approximately two million."

"Can there be that much?"

"Oh my, yes. That property would easily bring five or six million."

"Thanks," I said and hung up. Back in the Blazer, I struggled through the evening traffic, back onto the freeway. How many Californians owe less than half the value of their property? Finley Quale was doing better than most.

I found an art supply shop and purchased what the willing clerk suggested, including paper and watercolors. Drawing might ease Lori's fears by giving her something to do. The short stop earned me an extra delightfully delicious hug and kiss when I spread my purchases out on Ned's kitchen table.

After a modest meal, gleaned from Ned's slim cache, I drove the Blazer up the rocky draw. Bobbie was delighted to see me. She stayed at my side as I opened the safe and counted out seven thousand to go with the three in my pocket. The others would have more; I'd be at a disadvantage. But this was my personal limit. Sitting on the porch, waiting for Tony, I tried to ignore the growing conviction the odds were shifting against us.

Rosta would want me badly, since yesterday. He didn't even know my name, but Hank Krutz soon would. By the end of the evening, Krutz would know a good deal about me and could, if he wished, find out about this house. He wouldn't find it through normal channels. My published address is a rented mail slot in an office offering secretarial services. And the phone is set up on a calls-forwarding basis that's nearly impossible to uncover. Even my service doesn't know my address or the number their equipment dials when someone asks for Nelder, Inc. But around certain green circles of felt I'm well known, and Krutz had access to those circles.

If it was not yet time to seek another cave, it soon would be. And we should separate. That would be rough. For both of us. She'd worry incessantly but she'd be safe. I'd worry, too, but I'd be free to move. If something didn't break soon, I'd do it. Get hold of Lencho Cabral, that stalwart giant of great heart who'd stood beside me in Nam and stood beside me still. If Lori would agree, Lencho could hide her in the city's Mexican subculture indefinitely, beyond the reach of any hood or cop.

Haggen's cherry red Porsche rattled across the

cattle guard and stormed up the hill, startling
the colts, trailing a small cyclone of dust. He
slid to a stop by the porch. "Ready?" he asked
through the open window.

I waved dust away from my face, walking toward the car. "Best let me drive."

"Hell. We'd never get there."

"With you driving, I know where we'll likely
get and there aren't any angels there."

Tony chuckled. "Hey. I haven't killed anybody
in a month."

"It's not others I was thinking about," I mumbled, walking around the front of the car.

I climbed in and reached for the combination
seat belt and shoulder strap. The car was moving before I could get a grip on it. The dirt drive
never seems as rough as when Tony's behind the
wheel. I managed to buckle the belts as we
thundered over the first cattle guard. By the
time we jounced over the second, I had my left
arm locked against the dash and my right
through the open window, hugging the door
with elbow and forearm.

"Know what your trouble is?" Tony said
cheerfully over the rush of wind and scream of
tires.

"Expect you're going to tell me."

"You take life too seriously."

He eased the car out of the curve and gave it
more gas, a foolish move at best. Only his sergeant's shield kept him from collecting tickets

by the truckload. Only the luck of gods kept him alive. I earnestly hoped the luck would hold for one more run.

Besides Tony and myself, four other men had been sitting at the table for nearly three hours. Our host, the man on my left, must have had a name but I'd never heard him referred to as other than Slim. He wore a toupee that was at least ten years too young for him. Thin hairy arms were fully exposed. Since he'd been accused of cheating years back, he always wore a short-sleeved shirt. I'd met him often through the years and gained a little but never stung him badly. The hand was five-card draw. Slim opened for two hundred, laid his cards down, and watched the balance of play.

Harold Gison was a face I hadn't seen. He'd been introduced as a vice-president with IBM but had hastily pointed out IBM had an abundance of vice-presidents. He was a husky man of about fifty, who kept himself in shape. He called the two hundred, as did Hank Krutz and Jiles Hawthorne. Tony, on my right, folded. I raised three hundred and immediately drew concentrated attention from the others.

Only Hawthorne hesitated to meet the raise, studying his cards, then me, from under the baseball cap. His eyes in shadow revealed nothing. I'd not played with him before. Finally he met the raise, as if convinced he'd made a mistake.

Playing a four-card straight or flush is a fine

way to go broke. But I had an eight-high straight open at both ends and a four-card flush. Right or wrong, I love this hand. When they heard my call for one card, they showed interest. Slim and the others checked to me. When I bet five hundred, they took it seriously. Slim, then Gison, folded. Krutz studied my face for a clue, the eyes expressionless, the broad mouth curved downward in a dour expression. I hadn't seen him smile all evening. He raised five hundred and Hawthorne dropped. I called. Krutz showed three kings, which lost to my little straight. Slim shook his head and tossed his cards to Krutz for the next deal.

Krutz was the only man wearing a suit coat. I couldn't remember the last time I'd seen a player wearing a tie. His was double knotted, cinched up tight against the starched collar of his white shirt. When he tipped his head down, his short neck folded over the collar.

With stubby, agile fingers, Krutz dealt two cards down and one up for seven-card stud. Light reflected brightly off his bald head and spectacles. Only two inches of thinning gray hair showed above his ears. The beard was thick, dark gray in color. The cheeks lay forward in heavy folds on either side of the nose. The folds blended into the corners of the down-turned lips. He opened on a king for five hundred. Hawthorne went along. I folded a losing hand, content to study the stout balding man across from me.

I also considered the two well-dressed athletic

types seated by the door. They'd entered the room ahead of Krutz, pulled chairs next to the wall, and sat down. They'd been statues since, except for one trip each to the john. Armed bodyguards were the price paid if you wanted to play with Krutz.

There were a dozen questions I wanted to ask him. Any one might lead to a dozen more. Ruthlessly I shoved these thoughts aside. This was poker. A mental slip could cost me dearly. Outside this room, every player might be someone's guardian angel. Here they were hawks looking for the prey of weak play.

Two o'clock slipped past unnoticed. Not a bottle on the well-stocked bar had been opened. Tony, Krutz, and I had gained at the expense of the others. Tony and Hawthorne maintained an easy banter. Slim, Gison, and I said little, while Krutz said nothing at all, except with his cards and dollars. Tony anted and dealt three cards for seven-card stud.

Mine were all hearts, ace and king down, the nine up. Tony opened for five hundred. No one was scared out. I picked up the eight of hearts on the next card and began to take the hand seriously.

I wanted to bet. I had that feeling; this could be the game-breaker. Caution overruled. There was potential power in the cards face up on the green felt. I checked but called all raises to two thousand.

My next card was the ten of clubs. The bet to me was two thousand. I raised another two, hoping they'd believe in the eight, nine, ten straight. They did; they stayed. Krutz seemed the one to beat. His last card up was the queen of spades and he showed two other spades to a flush. If he had the ace and king down, I was beat by the queen. Slim folded what seemed to be developing into garbage. Gison folded three fives. Krutz bet two thousand and Hawthorne raised two thousand on his three tens, a possible full house. Tony folded and leaned back in the chair. I called.

My next card was the six of hearts; I now had a four-card straight showing and the ace-king flush hidden. If Hawthorne had his full house or Krutz had the king of spades down, I was dead. Krutz bet four thousand. Hawthorne apparently didn't have the full house or didn't like his chances. He folded. I called and raised four thousand more. Krutz studied me closely. I sensed he wanted to raise but he only called.

My last card put me in charge. It was the king of spades. It was no help to my hand but now I knew my flush would beat Krutz. I bet six thousand, the largest bet of the evening. Krutz raised an eyebrow, then matched the six and shoved another eight. I wanted to raise again but I had only enough to call.

Krutz showed his flush, ace-queen high. When I turned my ace and king, Krutz spoke for the first time since the game began. "Well done, young man." He glanced around the table and said, "That will be enough for me, if you gentlemen do not object."

"I'll go for that," Slim said.

The others stood and stretched as I gathered in the pot, stuffing bills into my pockets. "A drink, Mr. Krutz?" I asked politely.

"Fine."

I walked with him to the small bar. Krutz reached for the Scotch and poured liberally, disdaining mix or ice. I poured a dash of bourbon over two cubes.

"Tell me," Krutz asked. "Are you lucky or good? I couldn't decide."

"A little of both, probably."

Krutz shook his head. "I'm glad you didn't raise. I'd have called."

He'd followed me over to the window. We looked out at the lights of the city. "If I'd raised, you'd have thought it over."

"Indeed. But I have a stubborn streak. I hate to admit I'm wrong."

"Who does?"

"You cleared over twenty thousand dollars. Tell me, is that a lot of money to you?"

"I can't see it's your business, but yeah. To me, that's a lot of money."

"I didn't mean to be rude. I simply need to know more about you. The significance of the amount to the man making the bet is an important clue to his hand."

"Why do you need to know that about me?"

"Because, young man, I intend to beat you badly as soon as we can arrange a time." Krutz's slight smile was hardly a smile at all. There wasn't much friendliness in it either.

"If you're talking about poker, Mr. Krutz, I'm ready." I was surprised how easily "mister" applied to this stout, balding man of sixty plus. He radiated power and confidence. His stance was regal, demanding.

Tony was entertaining Slim, Gison, and Hawthorne at the bar. Only the bodyguards were watching me. I reached into my hip pocket, pulled out the wallet I'd taken from Sergio Landis, and handed it to Krutz. "It belongs to one of your people."

The eyes were instantly wary, watchful, and thoughtful. He turned to look at the four men at the bar, then glanced down at the wallet he'd opened. He folded it and slipped it into his coat pocket. "At the time, I was puzzled at Slim's insistence I play tonight. I imagine you arranged this."

"I wanted to talk, if that's what you mean."

"Did you know Landis nearly died from that blow? Your blow?"

"That's his problem. I'm fond of the woman." Krutz seemed less concerned about Landis than I was. "How did you know she'd visit that particular bank?"

"Mr. Macklen, I know a good many things."

"Tell me what you're looking for."

"I see no reason to do so. You're intruding into a game that's none of your affair."

"Mr. Krutz, I've been shot, Rosta tried to kidnap the woman, and three people I know of are dead." The grim face in front of me gave nothing. "The only way to get me out of this game is to tell me what you want. If I can find it, I'll do it and be glad to get out, along with the woman."

"There are ways to deal with interference," Krutz commented. "But let's assume for the moment I'm a kindly old man who wants everyone to be happy."

"That's a bit heavy."

Krutz chuckled, an unpleasant raspy sound from deep in his throat. "Yes. It is. But assume it's true. Precisely what do you want?"

"To know what you're looking for, what Matt Livingston was offered five hundred thou for. I want the woman left alone for forty-eight hours. And if I find what you want, both of us are out of it."

Krutz took a deep swallow from his glass. "I'm not sure why, but I like you, young man. Perhaps it's your straightforward approach, the absence of threats and bad manners so common these days." He turned and looked out the window as if at something he could not see from where he stood.

"Somewhere in this city is a dagger of religious significance to the Islamic world, that fourth of the earth's population who fervently believe there's but one God, Allah, and that Mohammad was his Prophet. Supposedly the dagger belonged to Mohammad himself, a gift from Abu-Bekr, his favorite disciple, on the eve of their flight from Mecca to Medina that marks the beginning of Islam.

"Reputedly the dagger has been passed down

through the ages to the present House of Saud. The original iron blade has been replaced with fine Damascus steel, the hilt with intricately carved gold, and the present scabbard is encrusted with jewels. With these, shall we say, enhancements, the claim this dagger was Mohammad's amuses me." He turned back to face me.

"Further, since the Arab world is not into icons, the legend is suspect. In fact my sources suggest the dagger is of far more recent origin, the creation of a zealous artisan of our time at the request of a certain religious fanatic, Prince Aba al-Saleh." He shrugged. "However, Arabia is not my home, nor am I interested in Islam. What I believe is of no importance. What is important is that Prince Aba al-Saleh, the appointed caretaker of the dagger, is the favorite nephew of the king. Hence the dagger has value to me. I'll pay five hundred thousand dollars if you can bring it to me."

"The paper said it was worth forty million. Why would I let you have it for five hundred thou?"

"Because it can't be sold openly. And the millions the paper speak of are not real. At honest auction, the piece would bring little more than I'm offering. Of course, it's worth a great deal more to Prince Aba al-Saleh."

"And you'd sell to him?"

"That is my business. It need not concern you."

"How do you know it's in the city?"

"Information is the key to my success. It's here."

"Can I have the forty-eight hours?"

"Yes. There are many places to look and few people to do the looking. My people will stay out of your way."

"And Rosta?"

"What makes you think I have any say over him?"

"Dell Vickers was at the bank with your man. Rosta's working for someone."

"Thus you assume he's working for me?" He raised an eyebrow, as if jeering at ignorance. He shook his head in mock sadness, produced a business card and pen, then scribbled briefly on the back of the card. "I'll leave you with your assumptions." He handed the card to me. "You can reach me by calling that number."

He turned and walked back to the bar, spoke briefly with the four men, then strode briskly to the door. One bodyguard opened it and stepped into the hall. Krutz followed. The second guard closed the door behind them.

I was left with the feeling I'd gained nothing, which was ridiculous. I had a free hand for forty-eight hours and I knew what to look for. It was a great deal more than nothing, but it left the empty feeling in my stomach unexplained.

I joined the others at the bar, accepted congratulations on winning, and waited, not listening to the talk. When Tony suggested we call it a night, we shook hands all around and left.

In the car I strapped myself in but, preoccu-

pied with my thoughts, didn't notice the needle
of the speedometer upward bound until we'd
turned onto the freeway. Even when I did notice,
it seemed unimportant. I repeated my conversation with Krutz.

Tony said thoughtfully, "I've got to take this to
the feds, buddy. I don't know much about
Saudis and oil and all, but there's government
types who think they do."

"We don't need them. They'd be in the way."

"They're always that," Tony snorted.

"And if they got to Lori, they'd slam her into a
cell as a material witness. When they'd finished
with her, they'd arrange a reunion in Texas,
along with headlines in the paper."

"That's fact, for sure."

"Can't you stall some?"

He was silent for several moments. "Hell.
Why not?" he replied, grinning. "I'll make it a
written report. And you know how slow I write.
It'll take weeks for them to get back at me."

I nodded my thanks and was silent for several
miles, vaguely aware of the light traffic Tony
passed as if it were parked. "I wonder why
Krutz wouldn't admit Rosta was working for
him?"

"I said his word's good. I didn't claim he
always tells the truth."

"It leaves me hanging. I don't know if he's
talking for Rosta or not."

"Count on one thing. Rosta will try for Lori.
He won't pay any mind to Krutz or anybody
else on that. He flat doesn't like witnesses."

"It might be time to stash her someplace."

"You've got to."

I gave him the card on which Krutz had written the phone number. "Can you find out where that phone is?"

"Easy," Tony said.

Neither of us spoke again until Tony skidded to a stop in Ned's drive. "I'll be by in the mornin'," he said grimly. "It's time to show you somethin' special."

"What's that?" I asked, releasing the belts and opening the door.

"It'll wait." He backed out and tires squealed as he accelerated down the canyon. I watched after him until the taillights disappeared around the bend, then turned up the dirt drive.

Fifty feet from the house, Ned stepped out from behind the trunk of a eucalyptus tree, the carbine nestled in the crook of his arm. "Howdy," he drawled slowly.

"Any trouble?"

"Like Sunday in church." He tucked a cigarette into the corner of his mouth and the wooden match flared.

"How's Lori?"

"Sleepin', I reckon. Leastwise she was a noddin' heavy, last I saw. She's been a workin' with them colors, ever since ya left." He took a deep drag, the coal of the cigarette glowing brightly in the night.

We started toward the house. "She tol' me most of it. Ya gittin' anywhere?"

"Not really."

"Then I'd git at it."

"That's the plan."

Ned followed me inside. Lori had fallen asleep, her hand on the table a pillow for her cheek.

"I sorta like thet one," Ned said, pointing to the impressionistic watercolor of an old cowboy on a great black horse. "Quite some woman, here."

I nodded agreement. Sketches covered the table, some roughly fleshed out with colors. I reached down and kissed her lightly on the back of her neck.

Her head snapped up.

"Sorry," I said. "But it's time to go."

She shook her head vigorously, her hair floating, rubbing sleep from her eyes. "Yes. A bed would be delightful." She stood up, looking down at her work, frowning.

"Why not let it be?" Ned suggested.

She kissed the old man on the cheek, then started toward the door, only half-awake. I grinned at Ned, fingering leathery hide where she'd kissed him, then hurried to catch up with her.

Saturday

IIII IIII IIII IIII IIII

I lunged up out of restless sleep, shook my head to clear it, and stumbled toward the window. Someone had driven over the cattle guard. Tony's red Porsche was charging up the hill. Lori and Bobbie were not inside. I stood naked, exposed, breathing deeply, waiting for the pulse rate to slacken. Back in the bedroom, I slipped on yesterday's pants, ignored the shirt, and walked out onto the porch. Bobbie rushed forward to greet me, changed her mind, whirled, and ran back to Lori, walking down from the oak.

She was wearing the white ducks again and, even with the grumps, I liked the way they hugged her waist. Admiration turned to envy. Why couldn't I spend my time cuddling close like that? I was vaguely aware she was wearing a long-sleeved wine-colored blouse I hadn't seen before, as I turned to face the Porsche, sliding to a stop in front of the porch.

This early in the day, Tony's tie was snugged up to the first button on his shirt. He showed no sign of late hours last night as he slid from the car into the dust cloud drifting toward me. "How's it go?" he called.

"It's early, don't you think?"

"Hell. It's near nine. We've got things to do."

When Tony moved up the draw toward Lori, I turned back inside. Hopefully they'd have a lot to talk about; it might take a couple of hours, even.

Cleaning up didn't improve my mood. I stumbled twice on the way to the kitchen. I tried to ignore Lori and Tony at the table and poured coffee, adding cold water from the tap. I scalded my tongue. When I added more water, it was too cold.

"Would you like something to eat?" Lori asked.

"It's too early to say."

Tony leaned toward her. "Try this. Cook it. Set it in front of him. And see what happens."

"That's a wonderful idea," she said. "Would you like something?"

"It wouldn't hurt even a tiny little bit," Tony replied, grinning.

It was difficult but I did a fair job of ignoring them. Clouds drifted over the mountain peaks, obscuring the sun. It looked like rain. It fit my mood.

With breakfast on top of my third cup of coffee and another cup in hand, I listened as Tony told Lori what Hank Krutz had said last night. I summed up my visit with Finley Quale and waited for someone to pick up the conversational ball.

"I've a little news," Tony said finally. "Captain Greer got together with a couple of wheels in the department. The priorities got reshuffled."

"How's that?" I asked, attentive now.

"They want Rosta. The boys are diggin' hard for anythin' about Rosta or Krutz. And both of them are bein' covered round the clock by the best we've got. If there's any way human critters can make a case, we'll get it done. And the D.A. bought off on Lori tradin' testimony to avoid extradition. All we need's a little luck and she'll be clear."

"Is anyone checking on Quale?" I asked.

"His name never came up. Should it?"

"Expect not. You'd want reasons and all."

"What have you got?"

"A feeling, Tony. Just a feeling."

"And that is?"

"Maybe you ought to wander out and take a look at his woman. Something about her eats at me. Tough doesn't come close to describing her."

"So he likes tough broads."

"If Vance Coggswell's right, he burns a million a year."

"So?"

"His house needs paint."

"You've lost me."

"You ought to call Vance. You might hear it different. But maybe Quale needs a good score, like collecting for that dagger."

"But the man's worth millions."

"Vance says there's not so many now."

"I can't make a dime buckin' your hunches, buddy. But I can't grab hold of this one." He took another sip of coffee. "Still, Matt did work for him."

"He did. And he was in Kuwait."

"Are you saying Matt smuggled the dagger out for Quale?"

"Hell. I don't know. It's possible, is all."

"Okay. It's probably a waste but I'll see what I can do." He turned to Lori. "You're sort of quiet. How's this all sound?"

"Encouraging," she replied. "But there seems so much to be resolved. Too much." I reached out and gathered both her hands in mine. She freed one and lightly stroked my wrist.

"Which brings us to a point," Tony said.

"And that is?" she asked.

"Did Scott say anythin' about you gettin' out of sight?"

I met her look. It's hard to face accusation from a soul betrayed. "No. But it's time," I said.

"I hope you don't mean what I think you mean," Lori snapped.

Tony leaned toward her. "Scott and I have this longtime buddy, Lencho Cabral. He owns a bar with gamblin' out back. He's somethin' of a god-father to a lot of Mexicans in the Valley. He can hide you so deep nobody'd ever find you."

"I feel safe with Scott."

"He's good, Lori. But he's only one man."

"They've seen my work," I added. "They'll send more next time."

"Who knows where we are?"

"I stay low. But there's people who know me. Some would talk if the bucks or the pressure were right."

"There's somethin' else," Tony said. "Some-body's been nosin' into stuff on my desk."

"Are you sure?" I demanded.

"I'm sure. We're always pawin' through each

other's stuff, but this time somebody tried to put everythin' back like he found it. Captain Greer was real interested. He's got Internal Affairs workin'."

"Rosta said he had a connection with the police," Lori said. "He claimed I'd be killed if I went to them."

"I remember," Tony said. "It's what made me sure somebody's buttin' in and doesn't want me to know about it."

"This could get a lot worse before getting better," I said to Lori. "It's time to tuck you away."

"Don't I have something to say about it?" She glared at Tony, then at me. "Would you ask me to hide if I were a man?"

"Damn it, Lori," I said. "What's that got to do with anything?"

"I might have what you'd call the final argument," Tony said. "I've been tryin' to decide if you need it." He spoke so softly, both Lori and I had to strain to hear.

"There's another side to all this. Sexual perversion, the worst our team ever saw. Your sister's death, Lori, more than anythin' else, got the big wheels to move. If there's even a chance Rosta's connected, we want to find out how. You know your sister was beaten and raped. But did you know it took eight, maybe ten hours of the worst sort of physical and sexual abuse to kill her?"

Lori's face paled. She pulled free of my grasp and pressed her hands flat on the table, tendons taut.

"Some ten years back, a squad car answered a disturbance call. By the time they got in, everybody'd skipped. Except the girl. She was dead. They found a reel of film under the bed, overlooked by people leavin' fast. The coroner claims two men savaged her for nearly three days. The drill probably started with some simple porn, then got harder a little at a time. The reel we've got is real kinky and ends with a hand shoving a Jap sword into her tummy, about a quarter of an inch at a time."

"My sister died that way?"

"I don't think there were any pictures. But the action's the same and nearly a duplicate of another case, about three years back."

"If you're trying to frighten me, it's working."

"You'd look good on tape, Lori." Tony accented each word. "You should drop out of sight for a time."

Silence mounted between us. Lori stared at Tony, rigid in her chair. He met her frightened look with a toughness he'd not shown her before; there was no warmth or friendliness.

"The film's in the car," he said vacantly, "if anybody's dumb enough to want to see it. Most barf after a minute or so."

"Do you have more shells for the pistol, Scott?"

I studied my empty cup until the weight of the silence forced me to look up at her frightened face, turning grim in tiny little ways. I went into the living room and dug out a hundred rounds from the back of the cabinet.

When I returned to the table, I laid the two boxes of shells near her arm. She stood decisively, reaching for the shells. "Now, if you'll excuse me." She walked briskly from the room.

"Stubborn?" Tony asked.

"It seems that way."

"She's got the tough to match it, though."

"That, too." I poured more coffee and asked, "What sexual habits go with the names we've got?"

"Rosta goes for high-class hookers. The girls have no complaints. Never any kinks. If anythin', they think he's old-fashioned. Real straight stuff is all he wants.

"Krutz is longtime married, his family grown and gone. I don't know how he gets on with his wife but there's a girlfriend he seems to keep busy and happy."

"And Quale," I added. "He doesn't need more than Char Killen can dish out." Involuntarily I shuddered.

"But now it's a whole new ball game. The boys are swarmin' on everythin'. We all want this guy. Beth Dobsen's our best lead ever. A lot of new names will come up. Any one could break it wide open."

"Did you get a look at Matt's photo album?"

"Yeah. I did."

"Any chance he was the weirdo?"

"No. He was keepin' score. I checked; none of the faces match the victims we've got."

The six hard slams from the .38 startled us.

"She seems determined. Can she hit anythin'?" Tony asked.

"She does pretty good."

He shook his head. "She needs to be better than that."

This time the shots were spaced further apart. She was taking it seriously. Any reservations left from yesterday had been set aside.

"So what's next?" Tony asked.

"I thought I'd check out Lori's house and Matt's apartment again. I've wasted good time in worse ways."

"Want company?"

"Sure. It's your kind of game."

"Good," he said, standing. "Let's do it."

"First, I want to see that film."

"Are you shittin' me?"

"I've good eyes and know some players. I might see something your people missed."

He sighed. "If you want it, you've got it. Not me. I'll go help make a killer out a Lori."

As he headed outside, I went to the phone and dialed.

"*El Oso.*"

"Macklen here. I need Lencho."

"*Un momento.*" Glasses tinkled near the phone as they were tucked away behind the bar.

"*Jefe,*" Lencho's deep bass pounded over the line. "What's happening?"

"I need some of your special talents."

"*Si?*"

"If I can talk her into it, I'm going to drop a woman off at your place. Her name's Lori Livingston. I want her hidden. If there's any trace of her, folks could die."

"Is it necessary for me to know why?"

I gave him the high spots; he needed to know what he was up against. When I'd finished, he said, "It's a simple matter. But you, *Jefe*. You are also in danger. No?"

"It's nothing I can't handle."

"You could use a couple dudes to watch your back. Ramirez and Acencio are the best. They stay close to Del's. Doc knows them."

"Thanks. I'll call if I need them."

I hung up as Tony came back into the room with the projector.

Rain clouds darkened the room; the projection on the wall was sufficiently clear. What I was watching was late in the proceedings. The girl was blond, full breasted, with broad hips and powerful legs. Scabbed scars from previous beatings with a whip marred pale white skin. She was bleeding at the wrists, tied to the posts of the giant brass bed, writhing in fear of someone approaching. Her feet were out of the picture but obviously tied to the bottom of the bed, her legs forced wide.

I watched with rigidly maintained detachment as she was assaulted with an enormous penis. Penetration brought blood, caught in close-up. The camera work was professional. All that was seen of the man was powerful thighs and the huge organ they supported. I didn't know if there was a sound track and had no wish to find out. The terrified woman was obviously crying out in anguish, probably hoarse from similar previous cries.

Occasionally a rope was slashed and retied, to give different access to the beaten, battered body. Light glinted dully off the broad blade. I could see it in her eyes as she watched the knife; she wanted death now, not later.

When I saw the clawlike hand move the glowing tip of the cigar toward her breast, my composure broke. I could almost hear her wail of anticipated agony as the camera zoomed in on the nipple, the clawlike hand, and the glowing cigar tip. I watched in horror as the hand grew, drifting out of the picture, until only the fingers and cigar were visible. Two deep scars were etched across the middle finger. I couldn't bring myself to look beyond the scars, as the camera closed on the glowing coal and the heaving nipple beneath it.

I snapped off the projector, my shirt drenched with sweat. A deadly calm encompassed me. I could still hear her screams as I looked at the now-blank wall. If I met such men, they'd die. It'd be mere extermination of mad, vicious animals. For a moment I felt an odd new closeness to Tony and his partners. I'd been subjected to feelings they knew too well. I rose slowly from the chair, picked out clean clothes, and headed for the bathroom. At least the shower could erase the sick-smelling sweat. Nothing would wash the film from memory. I was somehow cheered by the slam of six fast shots from the .38.

In the end, I gave up. Lori steadfastly refused to leave or even discuss the matter further. After a long silence during which Tony and I pretended not to notice her wiping dampness from the corners of her eyes, Tony tried to explain about the gun. That to use it in one's home to protect one's life was one thing. And legal. But to carry it in her purse was another matter, and illegal. She made no reply but the look in her eyes invited him to return to the planet from which he'd come. She picked up her coat and walked outside, the heavy purse gripped tightly in both hands.

I looked out at the gathering storm clouds and stopped to slip into the hip-length corduroy saddle jacket, then followed her. Because Tony had an afternoon appointment, we took both cars. Tony followed; the Blazer was no match for the Porsche. Lori was silent the entire way, her eyes focused beyond what could be seen through the windshield.

When we pulled up in front of the house that had been her home with Matt, Tony and I got out and examined the neighborhood. If there was a resemblance to two bird dogs testing the breeze, it was natural. We'd stood this way in other times and places, not to continue until both of us were satisfied with the feel of it. When I looked at Tony, he nodded and started toward the house.

For a city lot, this one was large, at least a
hundred and thirty feet wide. The house itself
was a low, rambling stucco structure, capped
with heavy shakes. Plantings were minimal but
well kept up. It was the wrong time of year for
cut flowers but I could see the beds Lori had
worked at. Tree roses, neatly pruned, lined the
walkway to the front door. I didn't know values
in the area but guessed I was looking at something close to a million worth of property. Lori
walked stiffly beside me, her arm tucked in
mine, eyes locked to the front.

When we got to the porch, Tony snapped the
police seal. Lori fumbled for a key and unlocked
the door. Inside, I watched her look about as if
visiting a stranger's home. She seemed uncertain, ready for flight, as if she were an intruder.

"Any tools around?" Tony asked.

"In the garage," Lori replied.

I followed Tony. He broke through another
seal on the back door. As he snapped the one on
the garage, he said, "We shouldn't have brought
her. She's hurtin' good."

"We didn't have much luck dumping her."

"You've got to get it done."

"I know. I only wish she did."

Inside the garage, I found a flashlight and
snapped it on. Matt's work area looked like a
window display in a department store. The long
workbench was clean. A good grinder and a
heavy vise were securely mounted to one end.
Every tool was in its proper place on the wall of
plywood behind the bench. We gathered up

screwdrivers and anything good for taking a house apart, including two clawhammers and a crowbar, then returned to the house.

Tony paused to check the main power switch; it was off. Inside, he said to Lori, "This will be ugly. We've got to tear it up."

"Do it," she responded grimly.

"Remember," I said, "we could be looking for a key, like to an airport locker."

"But it's either that or the dagger, nothin' in between," Tony said, turning to Lori. "You could pick up a few personal things."

She shook her head. "Not now, thank you."

"Are you sure?"

"Quite sure."

"Then stick with Scott. If you have an idea, sound off."

Tony turned to the walnut paneling in the living room and began ripping it loose with the crowbar. It had to be done but the splintering of expensively finished walnut grated like fingernails on a chalkboard.

"Do you have a stepladder, Lori? Or a stool?" I asked.

She went into the kitchen and returned carrying a three-step ladder with a waist brace. "Will this do?"

"Yeah." I handed her a screwdriver. "Take the plates off the wall fixtures." I watched her hesitate at the light switch in the kitchen. How many times had she turned it on or off? Once started, she continued doggedly. I went to work on the ceiling light fixture.

We worked for over an hour, exploring under or behind anything removable. I checked the attic crawl space and later climbed up on the roof. The garage received the same treatment. With shovels we dug in likely spots in the yard, ignoring dirt or plantings untouched in weeks. The dagger hadn't been in the country more than a few days.

"Any ideas?" Tony asked, as we gathered near the garage, looking about the yard.

"Only Matt's apartment," I said.

"It's probably a waste of time," Tony said, glancing at his watch. "But I've time to get you inside. Then I need to get back to the office."

"Let's do it," I said.

At Matt's apartment, Tony picked up the key from the manager, broke the police seal, unlocked the door, and stepped inside. I followed him. Lori entered hesitantly, looking about the room so recently filled with violence she had not seen but could easily imagine. I hoped she wouldn't catch the meaning of the cracked wallboard behind the television set, or notice the bloodstains on the faded blue carpet.

"Do you think Rosta might send his people back here?" Lori asked.

"I doubt it," Tony replied. "He knows we've been all over it, that it's sealed."

She nodded but remained uncomfortable, uncertain.

"I can get a squad car to cover," Tony said.

"No. I'll be fine."

"Are you sure?" he asked.

"Yes," she replied, more firmly.

"Then I'll be gettin' along. Let me know how you make out."

"Will do," I said.

We watched the door close behind him, both of us feeling lonelier and more vulnerable. "We ought to get to it," I said.

We repeated the procedure used at her home. It didn't include replacing anything removed. I was working on the medicine cabinet in the bathroom when she called from the other room. "Scott. I think you ought to see this."

When I walked into the living room, she was looking down at the top of the desk. "Where did these come from?" she asked. "I don't remember seeing them before."

Several pieces of paper had been laid out on the desk. They'd been previously crumpled, then flattened.

"They could have come from the wastebasket. Tony's folks may have found them." I looked at them one at a time. "I don't see anything special."

"Remember the invoices in the safe box from Stillson Imports?"

"Sure."

"This letter, on Stillson Import stationery." She reached for it, then continued. "Matt didn't receive it; he wrote it. I used to edit his correspondence. That first line was a typical opening."

I read out loud. "I appreciate the time you

have so graciously given and believe it will result in mutual profit." A glance at the balance of
the page showed it must have been a draft of
sorts; there was no mailing address. "You're
saying Matt was Stillson Imports."

"It looks that way, don't you think?"

"It does. But Stillson Imports is a vacant lot.
What does this give us?"

"A different address."

"You've sharp eyes. Yes, indeedy." I folded the
letter and tucked it into my pocket. "Let's finish
here, then check out this address."

She nodded agreement but there was no enthusiasm.

An hour later we stood in the middle of the
living room, looking about us. "What do you
think?" I asked. "Is there anything Tony would
have done that we missed?"

"No. I think we covered everything."

I nodded slowly, vaguely dissatisfied. Most of
the day was shot and we were no better off than
when it began. Krutz had only promised forty-
eight hours. We were running out of ideas as
well as time. "It's probably another dead end
but let's check out this address."

Lori slipped into her coat and headed for the
door. I gathered up the tools and followed. As
we started down the steps, it began to rain.

It was raining heavily when we drove by the
front of the three-story office building in North
Hollywood. That the building existed was a
good sign; maybe the office did too. The streets

were crowded with people homeward bound. But there was no room to park in front. I took the first right and pulled into a spot beyond the service alley behind the building.

I like rain. It adds a special softening privacy wherever it finds me. And I like watching others deal with it. Some run and collect more drops per unit of time. Some, with coat collars high, crouch as if to duck it. Only a few umbrellas were out; Southern Californians don't usually own them. I walked with my head up, enjoying the feel of the rain against my face. Lori, her arm tucked in mine, also held her head high.

Inside, we took the stairs to the second floor. We were looking for Suite 209. Offices were laid out on either side of a hallway that was a square on the building floor. The linoleum was worn. There were breaks in the roll along the walls. We followed the numbered arrow to the left, then turned toward the rear of the building. Some of the offices had glass fronts, others only a door. From the names displayed, the building seemed a gathering place for salesmen and distributors.

We found 211, realized we'd passed 209, and turned. We hadn't seen the number because the door was open. The front was glassed in. A middle-aged woman, with hair dyed red, sat at the large desk in front of the door. To her left was a small table upon which a switchboard system was mounted. She was wearing a headset and was typing. As we watched, she took a call and made notes on a pad.

Behind her, there were three rows of smaller desks. Each had a phone. A few were cluttered with papers and files. Most were cleared as if the day's work had been dumped in a drawer. Along one side of the room was a row of filing cabinets, on the other, a row of wardrobe closets. Only five desks were occupied at this late hour. Two men struggled with paper and pencil, their desks littered. Three others were on the phone. One looked to be offering the world at half price with no takers.

"We must have made a mistake," Lori said.

"Maybe not. Rent a desk. It comes with a secretary. And you're in business. That's how I set up Nelder and there's not even a desk."

Inside, we waited for the redheaded woman to finish with the phone call. She wore dangling brass earrings stamped from a modern mold that left them without any sense of meaning, only the color of brass. Her pale blue dress was practical and worn.

When she finished she looked up, a professional smile of greeting glued to her lips. "May I help you?" Her voice was her strongest feature, assertive, well-modulated, and pleasant to the ears. The eyes were watchful, calculating.

"I hope so," I said. "Does Stillson Imports have a desk here?"

"Yes, but their representative, Mr. Livingston, is not in. May I take a message?"

"I didn't catch your name."

"Ms. Falward."

"I'd like to introduce Mrs. Livingston," I said, nodding toward Lori.

"I'm glad to meet you," Ms. Falward said flatly, appraising the young woman as if she were a chicken to be plucked, then sold at auction.

Lori nodded in reply. "When was the last time you saw my husband?"

"I don't recall. He's here so seldom."

It sounded as if she'd give a similar answer if the question were asked of any of her clients. "If you could help, we'd appreciate it," I said. "Mr. Livingston seems to be missing. No one has seen him in several days."

"I'm sorry. But I don't concern myself with the personal affairs of my clients."

"Could we look through his things?" Lori asked.

"Do you have identification?" Ms. Falward asked.

Lori reached into the bulging purse and produced the wallet. She opened it and laid it on the desk. Ms. Falward glanced at it briefly. When she looked up, the eyes were bright. "For a hundred," she said bluntly, "you can take anything you find. It's the last desk on the right." The phone rang. She responded, ignoring us. I laid a hundred on the desk and followed Lori.

She sat down at Matt's desk and began examining the contents of the drawers. I noticed the extension number on the phone was ten and that the filing cabinets on the other side of the room were numbered from one to thirty.

I walked over and opened the top drawer of cabinet number ten. It was empty. So were the others. I removed each drawer, examined the underside and the interior of the cabinet. Nothing. Ms. Falward kept up with what we were doing. It puzzled me when I caught a look of smugness on her face.

Thoughtfully I walked across the room toward the wardrobe lockers. What did Ms. Falward have to be smug about? A hundred bucks that shouldn't have been required didn't make it. Lori was looking through a folder of clippings, correspondence, and invoices. "Anything?" I asked.

"Nothing yet," she replied.

The wardrobe was empty, except for the pair of light blue step-in coveralls that zipped up the front. The red hand-embroidered emblem in script read STILLSON IMPORTS. What would Matt need these for? The coveralls were standard but the embroidered logo was a costly addition.

There was a Bic ballpoint pen clipped to the upper pocket. All the others were empty, except one. I pulled out an invoice, like the ones Lori had found in the safe box. A shipment of thirteen cartons had been delivered to Technical Devices in Reseda.

"Look here, Lori," I said, laying the coveralls across the corner of the desk. "I wonder what Matt needed these for?"

"I've no idea," she replied, examining the embroidered logo.

"Can you read this?" I asked, pointing to the

bottom of the invoice. "Is that twelve or thirteen?"

"It looks like twelve to me. Is it important?"

"I don't know, but the original shipment was thirteen cartons." I reached for the phone.

"Yes?" Ms. Falward asked from up front.

"Can I make a call?"

"The number, please?"

I read from the invoice.

"I'll connect you."

"Technical Devices," the receptionist answered.

"I know it's late," I said, "but I was hoping to catch someone in receiving."

"Dave may still be here."

I was placed on hold. Moments later, a young-sounding voice said crisply, "Shipping and receiving."

"Dave?"

"That's me."

"I know it's late but I've a problem. On the sixteenth, last Friday, you received a shipment from Stillson Imports. That's us. My records show we shipped thirteen cartons. But you only signed for twelve. Is there any way to tell if the shipment was complete? We might owe you a carton."

"Do you know what you shipped?"

"The invoice says 2200 PC-144A. It's nothing to me. Does it mean anything to you?"

"Sure. That's the controller board for our Model IV series. I'm pretty sure we got them all. Let me double check."

I was placed on hold. When I looked up, Ms. Falward was turning back to her desk. She'd been watching again. Was it more than simple snoopiness?

"It's cool," Dave said, interrupting my speculations. "We received twenty-two hundred and they all checked out good."

"That's great," I said. "So you got all thirteen cartons?"

"Nope. Twelve."

"I wonder what the screw-up is?"

"What's the diff?" Dave asked cheerfully. "Put my name on that invoice and file it. Who'll ever care? The last name's Rogers."

"Thanks, Dave. I appreciate the help."

"Any time."

The line went dead. If there had been thirteen cartons shipped, where was number thirteen? It could be a mistake. Or a couple of cartons could have been damaged and repackaged as one. Whatever, Dave Rogers was certain: Technical Devices had received the full shipment.

"Anything at all, Lori?"

"I don't think so. It might help to compare what's here to the invoices in your safe. Some of this may relate to them."

"Bring the folder. We can check, back at the house."

"There is one thing. Someone else has already looked through this desk."

"How's that?" The last diehard tenant slipped on his coat and walked tiredly toward the door.

Lori backed away from the desk and opened

the top drawer. Pens, pencils, paper clips, and the like were scattered about the nearly empty drawer. The sectioned tray at the front was empty. "Matt was something of a neat freak. He wouldn't leave things like this."

I remembered the orderly array of tools in Matt's garage. I looked around the empty office, then at Ms. Falward's back. I suddenly felt uneasy.

"And this file folder," Lori continued. "Things have been inserted randomly. Matt always organized by date of origination."

The smug look I'd seen earlier loomed full before me. "Let's move it, Lori. Fast. Ms. Falward may have called someone we don't want to talk to."

I scooped up the coveralls and started for the door. Lori followed with the file folder. I undid the bottom two buttons on my coat and tucked the thumb in the waistband, next to the butt of the Colt. Ms. Falward did not look up as we passed.

When I turned toward the rear of the building, Lori looked at me sharply. "There must be a back exit," I said. "I don't want to meet anyone coming up the front." I didn't tell her folks might also be coming up the rear.

I pulled the Colt from under the heavy jacket and stuffed it into the oversized pocket. I dug out the keys to the Blazer and handed them to Lori, along with the coveralls. I wanted both hands free. "I've got that feeling, Lori. If things come apart, do what I say."

She nodded and glanced worriedly behind us.
"Two men just went into Ms. Falward's office.
They were in a hurry."

I turned right toward the stairs, then stopped
on the landing. I pressed Lori to the wall beside
me and drew the Colt. I felt her trembling and
wished there was a way to ease her fear.

I could hear them running toward us. I
waited, feeling the palms of my hands begin to
sweat. I wanted them close. I concentrated,
judging distance by the growing sound of
pounding feet. I lunged around the corner, the
pistol cocked in my fist.

The two men froze as if they'd smacked into a
wall, four feet from the muzzle of the Colt. "This
here rabbit's got good teeth."

Both men had guns in their hands but the
muzzles were pointed toward the floor. They
tensed, gathering themselves.

"Don't," I snarled. "It's a lousy day to die."

They hesitated, uncertain.

"Drop the guns. Now!"

Without volition, my finger tightened on the
trigger. I leaned toward them. First the pistol,
then the heavy automatic, bounced against the
floor.

I heard it as Lori said softly, "Someone is
coming up the stairs."

I took three quick steps, catching the two
hulking figures off guard. Behind them, I
palmed the Colt and slammed first one, then the
other at the base of the skull. They crumpled to
the floor in a bizarre embrace.

"The front, Lori. Run!" She did, trying not to look at the unconscious figures. I followed, digging for a speed loader, keeping myself in line with Lori and the back of the stairs.

Two shots rang out, the crashing thunder reverberating from the walls, floor, and ceiling. Lori turned down the stairs and stopped uncertainly. The rounds had smashed into the wall in front of me.

Instinct and training took control. I dove for the floor, rotating in a sliding turn, until I was able to bring the Colt up and on line. Another round notched a deep groove in the linoleum next to me. I squeezed off two rounds. The roar of the overloaded magnum erased all other sound. The big man halted abruptly, two rounds in his chest, exploded by mercury. The top half of him was tossed backward, his feet yanked from the floor. He was already dead when gravity overcame inertia. The body crashed heavily, awkwardly to the floor.

The second man had whirled toward safety in the stairwell. I had a clear shot but held back, wondering what it might cost me to let him live. When the rushing figure disappeared around the corner, I lunged to my feet and dashed down the stairs. Lori's hand was buried in the purse. She gripped the .38 tightly. Her face was chalky white. She needed no encouragement to follow.

When I rushed into the lobby, no one was in sight. I dashed through the main entrance, turned right, then stopped abruptly, my back to the outside wall of the building, hidden in shadows under the rain-filled sky. Lori stopped beside me, breathing heavily. The Colt was still in my hand, still cocked, but my arm dangled at my side. The few people who passed were more concerned about ducking rain than in what Lori and I were doing.

How many had been sent? Four was a reasonable number. But there could be a driver, even a second car. I studied the street from left to right. No one was visible in any of the parked cars.

"I don't see anyone, but you never do," I said. "They're looking for two of us. Let's gamble they still want you alive. Head for the Blazer and get it started. But cross the street at the corner, so you don't have to walk past the mouth of the alley in back. You drive and forget the lights. And hang tight to the .38. If you have to use it, don't try to pull it. Just hold onto the gun and let the purse fall. Got all that?"

She nodded and stepped out. I looked back and forth at the street and buildings in front of me, searching for any unusual motion. I'd planned to give her a fifty-foot lead, but I was moving before she was thirty feet away.

She was nearly across the street when I reached the corner and turned toward the Blazer. I paused, waiting for her, the eyes shifting restlessly between the intersection and the mouth of the alley at the back of the building. I risked a quick look around the corner, back toward the entrance. No one was coming this way. I moved out. I wanted to be past the mouth of the alley before Lori recrossed the street.

Short of the alley I paused, listening intently. The two men I'd clubbed were of no concern. But the slender man I'd let flee down the stairs and any others not seen were still a threat. I could hear nothing except early night sounds. When Lori started across the alley on the opposite side of the street, I stepped out with the open darkness to my right.

It wasn't much of a sound, almost like a cat landing lightly on the edge of a trash bin. The cause didn't matter one bit. Wondering can get you killed. I launched myself forward into a tumbling roll, twisting as I came out of it so as to be facing back toward the alley.

The bright cone of flame and fire stabbed at me through the wet night. The roar of the shot was curiously subdued by the wet night air. Still twisting, I brought the Colt up. I felt my body slam flat to the concrete walk only as the end of motion. The magnum roared. Four rounds were launched at the spot from which the bright orange cone had originated.

I rolled clear of the alley entrance, still facing it. I snapped open the cylinder, caught the dumped casings, and rammed home a full load. A sound that could have been someone crawling was erased by the roar of the engine behind me. With the gun up, cocked, and pointed at the middle of the alley, I stuffed the casings and empty speed loader into my pocket and began inching back toward the Blazer.

Nothing moved. Tires squealed at the intersection as someone stopped late on the light. The door of the Blazer opened behind me.

I lunged up and dove feet first, belly down, into the passenger side. With my chest hanging out, I grabbed the open door with my left hand. "Go," I commanded. My right hand directed the Colt toward the alley entrance.

When Lori shoved the accelerator to the floor, I nearly tumbled from the precarious perch. Seconds later, the view of the alley was blocked by parked cars. I laid the gun beside me, used the back of the seat to pull myself inside, and closed the door. With the gun back in my fist, I watched through the rear window.

"Take your first right, then a left."

Lori began to turn even before I finished the sentence.

"Hit the lights." The switch snapped on; my eyes remained riveted on the view through the rear window. Lori took a hard left. There wasn't a car in sight behind us.

"I think we're clear. Follow the rules and get over to Sepulveda." Three turns later, I was certain; we weren't being followed.

I turned back to face the front, slumping deeply in the seat. I stared vacantly out the windshield, unseeing, gripping the Colt in my lap with both hands, waiting for reaction.

"Are you hurt?" Lori asked anxiously.

"No. A few bumps, is all." I turned to look at her face in profile, alternately brightened and shadowed by the lights from approaching traffic. I tried to remember the last time she'd laughed. I gave it up, turning back to look out the windshield.

"How many did you kill?" she asked softly.

"I can't say," I said tiredly. I wasn't lying. The big man in the hallway had been dead before he'd hit the floor. Or even as he entered the building. Or when he went to work for Rosta or Krutz. Or when he stole his first car. I'd fired at the source of a cone of deadly brightness in the alley. I couldn't say it was a hit. Who'd want to know? She could go back and make the body count if she wanted to.

"And there'll be more killing, won't there?"

"How in hell do I know?" But I did. Tony had been wrong. Krutz had already broken his word. Others would come for us soon.

"How will you live with it?"

I straightened in the seat and turned to her. "Lori, are we quarreling? Did I miss something? Or weren't those bastards trying to kill me?"

"I only want to know how you'll live with it," she said, her voice trembling with her own reaction.

"Just as with the others. They'll become faceless memories."

"And you'll wake up screaming when you dream about them, won't you?"

"It's not likely. Those weren't men. They want that dagger and they'll kill anyone to get it. They aren't fighting for a better way of life or the right to enough food. Those bastards will steal your virtue or your money or your life, whenever it suits them."

"But the violence, the whole of it? How will I live with it?"

"That's it, isn't it? You somehow still think all this is your fault."

"Part of me does."

"Would it do any good to say you're wrong?"

"No."

Maybe I should have explained the only alternative to shooting the man who'd lain on her belly in Houston was brutal, violent rape, and quite possibly her death instead of his. But I said nothing. She was right about living with it being too damned hard.

It was after six when we stepped inside the house. I responded to Bobbie's welcome, then went to the phone and dialed.

"Foothill Division. Sergeant Haggen."

"Macklen here."

"There's a big squeal in North Hollywood. Know anythin' about it?"

"Maybe." I explained about the search of Matt's apartment and the crumpled letter Lori had found that had led to Ms. Falward and Matt's office desk.

"You must have been right busy," Tony commented. "Incidentally the body count is two. You nailed the guy in the alley with three rounds."

"Is anyone looking for me?"

"No way. That Ms. Falward?"

"Yeah?"

"She described you as slender, five-eight, and blond. She didn't mention a woman."

"Then she did set us up."

"It looks that way. Later, I'll stop by for a little chat. The two guys you clubbed were still out, last I heard. Our team tied them and the stiffs to Rosta. So maybe that woman can give me the link to him. All I need's the right button to push."

"So you figure I'm clean?"

"The description doesn't fit. And those slugs you use don't leave anythin' for ballistics to work with. Besides, nobody's goin' to get excited about two assholes bein' burned. If it comes to it, the lab team knows who started the shootin'."

"It looks like Krutz lied. It hasn't been near forty-eight hours."

"It's like I said. They were Rosta's boys. He could have been actin' on his own."

"Or Krutz is a liar."

"Then again, Rosta may not be workin' for Krutz."

"That doesn't fit with the bank scene. It's hard to believe Krutz's man being there with Rosta's was a coincidence."

"True enough. But face it. We don't really know."

When Tony hung up I dialed again, aware of sounds and smells from the kitchen that come from food cooking. But food was low on the present list of priorities.

"Dr. Tilden's office."

"Macklen here. I need Doc."

"He's finishing with a patient, Mr. Macklen. Can he call you back?"

"Sure thing."

I hung up. Rain chilled the February night. I made three trips to the woodshed out back. Bobbie helped; she carried a good-sized chunk each trip. Minutes later, fire filled the Franklin stove. I looked at the stack of wood, decided it'd last until morning, then walked into the kitchen for a beer. Lori was frying potatoes.

"I'll have this ready in a few minutes," she said, not looking up.

"Okay," I said, not much caring if I ate or not. Sipping the beer, I walked into the bathroom and opened the safe. I removed the six invoices Lori'd found in the safe box. I hadn't thought to give them to Tony. I'd have to do that, first chance. There might be meaning in them that professionals could read. I locked the safe and replaced the medicine cabinet as the phone rang. I caught it on the third ring. "Yeah?"

"Dr. Timothy Tilden, sir. At your service."

"You either just collected a big fee or you're expecting one from me."

Doc laughed. "It's nothing of the sort. I have finished with a last-minute patient and am about to join the rabble in the bar downstairs to partake of some uplifting conversation."

"Go slow, Doc. Remember what tequila can do."

He laughed again. "But this is Saturday night, Scott. Even God rested on the seventh day."

"I bet he didn't start Saturday night the way you're planning."

"Different gods have different habits."

"Uh huh. Could we get serious for a second?"

"I believe I can manage that."

"Lencho said you could get hold of Ramirez and Acencio."

"Done. One or the other is probably downstairs this very instant, while I'm here wasting valuable time."

"If it doesn't interfere with your drinking, have one of them call me."

"Certainly. Is there anything else?"

"Yeah. Watch out for the worm in the bottom of the bottle."

Doc laughed again and hung up.

Lori was serving when I entered the kitchen. I sat down at the table and spread the invoices off to the side, leaving room for the plate she was preparing. I dug out the folded invoice I'd found in Matt's coveralls and laid it beside the others.

I compared each invoice to the one I'd just found. When I finished, I started over. I didn't realize I'd been eating until Lori replaced my plate with coffee. I rearranged the invoices in a row across the table in front of me. One by one, I compared them once more. All I could see was that each shipment had been carried by Flying Tiger during the last leg of its journey and that the number of cartons delivered was noted in a virtually undecipherable scrawl.

Lori came back into the kitchen with the folder taken from Matt's desk. "May I look at them?" she asked.

"Go ahead. If there's something there, I don't see it." I grabbed an invoice and handed it to her. "Down at the bottom. Can you make out the number of cartons signed for?"

"It looks like four."

"The original shipment was five. Some of the sign-offs I can't make out at all. Matt's job with Exton kept him moving. His travels put him in a great position for a smuggling operation. He could have been using Stillson Imports as part of it. Hell, Quale didn't care who shipped the goods. The question is, how did he manage it? Maybe he used the balloon device to get what he wanted out of whatever country, then shipped an extra carton on each invoice to get it into the States."

"That's as good an idea as any. But even if you're right it doesn't tell us where the thirteenth carton is."

"I know."

As Lori compared documents in the folder to the invoices in front of her, I stood and dumped the remaining coffee in the sink. Bourbon better fit my mood. I poured liberally and sat back down.

When she closed the folder and looked up, she said, "If there's a connection, I can't find it."

I leaned back in the chair, looking up at the ceiling. "We've pushed luck far enough. You've got to hide someplace."

"That seems the sensible thing to do."

I looked at her sharply. "Then you'll do it?"

"No. I'm too frightened. I wouldn't feel safe with strangers."

"But it's not safe here! By now, whoever wants us could know about this place or at least be close to knowing."

"If necessary, I can hide in the hills. I don't want strangers involved."

"You mean you'd rather see your friends killed?"

"That's not quite fair."

"No. It's not. But ..."

"But nothing. You said you could hold off an army with those rifles over the door. Let Sergeant Haggen deal with the rest of it."

We argued quietly, each remark less reasonable than the last. In a matter of minutes, we were ripping and tearing at one another, logic and sensibility set aside. When she could no longer deal with it, when she failed for the third time to find a suitable telling remark, she rose and left the kitchen.

When I heard the shower turned on, I finished the rest of the drink, then poured another. In the living room, I hunted up the cleaning gear and started in on the Colt. Ten minutes later she came out of the bathroom, walked to the big bed, and crawled under the blankets. When I could take nothing more from the cold steel except the bluing itself, I reassembled and loaded it. Tonight I'd sleep with it in my hand. I put the cleaning gear away, walked to the kitchen, and poured another drink I didn't need. I don't know how long I'd been standing, looking down at the invoices, when the phone rang. I crossed the room, picked up, and said, "Yeah."

"Jaime Ramirez. Doc said I should call."

"I'm glad you did," I said, thinking of how this must be said. "Have you talked to Lencho?"

"This morning. He said he'd eat my ass, raw, if I screwed up. What do you need?"

"You and Acencio both, maybe even an army. The party is getting out of hand."

"What can you tell me?" Ramirez asked. There was curiosity but no sign of concern. I told him in brief outline all that had happened. A man risking his head has a right to know why. I ended with, "They sent four this time; two are down for good. Next time, there'll be more."

"What you should do is let Lencho hide her."

"She nixed that idea."

"That's too bad." I thought that an understatement, but I couldn't think of anything to add. Ramirez said, "I guess I don't know how we can help."

"You fellows are good, Lencho tells me. And willing to take a chance."

"That's true enough."

"Do you know the old man who raises horses up here, Ned Early?"

"Your neighbor, isn't he?"

"Yeah. Meet me there about nine in the morning. Maybe I can talk some sense into her by then. If not, the people looking for her may not figure to look there. Even if they do, there's good cover. How's it sound?"

"We'll be there."

"I want to thank you for your help."

"That can wait until it's over."

The line went dead.

I had switched back to coffee an hour ago. I sat by the window, watching moonlight sneak through an occasional break in the heavy cloud cover. It had stopped raining. The clouds proclaimed there'd be more.

We had quarreled twice tonight, if the unkind words in the car were to be counted. I loved her and she loved me. It was not words spoken in the night or that we'd made love. It was in the manner of our lovemaking, the way of our words, and in the fullness of this house, empty until now. It was in her eyes and in the hollow feeling in my gut whenever I saw the sadness so commonly reflected in them. The night would not last long enough to list the proofs. Why, then, would she not do as everyone urged? Take advantage of Lencho Cabral's near-inexhaustible supply of cousins and friends? Be safe?

It was late when I showered and eased into the bed we shared. She wasn't asleep. When she spoke, I knew she'd been crying. "I simply can't explain it," she said softly. "I feel death is near to one or both of us. I can accept that but not with strangers. I want to be with you as long as I can."

I reached and pulled her to me. I felt her tears on my bare chest as I tried to stroke the tension from her back. Maybe she was right. Maybe she was marked for death. If so, someone would pay the ultimate price.

Sunday

|||| |||| |||| |||| ||||

The car rattling across the cattle guard jolted me awake. I grabbed the Colt from under the pillow and padded naked across to the window, breathing heavily, aware of Lori coming from the kitchen to stand beside me. The light brown sedan struggled up the road, slipping and sliding in the muddy stretches. The skittish colts stayed well clear. Heavy clouds darkened the day. The clock said ten after eight. I wasn't expecting visitors and strangers have serious business if they make the long trek up to the house.

"I don't like it," I said, my voice filled with sleep. "It feels wrong." I turned to her. "Get out the back and down to Ned's."

She followed me into the bedroom, picked up her coat, and started toward the back door. She held the bulging purse tightly with both hands. I slipped into yesterday's pants and pulled the corduroy coat on over bare skin. I tucked the Colt into my waistband and trotted to the front door. The back door closed behind Lori as I reached up for the side-eject Winchester 94. The car rattled over the second cattle guard. I shoved an extra box of shells into my coat pocket and paused to scratch between Bobbie's ears. She'd been trained as an attack dog before I'd inherited her but I hadn't kept it up. Now I wished I had. "Stay," I commanded. Reluctantly, the dog lay down.

Outside, I ran down the knoll, away from the house, then dashed up the draw in what had become a small rushing stream of rain gathered from the hills. I slanted to the right into the smaller draw, my feet soaked and slippery. Footing was better when I clambered out of the draw and ran at a crouch toward the large outcrop of rock a little below the level of the house. Through a narrow slot created by one slab of granite tumbled up against another, I had a clear view of the fifty yards to the house. I could hear the car on the last rise, its engine struggling. I checked; a round was chambered. I cocked the rifle.

The car slowed to a stop short of the porch. Only one man was visible. He turned off the engine and got out. He was tall and beefy; his cheeks puffed out like a greedy squirrel. While studying the man, I watched the car; someone could still be inside. He examined the terrain, then walked past the front of the house and looked down at the draw. Rain beaded on thinning curly black hair. He looked to be about fifty, carrying unneeded pounds. He seemed unaware of rain streaking the light blue suit, painting it a darker shade.

He walked to the front door and knocked. There was no sign of anyone else in the car. I moved out silently from behind the rocks, checking the hillside stretching down to the road. Nothing moved except the colts. I steadied the carbine on the figure before me, my forefinger firm on the trigger. He knocked again. I kept moving. When he knocked the third time, I was fifty feet behind him, at the edge of the gravel. "Looking for someone?" I demanded, continuing toward him.

He turned slowly, as if he faced at least three stalking men each morning before breakfast. He didn't appear to notice the rifle sighted on his gut. He reached into his inside coat pocket, produced an I.D. wallet and let it dangle. "The name's Nunis. Captain Nunis. L.A.P.D. And you are?"

"Scott Macklen. What's a captain doing here on a Sunday morning in all this weather?"

"We're looking for a woman," he replied, a scratchy sound to the voice.

"Who?"

"Mrs. Lorraine Livingston, it says on the warrant."

"Does that warrant give you the right to go inside?"

"It does."

"I don't see it."

Nunis reached again under his coat and produced the warrant. I glanced toward the car, then moved closer. I took the warrant with my left hand, shook it open, and scanned the cold words. It was one thing to hear her name and the word "warrant" in the same sentence, another to see it typed boldly amid the legal jargon of the state, along with the word "murder." I handed it back and yelled, "Bobbie!"

Nunis was unperturbed by the yell. And uninterested in who or what Bobbie was. He ought to be. I've seen the wilderness look in her eyes when watching someone I wasn't fond of. Moments later, the dog dashed around to the front of the house and slid to a stop beside me, all attention focused on our visitor. He ignored her. "Go on in," I said.

Nunis turned and went inside. I followed, Bobbie at my side. He stopped and searched the large room with his eyes. I went into the kitchen, picked up a towel, and painstakingly wiped rain off the carbine. I returned it to the rack over the door and the box of shells to the shelf. Coals remained in the stove. I stuffed kindling and three small chunks of wood inside and stood warming my hands, watching the captain walk into the bedroom area. Bobbie sat by the day bed, alert, trembling slightly, never taking her eyes from the beefy man. It was the position she'd been trained to take while awaiting a command.

I went into the kitchen, poured coffee, returned, and sat down in the chair nearest the stove. Bobbie hadn't moved. Her ears adjusted frequently to sounds people don't hear. I heard a rustle that meant Nunis was pawing through the clothes closet. He reappeared, then disappeared into the bathroom. The shower door opened and closed, then drawers, and finally the medicine cabinet.

Back in the main room, he looked around once more. He walked to the window and opened one of the cabinets.

"Do you think she's in there?" I asked. Bobbie, sensing my mood, braced her back legs for a fast start, her hind end lifting off the floor.

Nunis closed the cabinet. "I wouldn't think so," he said, his face expressionless.

"Then stay out of my things."

"Have you ever heard of Salvadore Rosta?" he asked.

"So?"

"He's looking for something. I believe it's drugs. A fortune in white powder could be stored in any of these cabinets."

"If you want to look in cabinets, get a different kind of warrant."

"You're being uncooperative, Mr. Macklen. Honest citizens have nothing to hide."

"When was the last time you suckered some poor slob with that line?"

"You've dealt with police, then?"

"A time or two."

"Harboring a fugitive's a crime."

"Yeah. A real baddie. How come no one else has been by?"

"I'm working on a theory of my own. Who was the woman that was here last night?"

"A friend."

"When did she leave?"

"Late."

"Who's clothes are in the closet?"

"Some are mine."

"You don't seem interested in helping, Mr. Macklen."

"You're a bright fellow."

"You've been seen with Mrs. Livingston, on several occasions."

"Is that so?"

"Do you deny it?"

"I don't anything. If you want to talk, take me downtown. We'll do it legal."

"I don't believe you realize how important this is."

"I don't much care what you believe. The fact is, you should be on your way."

Captain Nunis turned to look toward the bedroom window that overlooked the draw. When he turned back, he was smiling, reminding me of a coyote on the scent of a rabbit close by. "Suppose I asked you to come along."

"You'd need a charge. Or else my lawyer'd stuff your ass with ground glass. You might never crap again."

"Are you threatening me?"

"Hell no. That's another one of your crimes."

He studied me for several moments, then shrugged and started toward the door. "Don't trouble yourself. I'll let myself out."

I didn't move but I felt uncomfortable with my back to the man. The latch came free. "Have a nice day," he said, then closed the door behind him. When the car started, I stood and watched until it turned right on the canyon road, back toward town.

I grabbed the phone and dialed Haggen. Who in hell was this fellow? Tony had never mentioned him. And what judge had signed a warrant for murder? If Tony was home, he wasn't answering. I tried the station. He was out.

"Come on," I said to Bobbie. I jogged out the back and down the draw. Even the dog knew it was important; she trotted at my side, ignoring wet exciting smells from the rocky draw.

As I cleared the last bend, Ned stepped out of the barn, his carbine cradled in his arm. I slowed to a stop beside him. "Is Lori inside?"

He nodded. "Trouble?"

"It seems likely. A cop showed to arrest her for murder. I think he knows she was up at my place, that she came down this way while he was driving up the hill."

Ned tucked a cigarette into the corner of his mouth and lit it, sheltering the match from the rain with his hat. "Reckon cops 're like others, mostly," he drawled. "Some good, some not."

"I can't say about this one but he hasn't got Lori's interests at heart."

"What ya figure ta do?"

"I seem to be out of choices. I wanted Lori to get out of sight. But she won't go for it. If we stay here, someone will get to us. The only thing I can figure is to take her someplace and wait for Tony to clean things up."

"Sounds reasonable."

"I don't like leaving this mess to someone else."

"Tony? He'll do good."

"Expect so." I looked around the familiar ground. Trees and outbuildings offered good cover. A broad patch of bare muddy ground surrounded the house. "Ned, I've got something to check out. It shouldn't take more than an hour. A couple fellows Lencho knows are due any minute. Could Lori stay here until I get back? Then we'll both take off."

"Ya gotta ask?"

"Yeah. I do."

"Don't ya fret none. With two good boys, we'll make out jest fine."

I turned toward the sound of the car coming up Ned's drive. I tucked my hand into my waistband. Ned's carbine was pointed at the car.

The driver pulled to a stop some fifty feet away. Two heavyset men climbed out, one carrying a carbine, the other a shotgun. Their eyes moved constantly, evaluating everything seen as threat, good cover, or meaningless. They wore heavy boots and long coats. They didn't seem to notice it was raining. They stopped in front of us. The taller man said, "I'm Ramirez. He's Acencio. What's the play?"

"Let's take it inside," I said.

The four of us turned toward the house, trudging through the mud. When we reached the porch, Lori opened the door, her face pale. Bobbie nuzzled Lori's hand until rewarded with a reassuring scratch between her ears. None of us bothered to wipe mud from our feet; the rough wood floor had dealt with worse. We sat down at the slab pine table in the kitchen. Ramirez chose a seat with a good view out one window, Acencio gazed out the other.

Lori found clean cups, nicked and scarred from long use, and poured coffee all around. She refilled the pot and started a fresh batch. With her own cup in hand, she took the empty seat beside me. Ramirez had been watching her. He glanced at me, as if approving, then turned back to the window.

I gave them a brief outline of what had led to my call. I reached under the table and clasped Lori's hand when I began to tell of the visit from Captain Nunis. I felt her shock at the mention of the warrant.

When I described Nunis' interest in the draw, both Ramirez and Acencio turned to look at me. "I know what you're thinking," I said. "If it's cops that show, you're out of it. Got that?"

Both men nodded, obviously relieved.

"I'm really only worried about hoods. Still, Nunis changes things. I wanted to stay, with you fellows to back me up. But we can't risk a shootout with cops and I won't take a chance on Lori being stuffed into a cell. So what I want is an hour of solid cover. When I get back, Lori and I will leave. That'll be the end of it so far as you fellows are concerned." The look on Acencio's face bothered me; at the mention of only an hour's risk, he'd relaxed. It could prove to be a fatal error.

"I don't know you two but Lencho says you're good. I hope he's right. If there weren't a warrant out for Lori, I'd take her with me. But there's cops where I'm going. So she stays here. I could be wrong, but if I were you, I'd set up as if trouble were on its way. If they come, there'll be half a dozen or more. From what I've seen, they'll be good."

Neither man was concerned about the odds. Acencio asked, "Do you have anything with more range than this shotgun?"

Ned gestured up over the front door. "Thet carbine hits good, if'n ya point it right. The shells are in thet little closet."

"There's a Springfield M1A with some forty-round clips up at my place," I said.

Acencio rose and walked toward the rifle, saying, "This will do. I've never used anything fancy."

"Suit yourself," I said, also standing. With my hand, I asked Lori to stand with me. I looked down at the old man. "I've got this feeling, Ned. Like I'm backing the wrong hand."

"Don't fret none. We'll do fine."

I nodded and walked to the door with Lori. When we were outside, the dog beside us, she asked, "Where are you going?"

I kissed her, then cuddled with the curve where her neck met her shoulder, kissing lightly again. "It's that damned dagger," I said. "It may be in that thirteenth case not delivered to Technical Devices. There's at least a possibility it's still out at the airport, a carton never picked up.

If it's there and I can get it, we can solve most of our problems. I've got to try. Running sounds easy but we both know it's not."

"Did you mean what you said? That we'd leave together?"

I pulled her close and hugged her closer. "Yeah." I didn't point out there didn't seem to be any other way to get her out of sight.

"I thought I'd never run again." She rubbed her cheek on my shoulder. "I can manage if you're with me." She sighed. "I'd like to leave right now."

I backed away from her and held her by the shoulders. "You stay in the house and keep the pistol handy. And Bobbie, too. She's fond of you; she'll help if there's trouble. I'll be as quick as I can."

"Do you think anything will happen before you get back?"

"I can't say. The fact is, part of me wants you to come with me."

"I'm even more frightened of police than Rosta."

"Expect you're right." But I wasn't sure. I wasn't sure of anything except that we should be long gone. I leaned forward and kissed her again.

"I love you," she said quietly.

"And I love you," I said, surprised at how easily the words fit my tongue. "Now get back inside."

She turned and walked toward the porch. The dog looked after her with a puzzled look. "Go,

Bobbie." She happily pranced through the door, ahead of Lori.

I hit the draw running. Once inside the house, I climbed into yesterday's shirt and into Matt's coveralls, then tugged on the heavy jacket. I grabbed the invoice, snapped it to a clipboard, and ran for the Blazer. I used four-wheel drive for a better chance against the muddy drive. There was nothing to point to, but the conclusion was clearly defined, immutable. The time we needed had vanished.

Sunday mornings are slow at the Burbank Airport. Steady rain separated me from the few people I saw. The air cargo offices are isolated from the passenger terminals. Despite a nearly overwhelming sense of urgency, I walked casually inside and up to the counter at Flying Tiger. There was no one in sight. I'd left the jacket in the Blazer. The blue coveralls, with the name STILLSON IMPORTS, boldly displayed, were zipped only an inch above my waist. Even so, it would be tough to get at the Colt. I propped myself against the counter, hiding the gun, waiting.

A sandy-haired youngster popped out from between rows of bins receding beyond view and sauntered toward the counter. He hadn't shaved in several days; it hardly showed. His name tag read BILLY. He glanced at the name on the coveralls and asked cheerfully, "What ya need?"

"Help, for sure," I answered. "I've a boss that's real unhappy." Billy wasn't measurably concerned with my problem but he did look at the invoice on the clipboard. "Down there at the bottom," I said, pointing. "Is that twelve or thirteen?"

Billy looked at the scrawled sign-off, then up at the printed thirteen. "It could be thirteen. Why?"

"Me? I think it's thirteen, too. But Technical Devices says it's twelve, that we're short a case. The boss says if I don't find it, I've got to find something else."

"What's that?"

"A job."

"Got ya," Billy said, grinning. "I'll check."

Billy ducked into the small office to the right of the desk. Moments later he emerged, waving a sheet of paper. "Looks like you're in. We show only twelve picked up. I'll look out back."

When he returned, he was carrying a cubical carton about a foot high. He tossed it onto the counter, grinning broadly. "How's that for service?" he asked, shoving a company invoice in front of me. "Put the old John Hancock right there and you've still got your job."

I took the offered pen and scrawled what I hoped looked like Matt's name. The hand was shaky. "You saved my life, Billy."

I turned with deliberate casualness and strolled from the building. Outside, it was all I could do to keep from running. My heart pounded against my ribs.

At the Blazer, I took time to strip off the coveralls and put the jacket back on before climbing inside. I ripped open the box. It was filled with small twisted chunks of Styrofoam. I dug gently through the packing, spilling some on the seat. My fingers touched a cold smoothness and eased it out.

Even in the rain-darkened day, the golden hilt gleamed dully. I don't know the difference between a ruby and red glass but the stones embedded in the scabbard looked real. Later I couldn't remember how long I'd looked at it. Forty million dollars, the newspaper had said. People had died for this. To the Arab world, it was sacred. Its loss meant unneeded tension between Americans and Saudis. To me, it meant Lori would be free of Krutz.

The thought of Lori brought me back. I stuffed the dagger into the box and hastily added the packing that had spilled. I drove off faster than usual. Once on the freeway, I let the Blazer wind out to sixty-five, max for a rainy morning and patrol cars.

We were free of Krutz. I'd get her clear of Rosta, one way or the other. Now I wished I'd brought her along. There'd been cops at the passenger terminals but none near Flying Tiger. She would have liked being part of this. Then again, it didn't matter. She'd share it with me soon enough.

I shoved the Blazer up the canyon at speeds that stressed the suspension. I'd tried to do some planning but hadn't been able to get past delivering the dagger to Krutz in exchange for having Rosta pulled off the hunt, as least insofar as the dagger was concerned. That Lori would remain a target because she was a witness, dangerous to Rosta, and that she was wanted in Texas, both seemed far away, things to be handled later with relative ease.

Abruptly I slowed. A late-model Pontiac was angled into the brush in front of Hotchkinson's place, Ned's neighbors to the south. They say it can't happen with homo sapiens but the hair on my neck felt as if it were lifting. The car didn't belong there. I killed the engine and coasted to the side of the road. I opened the door silently and let it close, unlatched. I stood, unmóving, listening for any hint of discord. There was nothing but the occasional grumbling cry from a wet, disgruntled bird. One of Ned's horses neighed, off to the right. The Colt was in my fist; I didn't remember pulling it.

Something was badly wrong. Or all senses had deserted me simultaneously. The urge was nearly overpowering but I couldn't charge into Ned's place. Someone might be waiting for me to do just that. The quiet assured me that whatever had happened was over. Wild ranging thoughts focused on the picture of Captain Nunis, looking down the draw. Then I knew. The best direction from which to launch an attack on Ned's place was from the south, Hotchkinson's place.

I ran, crouching, toward the parked sedan. Inside, ignition wires dangled, twisted together; the car had been stolen. It could have been abandoned by kids who'd grabbed it for kicks and driven until it ran out of gas or failed in some other way. But the notion didn't fit. Kids don't joyride Sunday mornings on lonely canyon roads with only two exits to the city below.

I ran another two hundred feet before turning up toward the barbed wire fence bordering the road at the south edge of Hotchkinson's place. Ruthlessly, all thoughts of Lori, of Ned, were forced aside. But oh, sweet Jesus. If they had her.

Using a fence post for balance, I vaulted the barbed wire, charged into the small culvert, and ran up toward the house. I pushed harder on each stride, lungs burning, aching, until fifty feet above the house.

I dropped to the ground at the edge of the culvert, studying the house. Lights were on, to be expected on this rain-darkened morning, if anyone was home. To the left, a fantail off the hills extended below the house, blocking any view of, or from, Ned's place. Nothing moved in the house or on the hillside.

I charged the rear of the house, wishing desperately for more firepower than the Colt. One glance through the window was enough. Hotchkinson lay on the floor by the open front door. Pooled blood under his neck and chest announced death in a convincing fashion. There was no sign of his wife but she seldom left the house. She'd probably leave only once more, never to return. The attackers had effectively covered their rear.

I ran for the fantail. Someone could be waiting for me but my gut said otherwise. Anyone on the other side of the hill was dead or down. Still I took the time to move silently.

At the crest, I threw myself to the ground, peering through the rain. Ned's barn blocked the view of the house. The lights were on. Nothing moved, except a horse shifting position in the corral beside the barn.

The attack had come from this ridge. Low chaparral gave ample cover down to Ned's property line, marked by the split-rail fence. Where would they have positioned themselves? Ned would have been near the barn. Ramirez and Acencio would have split up, one covering the road and access through the trees, the other watching up the draw.

I crawled cautiously down to the fence. I watched intently for any movement. As I became more convinced there would be none, I moved more quickly. I slipped under the fence. Acencio lay sprawled face down, a dozen feet from where I crouched. If the man had not listened to cautions rendered, if he'd been careless, it mattered little now. He'd paid the final price.

To my right, all but the roof of the house was hidden from view by the barn. Nothing moved. I lunged from cover, stuffing the Colt into my coat pocket. I scooped up Acencio's borrowed carbine, grabbed the box of shells that had fallen from his pocket, and tried to load a cartridge. A live round lay under the hammer. Acencio had not heard his attacker. I rolled the body over.

The head was nearly severed from the shoulders.

I moved silently down the draw, knowing the effort was meaningless. As the house came into view, I saw three more bodies. One sprawled brokenly across the steps. Another lay in a crumpled shadowy heap on the porch near the half-open door. The third lay with the face buried in mud, halfway between the house and corral.

At the far side of the barn I found Ned, sightless eyes staring up at the rain-filled sky. He'd taken a round in the shoulder, close to the heart. Anxiously I knelt and felt for a pulse in the tough leathery neck. It wasn't much, but it was there. The old man looked too small, too frail, to take such a blow and live.

When I stood up, the carbine dangled uselessly in my hand. I surveyed the yard through tear-filled eyes. I should have done as she asked, leave this morning. Or I should have taken her with me. Or any of a hundred other things. But not this. Anger and frustration conspired to confuse thought. Rain washed away the tears but did not slow increasing rage.

A hundred feet toward the road lay another figure. It could be Ramirez. I ran swiftly toward the downed man. He'd been hit from behind, easily a killing shot, and twice in the left leg. He was unconscious but alive.

With grim foreboding, I dashed toward the house. For an instant, I couldn't bring myself to move through the doorway. I nearly gagged at images of what might lay inside. I slammed into the partially open door. It crashed against the wall, one hinge tearing loose.

Bobbie would rush to greet me no more. The great black dog was dead, shot in the chest and head. The man with the bloody knife had lost his throat to the dog, in one savage, brutal swipe, perhaps justice for the way Acencio had died. I stepped further into the room and scooped up the .38, trying not to think of the raging terror that had been Lori's, alone, facing the assault. I thumbed the cylinder open and dumped it. All rounds had been fired. I tucked it into my waistband. There were two other bodies.

One had been hit squarely in the chest, the other had taken four rounds. Both showed signs of Bobbie's powerful teeth and jaws on wrists, hands, or face. The dog could have done no more. And Lori'd done fine. There had been too many.

Rosta had Lori. And it was meaningless. I had the dagger that had triggered all this dying.

I walked to the phone and dialed. It rang six times before the receiver was picked up, then dropped. A moment later, I heard, "Who the hell's this?"

"Macklen. Get your feet on the floor, forget the hangover, and listen up."

A moment later, Doc responded, sounding more like himself. "Yes, Scott. What is it?"

"Get an ambulance out to Ned's place. He and Ramirez have been shot."

"Oh my God."

"If you move it, you might keep them alive."

"I'll move," Doc said emphatically.

"And the horses, Doc. Get someone good to look after them."

"Done."

Doc hung up. I dialed again.

"Foothill Division. Sergeant Kramer."

"I need Haggen. Real bad."

"Your name?"

"Macklen."

"Hang on. I think he's out in the hall."

Moments later, Tony said cheerfully, "So how's it go?"

"Fuck that shit. Bobbie's dead, Ned's damn near it, and Lori's gone. There's enough bodies here at Ned's place to start a cemetery."

"What happened?"

"You get out here and tell me. Is Rosta covered?"

"Absolutely. He hasn't moved from his office since yesterday."

"I can feel him. His paws are all over this. Pull your men off. I want to talk to him. And pull off Krutz, too."

"For Christ's sake, buddy. Cool it! This isn't a jungle."

"The fuck it's not. You get out here and make the body count. If this isn't war, you can tell me what is."

"Come on. Let me take Rosta!"

"And his attorney? In two hours he'll make bail or get loose some other way." Into the brief silence I asked, "How long do you figure Beth Dobsen lived?"

"You've a point. But if you kill him, there goes the trade of testimony against extradition."

"You're not thinking. What's to trade when the body's cold?"

"I can't argue that."

"It was Captain Nunis that set it up. He was out this morning. He knows Lori slipped down the draw."

"What are you sayin'?"

"He was recon, buddy. He scouted the ground, then told the mothers how and where to hit. They sent in a good team, killed the Hotchkinsons, Ned's neighbors, drifted in over the hill, and nailed two fellows Lencho sent before they knew what was happening."

"How many bodies you got, for Christ's sake?"

"A bunch. Now, are you going to pull your people or should I plan to go through them?"

"I'll pull them. But Jesus, Scott. Take it slow. You know how you are when you lose control."

"I'll do it right." I didn't tell him it would also be fast and hard and efficiently ruthless, because Tony would expect nothing less.

"One more thing?" I asked, all hardness gone from my voice. Tears filled my eyes. I rubbed each one briefly, briskly.

"I'm still here."

"The dog, Tony. Even if you've got to do it yourself, get her buried. I don't want her in someone's trash. The ground uphill from the big oak, it's not too hard."

"Yeah." The silence dragged on. "I'll get it done." Tony sighed and the line went dead.

With the disconnect came the other familiar feeling, isolation. I was free of command, of the whims and demands of others. I dropped the receiver, letting it slam against the worn wooden floor. I turned and surveyed the scene of carnage one last time.

"I'm coming, Lori," I said out loud.

I yanked two blankets off the cot next to the phone and ran. I grabbed Ned's raincoat as I dashed through the door. Inside the barn, I fumbled for the coil of wire Ned leaves on the hook by the door.

Kneeling once more beside the old man, I gently searched for a pulse. It was there. I wasn't sure it was as strong as before. I doubled one blanket and tucked it down around the thin wiry frame, then ran to Ramirez. His head moved slightly from side to side. I dropped to one knee and lifted it.

"Sorry," he gasped. "So god damned fucking sorry."

"There's an ambulance coming."

A hand gripped my coat, surprisingly strong. "They thought I was dead," he said. "Look for a punk with a bad leg and another I nailed in the shoulder." His grip loosened. His hand fell away, slapping grotesquely into mud. His voice faded to a near-soundless murmur. "Burn them. Burn those motherfuckers. For God's own soul, you've got to . . ."

He drifted into unconsciousness again. I laid

his head back gently on the ground and tucked the second blanket around him. Lencho hadn't been wrong. Shot in the back, damn near dead, Ramirez had slowed at least two of them.

Where Interstate 5 comes down from the Ridge Route, drivers can continue on into the heart of the city or turn south across the San Fernando Valley. From the freeway, just short of this junction, travelers looking south will see the Van Norman Reservoir, a lake of water for the desert city. On Roxford, I drove toward this junction. Cold rain-filled air rushed through the open window. It cleared my mind, helped the concentration on those few thoughts allowed. Red rage and fear for Lori blocked most thought. There was nothing of the rain or tomorrow, only of the dog, Ned, and how I would find Lori. The notion I might fail was not allowed. It would start with Rosta. I couldn't see beyond that.

Traffic on Interstate 5 was light. I drove under the freeway, pulled off onto the wide shoulder, and stopped. I grabbed the dagger, hastily wrapped and wired in Ned's raincoat, along with some rock. I lifted the hood to show the Blazer had failed and waited for a break in traffic flowing on and off the freeway. When no one could see, I rushed across the grassy knoll, angling to the right. Each time a vehicle showed, I dropped to the ground, waiting. As I gained distance from the Blazer, I gained cover.

At the fence, I tossed the oddly shaped package to the other side. Here I couldn't be seen, unless someone pulled to a stop at the edge of the highway. The chain-link fence that protects this part of the city's water is topped with three strands of barbed wire, slanting outward. The barbs discourage climbers.

I wiggled out of the heavy coat and tossed it across the wire. I leapt for the fence top beyond and below the barbed wire and pulled myself across the coat. One barb tore through the shirt, drawing blood. I let myself slide, head down, placed a hand on the inside of the fence, and let my feet fall outward in a cartwheel to the ground. I grabbed the package and ran.

At the water's edge I gripped the free corner of the raincoat and spun, as in the hammer throw, driving on each turn, then let go. The package splashed into the water sixty feet from shore. It floated out onto the lake. I waited anxiously, holding my breath. It had to sink! There was no time for swimming. Suddenly it settled, as if becoming comfortable. Then it was gone, leaving only ripples of water disturbed. The dagger would bury itself in the muddy basin, lost to all the world but me.

Back in the Blazer, I gunned it to avoid a truck turning south onto the freeway.

Morning

‖‖ ‖‖ ‖‖ ‖‖ ‖‖

I had stopped for boots, climbing gear, and a wetsuit. I'd tucked my purchases into the flight bag, now resting on the seat beside me. The black stocking cap was pulled down to my eyebrows.

In light traffic on Santa Monica, I drove past the front of The Office. If Tony was right, Rosta was in his private office. If Tony was wrong or Rosta had moved, even to walk downstairs, I was probably already dead. I shoved the thought aside and studied the second- and third-floor windows. Even though clouds and rain blocked the sun, creating a morning twilight, most of the drapes were drawn. Dim light showed faintly behind only two windows.

I turned right at the corner, then right again into the alley behind the building. Rosta's Cadillac was parked in front of the service entrance. The first two windows on the second floor were brightly lit. Drapes covered the second one. I wanted to stop and study the scene, but the sight of two men in the brown sedan parked at the back of the service area urged me on.

They could be cops but Tony had said he'd pull his men. Besides, cops wouldn't be that close. These two must belong to Rosta, securing the back through which I'd entered with only a cook's apron for cover.

I drove around to the front once more. There

was no other sign of Rosta's people. The only
pedestrian on the block was an older man, leaning heavily on his cane. The few cars parked
along the street appeared to be empty. I turned
right and pulled to the curb a few feet beyond
the alley, beyond sight of the two men in the
service area. I looked up at the two lighted windows to Rosta's office. I paid particular attention to the window nearest the corner of the
building, the one with the drapes open.

A face showed briefly and was gone. I smiled.
It was Rosta. There was no mistaking the
drooping mustache. Whistling softly through
my teeth, I drove on, still smiling. I didn't have
to check in the mirror to know it wasn't a nice
smile. The tune was a blues version of a black
New Orleans funeral dirge, one played on the
way to the cemetery with the casket held high.

I pulled back onto Santa Monica and parked
in front of the four-story building next to The
Office. I grabbed the flight bag and walked toward the entrance. Rain-wet sidewalks hid the
sound of new boots. An older man and younger
woman stepped outside as I reached the door.
The woman gave me a streetwise inspection as I
slipped inside. The man didn't notice me.

The carpets were worn and frayed, with none
at all on the concrete stairs. Even in the dim
light, paint peeling off the walls was noticeable,
adding to the shabby look. The tenants were en-
trepreneurs, working at an ancient trade, an extension of Rosta's place next door.

On the fourth floor, the stairs ended. I walked

down the hall to the end. I needed access to the roof. There had to be one; all depended on it. And I needed it now. How long would Rosta remain in his office?

I walked more slowly back the way I'd come. All the rooms seemed to be about the same size. The door opposite 412 had no number, no markings of any kind. The doors on either side were marked 411 and 413. The unmarked door was either the entrance to one of three much smaller rooms, a closet, or access to the roof. I'd have to gamble and I'd have to be right. There was no time to deal with error.

At the door, I tried the knob; it was locked. I backed off and slammed my boot into the latch, filling the hallway with throbbing echoes. It gave but did not open. I slammed into it once more. The door flew open, revealing a narrow flight of stairs. I was through in an instant, closing the door behind me. I yanked the fire extinguisher loose from the wall and propped it against the door to keep it closed.

I rushed up the narrow dusty stairs. The door at the top opened. It was locked only to entry from outside. I walked flat-footed to the edge of the roof nearest The Office. I glanced briefly at the roof below, then stooped, zipped open the bag, and dumped the contents at my feet.

The movements were swift, automatic, unthinking. My mind was full of her. I watched her move in the white ducks. I pictured her lovely nakedness cuddled against me in the night. I rejected the image from the film of the broken, beaten blonde with terror-filled eyes, pleading for death. I must not fail. The consequences were unacceptable.

I pulled the Buck knife, measured thirty feet of rope, then cut and coiled it around my neck. I stuffed the stocking cap inside my coat and laid the Colt on the roof. Preparing the wetsuit was tricky. I cut from the armpits to within an inch of the wrists. Then I cut from the crotch to ankle on the inside of each leg. I had to be sure I could be free of the suit in moments. Even though the knife was razor sharp, the task was tedious, the rubbery material unyielding. I was counting on that.

Pulling it on was still a struggle. I used twine to tie the slashed sleeves and legs securely. I tucked the front of the coiled rope about my neck, under the suit; it wouldn't do to lose it. I pulled the zipper only to the middle of my chest, then taped the Colt to the inside of the suit. I practiced, yanking at the butt to pull it free, knowing I'd need to regrip it to fire. It could take time, too much time. I had to count on surprise. The .38, reloaded and tucked into my waistband under my coat, would be impossible to reach in a hurry.

I hooked the climbing belt to my waist and cinched it tight, then attached the remaining fifty-foot rope to the belt. I tucked the open knife through the slash in the wetsuit into the top of the boot. When I put on the face mask and stood, testing the gear, I was a grotesque figure,

a monster to frighten small children. The wetsuit bulged in spots and folded over on itself in
others; it was not designed to be worn in such
fashion or for such purpose.

With the rope doubled around a sturdy metal
vent, I slid over the side of the building. I rap-
pelled down the windowless wall to the top of
The Office, careful to land without sound.

The wetsuit felt awkward, uncomfortable. It
had made the simple task difficult. I yanked the
rope free, recoiled it, and walked silently toward the edge of the roof of The Office. From
behind the cooling unit, I peered down at the
car below. The two men in the front seat were
alert and watchful. I pulled back out of possible
view and began drawing imaginary lines of
sight. The man below wouldn't see me if I kept
close to the face of the building. If they did see
my last push away from the wall, they'd be too
late.

I estimated the distance of the window in
Rosta's office from the service side of the building. I had to be right. There'd be no second
chance. And if a desk stood in front of the window, the action would be exciting, if not fatal. I
tied one end of the rope securely to a two-inch
galvanized vent pipe.

It would have to be a fast descent in order to
gain momentum. I'd have to lengthen the distance traveled on each contact with the wall. I
stood motionless near the edge of the roof, rehearsing my path, the pattern of fall, and the
all-important landing.

I moved to the edge, laying out full-length on top of the wall. I added a last bit of tension to the rope, then slipped off the edge, scrambling to bring my feet flat to the face of the wall, my back arched out against the rope. As I moved down I shifted to the left, to center myself between the two third-floor windows. With each touch of boots to the wall, I allowed my legs to bend further, to gain greater distance from the wall with each thrust.

As my waist came even with the bottom of the third-floor windows, a woman screamed. I didn't know what this might mean to anyone in the room below. I was three feet below where I had intended to be, and a little left, when my boots landed soundlessly against the wall, a foot above Rosta's second-floor window. I compensated by kicking out harder with my left leg and tightening my grip on the rope to reduce the fall.

Feet together, I crashed through the plate-glass window, a foot above the sill. Only carpet lay between me and the opposite wall. I let line slip rapidly for an instant, then gripped hard. Rope stung my hands as I followed my feet through the hole they'd created in the heavy glass. I was moving downward, relative to the cloud of shattered glass. Small shards nicked my face and a larger chunk sheared through the wetsuit and my pants, slashing a gash in my thigh. I used every ounce of strength in my arms to hold back, to land on my feet.

But I was going to hit too hard, despite burning hands tightly gripping the rope. Rosta was to my left, rising from the chair behind the desk. The short, balding man stood by the door to the hall. His mouth hung open, his chin nearly touching his chest. Short pudgy arms were lifted to protect the face from flying glass and the eerie black figure swinging into the room. I let loose of the rope the instant my feet touched the floor and pushed off, tucking my head to my chest. I grabbed for the Colt and yanked. The rope slid easily through the belt loops, drifting my rolling tumble slightly left. The Colt came free on the second yank, as my shoulders and neck hit the floor.

I rolled back up to my feet, twisting away from the wall so that I crashed into it with my back, distributing the shock from waist to shoulders. The man at the door had recovered sufficiently to grab for the gun in his shoulder holster. It came free of his coat as I brought the muzzle of the Colt up in line with his chest.

He should have known he was beaten but the muzzle of the automatic kept coming around. Maybe he thought he'd be lucky. Maybe he thought I'd hesitate. Whatever he thought didn't matter. He was wrong. The magnum roared, pounding fierce echoes about the small room. The round took him in the center of the chest, lifted him inches off the floor, then slammed the body against the wall.

Rosta halted the movement of his hand in the top drawer of the desk, watching the dead man slide slowly to the floor, painting a broad streak of crimson on the wall. I swung the Colt toward him, waiting. Fleeting thoughts of Lori would be ignored, if the huge hairy arm in the white shirt made even a suggestion of further movement.

"Do it, punk," I snarled, a strangely hopeful feeling taking hold. He got the message. Tension eased in the massive shoulders. "Hands behind your neck. Now!"

Slowly he moved his hands up, clasping them behind his neck. I took two steps toward the desk, noticing the second door for the first time. It had been hidden behind a short partition; it led to an adjoining room.

Mentally I examined myself. The gash in the thigh was bleeding but there was no loss of mobility. The cuts in the lower part of the face, below the mask, weren't serious. The wetsuit had done its job. Now I needed to be rid of its restriction.

Rosta's face was a blend of rage and hate. I held the Colt steady in my right hand, pointed at his belly. With my left I unhooked the climbing belt and let it fall, then ripped off the face mask and dropped it. I unzipped the wetsuit and reached on down for the knife in the boot. I felt better; I had access to the speed loaders in the jacket pocket and the .38 in the waistband. I grabbed the knife, slashed the ties on arm and leg, and cut the wetsuit free of ankle and wrist. Throughout, the Colt remained centered on Rosta's belly.

I shifted the gun to my left hand, the knife to

my right, and began cutting my left side free. I'm a lousy shot with my left. It was the time for Rosta's move but he made none. The rope draped around my neck interfered with movement but I left it where it was. I planned to live long enough to need it. I reversed the gun and knife and, seconds later, was free of the wetsuit.

I had ignored quiet knocks on the door. Now they were louder. A voice cried out, "You okay, Mr. Rosta?"

"Tell them to stay clear," I said.

"You tell 'em, asshole."

I whirled and fired. The slug blasted a hole in the center of the door, waist high. I whipped the gun back to cover Rosta. Yelps and cries and screams from the hall suggested other bloody holes existed, created by scattering fragments of the mercury-loaded bullet. Rosta's snarling features were softened with caution.

I glanced again at the door to the adjacent room. I had planned to use Rosta as a shield, at least long enough to get out of the office, even clear to the street. The second door was an unexpected option. I listened intently for any sound beyond it. Could it be that those in the hallway didn't know about this exit?

I moved toward the desk until my thighs touched the edge. The muzzle of the Colt was steady, pointed at the big man's belly. "Where's the woman?" I snapped off each word as if short of breath.

"Fuck you, asshole."

"I've got the dagger. We can deal." The offer brought bile surging up in my throat.

"What dagger?" Rosta asked. Caution blended with other expressions in the dark eyes.

"The one you thought was in the package you took from Matt Livingston."

"I shoulda checked. It wasn't nothing, just a fucking balloon thing."

"You made a dumb move there. Don't make one here."

"How do I know you got it?"

"I've got it."

"Where's it at?"

"Where's the woman?"

"Christ, you are an asshole. What's one broad against forty million bucks?"

"That's the offer."

"What the fuck's that mean?"

"You get the dagger. I get the woman."

"Woman? What woman you talking about?"

I tilted the muzzle up and fired. A three-inch slash of red burst forth across the right cheek. The earlobe disappeared. He staggered, his hand reaching for his face, smearing the even, downward flow of bright redness. He looked at the bloody palm in confused disbelief. As a magnet points north, the Colt was again centered on his belly. "Next is your gut, punk, if you don't know what woman." My voice was softer, all harshness gone. In hasty judgment, one could believe there was even kindness in it.

"You'd never get out of here alive," he stam-

mered, still looking at the redness on his palm,
dripping to the floor.

"That's a nice original line."

"I got a fucking army out there."

"There's not as many now. Where's the
woman?"

That part of his face not bloodied was pale.
"Can I put my hands down?" he asked haltingly.

"I like things fine this way. Where's the
woman?"

"Shit. You sound like a broken record."

"Where is she?"

"I dumped her on the guy that wanted her,"
Rosta answered finally, his eyes etched with
fear. "I can't get her back. It'd take an army,
which I ain't got right now, like you said."

"Who?"

Rosta grinned evilly, confidence returning. He
was in a position to bargain after all. "You know
him. They tell me you're practically buddies."

"Who?"

"For the dagger?" Rosta asked, gluttonous
greed fading fear in the eyes.

"Yeah."

He wasn't a bright fellow. Faced with choice,
he was confused. What he wanted was the dagger and to stay alive, preferably with me dead.
His forehead furrowed in concentrated effort at
thought. Slyness mixed with other expressions
in his eyes and face. He never had time to think
it through.

Two men crashed into the door, slamming it
flat to the floor. The small office roared with a

duet of .38 and .45 automatic pistol fire. The rate of fire was too fast for accuracy; fear charged with them.

I fired once, diving for the open floor to the left rather than toward the cover of the desk, hoping the move would be unexpected. I crashed to the floor and fired twice at the confused jumble my first round had created when it slammed the first man back into the second one.

Rosta made a mistake. He was right; the Colt was empty. But as his hand dove down from behind his neck toward the desk drawer, I dropped the Colt and dug for the .38. "Don't try it!" I shouted. Rosta's hand flashed downward.

Without Rosta, Lori would die, slowly, horribly, in painful agony. "Don't!"

Rosta had the gun in the desk drawer in his hand and a hard, confident smile on his face. He was in control now. He had the high hand. When he saw my .38 come free, he rushed his move. The barrel of his gun clunked against the top of the desk.

I brought the pistol on up. Surely the man could see he was beaten! Rosta must live! "Wait!"

When his gun cleared the desk, choice ceased to exist. Three rounds from the .38 built a triangle of red, four inches to the right of the bright blue tie. The huge man collapsed forward onto the desk, the gun in his hand forgotten.

I fired at the light fixtures overhead, then again. The fluorescent lights went out. It didn't bring darkness but the dim light from the shattered window left the desk and the door to the adjacent room in deep shadow.

I scooped up the Colt and dove for cover behind the desk. Maybe I'd already lost, but if I could get free there was a chance. There was Krutz. I reloaded the Colt with a speed loader. Could I convince those in the hall I was trapped?

I waited for a head to peer around the door or a hint of motion. There was still no sound from the room beyond the door at my back. Someone had turned out the hallway lights but a dim glow filtered up the stairway from the first floor. I could see out better than they could see in. A faint darkness rushed across the doorway. I fired the last round from the .38 and was rewarded by an awesome scream.

I reloaded and jammed the gun into my waistband. For distraction, I tossed the desk chair into the draped, unbroken window. Glass exploded outward, making a furious racket. The chair slammed back to the floor. Running feet dashed down the stairs. I lunged up and charged the door to the adjacent room, trying to guess what lay on the other side.

Both feet left the floor and crashed into the door near the latch. It gave readily. I fell and rolled to my feet in the darkened room. My luck held. The room was empty. Light filtering through the heavy drape was sufficient for me to dodge furniture in the small apartment, as I rushed toward the hall door.

I opened it silently, only half an inch, listen-

ing. Sounds of whispered debate came from the
right, near the entrance to Rosta's office. How
many were there? How many others were scattered about in places I hadn't considered? I
opened the door further. I needed to know if dim
light from the room could be noticed in the hall.
It didn't seem so. And no one in the hallway appeared to know of this exit.

I would have to dash to the left, toward the
far end of the hall, rolling and tumbling as necessary. I wanted to get into a room on the street
side, guessing the alley would be well covered.
Suddenly running was an unnecessary risk. The
door directly across from me opened. The pale
face of a man tilted toward the faint sounds at
the office entrance.

With three strides I was across the hall, the
Colt in the man's face. I grabbed the door by the
open edge and forced it back enough to slip
through, shoving the man before me. I heard
nothing to suggest anyone had seen me cross the
hall. The woman on the bed screamed. I didn't
need that. As I locked the door, she screamed
again. She crouched, hugging a pillow to her
nakedness, gathering breath to scream again.

"I'll say this only once," I said, dashing across
the room to the small sink. The woman stopped
sucking in air. "You both better get to the floor
near the wall." I lifted the rope from around my
neck, stooped, and tied one end to the pipes
under the sink. "When those punks get in here,
they'll likely shoot anything they see."

I stepped to the window and opened it. No

screen! It meant no noise. I peered cautiously outside. There was no one in sight. The man and woman had heard me; they were scrambling frantically to get down on the floor next to the hallway wall.

A foot or shoulder slammed into the door. I fired twice. The slugs hit a foot apart, near the knob. A scream of agony rose in a wailing, whirling storm of pain. I tossed the other end of the rope through the window, tucked the Colt into my pocket, slipped over the ledge, and burned my hands once more, dropping rapidly to the sidewalk.

I ran for the Blazer. No shots came from behind. Driving hard, I fumbled for the keys. As I clambered in under the wheel, jammed the key into the ignition, and fired the engine, I watched the entrance to The Office and the window through which I'd fled. I rammed the Blazer into the car behind me. I saw the gun barrel in the second-floor window as I yanked the trans into first and shoved the accelerator to the floor. The heavy tires squealed, complaining on the hard U-turn. I heard shots but no hits. I turned right and was clear.

I tried to ignore thoughts of how long Lori'd been gone as I pulled up to the curb in front of the phone booth. I'd chosen an area poorly lighted. It wouldn't do to have a cop see me. There'd be questions. My face was cut in at least three places. Blood had flowed freely and dried, intermingled with unshaven whiskers. The large dark brown stain spread down my pant leg from the gash in my thigh. I pulled the stocking cap down over my ears and climbed out into soft rain.

I dialed mechanically, thinking of what lay ahead, of Krutz. And Lori was there, watching, with fear in her pale blue eyes. Was there pain as well? Or was that yet to come? When the operator announced the charges, I dropped the coins in my hand.

The phone was answered on the first ring. The voice asked, "Who's calling?"

"Macklen. I need Haggen."

He put the phone down. I knew where he'd laid it, on the windowsill, across from where I'd last seen the black dog, where I'd picked up the .38 from the worn wooden floor, where dreams had died.

The operator came on the line, asking for more money. Tony interrupted with, "Reverse the charges. Police emergency." He gave his name, division, and badge number. When the operator left the line, I couldn't find the energy to say anything.

Tony broke the silence, his voice tight. "You told it true, buddy. There was a dandy little war here."

Again he waited, then continued. "It looks like Ramirez nailed two. Ned got three. I guess you know how Lori and the dog did."

The silence was longer this time. "For God's sake, what happened with Rosta?"

"I fucked up." There was an unusual hoarseness in my voice.

"What the hell's that mean?"

"He's dead."

"Holy Mother of Jesus. Did you get anythin'? Anythin' at all?"

"He claimed the fellow that's got her is a friend, at least someone I know. The only name that comes to mind is Krutz. I'm headed there now. If I don't make it, it'll be up to you."

"Hold up. Slow down, buddy. Let me go in with you. I haven't anythin' to go on. If you blow it, all I can do is look for her body."

I knew what he was trying to do. To help, to slow things down to a reasonable pace. But the velvet red curtain of rage drifted downward toward the mental stage upon which conscious thought performs. It was too much, too hard, to pull at the edges of thoughts pushing out from beneath it.

"Scott, buddy. This is Tony talkin'. You're losin' it. I can hear it in your voice. You're too tore up to think straight. You've got to listen!"

I hung up and looked at the threatening skies. The soft rain soothed my face but nothing more. I stumbled twice, getting back to the Blazer.

The address Tony'd given me for the number Krutz had written down turned out to be an expensive tourist trap. The floor-to-ceiling window displays were littered with a vast array of unneeded items, boldly labeled imports. I drove

past the front of the shop and turned down the
alley alongside it. At the back of the building,
the alley joined another. I turned right again,
past the rear of the shop.

I was beat, too exhausted to try anything like
the entry to The Office. Besides, there were no
windows in the side or back of the building,
only locked doors. And there wasn't time for
anything clever, nor was there the psychic energy to deal with complexity. I drove past the
front once more. There was someone inside. I
could see movement. The large sign on the door
said CLOSED. Since it was Sunday, maybe they
didn't open until later. Maybe they didn't open
Sundays at all. It didn't matter. The phone was
inside. Whoever was there to answer it would
tell me where to find Krutz. That was as certain
as death.

I pulled to the curb, tucked my arms over the
top of the wheel, and leaned my head down.
Rosta had been the key and I'd dropped it. Now
Krutz was all I had.

I sat back and took three slow, even breaths. I
reached into the backseat, grabbed the box of
magnum rounds, and replaced the two I'd fired
through the door before fleeing out the window
at The Office. I reloaded the empty speedloader,
hands shaky. I tucked the Colt between my
thighs and turned to look through the back window. I needed the element of surprise. It wasn't
much of a plan. It would have to do.

In four-wheel drive, I jammed the trans into
reverse. I laid my right arm across the passen-

ger seat and looked through the rear window. I
couldn't stop it. The blood-red curtain slipped
down and locked in place, blocking all conscious thought. Rolling backwards, the Blazer
picked up speed. When the wheels hit the driveway to the alley beside the shop, I floored the
accelerator. The heavy tires grabbed, pulling me
up across the sidewalk.

The Blazer slammed through the window and
displays behind it. Glass, china, and knick-
knacks became debris, showering the floor of
the shop. The instant the door was clear, I
scrambled out of the car. In domino fashion, the
entire window display crashed to the concrete
floor behind me in an awesome crescendo of
sound. I dashed past the front of the Blazer,
slowed by each display it hit. It stopped
abruptly against a counter too large to be
moved by the engine at idle.

Two men, twenty feet away, each had an arm
up under his coat, reaching for a weapon. They
froze. It could have been the Colt, rock steady in
my fist, that did it. Or it could have been the
look on my face, teeth bared. It really didn't
matter. Both were statues, even seeking to
breathe slowly. Peripherally I was aware of rows
of shelves to the right, laden with showy products in a variety of sizes and colors. I could not
have identified any item. All my attention was
focused on the two men I faced and the hallway
behind them, extending toward the back of the
building. If anyone else was here, they were
down that way.

I moved toward the two men, shuffling my boots through scattered debris. I'd seen them before. Krutz could be here. They'd been with him at the poker game, sitting the night through by the door.

In the hallway behind them, a door opened and Krutz stepped into view. He didn't have a gun. He radiated confidence in his determined advance, a confidence that was puzzling, since I was the one holding death in my hand. He was immaculately dressed in a light brown suit and dark tie. The hallway lights bounced off the balding pate and reflected off the glasses, hiding the eyes. The heavy folds triangling down from the sides of the nose to the lips were deeper than I remembered. The dour expression was much as it had appeared across the green felt.

He stopped a few feet from his men, glanced briefly at the havoc created by the Blazer, then placed his hands on his waist, elbows extended, posturing in a manner that may have had meaning for him, but none for me. I could see the eyes now. They were bright, intense, and grim. There was something more, but I couldn't read it.

"They say your word's good," I said, my voice raspy, my mouth dry. "But you lied."

"I have not lied to you," Krutz responded, with a calmness unnatural in a man facing a .357 in the hands of another, eager to use it.

"You said I had forty-eight hours."

"I've made no move against you."

I could make nothing of the odd look in the eyes. "I want the woman."

"And much more, I think," Krutz answered crisply.

The response confused me. There was meaning here I couldn't capture.

"Yes," Krutz continued calmly, as if unaware of the Colt, the hammer back. "You've decided correctly." He nodded in the direction of the two bodyguards. "You'll kill the shorter man first. With a pistol, he's far the most dangerous of the two. His name is Rosenburg, incidentally."

What was he doing? How could he possibly know that if either man hinted at movement, Rosenburg, at least, would die. What is this clever little man saying now?

"...the other? He could draw and kill you where you stand. But you wouldn't be standing there, would you?"

I wanted to strangle him, to stop the source of unwanted jabs that demanded response I did not want to make, response requiring quick use of cautious, conscious mind.

"I'm very much afraid," Krutz continued, watching me closely, "that I have the advantage over you."

"I don't see it that way," I said, as if speaking across a great distance.

"You can't. Emotional resources have been exhausted. Rage separates you from yourself. You can't see or do anything, in any real sense." He paused, lifting his shoulders in an elegant shrug.

"For example, what can you do with that pistol, apart from killing me?"

"That ought to be enough."

"Death comes in time. I've seen her close by." He stepped forward and pulled up his sleeve. "Dachau," he said, stabbing with a stubby forefinger at the pale blue numbers tattooed on his forearm. "And I know something of rage." He pulled his sleeve down, watching me. "It's a marvelous tool when controlled by a thinking mind."

I could not react.

"At the moment, young man, you are mad. Quite mad. Incapable of thought or rational action."

The words. What did they mean?

"Now you must leave," Krutz said. "Or try to kill us all. You must choose."

What did he mean, try to kill? It was certain they'd die. Death was as close as the forefinger of my right hand. Could no one see it but me? It was only a matter of pulling the trigger three times, with a slight, almost automatic adjustment of the muzzle of the Colt. It would be easy. Death would claim what remained.

"Or forget the gun and come into my office." Krutz turned abruptly and strode away down the hall.

I was paralyzed, incapable of motion. I was holding my breath for no reason I could discern. The two bodyguards were motionless. Their hands under the coats had not moved. Krutz.

The man who had Lori. The man I'd kill if she were not freed. He was slipping away. Krutz!

I gasped for breath, shaking my head hard. I looked up at the two sets of eyes facing me. Both held an odd calm I'd seen in Krutz's eyes. They wre ready to kill or die as the fates might decree. I could see that much. What was I missing? It could not be compassion or pity. Men with guns do not allow such feelings. I tried to think, to find a rationale, however strange, for what was happening. I glanced down at the Colt. My fist was whitened by its grip on the butt. I looked back at the two men. How long had I been looking down at the gun, ignoring both of them?

Krutz had opened his door and was standing, waiting for me or a bullet. Why hadn't he stepped inside? Behind a door, armed, he had a chance to save himself. What in hell was he doing?

"Grab the backs of your necks," I commanded the two men. Both moved only their heads, slowly, to look at Krutz, who nodded. Moving with care, they did as directed.

I should disarm them, even knock them up alongside the head. But it wasn't necessary. I had Krutz. It was all I needed. There was another reason it wasn't necessary to cage these men, but I couldn't quite pull wispy strands of thought together into whole fabric. I was trying. Sweat beaded on my forehead and more gathered under each arm, trickling down my ribs.

Carefully, sliding my feet ahead of me, eyes

steady on the two men, I shuffled past them,
sideways. Tension mounted with each step. I
reached and passed a point midway between
them and the older man. Tension became overwhelming confusion, halting motion.

I had to think. I could not continue to cover
both the men behind me and the stout little
man in front. Finally I made my choice, realizing it to be conscious choice.

I turned my back on the two gunmen, leveled
the Colt at the stout man's belt buckle and
walked toward him swiftly. I stopped three feet
short and glanced down at the Colt, as if seeking
reassurance. The whiteness had faded from the
fist on the butt. Krutz had been right. I could
feel the emotional exhaustion now, as rage diminished. I must be careful not to let that rage
fade too far. I looked up at the man's eyes. Was
there a hint of triumph in them? Even humor?
There might be.

"Won't you come in, Mr. Macklen," Krutz said.

I motioned with the gun. Krutz smiled and
stepped inside. I followed, closed the door, and
leaned against the wall. The old maple desk was
large, of simple design, with an inlay of ebony
around the outer edge. Three upholstered chairs
faced the desk. A boldly patterned oriental rug
covered most of the floor. The bookcase filled
one wall and the wet bar with a coffee maker
dominated the opposite wall. Beyond the partially open door behind the desk I could see part
of the luxurious apartment.

Krutz stood in the center of the room, waiting. Finally he asked, "The gun?"

I looked at him, puzzled.

"You were going to put it away, were you not?"

I tucked the Colt into my waistband. I left my hand on the butt.

"That's much better," Krutz said. "Would you like a drink?"

I nodded, then shook my head, hard, trying to clear mental cobwebs. I watched intently as he stepped behind the bar. There could be a gun there. Something told me there wasn't.

"Bourbon, isn't it?"

I nodded again. He had a good memory. With the drink in hand, he asked, "Won't you sit down?"

I hesitated. I was comfortable with my back to the wall. Slowly I moved to the nearest chair and sat, slumping tiredly. My right hand was relaxed but it still rested on the butt of the Colt. I took the offered drink with my left and swallowed lustily. It burned nicely, landing in my stomach with reassuring warmth. Krutz rotated a chair to face me and sat down.

"You're damned smooth," I said.

He smiled, settling himself more comfortably.

"You almost died out there."

"No. You want Lori Dobsen too badly."

"So you know her name and that she's gone. Maybe you know too damn much."

"One can never know too much," he responded bluntly. "One Hitler in a lifetime is enough. I pay a great deal of money to a great many people to stay informed. It keeps me alive and adds to profits. I know of Lori Dobsen Livingston because I was seeking an agreement with her husband. I know she's missing because you're here."

"Rosta wasn't working for you, was he?" I eased my hand out from under the coat and grabbed the drink with both hands.

"No. Thugs are unreliable. I never use them. I gather Rosta managed to take Lori and that he's dead."

I nodded, sipping the drink, no longer surprised at the accuracy of his conclusions.

"And it was in rage that you killed, was it not?"

"Like they say, it came down to him or me."

"Would you tell me about it?"

In a quiet monotone, I sketched the attack, the shooting, and the escape. Part of me wondered why I did so. Another part pondered how I'd come to be sitting in this chair.

"Remarkable," Krutz commented when I'd finished. "Few men could have come out alive."

"Lucky, is all."

"Possibly. But unlike your entrance here, you were in control of your rage when you faced Rosta."

I swallowed the rest of the drink. Toying with the empty glass, I said quietly, "I've had about enough of that. You may have lived with rage longer than I. But I've dealt with it often enough. All I'm interested in is Lori. I thought you had her. I was wrong. If you can't help, I'll be leaving." To where, I hadn't a clue.

"I'm a businessman, Mr. Macklen. Suppose I could be of assistance. What might I gain?"

Hope and a rush of undefined emotions flooded over me. He did know something. This was suddenly the biggest game of my life. I concentrated on hiding any clue to my feelings. "People have died and you talk of profits?" I kept my eyes fixed on the rug.

Krutz shrugged. "People die day in and day out. I'm not the world's keeper. That aside, animals like Rosta are not men. His passing will be unnoticed."

"What about Lori's sister, Beth Dobsen? And Rachelle Nestrum?"

"Yes. A beautiful young woman. Ms. Nestrum, I mean. Far too fine a woman to be wasting time with the likes of Matt Livingston. Was Beth Dobsen also beautiful?"

"That's what they say. So what?" It was difficult to bury impatience deeply enough.

"Nothing, really. I'm stalling, I suppose. You wouldn't by chance have something to trade, say a golden-handled dagger?"

"No," I replied. "I have nothing." I stared at the empty glass in my hand, willing my fingers to hold it loosely. I know how to run a bluff. I kept my face turned down; I didn't think my eyes were up to the task at the moment.

"That's unfortunate. By returning it to Prince Aba al-Saleh, I could have made a fine profit."

I looked up at that, knowing what my eyes revealed now.

"No. No, Mr. Macklen. You misunderstand. I would have returned it as a gift." At my puzzlement, Krutz continued. "You see, he would have been in my debt, a debt of gratitude, one the prince would have felt obligated to pay, graciously and generously. I could have arranged a good many profitable contracts."

"Netting more than the five hundred thou you offered?"

"Oh my, yes. Much more. Probably many millions."

I looked back down at the floor. "Someone's probably already got the damn thing and you'll never see it."

"You may be correct." Krutz leaned his head back and looked up at the ceiling.

I watched him out of the corner of my eye, wondering how to persuade him to tell what he knew. Would it take more than words? I thought of the Buck knife and the tricks I could make it perform. Something told me horrible methods had been tried with this man and that they'd failed. When he looked back at me, there was a brittle brightness in the eyes. "I'm more into survival—mine, that is—than saving souls or anything else. However, I'll share a suspicion, if you'll agree to my terms."

"I'm listening."

"You must control yourself. If you kill the man I have in mind, I'll lose three hundred thousand dollars. If he dies, you'll have to settle the account."

"I'm still listening."

"But did you hear the terms?"

"I heard."

"Do you agree to them?"

"My best is all I can do."

"That will suffice, I believe." He paused. "The man you want may be Finley Quale."

The idea stunned me for an instant, then settled more comfortably, an intriguing notion. Images of Char Killen filled my mind. "What are you thinking?"

"For one thing, the comment Rosta made, that it would take an army to get Lori back. Have you seen Quale's estate?"

I nodded. It would take an army, a miracle, or both.

"I assumed Lori had been taken to obtain information about the dagger. That's undoubtedly the case, but Rosta could have dealt with that. Since he gave her over to someone else, there may be an additional purpose."

"Death flicks?"

"I've heard only the merest whispers."

I stood, walked unsteadily to the bar, poured more bourbon, and sat back down, surprised at the difficulty of the simple task. I took a goodly swallow, then looked up. "Best tell me the rest."

"Yes. I believe I must." He paused. "Quale believes he's an excellent poker player. Unlike you, he loses. Hence the debt he owes me. At first, I thought nonpayment was but the stinginess of some millionaires. When it occurred to me he could not pay, I had people check.

"Exton is little more than the gutted shell of past greatness. On forced sale, Quale would receive very little. Perhaps not by your standards, but by his, surely, the man is nearly broke.

"Then we found something truly astounding. Quale arranged to have the dagger stolen. He plans to sell it back to the prince. I approached him and suggested Livingston as a courier. I'd known Matt for years. He was an accomplished smuggler, using his job with Quale as cover. Even as I made the suggestion to Quale, I was hoping for a private arrangement with Matt."

"You planned to hijack the dagger?"

"That's putting it crudely but in fact sums up the matter. When Matt returned, he called. He had the dagger and the call itself demonstrated his interest in my offer. One of my associates, Alex Jacobs, is the best negotiator I've ever known. I asked him to meet with Matt. When he didn't report back, I set my people to work.

"Sergio Landis's task was to watch for Matt or Lori at the bank. When you assumed Rosta was working for me because Dell Vickers was also at the bank, it put me to thinking. Rosta was never a man of insight but Quale has his moments. I reasoned that Quale had guessed what I planned and asked Rosta's people to follow mine. Accordingly I alerted my people. A very unlucky thug was caught at the game and persuaded to tell what he knew." Krutz's smile was not pleasant to look at.

"He readily admitted working for Rosta. And he was one of the men who cleaned up after Rosta killed Alex and Matt. Unfortunately, he knew nothing of Rosta's connection with Quale. Still, I suspect Rosta intended to keep the dagger for himself."

"And the sexual bit?"

He sighed, then continued, speaking softly. "We found Quale has been abnormally active sexually. There is evidence of adventures most would call violent. And he's heavily into drugs. He's gone through most of his inheritance, given up public life, and now seldom leaves his estate. My sources believe his self-abusing life-style has left him impotent.

"I have a different theory, based on a single incident. A young woman entered Quale's estate somewhat over three years ago and was never seen again. I saw little significance in the matter until now."

"You don't think he's impotent. He only needs heavier kinks to make it."

"Yes. Something like that."

"I doubt there's anything kinkier than making death flicks."

"I wouldn't think so."

"With Lori in hand, he gets to find out what she knows about the dagger and can then star her in a new film. A two-for-one bargain, you might say."

"It's a distinct possibility."

I stood up, feeling as if my weight had doubled. Krutz also stood. "It fits too well, doesn't it?" I asked.

"It seems to."

"I don't know what to say. Thanks doesn't make it."

He moved to open the door. "I'll send a bill for the damages here."

"Do you want the address?"

"I had that before I sat down at the poker table with you."

"That figures." I paused. "Why did you do it?"

"You mean why did I tell you of Finley Quale?"

"Yeah."

"Possibly I believe a relationship with you could be profitable."

"Crap."

"Yes, it is, isn't it?" He looked down at the floor, then back at me. "The world abounds with evil. For the most part, it must be ignored. But what Quale appears to have embraced needs to be stopped. Ms. Rachelle and Lori are, or were," he added grimly, "lovely young women. Quite different, of course. But each beautiful in her own way. There have never been too many lovely young women, Mr. Macklen. They are to be cherished. Let me believe I acted in hopes you might keep these two alive."

"Do you think Quale's got them both?"

"I don't know that he has either one."

I nodded and stepped through the door.

Krutz called after me, "Remember, Mr. Macklen, the bill will be considerably higher if you kill the man."

I nodded again without turning. I ignored the two bodyguards leaning alertly against the wall of the hallway and walked out into the chaos I'd created. The Blazer's ignition had been turned off. I probably should have thanked someone but my thoughts were too busy bumping and stumbling over one another. I crawled behind the wheel and fired the engine. They'd had Lori for nearly three hours. It was all the further I could take that line of thought. I tried to ignore the ugly crunch from the heavy tires smashing through debris as I drove out through the broken window.

I directed all thought to the problem. There seemed no reasonable approach. Not even a starting point. I could raise an army with the help of Lencho and Tony, but what could be done with it? Nothing short of tanks and heavy weapons could penetrate Quale's defenses. Lori'd be dead before anyone could get to her. And I didn't even know for certain Quale had her. And if he did, was she at his estate? I'd bet my life on it, and her's, but not that of others. An army was out. I had to build a plan, and fast. All I needed for openers was a few small strands from which to build string, to be woven into stout rope of enduring strength and purpose. I couldn't identify even a single thread.

Afternoon

|||| |||| |||| |||| ||||

I was right. Tony was still at Ned's place. It didn't take him long to get to the phone. "Are you okay?" he asked anxiously.

"I'm all in one piece, anyway," I answered tiredly.

"What about Krutz?"

"He's one smart fellow. That's what he is."

"Then he's still alive?"

"Yeah." I told him all of it, then asked, "You can't do anything, can you?"

"No judge would move with what you've got. Face it. You can't even say for sure Quale's got her. And if he does, that's not sayin' she'd be at his estate."

"I called earlier. The man I talked to said Quale was out of town. I made the same offer I made to Rosta, Lori for the dagger. He insisted there was no way to reach Quale. I flat don't believe him. Quale's there. So's Lori. I can feel it." I was remembering the expensive video layout. Football tapes weren't all that were played on that giant screen.

"That's not much to go on."

"Try this. I'd bet heavy bucks there's not another place in those hills protected like his. He's either a classic paranoid or there's another reason. I like the second notion best."

"Tell me about it."

"Basically, it's the damned fence. Iron, eight

feet high and electrified. The only way in is through the gate, past two armed guards. The gate's too heavy to force with less than a Mack truck. Then there's cameras. So even if you took out the guards, there'd be people waiting inside."

I described the grounds. "There's a good field of fire from most any position to any other. There'll be people ready to do just that. Fire, I mean. Why else is everything kept trimmed so low? There's got to be weight sensors in the lawn near the fence. Most folks settle for some insurance, an electric gate, some alarms, maybe a dog and the neighborhood security patrol. Quale's plain got too much. He's making videotapes, Tony. And Lori's his new star."

"There's lots of citizens these days, not near as well off as Quale, layin' in pretty fancy barriers between the home place and the outside world."

"Remember the hand in the film, holding the cigar?"

"It'd be hard to forget."

"Remember the two scars on the middle finger?"

"Real good, as a matter of fact."

"Quale wears an oversized diamond ring, big enough to cover those scars. And he smokes cigars."

"You ain't got shit, really. But I've got that feelin', buddy. That crazy tingle that makes the backbone itch." He paused. "But what do we do? I can blanket the place with top surveillance teams. With that, and some diggin', we'd get him. But not soon enough to do Lori any good. Short of collectin' some favors and pullin' together an army, I can't think of anythin' we can do fast enough."

"Let me get out there and take a look. I'll get back to you in a couple of hours." I blinked back tears, thinking of how long two hours could be to Lori.

"Yeah. I'll see what I can get started at this end."

"Where will you be?"

"I'll keep the office phone covered."

"Do you know anyone that could get some hard stuff together right quick?"

"Just a sec."

I could hear him thumbing through the pages of his worn little black notebook. Most of the entries were numbers for his street contacts.

"Here it is. The Black Cat." He read the number. "It's a bar on West Seventy-ninth Street. Ask for Skimpy. If there's static, remind him of shotguns."

"What's it mean?"

"He ripped a shipment of a hundred autos from a Mafia type. One call and he's real gone."

"It sounds good. I'll catch you later."

"One more thing."

"Yeah?"

"I buried the dog under the oak, like you asked."

"Thanks, Tony."

I hung up. For several moments, my eyes were too blurred to dial the number Tony had given me. I couldn't tell what caused it—the dog, the hell Lori was living in, or my own frustration.

I hadn't been completely honest with Tony. I was going in and I had an idea how to do it. I wanted a closer look but I'd go in, as soon as it was dark. That would be relatively easy. It was getting out I couldn't figure. I remembered the look on the blond girl's face in Tony's reel of film, a wish for death. One way or another, I'd get that far. I'd put a hard end to that shit. And to any sonofabitch who got in the way.

I dialed. A husky voice said, "The Black Cat."

"I need Skimpy."

"Who wants him?"

"Tell him it's business." The phone was left dangling. Sounds of early drinkers crowded in.

"Skimpy talking at ja." The voice fit—high, tight, and squeaky.

"Haggen sends regards."

"So who's fucking Haggen?"

"The Haggen that knows about those shotguns."

"Got ja. What ja need?"

I read down my mental list.

"Don't see no big problems. Give me a couple days, ja know?"

"You've got a couple of hours. Haggen said you'd manage."

"That fucking shit."

"Haggen?"

"No. No. Not him, fer Christ's sake. It'll just cost like hell, what with no time and all."

"I didn't ask about cost."

"Ja didn't, fer a fact. Bring four G's. Can't say no closer fer now."

"Don't be late."

"Got ja. What ja look like?"

"Big, with a dark brown saddle jacket and a black stocking cap."

I hung up and walked back to the Blazer. There was one stop to make before heading for Quale's place. I needed a good pair of binoculars.

It began to rain again. I looked up at the clouds. It would get heavier. I hoped it'd rain like hell's ending.

I'd been lying at the crest of the knoll of the vacant lot behind Quale's estate for over an hour. I was bellied down in tall spring grass, looking with the B&L Discovers through the lower branches of a scrawny creosote bush. From where I lay I had near-perfect resolution over a hundred-foot field. Steady rain had soaked through to the skin. It didn't matter. It did matter that I hadn't brought something to dry the wet lenses. It was only a tiny oversight. But I'd already made too many mistakes. I might not survive the next one. The breeze picked up, bringing a shiver and tremble that jiggled the glasses.

The fence in back was a duplicate of the one in front, except the strip of grass on the inside was wider. It was nearly six hundred feet beyond the grass to the house. A dirt service road ran behind the property. The road proba-

bly accounted for the extra grass; Quale could
not use sensors outside the back fence.

The yard was unremarkable. No estate would
be complete without pool and tennis and hand-
ball courts. This one included a shuffleboard
layout. Plantings were colorful, all low-growing.
Most of the area was grass. Sprinkler heads can
be hazards in the dark. A study of the lawn near
the back fence showed Quale's were the pop-up
variety, heads resting at ground level when not
in use. There'd be no need to water tonight.

A small green utility shed with baked aluminum siding puzzled me for several minutes. A
garden shed was visible, up near the house. The
door had been left open and I could see tools.
The pool equipment was hidden behind a decorative rock partition, near the fence. What, then,
was in the utility shed?

While examining the power pole in the alley, I
got the clue I needed. Power lines passed from
the pole into the yard. I couldn't see beyond the
giant maple tree to where the line terminated.
Then a heavy gust of wind bowed the huge tree
and revealed the galvanized steel standpipe.
Quale's electrical and phone lines went underground at that point. When I spotted the red gas
can, I knew. The shed housed the gasoline generator for emergency power.

There were doors on each side of the house.
Even though I couldn't see them, the routes
taken by the few folks forced outside in the
weather proved they were there. Across the
center half of the back of the house was a porch,

some twenty feet deep. It was roofed and glassed in on all sides.

My hunch had been sound. Finley Quale wasn't out of town. In the rose-colored robe, he had stepped onto the porch shortly after I'd arrived. He was smoking a cigar. For a moment, I'd been unable to concentrate. Had he gotten my message? Could it have slowed down the action? When he came to the outer edge of the porch I was able to see with the light of the coaling cigar that he wasn't wearing his ring. I knew exactly why I felt suddenly colder; the games had begun. I couldn't get enough resolution in the dim light to see any scars but I knew they were there.

Char Killen had walked out to join him, braless, with only a flimsy bikini bottom for cover. I'd watched them fondle each other in coarse fashion, then looked away. When they'd turned and walked back into the house, I'd put down the glasses for several minutes and rested my head on my arms. Char was part of it. I refused to let imagination invent images of this cold animal near Lori, images that would cloud judgment.

I don't use a watch. But timing was critical. I glanced at my new Casio. Almost two. It was time to go. I hesitated.

Six cameras were mounted in the rear of the house. Two more were mounted at the corners of the back fence. It didn't seem as if they rotated far enough to pick up the alley itself. I'd counted people as best I could. I'd seen eight;

there'd be others. There'd been no sign of Otto
Gillis. I tried to picture what the man's massive
thighs might look like naked. They could be the
thighs I'd seen in the film.

I had determined the objective. Near the
center of the second floor, there was a curious
absence of windows. Large ones were distrib-
uted in fairly uniform fashion on either side, but
for a forty-foot section in the middle, there were
none. I'd examined the wall through the glasses,
inch by inch, and found what I needed. Cracking
plaster at one point showed the outline of three
sides of a window that had once been there. It,
and probably others, had been sealed over, a
reasonable move when one requires a soundproof room. When filming, Quale could not do
without one. Lori was behind that wall. I could
feel it. She was almost near enough to touch.

It was past time to go. I made a final pan of
the yard. I locked the glasses on the porch. The
man in the wheelchair was being pushed outside. The cast on the leg was bright white, even
in the dim gray afternoon light. It was a new
cast. I reasoned it was not more than hours old.
And the man pushing the wheelchair was
equally interesting. His left arm was supported
by a fresh white sling. Ramirez had been right.
He'd nailed these two, just as he'd said. I
couldn't stifle the hope they'd still be there tonight, that they'd get in the way.

I was going in. That was certain. But could we
get out? It seemed impossible. For the longest
time, I couldn't move. She was so close. She

needed help desperately. At last, reason took hold. The cover of darkness and a good deal more firepower than the Colt were essentials.

Reluctantly I eased back off the knoll. When below the crest, I crawled through the deep field grass on elbows and knees. I slipped across the low wall into the neighboring driveway. The house was unoccupied. I walked down the drive and climbed behind the wheel of the Blazer.

It was a forlorn hope but I had to try again. Even if all I could do was bother Quale, it might help Lori. Indecision can slow things down. I pulled up next to the darkened phone booth. Minutes later, the same voice answered. "Macklen again. Did Quale get my message?"

"No, sir. He hasn't checked with me. And, as I said, I can't reach him."

I struggled to hold my voice steady, wondering how many feet separated this man from Quale. From Lori. "You could add something."

"And that is?"

"There'll be no deal if the woman dies."

"I'll do as you ask. But I know nothing of any woman. I'm sure Mr. Quale doesn't either."

"Tell him anyway."

"If I hear from him, I'll deliver the message," the voice said formally.

When I turned back toward the Blazer, the world, filtered through harsh rage, had turned to shades of red and pink. I stood still, breathing deeply, until the last tinge of redness faded, until the Blazer was once more its true color, a faded, dusty, rusty charcoal gray. I glanced at my watch and ran for the car, fumbling for the keys.

When I walked into The Black Cat, it was two-thirty. It wasn't time to move but the nearness of it brought a familiar restlessness. I eased through the light crowd, predominantly black, picked a spot at the far end of the bar, and ordered beer. The fresh cuts, the torn and bloodied pants, were notable. No one paid any attention. It wasn't that kind of a bar.

A gray-headed old-timer pounded out crisp, bold rag on a battered and scarred baby grand piano. Two couples danced to his playing with more glee than style. Several men were staring at the television behind the bar. Someone got knocked on his butt on screen but I couldn't tell if it was boxing, basketball, or ritualistic dance. It wasn't important. Skimpy was, though, and no one had approached.

Then I saw him. He wore a greasy Dodger baseball cap pulled low over his eyes. A lot of mousy brown hair stuck straight out from the sides of his head. The face was pinched, as if he'd been cheated of a full complement of flesh and bone. His skinny frame matched the face. Black suspenders held worn jeans in place and looked absurd against the tattered dirty white dress shirt. The overcoat was a Salvation Army reject.

He approached cautiously, his eyes flicking suspiciously about the room. He paused in front of me, as if on his way to the john. "Ja looking for somebody?" he asked in a high-pitched half-whisper.

"Yeah. You, Skimpy." I turned on the stool to face him.

"Don't do that, man," he said, frightened. "I don't trade in no public-type place. Meet ja out front."

He shuffled on toward the rear. I laid money on the bar for the untouched beer and headed for the street. I leaned against the wall. I'd learned how to wait. I hadn't learned to do it easily.

When Skimpy came out, he ignored me and started walking up the street. I followed, thinking it was all a bit melodramatic. He turned into an alley. I shifted the Colt to my coat pocket. It was the kind of alley some walk into but not out of.

"Ja got the bread?" the slight, shadowy figure asked, still whispering.

"I've got it."

"Got wheels?"

"The Blazer we just passed."

"I got a van. Drag after me."

I followed him back toward the sidewalk, glad to be free of the alley. Behind the wheel, I fired the engine. The faded blue Volkswagen van, of indeterminate age, came up from behind and passed. Skimpy was driving. I followed. The van had been abused. Smoke billowed from the exhaust in accompaniment to the unhealthy racket from the engine.

Six turns and half a mile later, Skimpy drove into an empty parking lot. He pulled to the back, stopping in the shadows of a warehouse. I parked beside him and got out.

"Now be cool," Skimpy pleaded in his normal squeaky voice. "I couldn't get it all. Ja didn't give me time, man."

"What's missing?"

"I only got twenty clips for the Uzi. Clips is harder than the piece. Know what I mean?"

"What else?"

"The plastic." He seemed to shrink into the ground. "There ain't none in town. No C4. Nothing. Honest. I tried everywhere."

That was a blow. The whole plan required predictable explosives. "How about the radio control?"

Skimpy shook his head nervously.

Without remote-controlled detonation, the plan collapsed. I shoved my hands deep into my pockets and looked up at the cloudy sky. Was there any alternative? I walked a few feet away and squatted on one heel, facing the street. I picked up a rock and played catch with it. Dynamite was something I knew little about. It'd be easy to make a mistake. But I knew where there was a case of it. Ned had bought it to blow out rock for his trout pond. Could it be detonated remotely? Electronically? Without stringing the wire required for a hell box? I had the edge of an idea that might work, if I didn't blow myself into bloody, spongy fragments. I rose and walked back to the van and the skinny man fidgeting nervously beside it. "How much for what you've got?"

"How's three thou sound?" he asked anxiously.

"Two would be better. I need those damned explosives."

Skimpy nodded hasty acceptance. I could feel Haggen's presence. I pulled the roll of bills from my pocket and counted out the money. Skimpy stuffed it away and began handing packages out of the van. I dumped them on the back floor of the Blazer. When he handed me the silenced .38, I asked, "What kind of shape's this in?"

"Solid. Honest. And cold as hell."

I tested the rotation of the cylinder, checked to be sure it was empty, and squeezed the trigger twice. It was far from new but it'd do. The silencer would be effective; that was the greatest need. I tossed it into the Blazer.

When Skimpy handed me the Uzi, I unwrapped the oily rag and examined it intently. It was what I wanted, the original full-auto model. I'd been reluctant to pass on the Springfield M1A up at the house. With the Starlight scope, it's a fine killing tool. But it's best at range and it's only semi-auto. The Uzi can dump nearly five rounds a second. I'd need that kind of firepower against Quale's army at close range.

I checked every function that could be tested without firing the piece, trusting my ears to judge the health of the action. The bluing was flawless. I grabbed a flashlight and checked the barrel and rifling. It wasn't new, but close to it.

Skimpy had been holding his breath. He exhaled and tried for a smile when I turned back, having accepted the deadly little machine gun.

When the last item had been transferred I asked, "Have you a blanket or something?"

He disappeared into the van and returned with a battered piece of faded green tarp. "This do?"

"Yeah." I leaned out across the floor and tucked the tarp over my purchases. At least they were out of sight. I noticed the battered rear end of the Blazer as I walked around and climbed behind the wheel. Krutz's storefront was in worse shape but the taillights needed attention. It would be full dark soon. Before I could get the engine started, Skimpy had the van moving.

Taillight lenses aren't available late Sunday afternoons, even in Los Angeles. Red tape would have to do. The fourth gas station I tried had a roll. I turned on the lights and checked. At least no cop could say I'd ignored the problem.

It took longer than expected to find a black hooded raincoat. I bought the largest size and a pair of black sneakers. In a hardware store, I found a pair of heavy-duty bolt cutters. I also bought a dozen lantern batteries and a thousand feet of thin-stranded wire, insulated in black. Headed north once more, I reviewed the mental list. I checked three times. There was nothing missing, except the damned explosive.

I'd either have to make the dynamite work or give up the whole scheme. Since giving up was impossible, I thought about the dynamite.

With gut-wrenching agony, I at last came to grips with the certainty that Lori would have told about my place and that I'd left to try to find the dagger. I refused to consider what it might have cost her. I could deal only with the fleeting hope she'd not delayed the telling. Once past this barrier, I had to assume someone would be watching for me. Quale would still want the dagger, regardless of other plans for Lori.

I killed the engine and coasted to within a hundred yards of Ned's drive. With the Colt in my right fist and the knife in the other, I moved up the side of the road opposite my place. The rain helped; soggy leaves don't crumble underfoot. Still it took time, too much time.

Patience was rewarded. A cigarette glowed, near the cattle guard. I was certain I'd passed no other man. I continued on, needing a count of how many I faced. I found the car in the brush beyond sight of the entrance to my place. Nothing inside gave any hint of how many had arrived. There could be others, up at the house.

With infinite care, I crossed the road and moved back toward the position where the cigarette had glowed. The cigarette suggested I was dealing with a city-type, unaccustomed to being stalked in the woods. But I couldn't bring myself to move faster, even as thoughts of Lori flooded into my mind.

Twenty feet away, I could see the man. His back was to me, his attention on the canyon road up which I was expected to drive. I switched the gun and knife. I needed the fine control for the knife, offered only by my right hand.

Three feet from him, I grabbed the blade with my thumb and forefinger to limit the depth of cut. He heard my last step but it was too late. I dropped the Colt, yanked his hair back toward me and slashed his neck with the knife, close to his chin. Blood flowed over the knife, warming my hand.

"How many are here?" I asked, as if curious about the time of day. His entire body trembled.

"Christ, man. Easy with the blade, huh?"

"How many?"

"Just me and my partner up at the house."

"How do you get hold of him?"

"The radio in my pocket."

"Who sent you?"

"I work for Sal Rosta."

"Not any more. I killed him."

"Shit."

I added pressure to the knife. "Want to keep breathing?"

"Hell yes!"

"Get your partner down here. Do it your way but do it right."

"I need the radio."

"Be damn sure that's all you come up with."

He did it right.

"Hey, Joey. Did you get that?"

"Get what?" came the scratchy reply through the speaker.

"They got Macklen. Let's get out a this fucking rain."

"I didn't hear anything. You sure?"

I added pressure to the blade. "Hell yes, I'm sure. It must be the fucking mountains or something. I got it real clear. Stay up there and play with yourself, if you want. I'm leaving."

"Hold up. I'll be down."

I reached for the radio and threw it against a granite boulder. It disassembled in fine fashion. "Where's the hardware?" I asked.

"Shoulder holster. Left side."

A touch was all it took; he was well armed. I eased the .45 auto out and said, "Listen good, punk. The woman's a friend of mine. If I see you again, you're flat ass dead. You got that?"

"What woman you talking..." The voice trailed off, unable to continue. The slam of a .45 against the head disrupts many bodily functions.

I tossed the gun into the brush, tucked the knife away, scooped up the Colt, and began making my way toward the cattle guard. Lights flared behind the house. A car began moving down the muddy drive. It moved so slowly I wanted to rush up the hill, to close swiftly. An eternity passed, maybe two, before the front wheels hit the first loose rail. I tensed, then charged the car, driving the Colt through the half-open window, the muzzle into the man's ear. The car slowed abruptly and stopped. "Are you listening?" I asked.

"Real good."

"The name's Macklen. You're on your own."

"What the fuck you saying?"

"I killed Rosta. You're out of work, punk. Your partner's lying over there in the brush. Get him into this car and get your asses out of here before I forget killing bugs in human form is against some fucking law. Got it?"

"Got it."

"Then get to it."

He slid out of the car as if stepping into a nest of rattlesnakes. He didn't seem to notice when I lifted his .38 from the shoulder rig and dropped it through the rails of the cattle guard. With the muzzle of the Colt in his ear, I directed him to his downed partner.

"Sweet Christ. Look at the blood," he whispered. "Is he dead?"

"Not if you move it."

He slung the man over his shoulder and struggled back to the car. Seconds later, they roared down the canyon road. I ran for the Blazer.

I felt vulnerable and exposed, driving up to the house. I examined each window as I circled around to the back. All looked peaceful and empty and lonely. Bobbie would not rush to greet me. Nor would Lori. I climbed out of the Blazer and went inside through the back door, the Colt cocked in my fist. Moments later, I knew no one had been inside.

When I dialed, Tony picked up on the first ring. I filled him in on what I'd seen at Quale's place, then told him what I needed. We argued. Then argued some more. In the end, he agreed if one man couldn't get in, it probably couldn't be done. I verified the time on my new watch and hung up. He hadn't wished me luck. I'd have been surprised if he had. After training, planning, and preparation, it comes down to luck. Those who've been there know and won't waste breath on pointless words.

I dialed Doc's number. "How's Ned?" I asked hesitantly, remembering the old man lying in the mud by the barn.

"It's serious, Scott. But he had a great team working for him. If he's as strong as I believe he is, he'll make it."

"And Ramirez?"

"There's no question there. He'll be fine."

"Can you be in your office tonight? Say after six?"

"Yes. Do you want to tell me about it?"

I told him what he needed to know.

"Scott. You've lost your bloody mind. But I'll be there." He hung up abruptly.

Without realizing I was doing so, I found myself dialing Quale's number again. The same voice answered. "Macklen. Is there any word?"

"I'm so glad you called. Mr. Quale did contact me. He wants to speak with you. Is there a number where you can be reached?"

My heart pounded against my ribs as if to shatter them. "He'll deal then?" My voice was unsteady.

"Yes. He's very interested in the dagger. There's a gentleman here now, anxious to meet with you wherever and whenever you choose."

"You didn't mention anything about the woman."

"I'm afraid, sir, it's as I said before. Mr. Quale knows nothing of any woman."

I could feel the blood drain from my face. I had to grip the phone tightly to keep the hand from trembling. It was then I knew the calls had been useless. Lori could not live. No amount of money could offset her testimony in a courtroom.

"Mr. Macklen? Are you still there?"

"Yeah."

"Can I arrange a meeting, then?"

I could think of no reply.

Into the growing silence, the voice said softly, "We're talking about a great deal of money, Mr. Macklen. At the very least, you'd be a millionaire."

He was more subtle than Rosta had been. But he was saying the same thing. Forget about Lori and think about bucks. I'd been clenching my teeth so hard, they ached. The jaw muscles trembled with strain.

"Did you hear what I said, Mr. Macklen? We simply do not know of any woman connected with the dagger."

I did. In a short while, I'd knock on his door

and introduce him to her. Or her body. No. I wouldn't show him a body, just blow the fucking place apart. I took three deep, even breaths. "I need time to think on this. I'll get back to you."

"Sir, I think we should arrange something immediately. The gentleman with me is prepared..."

I hung up, realizing tears flowed down my cheeks. I rubbed my eyes with my soggy shirt and moved outside, locking the door to the silent house. I shivered when the gusting wind pierced my wet clothes.

With the Blazer in four-wheel drive, I drove down the draw to Ned's. The only sounds came from the horses. In the back corner of the barn, I uncovered the case of dynamite. I carried it out to the Blazer, placed it on the front seat, and drove back up the draw, taking more care than when coming down.

I pulled up in front of the workshop and began carrying in my purchases. I turned on the sixty-watt bulb. The shop was well below the crest of the hill; no one would notice. I glanced at my watch. It only confirmed I was late.

It all came down to Matt's balloon device. The first thing to determine was the range of the transmitter. I set the box on the ground and ran up the draw some three hundred yards. I pushed the button and ran back. The balloon was fully inflated. The range was ample.

Inside, I cut away the balloon and began taking the components apart. With the guts of it laid about me on the bench, I experimented, studying the way the transmitter activated the receiver. Twenty minutes later, I had three caps wired together with crude switches and linkage to a lantern battery. I stepped back a few feet and pressed the button. They all exploded. I'd have to assume the same result would occur at a much greater range. As I continued to work, I tried to formulate alternatives, should the transmitter fail. There were none.

Working rapidly now, more comfortable with familiar gear, I loaded the twenty clips. I notched the heads of a box of .38 shells with a hacksaw. I'd have rather used the magnum but a silencer on the Colt would have been a joke. The notched slugs would have to do.

I loaded the .38, rammed a clip into the Uzi, and hurried outside into the continuing rain. I used the paper target Lori had left. Wet, it cuddled against the old stump. From thirty feet, I fired six fast, near-soundless rounds from the .38, then trotted to the stump. The grouping was good, a bit low and to the right. Probably the weight of the heavy silencer. It would be simple to adjust for it.

I backed seventy feet from the stump and armed the Uzi. I was worried about who might hear and how they might react. I knew the weapon but I had to be certain of this particular piece. I'd have to risk it. Three- and four-round bursts destroyed the quiet of the late afternoon, the roar awesome, trapped in the small draw. Before the echoes had died, I was at the stump examining the results.

Patterns indicated a remembered lifting of the barrel. The hits from one three-round group were a quarter-inch apart in a near-vertical line. Two four-round patterns showed a greater change in elevation on the fourth round. It was a good piece.

I dashed back inside, reloaded the clip, and dumped all the gear into the Blazer. I turned out the light and climbed behind the wheel. Even moving, there was impatience to be dealt with. No one interfered with my exit or appeared to notice I was breaking the speed limit down the canyon road.

I drove up the street behind Quale's estate. In front of the mansion, beside the vacant lot from which I'd studied the back of his place, a black Cadillac was parked. Tony had delivered it. I'd wanted a less distinctive car. He'd argued that anything less prestigious would look suspicious to private or police patrols.

A half-mile further on, I took the right that would lead to Mulholland. Coming up on the entrance to the service road that ran behind Quale's property, I glanced at the watch. It was a quarter to five. It wasn't full dark but the rain and heavy cloud cover made it seem so. It was dark enough to get started. I stopped and turned off the lights, then backed up to the service road and into the entrance, killing the engine just short of the chain that spanned the road.

Once I made this first move, there could be no mistakes. If I was observed, it would end badly.

I hadn't seen anyone or anything move. I checked again. Nothing. I took a deep breath, grabbed the bolt cutters, and got out. The chain snapped crisply. I tossed the cutters into brush beside the road and turned back to the Blazer. On the third hard push, it began to roll backward. When clear of the chain, I used the emergency brake to stop; red lights flaring in the darkness could be noticed.

I grabbed a short length of wire and reattached the chain. Only close inspection would show the cut link. Yet ten pounds of pressure would break it loose.

Back in the Blazer, I released the brake. The grade was steeper here. Only a push with my left heel was needed to start it moving. In ghostly silence, it rolled backward down the hill.

It ought to have been simple but it wasn't. With the rain, it was impossible to see through the rear. I leaned out the side window, wanting to stay close to the side of the road, yet not wanting to smack into a wall or fence.

Where was that tree? The one that overhung the neighbor's rear wall? I must have been moving more slowly than I thought, for I'd about decided someone had cut it down, when I saw it. I backed under the willowy branches and stopped again with the emergency brake, close to the wall. I slipped outside and pulled branches out over the vehicle. In the dark, one could walk into it before seeing it. At least that was the plan.

I didn't want the coat muddied. Mud can create a fatal slipperiness. I took it off and tossed it into the Blazer. It was raining harder. Although wet and tired, I was cheered. Heavy, steady rain stifles random sounds and reduces visibility. I used the knife to cut two eye slits in the stocking cap and pulled it down to hide the whiteness of my face. I reached inside and carefully picked up three bundles of dynamite and batteries, wrapped in plastic, and the roll of wire. Cautiously I walked to Quale's property line and peeked around the corner. Near the house, large floods drove light through the rainy night, but the brightness faded long before reaching where I stood. I'd been right; the cameras at the back corners did not scan the alley.

At my feet was the low ground I'd seen from above, paralleling the fence about four feet from it. The high crown of the muddy road sloped downward below the level of Quale's yard. A stream of rainwater ran off downhill. I moved the Colt to the back of my pants. On my belly, I wiggled into the shallow depression and began the long crawl to the opposite side of Quale's property. Mud and water soaked through my shirt and pants. I used only elbows, knees, and feet to propel myself, holding my stomach to the muddy ground. It took time, but it wasn't a task to be hurried. Twice I stopped, once at sound that might have been voices and again at motion that might have been a dog. Each time, I had to write it off to wind, rain, or shadows.

At the corner of the property, azaleas were

clumped together. I picked a spot twenty feet
short of the corner. Unless someone inside was
specifically looking for it, they'd never see the
dynamite through the bushes. I attached the
wire, covered the bundle with muddy earth, and
began the long crawl back, uncoiling the wire
and covering it with mud as I moved. I placed
the other charges at equal intervals.

Back at the Blazer I gently lifted out the
fourth package. This was placed twenty feet in
from the near corner of the property, at what I
hoped was a safe distance behind the car. I connected the wire, covered the charge with mud,
and returned to the Blazer once more. I picked
up the last package, smaller than the others,
and attached the wires, then a separate fifty-
foot length. I tied a twelve-inch open-end
wrench to the other end of the last wire.

This was the risky part. I'd be exposed during
the final maneuver. The power pole was fifty
feet from the corner. My only protection would
be the rainy darkness. I crawled back down into
the ditch, again on my stomach, to within ten
feet of the pole. I rolled over onto my back. The
power line came off the pole some eighteen feet
above ground. I'd have to risk standing to be
sure of the throw.

The wind gusted heavily. Rain pounded me as
I rose and tossed the wrench, with the slender
wire trailing, and dropped to my back on the
ground. The wrench slugged into mud fifteen
feet away. I looked for any sign I'd been noticed.
All seemed quiet. I crawled to the wrench, half-

buried in the slick clay of the road. Flat on my back, I waited until first one, then the other camera began to pan from the fence to the house, then pulled swiftly on the black wire.

I didn't need the wind to catch the package and start it swinging, but it did. The swing lessened as it neared the power line. When I could pull it no further, I tied off the wire at the base of the pole. I made the last connection and crawled back to the Blazer.

I rolled up the stocking cap for better vision. I was covered with mud. I used rainwater from the ditch beside me and several dry rags to take as much off as I could. Then began the familiar routine. Webbed belts draped from my shoulders to the opposite sides of the waist and another draped around my hips. Clips for the Uzi, ten to each crossing belt. The holstered flare gun and cartridges, clipped to the waist belt. Fragmentation grenades to the left belt, phosphorous grenades to the right. The Uzi dangled by the leather strap over the right shoulder. When I struggled into the coat, only the bottom two buttons could be fastened. A few quick moves. Satisfactory. Nothing jangled. The silenced .38 tucked up under the coat behind the waist belt. Extra rounds for the Uzi into the right coat pocket, .38 shells into the left. The two speed loaders for the .38 into the top pocket, within easy reach.

I tugged on the black raincoat. It was a tight fit; I didn't try to button it. Black tennis shoes to the right-hand pocket, transmitter to the left.

The coat and shoes were for Lori, if she could walk. If she couldn't, it would be rugged. I'd have to carry her. If so, we might not make it. Hell. We probably wouldn't make it anyway. I refused to consider what might happen if she was dead.

Even with the best effort, it can go wrong. Each time I've faced death, I've known pure terror, as anyone would. Still, my own death does not overly concern me. It was the orders I'd given, the decisions I'd made, that fill night thoughts. Some had turned out badly for those who'd counted on me. Now Lori was at risk. Her life depended on the perfect execution of a complex, hastily constructed plan for which the probability of success was ridiculously low.

She'd been inside the estate for six, maybe seven hours. They had questioned her about the dagger. She must have told of my trip to the airport and what I'd hoped to find. Why else would Rosta's punks have been waiting for me? I hoped she hadn't resisted. But when she'd told them, the filming would have started. The sacrifice would have begun, Lori but another lamb at the altar of perverted lust. Would the action have escalated so soon to what I'd seen in the film? I shuddered. It turned into an uncontrollable shiver that had nothing to do with cold, soggy clothes.

Beth had lasted eight hours, maybe ten. I had no option but to assume Lori was alive. It was quite possible she'd already been forced to a degree of madness from which she'd never return.

It was absurd to speculate. I could not know, nor would knowing change what I would do.

I took a full minute to calm myself. There must be no thought of her. Surgeons are not allowed to operate on those they love; necessary objectivity can be lost in frightful emotions. The same rules should apply to the soldier. I had to execute the plan as a military exercise of no consequence beyond the object of winning. I'd done it times beyond counting. I wasn't at all sure I could do it now.

I glanced at the watch. I was five minutes late. Mistakes, even in timing, could not be tolerated. In a low crouch, I moved up the service road away from Quale's estate. I crossed the muddy road and dove into the weeds in the vacant lot. I crawled on hands and knees through the heavy grass and brush, clear to the sidewalk on the other side, then studied the empty street. When convinced no one would notice, I walked to the black Caddy. The interior lights had been disconnected and the seats wisely covered with heavy plastic. I wedged myself behind the wheel, started the car, and drove slowly up the hill. I turned right toward Mulholland. The chain across the service alley looked natural.

I turned onto Mulholland, after cutting the lights and engine, then opened the car door. I held the door closed but unlatched, while coasting down the hill, coming to a stop sixty feet short of Quale's drive. Nothing moved in the mirrors or the street ahead. I took a last breath, freed the silenced .38, and got out. I left the door ajar and crouched beside it, listening. I could hear nothing unexpected, nothing louder than raindrops gathering on tree leaves and plunging to the leaves below. I dropped to my knees and crawled into the ivy bordering the sidewalk. I couldn't say how it would end, but it had begun.

Evening

IIII IIII IIII IIII IIII

I hugged the bushes bordering the ivy, keeping as far from the street as possible. The bushes served the purpose I'd counted on; I was in total darkness. Not a glimmer from the streetlight behind reached my path. On hands and knees I made good time. A car roared up the street, high beams flooding all before it. I collapsed, pulling myself down against the ivy, closing my eyes against the brightness.

I continued, moving more slowly. The wet ivy gave little sound of my passing. Twenty feet from the guard house, I flattened and inched forward by pulling on the branches ahead. The ivy had been allowed to intrude onto Quale's property. I was grateful. I stayed with it to within seven feet of the guard station. Light flooded through the windows. The sills were four feet off the ground, leaving a band of black shadow next to the wall.

The streetlight, some forty feet ahead, was no help. There was three feet of open grass to be covered between the ivy and the short junipers growing beside the station. Until I was behind the junipers, I'd be visible.

I couldn't see the guards. I assumed they were sitting. It'd be better to know. I checked the .38 again, waiting. Another car drove past. There was still no sign of the guards. I could wait no longer. I moved on, the slight brushing sounds of motion hidden by the steady rain. Then I was behind the junipers, slithering over prickly fallen needles. I hadn't realized I'd been holding my breath until I was safely in shadow, gulping for air. I reduced the moves to cautious silent inches.

At the corner I peered into the grounds. The guard station protected me from the camera behind it and three Italian cypress hid me from the camera mounted at the other end of the fence. I'd have to move around the corner to get to the guards. When I did, the streetlight and floodlights on the gate would reveal me to anyone on the grounds. Rain blocked any view from the house. When I was certain no one was in sight, I eased out from cover, still on my belly.

Ever more slowly, I inched toward the narrow door. It was closed against the weather. If it was locked, I'd have to stand and assume added risk. I reached up toward the knob. It opened outward, blocking any view from the yard.

There was only one guard, tilted back in a wooden chair, rocking, reading a copy of *Play-*

boy. The pale blue uniform was neatly pressed. The black officer's cap perched at a jaunty angle atop curly brown hair. He lowered the magazine, his glance moving down until he saw the silenced .38 in my fist, the muzzle centered on his chest. He eased the front two legs of the chair down to the floor, his eyes on the gun.

"Open the gate," I said evenly.

"What the hell do you mean?" the guard demanded. "That'd cost me my job."

"A job, a life. You decide." The gate had to be open. There were no other options without this one. Peripherally I was aware of the array of monitors, switches, and dials. Could I find the right switch by myself?

"You've got to be kidding," the guard said in an awed voice. "There's a whole damn army in there."

"That's my problem. Yours is staying alive."

Confusion overflowed the broad face and dark eyes.

"No one would hear you go down," I pointed out. "I could open it myself."

"You ain't kidding, are you?"

"No."

Slowly he stood and moved to the console.

"If you get a call," I said, "say the gate just started to open. You don't know what went wrong."

"They ain't gonna believe that."

"Best for you if they do."

He reached out and touched a switch. The heavy gate began to roll open.

Seconds later, a gruff voice over the intercom demanded, "What the hell you doing, Donavan?"

"I don't know, Pete. The damn thing went off by itself."

The opening was four feet. "That's bullshit! Hit the stop button!"

"For Christ's sake, I tried that."

The gate was open to eight feet. It was enough. "Ah, screw it. Must be the damn rain. I'll get it from up here."

With my hand in the pocket of the raincoat, I pressed the button on the transmitter. Nothing happened! Oh, sweet Jesus! The range was too great! I could get inside. But how would we get out? I braced myself. I had to get through the gate. It stopped opening at twelve feet and began to close. Desperately, I yanked the transmitter from my pocket, held it high off the ground, and pressed the button again, holding it down, waving my arm in slow, gentle sweeps.

"What the hell you doing?" the guard asked, bewildered.

The rainy darkness at the back of the estate erupted in what seemed one thunderous explosion. Instantly all lights went out and the gate stopped moving. The sky above the house flared brightly. The streetlight did not go out. I sighted quickly and fired. The butt of the gun jolted against my palm but only a dull thud accompanied the cone of light streaming from the barrel. The streetlight exploded.

I lunged to my feet into the darkness, charging the guard. Donavan had thought of it; his hand was on the butt of his gun. Now that option was gone. "Do you want a knock on the head?" I asked. "Or would you rather walk?"

I couldn't read the expression on his face in the darkness but I could see the frown on the forehead.

"Walk, I guess."

I reached for his holstered pistol, lifted it free, and laid it on the counter. "Best get to it."

Without a word, ex-guard Donavan jogged out of the booth and down the street. The jog soon became a full-out run.

I turned to the control panel. I had no idea how much power the emergency generator would produce but I had to assume it would be enough to close the gate. It had to remain open. I fired the remaining five rounds from the .38 into the section of the control panel near the switch the guard had used. If closing the gate, even from the main house, depended on these circuits, the gate would remain open. I took time to reload individual rounds, saving the speed loaders.

I ran through the gate toward the unit that powered it. I tossed the transmitter over the fence, then bent down to examine the motor. I grabbed a grenade, pulled the pin, and jammed it between the rail and the motor. If the rail moved, the grenade would destroy the motor. At least I hoped so.

I dashed across the grass toward the small plantings and low shrubs. From behind the house came occasional shouts. They had no meaning for me, except that people were there. Hopefully attention was focused on the back and the blown fence. I moved at a crouch near the plantings, trying to watch all the yard. I was more vulnerable closer to the house, where the patches of grass were larger. I needed time to reach a side door before the generator was started. It could get noisy and bloody if the lights came on before I was inside.

I reached under the raincoat and unbuttoned the jacket. Still moving, I pulled the Uzi out and let it dangle. I crouched behind a tree trunk and armed the deadly little gun. From the rear yard, I could hear shouted contradictory commands aimed at starting the generator. It was probably not something regularly practiced. Hopefully it would take fumbling time to get it working.

I was about to step from behind the tree when two men appeared in the side yard. They rounded the corner and trotted toward the front door of the house, dark shadows against the white wall. Both men carried automatic rifles. They looked as if they knew how to use them.

When they reached the far side of the house, they moved cautiously around the corner. When they disappeared, I sprinted for the house, slid behind the oleander, and peered back into the yard. Faint light from streetlamps not blown provided a blurred image of the taller man, when he stepped back into the front yard. He moved in my direction, his back to the house, sweeping the grounds with the rifle.

I dropped the Uzi, letting it dangle, grabbed the .38, and struggled alongside the house behind the bushes. Remembering the leveled rifle, speed seemed more important to me than stealth. I plunged away from the wall through a gap in the plantings, crouched low on the grass, and ran. The first door was locked. There was only one other on this side of the house. I ran. If it was locked, I'd have to depend upon the silenced .38 for entry. The sounds of angry voices and the stubborn engine were distinct. I couldn't continue around to the back of the house.

The door wasn't locked. I gave a soft sigh of thanks and plunged inside, breathing heavily. With my back to the wall, I listened, slowing my breathing. I could still faintly hear sounds from the backyard. The man with the rifle could be near. I locked the door, hoping that if he checked, he'd continue to the rear, believing no one could have entered this way. I was in a hallway that spanned the width of the house near the back. The touch of lighter darkness ahead was light from windows at the far end of the hall.

Stealthily I started forward with short, flat-footed, soundless steps. The .38 was up and ready. Halfway down the hall, faint light flared through a doorway. Someone had found candles. A few feet ahead, I half fell over what proved to be a step.

There was no motion or sound from the house, as if those inside waited fearfully for light. The voices outside were muffled. I started up the stairs, desperately hoping I'd meet no one coming down. I might have no choice but to shoot. I didn't want that. Not until I had Lori. I placed the toe of my foot on the outer edge of the step, then slid it to the riser before putting weight on the foot. At last, my feet found the carpeted hallway on the second floor.

Feeling time running out, I shuffled toward the center of the building. This hall paralleled the one below, extending across the house. A hint of lightness filtered through windows at each end. With my back against the wall, I faced the rear of the house. In near-total darkness, I studied the pattern of doors in front of me. Only faint changes in gray shadows helped build the pattern. Lori was behind one of these doors. Which one?

The generator sputtered. The next surge rumbled on raggedly, then grew stronger. The noisy engine steadied into an even roar. The hallway lights began to flicker. Which door was it? I had to move. I also had to be right. As the lights began to glow dimly, I backed against the wall, studying the three most likely candidates. I was no closer to decision when full power hit, bathing the hallway in light. My eyes squinted against the blinding brightness. I was completely exposed, vulnerable. I had to decide. Take a chance. Now! Which one?

The door on my left opened and Finley Quale stepped cautiously into the hall, his face pale. My heart pounded fiercely, as if near bursting. I couldn't move. The gods are never so kind. Quale wore white linen pants. The upper part of the naked sagging body bulged over the beltline. As he turned toward me, I tensed. When he saw my black hooded figure, he froze, then began trembling.

With one stride, I was at his side, the silencer of the .38 tucked up under his chin. I ripped up the stocking mask. I wanted him to see my eyes and snarling lips. I wanted this pathetic specimen to see the soul he faced and thus know he had cause for fear and trembling.

"Where's the woman?" I demanded with a fierceness I could not remember hearing before.

"What woman?" Quale asked, his voice breaking upward in fright.

"Rosta asked me that. Then I killed him." I reached down and lifted Quale's right hand. It was limp and pudgy and there were two broad scars across the right middle finger.

I dropped the hand as if it were infected with a lethal virus, then jammed the gun up under his chin. His head bounced off the wall.

"No one's dead yet. No one has to die." It wasn't a lie, even though death hovered nearby, patiently waiting as only she can. "Maybe there's two of them, you sonofabitch. Is Rachelle Nestrum here?"

He tried to speak. No sound came from between his lips. Spittle dribbled out of the corner of his mouth where the lower lip sagged oddly. He managed a slight shake of his head.

"You real sure?"

He was more emphatic with his nod.

"Uh-huh."

I turned and looked at the doors across the hall. He could be lying about Rachelle, but I didn't think so. Even if she had been here, she would be dead by now. "Lori's here. Behind one of those doors." I accented the statement with the silencer. "Which one?"

Pressing down against the cold steel, Quale managed a nod in the direction of the door slightly to my right. Could it be a trap? Any one of the three could be the one I needed. I grabbed his flabby arm and pulled him along.

He held back but the silencer kept him on tip-toes. His strength was no match for mine. In front of the door I added upward pressure on the pistol and opened it slowly. Inside was a tiny cubical and another door. I checked the hall. There was no one in sight. I yanked him in beside me and closed the hall door.

"Any secret codes? A password, maybe?"

"Nothing like that," Quale stammered.

"Then go on in."

"I...I can't."

"Is that so?"

"I..."

He never finished. I threw the door open and shoved him inside. He stumbled, arms wind-milling for balance. I had a vague impression of a woman's red nakedness on the bed as I dropped the .38 and grabbed the Uzi. Automatic fire exploded from the left, stitching a row of bloody holes diagonally across Quale's naked chest. Using the sagging body as cover, I dove into the room, twisting sideways, the Uzi extended. I pulled the trigger as I cleared the falling body, sweeping the far side of the room, concentrating on the corner from which the shots had come. Even before I hit the floor, I had emptied the clip and was digging for another.

I hit hard, beside the huge bed. Air, in the form of a heavy grunt, was forced from deep within. I rammed the full clip home. I couldn't stay where I was and live. Would they expect me to try for the door? Maybe. I tucked my feet under me and lunged up toward the outside wall, the Uzi pounding.

I needn't have bothered. The man who'd cut Quale in half was clutching his throat where two rounds from my first burst had ripped at it. My glance flicked briefly over the woman on the bed, then my finger sought to pull the trigger and its housing out of the gun. In slow motion, shuddering under the impact of fire, still gripping his throat, the gunman fell, face down. Blood flowed forth from beneath the body, staining the pale pink carpet. There was no one else in the room except the naked woman tied to the bed.

It was Lori. Three cameras were pointed at her. I buried a burst in each, watching them disintegrate in satisfying fashion, then turned slowly back to the bed.

I could feel the blood drain from my face. I felt faint, trembly, shaky, unable to move. Her mouth was taped. She was screaming silently, her body stressed with effort. There was too much terror in the eyes, more than any human could bear. Her wrists and ankles were bleeding where they were tied to the bed frame. Blood stained the silken sheet between her legs. She'd been beaten with at least fists and lash. I'd expected the worst, even her death. I was totally unprepared for what I faced. Her entire body had been painted a blood-red color that reminded me of cheap lipstick. All of her trembled in pain and agony and terror.

I shook my head to restore a more effective pattern of thought. It occurred to me I might have to hit myself, hard, to regain control. I had to move. Now! Slowly I looked down at the Uzi and remembered it was nearly empty. I also remembered where I was. Even though the room was soundproof, the shots might well have been heard.

I'd accomplished the first objective. There'd be no more filming of Lori. With gradually increasing efficiency, I ripped a clip loose and reloaded. I glanced around, as if seeing the room for the first time. There was a side door. I let the Uzi dangle and reached into the top of my boot for the knife, watching both doors, listening.

In her eyes, terror was giving way to questioning puzzlement. I ripped the tape from her mouth and started in on the ropes. She whispered faintly, hoarsely, "Is it really you?"

I tried for a smile that must have been half

grimace and half snarl. "It's me." The heavy anger in my voice nearly hid the words. Seconds later, her feet were free. "Can you stand?"

She rolled off the bed, groaning. She'd have fallen before coming erect, if I hadn't caught her.

"Sit down. Move the legs." She began bending long slender legs, her face pinched with pain.

"Ignore the hurt as much as you can. I can carry you but it would slow us down."

I shrugged out of the raincoat, tossed it onto the bed, and bent down in front of her with the tennis shoes. She needed a narrower size, but they'd do. I laced them snugly. "Try again."

She handled it herself, weaving a bit, but standing. Gently, ready to catch her, I slipped the raincoat on and walked around front to button it. I shortened the bulky sleeves with the knife and knotted the belt tightly. "It's not much but it'll do."

She wasn't listening. She took three faltering steps, using her hand on the edge of the bed for support. She turned around and did better with another three. I stepped into the small entry and recovered the .38. When I turned back, she was looking down at what had been Finley Quale, as if regretting he was dead. I thought I understood. She'd like to have done the killing.

I closed the inner door and stepped to her side, offering the .38. She grabbed it firmly. "It's like the one you were using, except the silencer pulls the muzzle down a bit and to the right. Got it?"

She nodded.

"We've got to move. Ready?"

She nodded again and leaned heavily against me when I slipped my arm around her waist. She gained strength with each step toward the door. I could feel her wince with pain at every move but she didn't hesitate. I leaned her against the wall. "I've got to see what's on the other side. If anyone comes through there," I said, pointing to the door to the hall, "kill them."

Her terror-ridden eyes were clear and bright. Her nod and the grim set of her jaw reassured me, as did the way she gripped the pistol with left hand locked to right wrist, centering the muzzle on the closed door.

Cautiously I opened the door. There was another short hall to the second door. I plunged through into the adjoining room, firing. The room was empty, except for the elegant couch, two chairs, and bar. The outside wall was sealed, soundproofed. But against gunfire? I couldn't be sure.

I'd used three clips. Did I have enough left? It was silly speculation. There's never enough. I rushed back into the other room, scooped up the abandoned clips, and said, "Go, Lori."

She pushed away from the wall, struggling for balance. Every part of me wanted to reach out and help. But I held back. For a chance, she had to do precisely what she was doing: move, despite seemingly unendurable pain.

I began reloading a clip as I followed, closing both doors behind us. We were alone, safe for the moment. "It's got to hurt worse than hell's burning, but keep walking. We could have to run to get clear."

As if in a trance, she walked painfully back and forth across the room next to the wall, reaching out occasionally to touch it lightly. The .38 dangled at her side, the tendons in her wrist drawn tightly in the grip on the butt.

I stuffed the newly loaded clip into my pocket and began on the next one, watching her struggle but also gain something with each stride. My hands worked automatically, leaving my mind free.

The generator had to go. I'd hoped this room would have a window overlooking the shed. If we were spotted in the lighted hall, the risks would be high. We'd have even less chance outside the house. I finished the second clip and began on the third.

There were only three choices. Try another room on this floor, or one on the ground floor, or a direct attack through the door I'd used to enter. The latter wasn't much of a choice. The best bet would be a room on this floor. Lori couldn't move with sufficient quickness. It wouldn't do to be caught in light.

What I wanted to do was to take her in my arms, to assure myself she was really here in this little room with me. What I did was step over to the wall and put my hand on the light switch. I explained what we must do. She nodded, eager to be gone.

I snapped off the light and plunged through the two doors, the Uzi ready. The hall was empty. It was the tops of the stairs that concerned me. These were the most likely positions from which an attack could be launched. Hopefully most of Quale's people had no part in the happenings on the second floor and had been ordered never to come up here.

"Okay," I said over my shoulder. I watched the long length of hall, walking backward. She had the support of my shoulder and that of the wall. Nothing moved. There were no sounds but ours.

Her swift intake of breath was followed instantly by the thud of the .38. I spun around, driving hard. She had dropped to the floor as planned but contact brought gasping sounds of bitter pain. It was Otto Gillis, at the top of the stairs, both hands clasped to his chest in confused wonderment.

He was already dying, but I could keep Lori from knowing she was responsible. I fired three short bursts. The first stitched a pattern up from his belt buckle. The second slammed through his hands, on into his chest, within inches of where Lori's round had hit. The third burst blew out his left eye, splattering bloody gore against the wall behind him. He crumpled, nearly folding upon himself, into a motionless heap on the carpet.

I looked back down the hall, then rushed for

the last door on the back side of the building. I threw it open and charged inside. Video equipment filled tables along the walls. It looked like the editing was done here. There was one window. No lights were on. I rushed back into the hall and took a position beside Gillis's body from which I could cover the entire hall and both stairways. "Inside, Lori."

She struggled to her feet, her face drawn with pain. For several precious seconds, she looked steadily at the bloody heap that had been Otto Gillis, her face filled with loathing beyond anything I'd ever seen. There was no need for words. The late Mr. Gillis had been a participant. Lori turned stiffly and walked determinedly into the room.

The moment she was inside, I rushed for the door and closed it behind me. Crouching, I moved to the window to examine the shed housing the generator. Could I hit it with the flare gun? I'd never throw a grenade that far accurately through the window. A flare seemed worth a try.

I opened the sash window, used the knife to slice a hole in the screen, then loaded the flare gun. A man walked into the shed, carrying a five-gallon can of gasoline. It looked promising. I gave it a slow count to thirty, hoped gasoline was being poured, and fired. The shed disintegrated in a ball of yellow and orange flame. Lights faded. We again had the friendly protective cover of near-total darkness provided by the rainy, cloudy sky.

"Let's go."

She was unsteady but she was walking. I unlatched the door to the hall, set myself, flung it open, and burst out of the room, the Uzi ready. It was too dark to see anything not moving, but the hall seemed empty. "Okay."

When she was beside me, I said, "It's only a few feet to the stairs."

When I felt her arm on my sleeve, I moved toward the stairs, carefully avoiding what was left of Gillis. I stopped with my foot at the top of the stairs. I reached out and guided her down the first step. When I felt her grab the banister, I started down beside her, walking sideways, feeling my way with my feet. My job was the stairs above, hers those yet untraveled.

She moved slowly but steadily. I couldn't urge her on, even though we were dangerously exposed. I tried counting steps but lost track once past the landing. She slowed unexpectedly. "I think we're down," she said in a faint whisper.

I stood still, listening for any sound from above, then turned and felt my way past her to the main floor. I peered around the corner down the length of the dark hall. There was no sign of movement. The candlelight was gone. The excited yells from outside seemed far away.

"Like upstairs," I said. "Stay close to the wall. I'll cover the rear. We've got to make it to the end of this hall. Okay?" I didn't add, as I had before, that she should be quick to shoot. She'd shown she understood that part of her assignment.

"Yes," she said without hint of emotion.

She walked across the hall, placed her shoulder against the wall, and with increased confidence continued walking. Beside her, moving backwards, I could feel it; she was stronger. Still, it took time. The hallway was long and her stride short.

I didn't see it but I heard it. A door we'd passed opened, some twenty feet to my front. In the dim light through the windows of the room, a man was silhouetted briefly, revealing a triangle of whiteness, a sling. The man Ramirez had hit! Had we been seen? Heard?

The man fired an unseen shotgun. I shoved Lori to the floor, even as I returned fire, diving forward. I was sure I'd hit but was it a kill? It had to be. We'd been seen in the flare of exploding rounds. I lunged to my feet, ripped a grenade loose, yanked the pin with my trigger finger, and dashed down the hall, staying close to the wall away from the door. When I was even with the entry, I lobbed the grenade and allowed momentum to carry me beyond the opening. The blast rocked the house. Bright blinding light and smoke burst into the hallway.

I didn't have to check. No one could have survived. But I slipped inside, eased my back to the wall, and waited. There were no sounds of life, only the snapping readjustment of matter to new forms. The two crumpled bodies on the floor in line with the window were still. One had a white cast on the left leg.

I rushed into the hall. "We've got to move

fast." I reached down and grabbed her arm, urging her up and then to greater speed. She struggled determinedly. At last I saw it, the door to the outside.

What might be waiting out there couldn't be known. It all depended on the orders Quale's people had been given. If they'd been assigned positions and told to hold them, and if they'd done so, there was a chance. "We need to get out that door and a hundred feet to the wall, then seven times that to the back. Can you do it?"

"I'll do it," she said grimly.

"Then get to the door but don't open it."

She stepped past me and walked stiffly to the wall, turned, and put her back to it. I rushed the door, whirled, and studied the long empty hall. Fire spreading in the blasted room cast eerie flickering shadows. Nothing moved.

I opened the door a crack, standing clear. The rain was heavy and the wind had picked up. It would help. "Lori, take a look."

She peeked around the doorjamb. "I'm going for the hedge against the wall. When I disappear, you come on. Nothing fancy, like crawling. Just walk. If you hear shots, hit the ground."

"All right," she answered, her voice sounding more natural.

I pulled the stocking cap down, crouched, then rolled out across the porch, off onto the ground. Crouching, I rushed for the hedge and backed into it for cover. Lori moved outside and started down the steps. I guarded both front and rear, moving only my eyes, listening. In the

full darkness of night, the rain diminished visibility to little over a hundred feet. Nothing stirred
except Lori. As she closed, I could see her cringe
from pain at each step, but she never faltered.

In front of me, her pale face gleamed in the
night. I bent down and scooped up mud. "Sorry.
Skin makes a good target."

She nodded and reached for the mud, apply-
ing it as cold cream. When she'd finished, I
touched up a few spots and said, "Stay low."

I walked slowly, crouched, eyes alert. We were
nearly invisible against the hedge. My ears
guarded the rear. When I saw the pool equipment loom up out of the misty darkness, the
guilties hit. I would leave her here. I'd known all
along that if we got this far, I'd have to. It was
her only chance. It seemed unfair to lie to her,
with death on all sides.

I turned and reached out in the blackness,
gently pulling her head closer. "I've got the
Blazer out back, just left of this wall. The keys
are in the ignition. We've got to separate. Crawl
along the hedge. Shoot anything that gets in
your way."

I handed her the two speed loaders. I didn't
tell her that if she needed more rounds, she
wouldn't make it. A .38 against automatic
weapons isn't much of a contest.

"Take it slow when you get to the back. There
should be a man near the corner. If I don't put
him down, you'll have to. I blew hell out of the
fence a little earlier. If you can get by anyone
there, you're home free."

I wanted to go with her. But that had been decided. I would draw fire so she could be free. "If you get to the Blazer before I do, take off. The road's muddy but I've got it in four-wheel. There's a chain at the end of the alley. Drive right through it; it's rigged to give. Then get to Doc's."

"What about you?"

"Me?" I asked, wanting desperately to avoid the lie.

"Yes. What will happen to you?" There was a new firmness in her voice, one I hadn't heard before.

"Against the hedge, you'll be exposed. You've got to have cover. I'm going to start a little war. I plan to finish it, too, and beat you to the Blazer. If I don't, there's a car stashed on the next street over." If my estimates were correct, there were at least a half-dozen armed trained men in this yard. All of them wouldn't be unlucky. And there was no car except the Caddy out front, beyond Quale's little army.

"You don't believe you'll make it, do you?" she asked, with a curious absence of demand.

"I came in to get you out. Are you going to waste all this? All this dying?"

"No," she said, her voice hushed. "I'll do as you ask."

"Good," I said. "I'll drift off to the right and get things started. As soon as I can, I'll be back along this hedge. So don't shoot someone coming up behind until you know it's not me."

"I won't," she replied. "But why not wait for the police? Someone must have called by now."

"Rosta's dead; there's no chance to beat extradition. If the police find you here, you'll be halfway to Texas. As for me, how would I explain all this killing?"

I wanted to reach out and hold her. I wondered if she wanted the same thing. "Go on," I said gently. "It's time."

"It isn't fair."

"I know." I searched deeply for the good words. As usual, they alluded me. "You best move," was all I said.

Slowly she turned away, crouched, and began crawling along the hedge.

I felt old, alone, and friendless. As if all that mattered, all that would ever matter, was leaving me. Grimly I turned toward the yard. I'd always thought I was pretty damn good at this kind of game. I'd never have a better chance to prove it.

I crawled diagonally across the yard, pulling myself forward with knees, scuffling feet, and elbows. The objective was the back of the tennis court and the thick plantings around it. As I moved, I listened. I stopped, occasionally, when uncertain of the meaning of a shadow or sound. For the most part, I continued steadily. At least for now, I knew where I was going and what I would do. I'd create a tunnel of safety for Lori or never create anything again.

When the chain-link fence of the tennis court loomed up in front of me, I rose to my knees and crawled more rapidly, knowing the bushes added cover. It was looking better every minute. I was at least going to be able to give Lori a chance.

I stood up slowly with bushes behind me. The back of the lot was invisible in the rainy darkness but I'd estimated the distance from the vacant lot. I could see the shadowy outline of the maple tree against the sky. It was all I'd need.

I let the Uzi dangle, then pulled and loaded the flare gun. I yanked loose four of the phosphorous grenades. Someone might hear the clips snap but they'd have a tough time getting a fix on my position.

I planned each throw, relative to the misty outline of the maple tree. With quick, practiced motion, I pulled the pin on the first grenade and let it fly. I repeated with the second and third. The first one exploded in the far corner of the yard as I released the last one. A man screamed, nailed by phosphorous. I fired the flare in a high arc that would float it down close to the fence near the Blazer.

Someone pinpointed the source of the flare. But I'd already grabbed the Uzi, dived for the ground, and was rolling toward the tree to my left when slugs chewed holes in the bushes where I'd been standing. I returned fire and was rewarded with a yelp of pain as I rolled on to the cover of the tree.

It was then I knew our luck wasn't good. In the flash of the grenades, I'd seen only vague shadows. The descending flare revealed four men, scattered about the rear of the yard, all in good cover. There would be others behind me, nearer the house. Police sirens screamed in the street out front.

I dumped a three-round burst at each of the figures highlighted by the flare, then emptied the clip in the direction of the figure nearest Lori's path. The man surged up off the ground, hit, an easy straight-away target. Before I could be certain of the kill, I had to duck behind the tree to avoid incoming fire.

It sounded as if five weapons were still in action, two at the back fence and three closer to the house. Tires squealed to a stop out front and the scream of sirens faded. Immediately there was gunfire, pistols and shotguns against automatic rifles.

I reloaded the flare gun, rolled, fired while on my back, and continued to roll. I dropped off a short retaining wall onto a concrete walk. It caught me by surprise, stunning me. But it was cover. I peered over the top. Even in the rain, the flare made noonday brightness out of the night when it drifted close to the ground. I fired short bursts until the clip ran out, grabbed another and, ignoring returned fire, continued the pattern, swinging the gun quickly, concentrating on the corner near the Blazer, the corner Lori must pass through safely.

The heavy pounding of feet down the side of the house was not encouraging. I jammed a fresh clip home, listening to the last siren die. The rushing footsteps slowed. The plan didn't allow for cops. Had there been time for them to get this far since the squad cars had skidded to a stop? I couldn't see how. There were at least two men. Now they were clear of the back of the house, still closing. They had to be Quale's people, ducking away from the official attack out front.

I couldn't wait any longer. Whoever they were, they were too damn close. Even a random burst could wipe me out. I yanked a grenade, pulled the pin, and let it fly. I steadied the Uzi on the second man, highlighted by the explosion, beyond the body tumbling into the air. I fired and watched the figure crash to the ground. At least they hadn't been wearing uniforms.

I couldn't be sure; that's not possible. But the last clip might have done it. Whatever, I now had to escape the threat from the front of the house. I loaded another clip and, crouching, ran at an angle toward the hedge, aiming at a point Lori should have passed. I was already diving for ground when I heard fire from behind me. I hit, rolled, and waited. It was the last thing I'd wanted, to draw fire in Lori's direction. On the next flash, I emptied half the clip, circling the source of bright, deadly light. Had I hit? No rounds were returned.

I charged up along the hedge. I saw the faint shape of her, full length on the ground. "Say something, for God's sake!" she cried.

"It's me." I rushed up beside her. We'd had

more luck than I'd thought possible; I was back beside her. "Let's get out of here."

"I'd like that." Her voice was strained and tired and filled with pain.

"There's a problem."

"Yes."

"There may still be folks off to the right."

"I understand."

"Stay between me and the hedge. If anyone shoots, get down fast."

"I will."

I tucked my arm around her waist, lifted her, and trotted awkwardly toward the back fence. The fire in front of the house had risen in intensity. Maybe we were clear. Maybe I'd hit or discouraged all between us and the blown fence.

I didn't really see it, only felt it, a presence off to the right. I shoved Lori to the ground and brought up the Uzi. At the first flash of light, I fired a short burst. A volcano erupted in my shoulder and sharply defined cones of light probed determinedly in my direction. I fired again, ignoring the left shoulder, melting, a longer burst this time. A round hammered the left leg out from under me. I crashed awkwardly to the ground, landing too hard. Dizzy from fatigue and exploding waves of pain only slightly eased by shock, I rolled to my stomach and lifted my head.

"Crawl," I cried. "Get out of here." How bad was I hit? I could only be sure it wasn't good.

There was no sound of motion behind me. "Go! Now!"

I heard her begin to move. If I could hold right here, she'd have good cover all the way. The left shoulder throbbed unmercifully, the arm useless. I dropped the Uzi to the wet grass and fumbled for clips. I ripped three loose, then used the ground and my good hand to reload. I returned full attention to the field of fire, my vision blurred by the rainy darkness and near-overwhelming pain.

I could no longer hear Lori. She must be nearly clear, close to the Blazer. The roar of fire from the front of the house rose in a frenetic crescendo. It sounded like cops had taken weapons from downed defenders and were returning fire in kind.

I reached for the useless hand. Ignoring blinding starbursts of frightful hurt, I pulled the hand out in front of me and draped it over the Uzi. Hot steel scorched the palm. The fingers worked in detached fashion. I was able to loosely grip the top of the gun. I grabbed the weapon with my right fist and waited with the patience of death herself.

What I wanted most, what I was desperate to hear, was the roar of the Blazer engine. Lori. Move it. The plea died before reaching my lips. I could feel strength ebbing too rapidly. If I could only hear the engine, I could lay my heavy head down and rest. I struggled fiercely to hold it up and steady.

Three four-round bursts exploded from beyond the maple tree. I ignored the ugly slapping of slugs into the hedge behind me and concentrated on holding the position of the gun flashes with my eyes. Maybe she couldn't get it started. She should be there by now. Was she hit? Down?

I brought the gun up with my right hand, hoping there was enough linkage remaining to my left to hold the bucking barrel down. Where was Lori?

On the next flare of light, I fired. I held the trigger back, circling the barrel in a spiral. I managed to slip the left hand forward, holding down on the gun with little more than the weight of the near-dead hand. The little gun bucked steadily.

When I realized it was empty, I dropped it to the grass and fumbled in a fresh clip. Why hadn't the Blazer at least started? I had no choice. I had to know. I lurched upward but I'd forgotten the torn left leg. It collapsed. I crashed onto my left shoulder. Gasping groans of total agony punched unwanted from between clenched teeth, frightening me. I tilted over, rolling onto my back.

The rain brought coolness to my face and in time the dizzy, sick emptiness receded. Could I crawl? The wound was below the knee. I rolled onto my good shoulder and pushed myself to my knees, letting the Uzi dangle against the grass. I don't know how long I held the position. I only know time passed. Then slender fingers wrapped around my arm, pulling me upward.

Damn her soul! She was supposed to be in the Blazer. Gone. But I couldn't sustain my anger as she helped me up. I used her strength, eagerly, greedily. I was able to override the slamming pounding in my shoulder and drape the bad arm behind her neck. She gripped the wrist tightly. Now the pain that had blinded was an ally. My mind cleared with each step. She took much of the weight off my left leg. We were moving, stumbling haltingly, awkwardly, but moving. My eyes roamed the bleak blackness to the right, the gun up in the good hand. How many were still out there, able to fire?

Each faltering step increased hope. The wind shifted and heavier rain sheeted into my eyes, blurring vision. But we were past the fence. I felt her stop, pulling me around her. The Blazer! I could smell it. Could she drive? Her agonized breathing as she half carried me told me I couldn't ask. I'd have to manage. I sensed its closeness. I let the Uzi dangle and reached out, brushing the willow branches out of the way. "I'll be okay," I said, in quiet desperation.

I fumbled alongside the Blazer, using it for support. With teeth clenched, grinding against pain, I used the steering wheel and the good arm to pull myself inside. My entire left side was a sheet of scalding flame, useless, an object to be discarded. I waited only for the door to open on her side, then turned the key. The engine fired on the first crank.

I thought of the chain up ahead, falsely attached, cheering the merits of planning. We'd drive through it as if it weren't even there. But when I peered out from beneath the willowy

branches, there was nothing to cheer about. I
rubbed my eyes to erase what I saw.

The flashing lights of the patrol car blocked
the alley. Two misty figures drifted cautiously
down the road directly toward us. "Get down,
Lori. We've got more trouble."

I rammed the trans into reverse and backed
down the hill, dangerously close to the wall and
what was left of Quale's fence. And we were
backing into the field of fire of any remaining
gunman. I braked with the good foot and shifted
into low. Then I shoved the accelerator to the
floor and turned, sliding on the narrow muddy
road. The slam of service revolvers punctuated
the night. The Blazer roared up the vacant lot
behind Quale's estate, heading for the spot I'd
occupied earlier. We only had to make it over
the crest.

But the hill was too steep or the Blazer was
too old or I was too far gone to deal with it properly. We'd drifted too far right. Rounds slamming into the rear of the vehicle didn't help.
Whatever the reason, when I snapped on the
lights, the rocky wash was dead ahead. I yanked
the wheel hard left. I could feel it; we were
going to roll. The left front wheel dove into an
unseen depression, taking my breath away, accenting the turn and righting the Blazer. As the
rear wheel dropped, we gained traction and
speed.

Seconds later, we were rushing down the
other side. At the curb, I cranked a right the instant the front wheels fell away. The bounce was

frightening but we made the turn. We roared down the quiet residential street. I fought to steady the strangely erratic course.

I took the first left, tires squealing, then a right. "I think it's okay, Lori. You can get back up," I said faintly, my mouth dry, a pronounced buzzing in my ears.

White-hot swords from my left side seared into what little remained of my right. "Doc's..." My voice trailed off. What had I wanted to say? "Doc's waiting. At his ... office."

A fierce new storm emerged, enveloping the whole of my being. Desperately I jammed the good foot against the brake pedal, drifting the Blazer slowly to the right. Nothing seemed to be working. All was in slow motion as in a dream gone mad. A searing wave of pain blurred perception. We were accelerating, not slowing. Faster. Faster! I slipped off the edge into the well of hellish bottomless blackness.

I came to with infinite slowness, remembering only the fundamental rule: Be still. Mentally I ran inventory of critical parts. Everything seemed to be properly attached. But something was different. What was it? Drugs. That was it. I'd been given something to still the crashing cymbals of pain. The Cong wouldn't do that. Where was I? Determinedly I returned to testing, extending earlier efforts. Minimizing movement, I tensed the right leg, testing toes, then ankle, lower leg, knee, and finally the thigh. I repeated the test with my left. The near-unendurable pain was covered with drug; it hurt but it didn't matter. Everything worked. Lights were on. Where was I? The smells were clean, emanating from antiseptics, not the stinking rot and stench of another time. I continued. Arms, torso, and neck. It was while examining the torn left shoulder that it came to me. I opened my eyes.

Doc was sitting in a chair by the table, smoking. It was something he'd sworn never to do again. And he'd kept the vow for over six months. It was all coming clear. Fuzziness remained only in spots.

"It'll kill you, Doc," I said, my voice raspy, faint. I was surprised at how weak I felt and knew I shouldn't be. I moved the left arm tentatively. The shoulder was not as bad as it felt. When I lifted and bent the left leg, I reached the same conclusion.

"You're undoubtedly correct about the smoking," Doc replied. "But things have been getting to me lately."

"Like what?"

"Like treating the lovely young woman you so ungraciously passed out on, wondering if she'll ever be able to deal emotionally with her experience. How she was able to get you out from behind the wheel and drive all this way, I'll never understand."

"She'll be okay, won't she?" I asked, trying to sit up and falling back to the cot before lifting more than my head.

"She has severe bruises on nearly all of her

body. I'll need to check for internal damage. She was beaten repeatedly with a whip, one with multiple strands, each with a little sphere covered with sharp barbed points. A salt brine was rubbed into bleeding wounds. It must have been incredibly painful. She was raped, of course. Repeatedly. And with more than a penis. Some internal surgical repair will be required.

"Her wounds will heal in a matter of days. It's too early to say about the internal injuries. A plastic surgeon can do much to reduce the scars."

"And the scars on her soul?"

Doc shook his head slowly, dragging deeply on the cigarette. "I simply don't know. The physical injuries are of little consequence. But the rest of it?" His voice trailed off.

I looked unseeing at the ceiling. "After all that, she watched me kill half a dozen men, maybe more. How will she deal with that?"

"Scott, I can't say. She may end up hating or fearing you or both. Then again, she may decide she's to blame. I can't lie to you. The chance of her coming out of this without severe psychic scars isn't good."

Doc ground out the cigarette, then lit another. "Aren't you going to ask about yourself? You've been unconscious for nearly four hours."

"Are you forgetting something?"

"Yes, I suppose I am. This isn't new to you. But for the record, the shoulder will take two to three weeks and the leg somewhat longer. It will take another while for total recovery but there's no serious damage."

"I follow you."

"Lencho sent some men to drive you home. But you're welcome to stay here."

"Can I see Lori?"

"I don't think you should. Let her rest. Hopefully she's asleep by now." He stood and walked to the window. "You know, of course, she may never want to see you again. Trauma can do that. One seeks to block out all that preceded it." He turned and met my look squarely. "We'll have to wait and see."

I fought back the urge to cry. "Let's get me out of here, then." I grit my teeth, lurched into a sitting position, and nearly fainted. I grabbed hold tight with the good arm and it passed. I looked down at the pants I was wearing under the treatment smock.

"One of my patients left them. Your's weren't in very good condition. I put everything in that bag over there." He pointed to the table.

"I'd feel better with the .38 a bit closer."

Doc stepped to the table, fished about in the bag, then handed me the pistol, butt first, then the speed loaders. "Guns," he said. "It seems a hard way to live."

"Expect it beats dying, some way or other."

Doc nodded, walked to the door and opened it. Three young men filed in, Mexican, smiling politely, with a look in their eyes that said they'd been there and made it back. They seemed accustomed to the guns under their arms. The husky one gripped me under the good shoulder and muscled me up off the cot. Another grabbed the bag from the table and the bundle of wet clothes from the floor. The third picked up the crutch and stepped out the door, looking both ways before proceeding.

"Lencho wants these men to stay with you," Doc said.

"It's a good thought," I said, thinking of how helpless I was. "About Lori and cops? Can you keep her out of sight?"

"I'll take care of that."

I hobbled slowly toward the door, letting the big man carry most of the weight. From behind me, Doc said, "In the bag, Scott. There's something for the pain."

"Thanks." I didn't tell him the pain he was speaking of was an old acquaintance, hardly worth consideration. If I'd won it all and lost her, I'd won nothing at all. I'd lost everything. For that pain, Doc had no pill.

Monday

‖‖ ‖‖ ‖‖ ‖‖ ‖‖

The hills blocked the sun when I awoke in the day bed in the front corner of the room. I hadn't used the big bed I'd shared with Lori. I didn't think I would again.

Pounding pain and my swollen bladder had awakened me much too early. Now they conspired to drive me from beneath the covers. It worked. I rolled over slowly, holding my left shoulder, testing the left leg gingerly. It hurt like hell gone mad and the shoulder was worse. But the pain took my mind off other things. Like Bobbie. And Lori. And the emptiness of the house. I used the crutch and good arm. There was no sign of the heavyweights that had brought me home but the M1A was missing from over the door. I was covered.

I swallowed a pain pill, then struggled through a light shower, trying to keep the dressings dry. I didn't spend much time thinking before reaching for another pill. After a spotty shave, I struggled into clean pants and an old pair of loafers. I pulled a shirt on over the good arm and let it drape over the torn shoulder. I tottered back to the bed and grabbed the Colt. For a goodly while, I would go nowhere without this steel against my belly.

Curiously, I found myself watching the antics of the colts in the pasture below. I'd never paid much attention to them before. Rain clouds still

344

threatened but it was bluff. The storm was over. I hobbled into the kitchen and opened the refrigerator, thinking of food. One glance did it. I closed the door disgustedly and hobbled out onto the porch. Jose, the man sitting in the rocker with the M1A across his lap, looked up at my struggles and said, "It hurts some, don't it?"

"Yeah. But we've both been worse off."

He nodded, not surprised I'd read him so well.

"I appreciate your help last night," I said.

"Anytime." He grinned. "But with luck, not too often."

"I hear that." I looked about the familiar terrain and studied the hills as if seeing them for the first time. "I don't want to run you off but I can handle it now."

"You don't look that good," he said, as if he had serious doubts.

"Last night, we could have been hit by someone who didn't get the word. By now, anyone left knows Rosta and Quale are in the morgue. There's not much point in working for free."

"From what I hear, there aren't too many of the opposition still moving. But somebody could be pissed enough to make a try."

"It's possible," I acknowledged. "I'll be all right today. I'll give Lencho a call if I wipe out tonight. Mostly, though, I'm a light sleeper. It'd be tough for anyone to cross this gravel without me hearing them."

"It's okay by me but there could be a problem."

"And that is?"

"Lencho. He'd take my head off if you went down and I wasn't here."

"I won't push it. I'll call if I've any doubts."

"Like they say, you're the boss." He stood and propped the rifle inside the door. "That's a nice piece. It might do to keep it handy."

"I plan to."

He nodded approval and stepped down off the porch, moving toward the back of the house. He whistled with two fingers in his mouth, loud and shrill. One man broke cover on the hillside above the house. The other stepped into view in the draw. Minutes later, they drove off down the drive. Before the car reached the first cattle guard, I missed the cover they'd provided. But it was better this way. I didn't feel up to dealing with people. This was bear time—time for a cave, aloneness, and the licking of wounds.

I hadn't planned it. A crutch doesn't work worth a damn on a rocky slope. When I found myself up under the great oak, it surprised me. I looked down at freshly turned soil. I couldn't remember coming up the draw or when the tears had started. It was probably childish but I wanted to get a marker to commemorate Bobbie's loyalty and devotion. I ought to get one for Lori, too, one to mark love lost, destroyed in the violence cherished by death.

I rubbed the blur from my eyes and looked out over the valley, remembering the hills behind and the wilderness beyond them. It was a good place to live. If contentment couldn't be found here, I'd have to do without it.

I struggled back down the draw, the leg throbbing mercilessly. Inside, I stumbled into the bathroom for another pill, then to the chair by the phone. I dialed. The girl put me through immediately.

Stephen Weinberg's voice lacked its customary aplomb. "Will you be all right, Scott?"

"It'll take time, is all."

"Tony called. It's difficult to believe."

"Believe it," I said, knowing Tony would have lightened the telling.

"And Lori?" he asked, uncharacteristically tentative.

"She'll make it. I was hoping you could help."

"I can try. With Rosta dead, it will be difficult to prevent extradition. Do you have something else in mind?"

"Is your phone clean?"

"Yes. I have the entire office checked regularly."

"Is that damn dagger the Saudis are looking for as important as the papers say?"

"Let me put it this way. If diplomacy cannot resolve the issue and war is deemed unsuitable, there are those who say America will run out of oil in less than five years. There's much exaggeration in such statements because the oil will be sold to someone. Still, it will undoubtedly cost Americans a great deal.

"But the fundamental issue isn't oil at all. We need the Saudis. If the bottom falls out of the Middle East, they're the ones we can count on. The theft of the dagger, which some fanatical

Arabs even claim was a CIA plot, weakens the trust we've worked so long and hard to build. In the long run, that trust is far more significant than oil or dollars or trade."

"So the theft jeopardizes both our economic and military position throughout the Middle East, not just with the Saudis."

"Absolutely."

I turned it over in my mind, studying it from every angle. It didn't make sense to me but I wasn't Arab.

"Scott," Weinberg said. "You have something, don't you?"

"Maybe," I answered, still thinking. It was time to deal the cards. "Do you know someone in Washington with solid clout?"

"Yes," Weinberg replied cautiously.

"Are you interested in something a bit off the norm?"

"I'm not sure. What do you have in mind?"

I told him. In detail. When I'd finished, he laughed heartily. "I've always known you had unusual talents but I didn't realize you had such a devious mind. Not only am I prepared to do precisely as you ask, I'm going to enjoy it immensely."

"Do it right."

"Better than that, Scott. Much better than that." He hung up, his laughter pleasant to my ears.

I dialed Doc. The news wasn't bad or unexpected. It just wasn't good. Physically Lori would be fine. It was only the severe depression that was worrisome. Ned had regained consciousness; that was good. When I hung up, I concentrated on my coffee and keeping unwanted thoughts away. The last was difficult. There wasn't much I wanted to think about.

It was a grim, lonely afternoon. The clouds billowing up over the hills disappeared when they mingled with the valley winds. The sun peeked through occasionally. It didn't help.

It was nearly three when the silver Lincoln limo drifted sedately up the hill. The windows were smoked glass. I wasn't up to circling around to the rocks outside. Instead, I grabbed the M1A, checked the load, and waited. I couldn't see how any damage could be done until someone got out of the car or at least opened a window.

When the limo pulled to a stop in front of the house, two men got out, Krutz's bodyguards. The driver opened the back door. Krutz stepped out gracefully and surveyed the valley below. He turned, glanced at the hills, then walked with a short brisk stride toward the door. His bodyguards leaned against the front fender of the car, facing the house. I propped the rifle against the wall, rubbed the butt of the Colt, then opened the door.

"May I come in?" Krutz asked, with his version of a smile. The stout dapper man seemed as confident and capable in this open environment as he had been in his office.

I nodded and hobbled into the kitchen.

Krutz stepped inside, studied the large room, then followed me. He sat down at the table without invitation. "Very nice, Mr. Macklen. Very nice indeed." His wave encompassed the whole of the house and the hills and the valley. "You must find it peaceful here."

"It suits me," I commented, wanting to get on with it. "Would you like a drink?"

"No thank you. But you might." The corners of his mouth were flattened, erasing his usual dour expression. It wasn't really a smile but there was a hint of jostling laughter in the eyes.

I turned to the sink, poured bourbon liberally, and hobbled around the table to sit across from him. I slumped down in the chair, sipping the drink. "What brings you way out here?"

"Business. There is the matter of my bill."

"What do you think's fair?"

"Three hundred and fifteen thousand dollars is the amount I've arrived at."

"It's a nice-sounding number. Where'd it come from?"

"You did approximately fifteen thousand dollars damage to my shop that insurance won't cover. The balance is what Mr. Quale owed. Surely you remember I cautioned you not to kill him. It was conditional to my sharing information."

"One of his own killed him. Not me." I didn't feel compelled to describe how I'd shoved Quale into the room ahead of me.

"Even so," said Krutz, still smiling with his lips flat and thin, "the man would not have died if you had not intruded. No. You owe me, as we agreed."

"I haven't that kind of money."

"Of course you do. You can mortgage your little houses, and this place. As a courtesy, I would be happy to put you in touch with an innovative banker who would understand the situation."

His estimate was too high, regardless of how innovative the banker was. But not by all that much. Somehow I didn't think my being broke would bother him much. Had he really believed I'd pay what Quale had owed? A small part of me, buried deep within, issued stern warning; he expected more than words. But what? He couldn't seriously expect me to hand over everything I owned. Was he only bored, looking for excitement? Or was he a bit crazy? I dropped that notion quickly. This old fox was anything but crazy. Could it be simply a matter of pride? The need to wrest some profit from the shambles? A response was required, that was certain. "Excuse me," I said, standing with the help of the crutch.

"Certainly." There was an amused look of anticipation in the eyes.

I hobbled into the bathroom, removed the cabinet, and opened the safe. I set the briefcase on the sink and counted out fifteen thousand from the safe, then counted what was left. It wasn't much; it'd have to do. I stuffed the wad of cash into my pocket and opened the briefcase. I counted out a hundred thousand in the largest bills and returned them to the safe.

With the briefcase and half its original content, I struggled across the room to the cabinet next to the foot of the bed and picked up a deck of cards.

When I was again seated, I tossed the cards onto the table. "They say you play when the stakes are right."

Krutz nodded cautiously. Curiosity filled the eyes.

I pulled the wad of bills from my pocket and tossed it across the table. "I owe for the shop."

He glanced at the bills for only an instant, then raised sharp attentive eyes, waiting.

"I don't owe shit for Quale." I waited for response. Anything that might be hint to what was needed. The man gave nothing.

I lifted the briefcase to the table and opened it facing him. "There's a hundred thou there," I said. "It's not mine but I can replace it without bankrupting myself." I shoved the deck to the center of the table. "I'll cut you for it but win or lose, we're quits." If I was right, if Krutz was sitting here because of pride or in need of some gesture for fulfillment, this might do the trick.

"It's a fascinating offer."

"Think of it this way. To collect from Quale, you'd have had to discount the note."

"Hardly by two-thirds," he snorted.

"If that prince had found him, you wouldn't have collected at all." I paused, waiting, watching his eyes, as he looked at the case. I had no significant cards left to play.

"That is true," he said finally.

"Collecting from me might be tougher than you think."

He looked steadily at the money, never glancing at me.

"This way, you at least get a chance at something and risk nothing. I only said I'd do my best. This is it."

He looked up at me, wringing his hands expectantly, then reached for the deck and broke the seal. He shuffled expertly and offered the deck for a cut.

I shook my head. He smiled and fanned the deck across the table, studying the backs of the cards as if to read the other side. "Go ahead," I invited.

He reached boldly for the card he'd mentally selected and turned it. The queen of spades. He looked up. "A difficult card to beat."

"That's true." I reached out with a studied casual motion, hoping he couldn't hear my heart pounding fiercely. A hundred thou is a bit over my limit. I fished a card from the deck and flipped it face up on the table. The king of clubs.

"You do seem to be running in luck," Krutz commented softly.

"It's like that sometimes," I said, my mouth dry. If the man was disappointed, there was no hint of it.

"Well," he said, standing. "That appears to conclude our business." He reached for the fifteen thousand and tucked the bills into his pocket, eyeing the money stacked in the briefcase. When he looked at me, the eyes were bright and alert. "And what will you do with the dagger?"

"You'll hear about it."

"And you won't sell it to me."

I shook my head.

"You had it when we talked, did you not?"

I nodded.

He laughed, a deep, gutty belly laugh. "You'd have traded it for the woman, wouldn't you?"

I nodded again.

He sighed. "I greatly fear there's much more I must learn of you."

"Why?"

"For our next little game, as I've already explained. I'll need a great deal of information if I hope to win."

"Luck'll do."

He laughed again. "Do you realize how badly you've hurt my pride?" he asked. "First, you beat me at my best game, poker. Then I could have had the dagger. And now you talk me out of two hundred thousand dollars and take another hundred the queen said was mine. It's a severe blow."

"Do you remember Dachau?"

"Certainly."

"You got through that. You'll get through this."

He laughed once more, turned, and walked from the room. A few moments after the door closed, I heard the car start and move off down the hill. I stared at the money, thinking of Lori.

Tears streamed down my cheeks. She'd need clothes.

I hobbled into the bathroom and recovered the other hundred thousand. In the bedroom, I packed her things into a suitcase and placed the briefcase on top. After latching it, I dragged and pushed it to the front door.

Another pill and more bourbon helped the pain but did nothing to ease the guilties from putting it off. It was dusk, and well past time. I dialed.

"Foothill Division. Sergeant Haggen."

"Can you talk?"

"Sure thing," Tony replied briskly. "I called Doc. He says you're hurtin' but in good shape. Is that so?"

"That about says it." I paused, choosing the words. "I was glad to see you haven't lost your touch."

"How's that?"

"You were right on time at Quale's place."

"Hell. When we saw the gate openin' it was all I could do to keep the team from goin' in right then. I had to keep tellin' them to wait for the flare."

"I nailed two coming down the side of the house. They weren't yours, were they?" I realized I was holding my breath.

"Hell no. The boys knew the score. Nobody went anywhere near the back until we heard the Blazer was clear. I told them you were good and not too particular if somethin' was movin' at you."

"I could have done without those two at the end of the alley," I commented, keeping it light.

"A different team. Private cops for the neighborhood. Hell, you blew out power to twenty homes. It shouldn't have been a big surprise to find somebody checkin' it out."

"Is there any trouble headed my way?"

"I don't see how. Captain Greer wanted to know how come nine off-duty cops happened to be sittin' up on Mulholland Drive. I don't think he believed me when I told him I had a tip. But he won't press it. He likes the results. Internal Affairs nailed Nunis at the airport with three videotapes and a chunk of cash. He's not sayin' anythin' but our boys think they can prove he was makin' big bucks off Quale's work."

"Then I'm clear?"

"For sure. I'll bottle up any loose ends that pop up."

"What did you find?"

"If you've got a couple hours, I'll read the list. There was a ton of film and videotapes. We'll be able to identify most of the women. The blonde, Char Killen? She's bein' helpful. She's in some of the recent tapes and knows she's lookin' at forever in jail. She told us about an abandoned mine on a little place Quale owned in the desert, near Mojave. Our guys already got half a dozen bodies and they're not really into it yet."

"How'd the papers handle it?"

"Same shit. Gangland shootout. Somebody fed them a connection to Rosta. It was all the news hawks wanted."

"Do you think it'll all come out?"

"It might but I doubt it. Mass murders make good headlines but I think the big guns'll keep a lid on this. More than fifty good-lookin' women, gone missin' the last ten years, will be traced to Quale. Cops don't want to look stupid, any more than most people."

"Is there any sign of Rachelle?"

"We got lucky there. She's with her parents in upstate New York. She must have heard one of us." He answered someone in his office, then said, "Look. I've got to run."

"Stay in touch?"

"For sure," he said. "By the way, you haven't lost much, either. That was real pretty work." He hung up.

I sat unmoving, looking at the phone. Eventually it blurred into nothingness, which in turn was replaced by the image of whiteness snuggling slender hips and thighs. In time I realized moonlight was sneaking through the remnants of stormy clouds, and that I ached all over.

It was after two in the morning when I fell fitfully asleep from a combination of bourbon, pain pills, Seconal, and exhaustion. Sleep did not dim worried, lonely thoughts of Lori, nor erase the emptiness of the house, nor the cold, hard knot in my gut. I found that a new set of terrified screams had been added to my ample cache of memories, the raw materials for dreams.

* * *

Tuesday blended into Wednesday, then Thursday, without any good news. Doc answered uncounted calls, repeating patiently I'd have to wait on seeing Lori. Even the pain became boring.

Ricardo brought the Dodge. He loaded Lori's suitcase for me and took the Blazer, promising only to repair it, not rebuild it. I ignored the brightly painted new rear fender and shiny chrome bumper, struggled behind the wheel, and drove to San Fernando.

Doc sent his receptionist to get the suitcase and began redressing the shoulder. He doesn't usually have much to say, aside from a caustic remark here and there. Today he talked continuously, giving a detailed description of Lori's progress.

The vaginal surgery had gone splendidly and extensive tests had revealed no internal damage that would not mend naturally. The cuts and bruises were healing nicely. So well, in fact, there might be no need for a plastic surgeon.

He'd called in a psychologist—a good one, he claimed, a man who'd read Freud and understood him. He finished with the shoulder and turned to the leg.

Lori seemed more comfortable, now that she was at the clinic. She kept to herself and spent a good deal of time on the grounds and in the adjacent fields. Finally I asked, "When can I see her?"

"Christ, Scott. Why do you think I've been

running off at the mouth. I didn't want you to bring that up."

"Sorry, but I just did."

"Wait. Be patient."

"Won't she think I don't care? Or worse?"

"We're going to have to wait, Scott."

"Who in hell's we?"

"You, then."

He continued his chatter until he was able to usher me out the door with appropriate sympathies and another bottle of painkillers.

Days faded into nights, except that awake I was able to exercise some control over my thoughts. Nights were filled with restless, futile absurdities, mixed with silent screams, none of which were deterred by more pain pills, Seconal, or bourbon.

Each afternoon I found an excuse to see Doc. Each visit was more difficult for both of us. I did not get an invitation to visit the clinic. At the hospital, Ned was always glad to see me. I talked too much of Lori. Ned didn't seem to mind.

Another Sunday came and drifted slowly past, the second anniversary of my losing her, finding her, then losing her again in a manner I'd not yet been able to deal with. The third Sunday was harder than the others, filled with the conviction I'd never see her again. It left a strange kind of vacuum to be filled with a different hurt and a sense that the days ahead weren't worth looking forward to.

A few days later, the peace of the horse pasture was destroyed by selected phone calls. Men surged over the landscape with dozers, tractors, and shovels. Blasts shattered stubborn rock. A new well was dug and an electrical line was buried underground, from the house down to it. I contributed little beyond explanations of what Ned had planned.

About when the dam became a recognizable form, water began to rush down the hill from my well, mixing with earth and water, from the original spring. It all disappeared rapidly in discouraging fashion. If the ground didn't hold water, a certain high-priced geologist was going to be bothered some, answering more than a few questions about his report. But when the new well began to contribute, water pooled encouragingly in spots.

With the final troweling of the concrete spillway that would allow winter rains to rush on down the hillside without taking the dam along, the last of the workmen left.

The following morning, there was three feet of water in spots. One of Doc's friends arrived from the state fish hatchery near Bishop with a contraband load of young trout and a bonus of two dozen mature fish. After testing the water, he snapped, "They won't like it." He snorted disgustedly. "But the stupid critters will probably live. They might even grow some."

He gave me an hour of furiously rapid lecture, gesticulating wildly with his hands, on how to care for the fish and the water and why building a trout pond was about the dumbest thing a man could do. When he decided he'd said enough, he dumped the fish without ceremony, climbed into his car, and drove off without a backward glance.

I limped around the pond, idly moving a bit of dirt here and there with a shovel. The late afternoon sun warmed me in its special way. I was alone with the colts and the fish.

When filled, the pond would be nearly a hundred feet long and over fifty feet wide at several points. I fed the young fish as directed, tossing little packets evenly over the water. The containers dissolved rapidly, allowing the bits of food to spread outward in a circle. Rings made by jumping young fish gave hint of what the pond might look like filled with grown ones snapping at real or imagined food.

When Doc's car rattled across the cattle guard, my hand brushed across the butt of the Colt. With no noticeable enthusiasm, I turned toward the sound.

It wasn't Doc who got out. It was an eye-catching brunette in a simple blue dress, trimmed with white brocade. The image was one of tall slenderness. The hair was cut short, feathered back at the sides. It was the first time I'd seen the whole of her face. Some might think it too wide. It looked fine to me. Hesitantly, I walked toward her, trying to disguise the limp.

God, she looked good. I felt like a schoolboy, wanting to say something special to his first true love, so tangled in self-consciousness I couldn't say anything. I wanted to take her in my arms, to hold her tightly for as long as she'd allow. What I said was, " 'Lo, Lori."

"How are you, Scott?" she asked politely. I'd forgotten the rapid crispness with which she spoke and wondered how I could have.

"I'm good, Lori. You look fine."

"I am. Fine, I mean." She was flustered for no reason I could see. "What is all this?" she asked, indicating the scarred hole and new dam with a graceful wave.

"Ned always wanted a trout pond. We never got to it. Now seemed a good time."

"He'll be so pleased. I'm sure of it."

"I hope so."

For several moments, she surveyed the scene. She nodded briefly, indicating understanding, satisfaction, or both. When she looked at me, amusement flooded into her eyes. "Did you see the papers last week?"

I shook my head.

"The dagger was returned to Prince Aba al-Saleh with all cameras rolling. He and other Saudi leaders are trying to outdo one another in their praise of American investigative agencies. They're saying ridiculous things." She paused, then continued in a rush. "I so wish I could tell the world just who these agencies really are."

I smiled at her enthusiasm, wondering how Krutz had taken the news.

"Did you hear about me?" she asked excitedly.

"Hear what?"

Hastily she dug into her purse and produced

an official-looking document. "It's signed by the governor of Texas," she said in an awed tone. "It's a full pardon. Mr. Weinberg arranged it with the help of some people in Washington."

She was beautiful, so excited, all of her vibrant, radiant, and alive. But the smile and the eyes flashed signals of uncertainty I didn't quite understand.

"That's terrific, Lori. Absolutely fantastic."

She looked down at the ground and said, "I know it was really you who made it possible. Ned told me how you used the dagger as a political club."

"I never knew him to be the talkative kind."

"I've been visiting him every day. You're about all he talks about, as if you were the son he never had." She studied my face closely for several moments, her head cocked to one side. "I almost forgot," she said suddenly, turning and diving toward the backseat of the car. When she turned around, she held a small black puppy with symmetrical tan markings on its chest and short stubby legs.

Shyly, she set the pup on the ground. The long black tail wagged in friendly fashion. "I know she can't replace Bobbie, but I saw her mother and father. They are simply gorgeous. Both have won all sorts of prizes in the Doberman class."

She waited anxiously for a reaction. No words came to mind. I squatted down on my right heel and snapped my fingers. The pup charged headlong, ears flapping. She tumbled over a rock and rolled to a stop under my hand. She made no effort to evade my gentle scratching of her tummy. "That's real thoughtful, Lori. She seems like a good choice." I looked back down at the pup. "Has she got a name?"

"I thought Duchess might suit her but you can change it."

"No. That sounds about right." I hadn't thought of another dog. I probably wouldn't have. It might work out, though. Duchess might fill a little of the emptiness. I looked up at Lori, still scratching the pup, and asked, "Are you going to be all right?"

"I think so. I feel stronger each day. The pardon helped more than I'd have believed it could. I'm still shaky at times. But I believe Doc when he tells me that will pass."

I stood up, watching the puppy chew at my loafers. I'd have to put my good shoes up out of reach. Without looking up, I said softly, "Knowing how you feel about violence and all, I wasn't sure I'd see you again."

"Don't be foolish," she said firmly. "If you hadn't come for me, I'd have died, horribly. It's my problem, not yours. What bothers me most is that I've destroyed the peace you've so carefully built over the years. I've hurt you terribly."

"Do you have any plans?" I asked, as if changing the subject.

"Not really. I gave Matt's money to Doc. Whatever Matt did to get it, I think it must have been illegal, if not evil. I've seen what Doc does with his clinic. He'll use the money wisely."

"Yeah. He will." I paused, uncertain how to

put it. "While you're deciding what to do, you could stay here."

"Are you sure?" she asked hesitantly.

"You could look after this pup while I finish Ned's pond."

"Are you really sure? I mean, after all that happened to me, the way they savaged..."

"I'm sure. The house is a mess and I haven't any clean clothes. I've been eating poorly, too."

She took a hesitant step, watching my eyes, then jumped, tucking her arms around my neck. She lifted her legs off the ground when I kissed her back with equal vigor. I didn't mention she was tearing stitches out of the shoulder.

When she let herself down, I put my good arm around her waist and said, "You could start right now. I'm hungry. How about you?"

She nodded vigorously. We moved up the hill toward the house, walking slowly, her head tilted against my shoulder. The pup followed, happily tugging the lace loose on Lori's right shoe.

A Message To Our Readers...

As a person who reads books, you have access to countless possibilities for information and delight.

The world at your fingertips.

Millions of kids don't.

They don't because they can't read. Or won't. They've never found out how much fun reading can be. Many young people never open a book outside of school, much less finish one.

Think of what they're missing—all the books you loved as a child, all those you've enjoyed and learned from as an adult.

That's why there's RIF. For twenty years, Reading is Fundamental (RIF) has been helping community organizations help kids discover the fun of reading.

RIF's nationwide program of local projects makes it possible for young people to choose books that become theirs to keep. And, RIF activities motivate kids, so that they *want* to read.

To find out how RIF can help in your community or even in your own home, write to:

RIF
Dept. BK-2
Box 23444
Washington, D.C.
20026

Founded in 1966, RIF is a national nonprofit organization with local projects run by volunteers in every state of the union.

ADD A PAGEANT MYSTERY TO YOUR LIFE!

THE SILVER SETUP

A MIKE GARRETT MYSTERY

If Kathleen Turner were a mystery novel, this is the book she'd be! Join us as Mike Garrett checks into an out-of-the-way motel that features hot and cold running blondes, some menacing hired muscle, and a corpse—or will it be two?

ISBN: 0-517-00067-9   Price: $2.95

RICHARD BLAINE

AVAILABLE AT BOOKSTORES NOW!

EVIL IS LURKING...

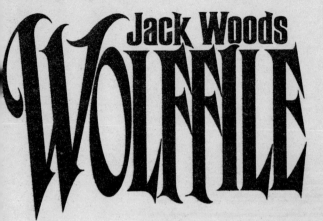

Jack Woods

WOLFFILE

Dr. Ian Sanders returns to his home off the coast of Maine for peace and tranquility. Instead he finds the island littered with bodies that have been clawed to death by a hairy, sub-human creature from whom the entire population is fleeing in fear. Will Dr. Sanders end the beast's ancient ritual of death or must he, too, become its victim?

0-517-00043-1 $3.50

ON SALE NOW
FROM PAGEANT BOOKS!

A NOVEL OF
UNSPEAKABLE HORROR...

DEATH ANGEL

ROBERT BLACK

A rural farming community in Depression-era
America is terrorized by a serial killer in this
harrowing first novel. As masterful as the
best of Dean R. Koontz, this riveting tale of
horror from Robert Black is one you won't
easily forget.

ISBN 0-517-00835-1 $2.95

FROM PAGEANT BOOKS!

A NOVEL OF PURE TERROR!

BLOOD FARM

by
SAM SICILIANO

From a stolen hour of feverish passion to a
harrowing dance with the emissaries of evil,
Mike and Angela are driven through a storm-
tossed night into the yawning maw of
hell! What terrifying evil lurks in the unspeakable needs and insatiable passions of the
undead? What ghastly savagery awaits them
when they accept the chilling hospitality of
Blut Farm?

0-517-00660-X $3.95

ON SALE NOW
FROM PAGEANT BOOKS!